'An ace undercover private... *Sunday Post*

'Witty, thrilling and heartwarming ... recommends her book to fans of Agatha Christie and M. C. Beaton. Comparisons to Charles Dickens and Wilkie Collins would be as apt. Ms Saunders's dozens of characters ... all social classes are sketched with sharp strokes, her ... dramatic plot turns are truly shocking and her heroine is ...t, capable and brimming with human sympathy. Sequels, ...se' *Wall Street Journal*

...nders immerses us in Victorian England in this delightful ... series. You'll love Laetitia Rodd and her charming cohorts ...ey unravel an intriguing tangle of mysteries ... I couldn't ... it down!' Victoria Thompson, author of *Murder in ...ningside Heights*

...ked with pithy observations about human nature ... Mrs ...d makes a genuinely likeable character you can't help but ... for' *Irish Examiner*

...nders evokes the period with witty references and shrewd ...hts. Mrs Rodd and her landlady Mrs Bentley already have ...sebook of mysteries. The author will do us a favour by writ-...hem up as quickly as possible' *Saga*

...norass of crooks, mistresses and murderers' *Country Life*

...ergetically written, it's the first of a series featuring the ...ventures and wit of this endearing Victorian detective – the ...xt one can't come soon enough' *Choice*

...r Dickens would approve!' *New York Journal of Books*

... does remind me of Miss Marple ... Clever, witty and alto-...ther likable ... I look forward to more ★★★★★' *San Francisco ...ok Review*

BY THE SAME AUTHOR

Night Shall Overtake Us
The Marrying Game
Bachelor Boys

A LAETITIA RODD MYSTERY

The Secrets of Wishtide

KATE SAUNDERS

BLOOMSBURY

LONDON · OXFORD · NEW YORK · NEW DELHI · SYDNEY

Bloomsbury Paperbacks
An imprint of Bloomsbury Publishing Plc

50 Bedford Square
London
WC1B 3DP
UK

1385 Broadway
New York
NY 10018
USA

www.bloomsbury.com

BLOOMSBURY and the Diana logo are trademarks of Bloomsbury Publishing Plc

First published in Great Britain 2016
This paperback edition first published in 2017

British Library Cataloguing-in-Publication Data
A catalogue record for this book is available from the British Library.

ISBN: HB: 978-1-4088-6686-3
TPB: 978-1-4088-7916-0
PB: 978-1-4088-6687-0
ePub: 978-1-4088-6688-7

2 4 6 8 10 9 7 5 3 1

Typeset by Integra Software Services Pvt. Ltd.
Printed and bound in Great Britain by CPI Group (UK) Ltd, Croydon CR0 4YY

FSC
MIX
Paper from
responsible sources
FSC® C020471
www.fsc.org

To find out more about our authors and books visit www.bloomsbury.com.
Here you will find extracts, author interviews, details of forthcoming events
and the option to sign up for our newsletters.

To the memory of my beloved mother, Betty Saunders,
who would have made a brilliant detective

'I was so young, I loved him so, I had
No mother, God forgot me, and I fell.'

Robert Browning, *A Blot in the 'Scutcheon*

'There has been a time since … when I have asked myself
the question, would it have been better for little Em'ly to
have had the waters close above her head that morning in
my sight; and when I have answered Yes, it would have
been.'

Charles Dickens, *David Copperfield*

One

IT WAS A BRIGHT, windy October morning, and Mrs Bentley and I were down in the basement kitchen making a rabbit pudding. The rabbits were a gift from Mrs Bentley's second son, whose daughter I had helped to place in a very respectable domestic situation with the Mayburys of Finchley, and when the doorknocker sounded I was up to my elbows in flour.

'Drat.' Mrs Bentley dropped the potato she was carving (she was infinitely patient about cutting out the black parts). 'You're not expecting anyone today, are you, ma'am?' She got up and went to peer out of the window. 'It's Watson – from Mr Tyson's office!' Her pale eyes were suddenly as bright and alert as a squirrel's. 'Shall I ask him to come straight down?'

'Yes, do.' I carried on rolling out the suet pastry, very glad not to be interrupted by a formal call, which would have meant handwashing and hairbrushing and the removal of my coarse apron. Despite my 'reduced' circumstances (that term always puts me in mind of sauces), the vicar's wife felt obliged to visit me, and I sat on several charitable committees with various local ladies. They all knew how reduced I was, but would have been horribly shocked to catch me in the act of cooking.

'Well, I hope this means Mr Tyson needs another little job doing.' Mrs Bentley beckoned Watson in eagerly, and I felt a flutter of anticipation as his great nailed boots came ringing down the area steps. Watson was a ticket-porter employed by my brother's chambers; the fact that he had been sent all the way from Lincoln's Inn to Hampstead could only mean a new case.

'Good morning, Mrs Rodd.' Watson pulled off his greasy hat; he was a stocky, grizzled, growling man, wrapped in a greatcoat that looked and smelt like a horse-blanket. 'I've a note from Mr Tyson, ma'am, and I'm to wait for a reply.'

'Thank you, Watson.' I banged my floury hands on my apron and took the single sheet of paper. 'Please sit down and rest for a few minutes – Mary, draw him a glass of beer.'

'Very civil of you, ma'am.' Watson was not an enormous man, yet he seemed to swamp the room and fill the entire house with the reek of stale tobacco; I would have to open all the windows later.

The note was the usual terse summons: 'Dear Letty, a matter has arisen. My carriage will come at five, yrs affect. F.'

I pencilled an equally terse reply: 'Dear F, at your service, L.'

Discretion was the foundation stone of my work; Fred and I were scrupulously careful about what we committed to paper.

Watson drained his beer, and was barely through the door before Mrs Bentley burst out with, 'Well, ma'am? Is it another case?'

'That's what it looks like.'

'Praise be! I'll get your good black silk out of the press.'

'Yes, Mary, if you would.'

'And you'll be staying at Mr Tyson's for dinner,' Mrs Bentley said. 'So we can keep the rabbit pudding for tomorrow.'

'Don't be silly – what will you eat?'

'I'll toast the rest of the bread and cheese; there's more than enough for one.' She scattered white pepper and salt over her bowl of meat and vegetables. 'I wonder what it'll be this time?'

'So do I, but Mr Tyson didn't give any details, and it's pointless to speculate.'

'The money will be handy, that's for certain – we'd never have managed till next quarter-day on what you've got left. The Bradshaw business was months ago and you didn't take enough for it.'

'That was light work; all I needed to do in the end was intercept a couple of letters.' The previous spring I had uncovered the younger Bradshaw daughter's plan to elope with her dancing master; my work could be described as the Management and Prevention of Scandal (my brother used to enjoy making up facetious advertisements for my services – 'Blushes Spared and Broken Commandments Mended!').

'Anyway, that was dull as ditchwater,' Mrs Bentley said. 'Let's hope the sins are bigger this time.'

'Mary!'

'I'm not wishing for any more sin in the world, ma'am – but there's never a shortage, so why shouldn't some of it come our way? You're too charitable, that's your trouble – and too blooming refined to ask for more money, when folk certainly ain't too refined to cheat you.'

Overfamiliarity is, of course, a dreadful quality in a servant; this was one of the first principles I had to get into the heads of the girls I used to train up for domestic work. 'You'll never rise out of the scullery if you take that tone,' as I told them. 'You'll be turning a mangle until doomsday.' But Mary Bentley was more than a servant to me. Mary Bentley was a friend I trusted with my life, and she had an endless fund of the plainest common sense; her shrewd eye for human falsity had been invaluable in all my cases.

I had been living with her in this narrow, sooty, inconvenient house in Hampstead for more than two years. On the day that I came to look at the place, my husband had just died, and our house in Bloomsbury had been broken up and sold. I had been looking for a small place near my brother in Highgate, but there was nothing suitable in Highgate that I could afford (Fred couldn't help me; his wife's lavish housekeeping ate his income up to the very limit), and I had come to Hampstead because it was busier than its sleepy neighbour, with cheaper lodgings to be had.

Well Walk was a bustling, workaday street and Mrs Bentley's house was practically next door to a tavern. I didn't see how I could possibly live in this shabby little terrace, with carts and drays rumbling past all day. I had done my best to put a good face on things, and I really don't think pride is one of my beset-ting sins, but at that moment, on that damp February morning, I felt how far I had fallen – Matt would have been so sad to see me. I had been as brave as everyone expected me to be, but there were times when my longing for him, and my sense of how solitary I was without him, pierced me like a knife.

The door of this unpromising house was opened by a small, spare old woman. At first glance I took her to be ancient. The thin frizz of hair underneath her cap was snow-white. Her brows and lashes were white and her pale eyes held only the

4

washed-out memory of blue. But she was wiry and vigorous, and simply pale in the way that very fair-skinned people and white mice are pale. Once upon a time (as she told me later), her hair had been flaming red. Her five sons and her tribe of grandchildren were all red-headed; she had scattered ginger across every north London village from Golders Green to Kentish Town.

Mrs Bentley was talkative, and while I was examining the fireplace in the front parlour, she told me that she had once, many years before, let rooms to the poet John Keats.

I was off my guard, aching for the lost half of my soul, and a great tenderness and sorrow came over me. Matt had a fondness for poetry that I often told him was unsuitable in an archdeacon. I was only teasing – it was our shared weakness for poetry that drew us together in the first place. I saw myself as I had been at twenty-two, dreaming my way through the long summer days of our engagement, reading Matt's letters that bristled with romantic quotations from Wordsworth, Crabbe, Young – but mostly Keats, the highest romantic of them all, whose verses he particularly loved.

Now Matt was gone, as thoroughly as if he had never existed, and I was a poor, childless widow of two-and-fifty – 'In drear-nighted December,/Too happy, happy tree,/Thy branches ne'er remember/Their green felicity –'

I found, to my mortification, that I was weeping.

Mrs Bentley said, 'There, there, ma'am!'

Ignoring my feeble protests, she marched me down to the kitchen, where the fire was, and told me that I needed 'something to keep the cold out'.

I sniffed that a cup of tea would be most welcome.

5

'Tea be blowed,' said Mrs Bentley.

She made a little jug of brandy and hot water, with a spoonful of sugar, and it warmed us into a state of confidentiality. I spilled out the story of my husband's sudden death, and the annuity he never got round to providing for me. Mrs Bentley told me about the rheumatism which prevented her letting her lodgings to anyone more demanding than a single lady. At this moment, the supposed social gulf between us was meaningless; we were two lone women, struggling for a place in this cold world. By the time the jug was empty I had even told her about Fanny.

'I'm living with my brother and his wife at the moment, and I can't endure much more of her.'

'Wants rid of you, does she?'

'Worse – she's counting on me to stay in that tiny room overlooking the stables and teach the children for nothing. She thinks that's what a poor female relation is for.'

'Oh, I know all about that,' Mrs Bentley said. 'When Bentley died, all my sons' wives were wild for me to give up the house and move in with them as an unpaid nursemaid. You should stand up for yourself more, ma'am. I could make a beautiful little place for you here, and you'd be at nobody's beck and call.'

And so the bargain was made and Fanny had to keep her expensive governess, much to her annoyance. I had the house in Well Walk thoroughly cleaned and repainted; I installed the few bits and pieces I had salvaged from my old home – most precious of all, the portrait of my beloved Matt by Edwin Landseer, which was presented to him by the Diocese of London the year before he died (and is so like him that it can still, after all this time, make me weep if I gaze at it too long).

Mrs Bentley's youngest son nailed up pictures, curtain rails and shelves. I discovered that my neighbours were an interesting mixture of busy tradesmen, out-at-elbow young writers, retired sea-captains, bankers, actors and vagabonds of every class. Matt would have loved it.

He would also have loved Mrs Bentley's stories about Keats and his two brothers, though her memories were not very poetic. More than thirty years earlier, the late Bentley had worked as the local postman. Mary Bentley had been a young wife bringing up five little boys, and to make ends meet, she let serviced rooms to gentlemen. Into this crowded house had come the poet and his two younger brothers – how they all fitted in is still a mystery to me. According to Mrs Bentley, the Keats brothers were very nice young men, though Mr John had the sauce to complain about the noise, and he once lost his temper when it poured with rain and she had to dry the boys' worsted stockings on the stairs. It was the last house, she said, where the Keatses had all lived together and been happy. Matt would have laughed at me for taking this as good omen. 'By God, Letty,' he would have said, 'what a romantic old boiler you are!'

The carriage rolled into Well Walk at precisely five o'clock by the church bell. It was a large four-wheeler built to accommodate my brother's ever-expanding family. I picked the stale remains of a piece of gingerbread off the seat and threw it out of the window. There were ten children at the last count, and Fanny was constantly stuffing them with treats in a vain attempt to keep them quiet; fewer cakes and another nurse-maid would have been my solution, if anyone had asked me.

The noise in that house was simply incredible; when the bigger boys were home for the holidays, Fred groaned that he lived in Pandemonium.

My brother, Frederick Tyson, was one of London's most celebrated criminal barristers, with a reputation for defending murderers; it was said around the Inns of Court that he could have 'turned' a jury in favour of the Emperor Caligula. Sketches of his large, flamboyant figure appeared in the popular press. In my mind's eye, Fred would always be my playmate: the plump little boy with eyes filled with mischief, and the dimples and curls of a cherub. He was still cherubic at fifty, though he had lost the dimples and the curls were grey.

Fred and his family lived above the stew of the city, in an old, red-brick box of a house that overlooked the green in Highgate village. He was waiting for me, prancing with impatience, in the panelled hall.

'Fanny and the mob are safely shut away upstairs – we won't be disturbed.'

'I thought it was strangely peaceful.' I took off my black silk bonnet. 'What's afoot, Fred?'

'Something absolutely tailor-made for you, old girl – it's a job that requires nothing more than a little genteel probing and perhaps a modicum of eavesdropping.'

'Oh dear, I'm never sure about the morality of eavesdropping, even in a good cause.'

His eyes still had that wicked gleam. 'Think of the money.'

'Fred!'

'Don't get prissy – there's plenty of it in this case.'

I'm sorry to say that the sum he mentioned blew all moral scruples from my mind. 'Good grief, who are these people?'

'Major bigwigs.' He lowered his voice. 'You're about to meet a Mr Filey – confidential lawyer to the parties in the case, and very much your traditional Old Family Retainer. He's in the library. Remember not to look shocked.'

'I know the drill, thank you.'

The library was at the front of the house; a comfortable, well-lit room, lined with Fred's heavy legal tomes. The green blinds were already tightly drawn across the three long windows (the house was built during the reign of Queen Anne, when people must have been very fond of draughts). A fat, rich fire – far too much on a day like this – blazed in the grate; I couldn't help thinking the coal bill must be colossal.

Mr Filey stood stiffly in the middle of the room, his hands folded behind his back. I took him in quickly. He was a hale, upright old man, with sharp, bright eyes in an intensely wrinkled face. He had an air of indignation held in reserve, as if he half-expected me to offend him (this was quite usual; my cases were invariably touchy about the situations in which they found themselves).

Fred made the introductions and we sat down around the big mahogany desk.

'Your brother tells me,' Mr Filey said, 'that you have been known to get to the bottom of certain domestic mysteries.'

I appreciated his delicacy. 'Yes, sir – though I'm not in a position to provide references.'

The craggy face softened for a moment, with what might have been a glimmer of humour. 'As a matter of fact, I've made some inquiries of my own. Certain people you have assisted praise your abilities to the skies – I say this most particularly in regard to the letter "H".'

Fred and I exchanged quick glances; he meant the Heaton case, our finest hour, when my investigations uncovered a wicked conspiracy and saved Colonel Heaton from the gallows.

'You are very discreet, Mrs Rodd. Everyone is agreed about that.'

'She's a veritable Sphinx,' Fred said. 'A rock couldn't be more inscrutable.'

(Matt used to say he fell in love with me because I had a 'poker face' and he took it as a challenge to make me smile.)

Filey cleared his throat. 'I have the honour to be connected to the Calderstone family, of Wishtide in Lincolnshire. You have heard, no doubt, of Sir James Calderstone.'

'Yes indeed.' I knew now why Fred had warned me not to look shocked.

Sir James Calderstone had an immense fortune, due mainly to his coalmines in the north. He had no official position in government yet he pervaded the political scene like an invisible gas; Matt used to accuse him of having half the Cabinet in his pocket.

Sir James Calderstone. Well, well, well.

The goddess of Scandal was no respecter of the Mighty; that was for sure.

'In a nutshell, Mrs Rodd, the son wants to make a very bad marriage. For various reasons it must be prevented at all costs.'

'I'm not in the business of preventing marriages.'

'No – but you do have a reputation for getting at the truth. That is why you are needed. The background of the lady in question is a perfect blank, except for some very worrying rumours. We want facts, but we can't be seen to search for them.

Do you understand? There has been far too much talk as it is. Your task would be to seek out the truth, without attracting attention.'

'I'm happy to do that. Please be warned, however, that if I find the truth you mightn't like it. Some people have blank backgrounds simply because their lives are too small to leave a trail. This woman may turn out to be guilty of nothing worse than poverty.'

'She may – and she may not.' Again, that glint of humour. 'Personally, I'd bet good money she has a past that would make your hair curl.'

'I can't say I don't know how it feels,' Mrs Bentley said. 'I remember how I felt when my boy Tom took up with a woman who was no better than a word I can't say in front of you, ma'am. She ran off with a sailor and I could've danced a hornpipe.'

Fred's carriage had dropped me back in Well Walk just before ten, and Mrs Bentley had been waiting up for me, dozing bolt-upright in a kitchen chair, as I had known she would be. I had changed my good black silk for a flannel wrapper and described my dinner (roast mutton and potatoes, apple pudding). We were now sitting cosily in front of the kitchen fire, with our skirts turned up and our feet resting on the fender. Mrs Bentley had made a fragrant jug of hot brandy – sensing an occasion she had borrowed a lemon from next door.

'All that money!' Mrs Bentley couldn't get over this; Mr Filey had given me a handsome sum to meet immediate expenses and she had gazed at it with her eyes bulging. 'They must be desperate for you to stop that wedding, ma'am. Why don't they just threaten to cut off the young man's funds? That's usually all it takes to kill true love.'

'You're a cynic, Mary – but whether you're right or not, the Calderstones apparently can't cut off young Charles. When he was twenty-one he came into his grandmother's estate, which provides him with a perfectly good income. He's an independent man of twenty-three and he claims not to care about his father's enormous fortune.'

'Well, why doesn't he just up and marry her?'

'She won't have him without his family's approval – and if Sir James did cut him off, Charles would lose more than the fortune. In worldly terms he would be a man without a future – yet he's apparently prepared to surrender everything for the sake of this woman.'

'She's playing a long game,' Mrs Bentley said. 'Holding out for the lot.'

'That's possible. It's also perfectly possible that she is acting from the highest motives.'

'She must be pretty.'

'Very, I'm told, and with the manner and appearance of a perfect lady. Charles met her when she came to the house to teach his sisters Italian. She also plays and sings as if she'd had the most expensive masters. But nobody knows a thing about her, beyond the fact that three years ago, in Italy, she married a clergyman named Orme, who died a year later. There's a perfectly good record of the marriage at the English Consulate in Florence. She still lives with his sister, Miss Winifred Orme.'

'But they think she's hiding something,' Mrs Bentley said.

'Exactly. They're pinning all their hopes on a rumour that she's already married to someone else.'

'Bigamy! We've never had that one before.'

'It's the merest wisp of gossip, very difficult to substantiate. I warned Mr Filey there might be nothing I can do.'

'You didn't turn him down?'

'Certainly not; I agreed to start immediately. I'm to go down to Wishtide next week, to put Mrs Orme and her history under a magnifying glass. As far as the rest of the world is concerned, I'm the new governess, come to "finish" the young ladies before they go into society.' I sighed rather crossly. 'It's funny, when you think of the lengths I've gone to not to end up governessing; I only hope those girls don't speak French better than I do. And I might find nothing – if Mrs Orme is as clever as she sounds, she'll have covered her tracks.'

'But there are always some things that can't be covered up,' Mrs Bentley said. 'Some secrets go off and stink the house out, like a dead mouse under the floorboards. If Mrs Orme is hiding something, someone in this world will know about it.'

Two

My dear Fred,

Here I am, sound in wind and limb, after a very long day of being shaken to pieces and covered with soot on the railway. As you may imagine, I was rather dreading my arrival at the Castle and fully prepared for the traditional trials of the governess – leftover food, meagre fires and insolent servants. My fears were groundless, however; please tell Fanny how well the Calderstones treat their governesses, which might give her pause for thought next time she expects your poor Miss Birch to dine upon broken meats in a cold schoolroom.

A comfortable carriage was waiting for me at Horncastle. Wishtide is situated in the southernmost part of the Lincolnshire Wolds, and in the chill, slate-coloured autumn dusk we drove through a country of wooded hills, with church towers and cottages clustered in the valleys. In the very last of the light we suddenly turned off the road into a great pair of gates. I was able to see how excellently the lodge was kept, which I always think significant. The woman who opened the gates was as neat as a pin and dropped a very civil curtsy. It was too dark after that to admire the famous lawns and trees of the park.

The house is enormous. It was built twenty-five years ago in the style of a castle, with squat turrets and mullioned windows. I walked up the steps into a huge, vaulted hall, where two Great Danes dozed and wheezed before a blazing fire, in a fireplace the size of my front parlour.

The housekeeper, Mrs Craik, came out to meet me. I was anxious to make a good impression on this woman – in my experience the housekeeper keeps the keys of a house in more senses than one (Thorpe, the butler here, is far too grand a personage to deal with a governess). Mrs Craik is a thin, grey-headed woman of about my years. She wears an apron of black silk, and is a little reserved in her manner, which is a shame from my point of view.

But she is kind, and evidently (as Mrs B would say) knows her onions – everything I have seen here is in the most beautiful order. I am writing this beside a generous fire, in my very pleasant bedroom. I have a high bed, an armchair, a desk, and plentiful supplies of coal and candles. The curtains and bed-hangings have seen some service, but are in good repair and spotlessly clean. My supper, brought to me by a decently spoken girl from the kitchen, consisted of game pie, baked apple cream and a glass of wine. I think in such easy circumstances I might even like being a governess.

I am to meet Sir James and Lady Calderstone after dinner, presumably to talk about –

There was a loud knock at my door. I laid down my pen. 'Come in.'

I was expecting another servant, and I was startled to see a tall young man in evening clothes, simmering with indignation.

'Mrs Rodd?'

'Yes.'

'I'm Charles Calderstone – and I may as well tell you straight out – I know why you're here.'

I said I had been engaged to teach his sisters.

'Pish,' said Mr Charles. 'You're spying for my father.'

Well, here was a fine beginning; did this mean everyone knew?

I stood up, very much on my dignity. 'Yes, I'm conducting an inquiry at the request of your father. Strictly speaking, I am indeed a "spy". If my position here is common knowledge, I'm afraid I won't be of much use to him.'

'It's not common knowledge – I've just had an almighty row with him and he told me. Everyone else thinks you're here for the girls.'

'And are you about to blow my cover?'

This piece of criminal cant (I picked up all kinds of expressions from Fred) surprised and disarmed him. He had burst into my room with his guns blazing, and was now uncertain. 'I – I don't know.'

'Before you make up your mind, perhaps you should steal a march on your father and give me your side of the story.' I gestured to the armchair beside the fire. 'Please sit down.'

He hovered. 'He'll tell you I'm a fool and it's a pack of lies.'

'I've already explained in my correspondence with your father that I am only interested in concrete facts, not hearsay or slander. Please do sit down, Mr Charles.'

'Well – all right.' The firelight was bright, and showed me what a handsome young man he was. His hair was of a rich dark brown; his brown eyes were large and tender, with long, girlish lashes, yet his jaw was strong and his mouth firm and stubborn.

And this fine young prince had fallen in love with a Nobody from Nowhere – as princes sometimes do, though not as often as romantic tradition would have you believe; we would never have heard of King Cophetua if kings were in the habit of marrying beggar-maids.

I moved my chair so that we faced each other across the hearth. Mr Charles harrumphed and reddened and looked at his knees.

'Let us be confidential,' I said gently. 'Tell me what you like, and don't worry that I'll report it to your parents.'

He glanced up hopefully. 'How do I know I can trust you?'

'You have my word as a Christian lady. If that's not enough, you can ask the Bishops of Ripon, Peterborough and Bath and Wells, all of whom have dined at my table, and seem to think I'm generally a good sort.'

Mr Charles smiled at this, and his smile was fresh and open and charming – he reminded me a little of Matt, my beloved, portly old archdeacon, back in the days when he was a slender young curate with all his hair (the idol of the parish; oh, my unbelieving joy when he chose me, the silent, black-browed girl in the corner; I never allowed myself to forget how it had felt to be young and in love).

'I hope you are a good sort,' he said. 'Nobody listens to me here. And I have to stop my father's vile campaign.'

'Campaign?'

'To blacken the name of a lady, and – and to stop me marrying her.'

I couldn't argue with him; this was exactly his father's campaign; the fact that he had engaged me was proof of his determination. 'But if you are to marry her, Mr Charles, your parents have a right to know about her background. For a young man in your position, an injudicious match would be a very bad step. They are only trying to protect you, surely.'

'No they are not!' His voice was tight, choking back fury. 'My father wants me to marry someone else – that's why he's so set on ruining the reputation of Helen Orme – whom I know to be as pure as my own sisters!'

His eyes were wet with tears of hurt and anger; he was working himself into a state, and I didn't necessarily wish the rest of the house to know about this conversation.

I made my voice soft and inviting. 'Tell me about Mrs Orme.'

'She's – I don't know where to begin. She came here to give the girls lessons in Italian. She speaks it like a native; it's astonishing to hear her.'

'Did she live in the house?'

'No, she has a cottage, near Horncastle. She shares it with her sister-in-law, and they live in a poor sort of way – genteel, you know, but they've only a hundred and fifty pounds a year between them, so it's a scrape.'

(I did indeed know, and had a pang of fellow-feeling for Mrs Orme.)

'I made a promise to my father,' ......es said, 'that I wouldn't do anything to cause talk in the villages. That means I can't take care of Helen – Mrs Orme – as much as I'd like. She'd rather die than take money from me – I send the girls round with little presents of game and wine and so forth, as often as I dare. But naturally the whole countryside knows where it comes from.'

Here was an interesting situation. The first mental note I made was that Mrs Orme had refused money. Perhaps this was a sign of her purity, perhaps of her intelligence. The second was Mr Charles's careless reference to his sisters.

'Do your sisters still call on Mrs Orme?'

'Yes, when the old man is away. Our mother tries to stop them, but the girls are fond of her and they keep disobeying.'

'So you'd say that Miss Blanche and Miss Elizabeth are in sympathy with your proposed marriage?'

Mr Charles smiled. 'They've been a pair of bricks. Have you met them yet?'

'Not yet.'

'Don't mind if Blanche is cross with you at first – she's furious to be getting yet another governess, and she says she doesn't want to be finished. But she's all right really.'

He had calmed down; when he spoke of his sisters, the impassioned lover changed back into a cheerful and good-natured young man.

'Thank you for the warning; I'll bear it in mind.'

'And you'll like Bessie, she's a dear old thing.'

'So it was your sisters who introduced you to Mrs Orme?'

'It wasn't exactly a formal introduction; I came upon them all in the garden, sitting on the big bearskin under the trees. It was like stumbling into Paradise – this sprite of a girl in a grey gown – an angel in Quaker's clothing –'

'A girl?'

I'd kept my tone light, but he knew what I was getting at and coloured angrily.

'She looks like a girl – she's as small and delicate as a fairy.'

'Do you know her age?'

'Of course – we don't have secrets. She's two-and-thirty, which is nine years older than I am, but I couldn't care a straw.'

'Has she talked much about her late husband?'

'Not much – but only because I don't like hearing about dead saints.'

19

'Was Mr Orme a saint?'

'According to Helen. But it wasn't a love match – in the romantic sense, I mean.' He looked away from me, to mumble, 'It wasn't a true marriage, if you understand.'

He was trying to tell me – blushing up to his eyes – that Mrs Orme was, so to speak, still in a state of maidenhood. I wasn't sure that I believed this.

But I nodded gravely. 'And she met Mr Orme in Italy.'

'Yes, and he died there.'

'Do you know what she did before her marriage?'

'Of course I do!' Mr Charles held his head up proudly. 'She was in your trade.'

'I beg your pardon?'

'Of course, you're only pretending to be a governess, but Helen was a real one. She lived with several aristocratic families.'

'I see.' I wasn't sure that I believed this either.

'She has nothing to hide, Mrs Rodd. Her maiden name was Lyndhurst; her father was a poor curate on the Suffolk coast. She was left an orphan at a very young age, and forced to earn her own living in other people's houses. There you are; that's all there is to know. It's shameful of my parents to hold her poor background against her; it's not her fault she's had a hard life.'

'No.' Nobody could help where they were born; it would indeed have been shameful of the Calderstones to object to Mrs Orme simply because she had been forced to earn her own bread.

But this puzzled me: if the story Mr Charles told was true, the match surely need not be seen as such a disaster. People would whisper about the fact that Mrs Orme was a widow, and older than her husband. But poverty is forgivable in a clergyman's daughter, and her essential gentility was beyond question; any social disappointment could have been very quickly absorbed. Why (as Mrs B would say) were his parents in such a taking?

And another thing: I had known many governesses in my time, starting with my own. They were all, to a woman, the daughters or widows of poor clergymen. The large majority were imperfectly educated and sadly lacking in the expensive accomplishments. How had Mrs Orme, this orphaned curate's daughter, turned herself into a polished lady who spoke perfect French and Italian? Her late husband was an educated man, but that did not explain it; they were only married a matter of months.

The clock on the chimney-piece chimed the hour; it was nearly time for me to meet Sir James and Lady Calderstone, and I became businesslike.

'Mr Charles, I must ask – I was told about a certain rumour.'

'What – that she was married to someone else before Edmund Orme?' He laughed angrily. 'Yes, I've heard all about that, and it's a pack of lies.'

'Do you know where the rumour originated?'

'No, and I don't care; it's arrant nonsense. I know it in the marrow of my bones.'

'Before I meet your parents, Mr Charles, I must know if you intend to stand in the way of my inquiries. I can't be of any use at all if you are set against me.'

'Oh, don't you worry about me. I'm happy for you to poke and pry all you like – I know you won't find a single thing against her.'

'And you won't tell anyone else why I'm here?'

'I give you my word I won't tell a soul. That's exactly what I said to my father. I told him I wasn't afraid of the truth, and neither is Mrs Orme. I'm going back to town this very night, and I wouldn't dream of standing in your way.'

'You won't tell Mrs Orme?'

'My word of honour. You'll see for yourself that she has nothing to hide.'

His belief in her purity was absolute; she was his spotless idol. I didn't like to think how he would feel if I found any blemishes.

Three

'It's the ingratitude that astonishes one.' Lady Calderstone was tearful. 'Edmund Orme was a cousin of mine. That's why I felt I had to do something for his wretched widow when she turned up on my doorstep. I thought the girls could learn some Italian – which always gives such a smart impression in society – and I could do my duty at the same time.'

'Two birds with one stone,' I suggested.

'Precisely. And to tell the truth, it was a godsend that she was setting up home with poor Winifred; otherwise one would have felt obliged to have Winifred here.'

'Lord. No,' said Sir James. 'Face like a horse.'

'I was pleased with Mrs Orme when I met her; she puts up a very convincing act. I had absolutely no idea she'd steal away my son from right under my nose.'

We were in a large drawing room on the first floor, and I felt as if I had landed in an *Arabian Nights* treasure-box of silks and jewels. It was a cocoon of luxury – windows dressed in great swathes and cascades of indigo velvet, chaises and armchairs like feathery clouds, and everywhere the gleam of polished walnut, fine china, silver and gold.

Lady Calderstone paced irritably, sweeping skirts of dark ruby taffeta behind her with a great rustle. She was a thin, nervous, peevish-looking woman, and I had to make an effort not to dismiss her as simply superficial and spoilt; when I exercised a little Christian charity I saw that there was sadness too – and a certain wariness towards her husband.

It was easy to see where Charles had got his looks. Sir James was an older version of his handsome son – broader and stouter, the luxuriant brown hair retreating, yet still fresh and energetic. He stood before me, a commanding figure in black tails and a capacious white waistcoat, clutching a pile of papers as if posing for a portrait.

'So you've met the boy, Mrs Rodd. I don't suppose you got much sense out of him.'

'He's a young man in love,' I said. 'And he is as eager for the truth as you are – he believes that when Mrs Orme's reputation is proven to be immaculate she'll agree to marry him.'

'Oh, that's just like her artfulness!' snapped Lady Calderstone. 'She knows what a chivalrous boy he is – it's just the thing to fire him up and make him think he's some sort of Sir Galahad!'

'There are a lot of very good reasons why Charles should not marry this woman,' Sir James said. 'I have the family name to consider.'

'He was on the point of asking someone else – a young lady that Sir James and I liked very much – and then he met this dreadful woman –'

'My dear,' there was a note of warning in Sir James's voice, 'Mrs Rodd doesn't need to hear all this; let's stick to the matter in hand.'

'I should like to know,' I said, 'about the rumour of another husband.'

Sir James extracted one piece of paper and held it out to me. 'Three weeks ago, I received this letter at my house in London.'

I took it, and read the few crude words: '*Your cousin married a WHORE. Her true name is MRS SAVILE. You will pay for my silence. WAIT and SEE.*'

I returned the filthy thing to him with a shudder. 'This is nothing more than malicious slander, surely.'

'I'm of the opinion,' Lady Calderstone said, 'that there's no smoke without fire.'

'Slander or not,' Sir James went on, as if she had not spoken, 'it must be looked into.'

'Do you have any idea who sent it?'

'None whatsoever – and my investigations drew a blank.'

'And there has been no demand for money?'

'No – not yet, at any rate. But this isn't just a matter of money. I have many enemies, Mrs Rodd – I think it's inevitable when a man's in public life. Someone is trying, as they say, to put the wind up me. If one breath, one squeak gets out that my son's woman is a harlot, that public life will be ruined. I engaged you because you can ask questions without drawing any unnecessary attention to yourself.' He chuckled suddenly. 'Nobody is likely to mistake you for a copper's nark.'

I couldn't help smiling at this. 'I should hope not.'

'You'll have all the assistance I can give you. Do you know where you'll begin?'

'I'd like to look into the story of her early life in Suffolk. I have some connections down there.' I added, to Lady Calderstone, 'Naturally, I'll give Your Ladyship due notice before I take myself off anywhere; I haven't forgotten I've also come here to teach your daughters.'

'Lord, that doesn't matter,' Sir James said briskly. 'Do what you like, and never mind the girls; if you can make them do as they're told without arguing, you'll be worth every penny.'

'How can you say it doesn't matter?' Lady Calderstone was fretful. 'Blanche will be coming out next year, and her manners are shockingly countrified.'

'Please tell me what you'd like from me in the way of teaching,' I said. 'My French is good – I spent a year in Boulogne as a girl. I know a decent amount of Latin and a smattering of Greek.'

'Oh no, not Latin and so forth,' said Her Ladyship. 'I don't want people to think they're a pair of bluestockings.'

'If you'll excuse me,' Sir James took his gold watch from his pocket, 'I'll leave all this to my wife and go back to my desk.'

Once he had left the room, Lady Calderstone dropped down on the nearest sofa, like a puppet with cut strings. After a pause, she said in a small voice, 'I hope you can save us, Mrs Rodd.'

'Save you?' The word startled me.

'I can't really explain – but Mrs Rodd, if Charlie marries that woman, we'll all be ruined. Simply ruined.'

Miss Blanche pulled herself off the sofa just long enough to touch my hand, mutter, 'How do,' and flop back against the cushions.

Miss Elizabeth blushed a little, embarrassed by her sister's rudeness to me. 'I'm Elizabeth. How do you do.'

'I'm very pleased to meet you both,' I said. 'I thought we could spend this morning getting to know each other, and finding out where I can help you.'

The gilt clock on the chimney-piece had just chimed nine. After an excellent breakfast in my room, Mrs Craik had appeared to escort me to 'the Young Ladies' Drawing Room'; a rather grandiose title for a pleasant, sunny sitting room that was still partially a schoolroom. There were armchairs, fresh chintz hangings and an elegant rosewood piano, but also an inky deal table and a globe, and a shelf of wax dolls, wooden animals and other childish things that had only recently been put away. I sized up the two girls, my official reason for being here.

Miss Blanche, an elderly and jaded eighteen-year-old, was very pretty, and very recognisably the sister of Mr Charles, with the same rich-brown curls and fine complexion. Her sky-blue silk gown and dainty muslin apron were far too splendid, I thought, for a schoolroom in the depths of the Lincolnshire countryside.

Miss Elizabeth, aged fifteen, was bulky and awkward, with a long plait of light-brown hair, heavy cheeks and little, anxious blue eyes. I gave her my friendliest smile; poor thing: fifteen was a trying age for the prettiest girls, and could be agony for plain ones. I had been a plain girl myself at that age (of the comically skinny variety, with enormous hands and feet and a nose that seemed to grow overnight like a mushroom), and I hadn't had an elder sister like Blanche to contend with. Miss Elizabeth wanted to like me, I decided, and would be the easier of the two to win over, just as Charles had predicted.

'You can help Bessie if you want,' Miss Blanche said, with a haughty toss of her curls. 'She's still doing things like arithmetic and geography – schoolroom things. I'm eighteen and I shouldn't be in a schoolroom at all.'

'I'm not here to give you lessons,' I assured her. 'Just to give what your mother calls a "polish".'

'Pooh,' said Miss Blanche, 'I'm not a brass doorknob. Mamma says I'm not "finished" and lack "polish", but as far as I'm concerned I ought to be out in society right this minute. I'm done with governesses – so you must forgive me, Mrs Rodd, if I ignore you.'

She picked up her book – one of those vulgar 'Keepsake' volumes, stuffed with sentimental verses and pictures of soldiers with huge eyes and wasp waists – and pointedly began to read.

The impertinent speech should have annoyed me, but I couldn't afford to be at odds with the little madam, and kept up my serene (I hoped) smile. I found myself wondering why Miss Blanche had not 'come out' this season, when plenty of other girls her age were already engaged to be married. It couldn't be a question of money: not in this house that might as well have been wallpapered with banknotes.

'I shan't be giving lessons this morning,' I said, turning towards Miss Elizabeth as if her cross sister had disappeared. 'We should get the measure of each other first. Shall we try a little conversation in French?'

'Now?' She was dismayed.

'Our French is perfectly fine,' Miss Blanche snapped. 'We spent six months in Paris last year – very tedious months, with no one but French servants for company – and we can jabber away with the best of them.'

I would have liked to retort that more was required of a young lady than 'jabbering', but pretended not to have heard. 'All this talk of "finishing" makes me smile,' I said cheerfully. 'It reminds me of my dear, naughty friend Minnie Gilmore, from my own schooldays in Boulogne. The first time I ever saw Minnie, she was sitting on the windowsill of our bare bedroom in our dismal *pension*, shouting to all and sundry that she didn't need finishing, and she had only come to France because she meant to elope with a poet.'

Miss Elizabeth giggled at this, and – more importantly – so did Miss Blanche.

'Oh, Minnie was absolutely shocking,' I went on. 'She was always hungry, and she used to sneak out to the market in the evenings to buy cakes and pies. And she was always sighing over handsome bandits in sentimental novels.'

Miss Elizabeth giggled harder – all she had needed to like me was some sign that I hadn't forgotten how it feels to be young.

Miss Blanche dropped her book. 'Did she elope with a poet – or anyone?'

'No, I'm glad to say.' I turned to face her. 'By some miracle Minnie managed to stay more or less out of trouble – though she was always dreaming up new mischief, and laughing at me when I begged her to be careful.'

'I think she sounds delightful. What happened to her afterwards?' Miss Blanche's face was alight with curiosity.

'She went home,' I said, 'and married the curate.'

'Oh!' Miss Blanche let out such a cry of disappointment that I could not help laughing outright.

She pouted crossly for a couple of minutes, and I was afraid I had spoiled any chances of winning her confidence. Like her brother, however, the young lady had a good, commonsensical nature underneath all the dramatics, and her pretty face melted into a charming, unselfconscious smile. With a great rustle of her sky-blue skirts, she jumped off the sofa and came to join us at the round table – forgetting she had decided to be cross with me.

'Why on earth did the poor thing end up with the curate?'

'Believe it or not,' I said, 'she fell in love with him. And "ending up" with the curate isn't such a terrible fate – I did exactly the same thing myself.'

'Oh, don't! I can't picture it, that's all; our curate here is a hideous, bony fellow with a face like a Jack-o'-lantern. I'm sure I hope yours was a great deal handsomer.' She turned to her sister and said, in French, 'Bessie, let's show Mrs Rodd how good our French is – the weather is grey this morning, but not wet; we shall take the carriage out this afternoon. See? We speak it like natives.'

'Very – very nice,' I said faintly, doing my best to hide my horror. Yes, she spoke French 'like a native' – and that was just the trouble. She was fluent, but she had the accent and diction of a Parisian guttersnipe; everyone in society with even half an education would notice it at once, and this pretty girl would be a laughing-stock. I resolved to do what I could about it, just as if I were a genuine governess.

These girls appeared to be as pampered as a pair of poodles – but I had an impression that they had been ignored and left to themselves for far too long. Expensive teachers are no substitute for proper parental supervision. By the time the clock struck ten, however, I had made an assessment of their accomplishments and decided that the situation was far from hopeless; they were both quick and intelligent, and when I asked them to read aloud to me from *Paul et Virginie*, they responded well to my criticisms of their accents. After the French we moved to the piano, and that was even better; no amount of money can buy

30

an ear for music and both girls played and sang nicely. Miss Elizabeth had the makings of a very sweet voice.

'And I know some Italian songs,' said Miss Blanche.

Here was an opening to the subject of Mrs Orme, whom I was determined to meet before the day was over. Without comment, I played the sheet of music that Miss Blanche set before me – Mozart's 'Batti, Batti', perhaps not entirely suitable for a young girl, but I was impressed by the freshness and simplicity of the performance.

'That was charming,' I told her, with absolute sincerity. 'You've evidently been very well taught, I presume by one of the fashionable Italian masters in London.'

'We never go to London,' Miss Blanche said. 'Our teacher lives only a few miles away. She's a sort of cousin by marriage; our lessons had to stop when our brother fell in love with her.'

'Blanche!' Miss Elizabeth hissed.

Miss Blanche rolled her eyes impatiently. 'Oh, I know – we're not supposed to gossip about it. But what's the point when the whole countryside knows? Mrs Rodd might as well hear it from us. And you might as well be clear,' she added to me, holding her head up proudly, 'that I know nothing against our cousin, and fully intend to carry on visiting her.'

Here it was; the knot of conflict at the heart of this puzzling family. It took me a couple of minutes to decide what to say next. Why was Blanche so vehemently at odds with her mother? And why was she allowed to defy her – did Lady Calderstone have no authority in her own household?

Regrettably, it was necessary to lie. 'Her Ladyship mentioned nothing of this to me; I'm sure she trusts you not to call upon anyone unsuitable.'

'Her name's Helen Orme,' Miss Blanche said, with an air of challenge. 'And we like her very much – don't we, Bess? Before she came, Wishtide was the dullest place in the world. Our mother wants us to stop seeing her, but I refuse to cut her off unless someone gives me a proper reason.'

'The business with your brother –' I hinted.

'That's not good enough. I don't see why she should be blamed for it. She didn't ask Charlie to fall in love with her, and she utterly refuses to let him say they're engaged. It's just not fair!'

The 'not fair' had a childish sound, but Miss Blanche was quite right – she had stumbled against one of the great injustices of life, namely that in situations of this kind, the blame always falls upon the woman. And when a woman is young and poor and friendless, a pretty face is not necessarily a blessing to her. I liked the child more for her honest indignation, and her loyalty.

Now I had to think quickly. The two girls were my passport to Mrs Orme, and Mrs Orme was the reason I was here – but how could I visit her, without appearing to condone their defiance of their mother?

'I assure you, Miss Blanche,' I said, 'Lady Calderstone has not said anything to me about whom you may or may not visit.'

At this moment, to my relief (I did not enjoy lying to these innocents), there was a brisk rap at the door and in came Sir James. 'Hello, my girlies –'

Blanche and Elizabeth leapt up and launched themselves at their father with shrieks of joy; he put an arm around each of them and hugged them until their little boots lifted off the floor.

A great deal can be learned about a man if you watch him with his children; it gladdened me to see the way Sir James's face softened and glowed as he embraced the two girls.

He said, smiling over their heads, 'Good morning, Mrs Rodd; I'm sorry to interrupt, but I'm off to London and wanted to kiss my girls goodbye.'

'I wish you didn't have to go again,' Miss Blanche sighed. 'And I do so wish I could go too!'

'Not this time, my pet.'

'But how will I ever be married? By the time I have my season all the good husbands will be gone!'

'Nonsense – you'll be the toast of society and all the young blades will fight duels over you.'

'I don't think I want a husband,' Miss Elizabeth said.

Sir James tweaked her nose affectionately. 'Nobody's good enough for my fat little mouse. You can stay at home and take care of your poor old papa.' He glanced at the clock. 'I'll stay for a cup of French coffee – Blanche, tell that woman of your mother's.'

Miss Blanche jumped up, in a flurry of blue silk skirts, and tugged at an embroidered bell-pull; a very short time later, a female servant appeared. The woman had a hard red face and a foreign-looking cap, and as soon as she opened her mouth she revealed herself as the source of the guttersnipe accent; this is too often what happens when you leave impressionable young people in the company of servants. Mlle Thérèse stood in an insolent manner with her hands on her hips, and her response (in French) to Miss Blanche's request was, 'Coffee for how many? Is the old widow to have it too?'

Old widow, indeed! I did not take to this woman, with her small brown eyes watching me under a single, hairy eyebrow, and had an instinct that she was not to be trusted. Here was another puzzle – how could a man like Sir James Calderstone make such a bad choice of servant? I made a mental note to ask a few discreet questions downstairs.

He didn't really understand Mlle Thérèse, of course; he had made a Grand Tour as a boy and read French fairly well, but he couldn't actually speak the language, and as far as he knew, the words that tumbled out of her mouth might as well have been Sanskrit.

The Frenchwoman made coffee far better than most English servants, in the French style with hot milk (which made me remember the delicious bowls of coffee we had at Boulogne on Sunday mornings).

Before Sir James left for London, he asked for a private word with me, and we had a hurried conversation in the corridor outside the girls' room.

'When were you planning to make your investigations down in Suffolk?'

'I haven't made any plans yet, Sir James. And I don't like to leave your daughters when I've only just arrived.'

'Pish – I told you, that doesn't matter. The other business is far more pressing.'

'I'm thinking of appearances,' I reminded him. 'You don't want people to talk. And they will talk if the new governess suddenly leaves.'

Sir James shrugged impatiently. 'Don't people have anything better to do?'

'That never stopped anyone.' Half this man's mind was stuck in Westminster and I had to make him see that what went on in the country was of equal importance to this case. 'I don't think you quite appreciate, Sir James, how every single happening in a great house like this will be scrutinized by every man, woman and child for miles around – from the Mayor and Corporation down to the old women in the poorhouse. Appearances must be kept up.'

'Very well, if you have to leave in a hurry, I'll get my wife to take the girls off on a visit somewhere. Will that satisfy Mrs Grundy and her friends?'

'Perfectly,' I said. 'Where may I contact you, if I need to?'

'Write to me care of Filey – I gave you the address of his office. He has my entire confidence.'

'Very well – and I'd like to be clear about the steps you took relating to the anonymous letter.'

'Not many.' Sir James sighed; the energy momentarily died out of his face and he looked years older. 'One of the footmen at my London residence claimed to have caught a glimpse of the man who delivered it, dressed in the livery of a well-known stable down in the City.'

'Which one?'

'Which –? Dear me, Mrs Rodd.' He was smiling again. 'I had no idea you'd be familiar with such a section of society. It was the Cross Keys, near Leadenhall Market. Naturally I made inquiries – but the livery is a common one, and anyone might have borrowed it to disguise himself. I didn't go into it too deeply; I can't afford to have my business bandied about in stables and taprooms.'

He was quite right that the inns were the most notorious gossip-mills in London. A man of Sir James's standing was well advised to keep his name out of such places.

'You may leave the matter with me,' I said. 'I shall make a few inquiries of my own.'

My dear Mary,

I hope you are well and assure you that I am in rude health.

I left in such a flurry that I forgot to remind you about the window on the second-floor landing; the sash cord is hanging by the merest thread. I also meant to mention the back door. Please ask your youngest son to repair them, and pay him from the money I left in the little box with the picture of Windsor Castle, on the top shelf of the kitchen dresser.

I also have a small job for your son Joe, in his capacity as the under-manager of the stables at the Blue Boar in Smithfield. Could Mr Joe, with the utmost discretion, ask if any man from the Cross Keys at Leadenhall Market has ever been engaged to deliver a letter to the London residence of Sir James Calderstone? Or if any man has ever lent out his livery to another party? Or if he has ever heard the name Savile? Tell him he may feel free to jog memories with half-crowns. If he discovers anything he is to contact Mr J.F. Filey, at his office in Paget Court off Cheapside.

My situation here is very comfortable. For breakfast this morning, I feasted on soft white rolls and creamy butter, and I wished I could share them with you. I am afraid, dear Mary, that you don't take sufficient care of yourself while I am away. Make sure you are eating enough and keeping warm; I know we have been poor in the past, but now that I am working, I expect you to spend the money I left on things like good mutton chops. There was plenty of coal when I left and I beg you to build yourself a decent fire; the damp autumn weather is bad for your rheumatism.

The pickled cabbage on the third shelf of the pantry needs using up.

It would be nice to have a bushel-basket of russet apples before they are quite over. Please pay one of your grandsons to carry them from the market and – this is *VERY IMPORTANT* – to spread the apples out in the loft-space under the eaves on some dry straw *BY HIMSELF.* If I hear that you have tried to do any of this, I shall be downright cross with you – don't you even *THINK* of going up that ladder!

Dear Mary, I worry about leaving you alone; please take good care of yourself.

Yours,

Laetitia Rodd

Four

'I WAS SORRY TO HEAR that your mother is ill,' I said. 'I tried to ask her approval, but Mlle Thérèse said she wasn't to be disturbed.' (I did not add that the Frenchwoman had turned me away from Lady Calderstone's rooms in a most insolent manner.)

'Oh, she always rests in the afternoon,' Miss Blanche said dismissively. 'She won't make a fuss about it because Charlie's not here with us.'

Miss Blanche, Miss Elizabeth and I were in the carriage, which was taking us to call upon Mrs Orme and her sister-in-law. The afternoon was grey and gusty; wet brown leaves slapped against the windows. The fields that 'clothed the wold and met the sky' were bare; Matt's first parish was situated in a rather flat part of Gloucestershire, and when the fields were bare I always felt our rectory was marooned in a vast sea of gravy. The sight depressed me now, and the ambiguous status of the outing was making me uncomfortable.

'Mamma hasn't absolutely forbidden us to visit her,' Elizabeth said, surprisingly. 'She doesn't really make rules these days.'

'Oh.' I kept my voice neutral, but was puzzled by this. Lady Calderstone had not struck me as a woman who did not care about the education of her daughters; why did her wishes and opinions have so little weight? I made a mental note to ask some questions down in the servants' hall.

'It's since she was ill,' Blanche said, as if this explained everything. 'Four or five years ago Papa sent her away to the Alps to recover her health. But she's never been quite the same since she came home.' The carriage slowed and she leapt out of her seat. 'We have to walk from here, Mrs Rodd – the lane is too narrow for the horses.'

Mr Charles had said that Mrs Orme and her sister-in-law lived in a 'poor sort of way', but I was not prepared for the rustic appearance of their small cottage, with its dirty walls that cried out for a coat of whitewash and a thatched roof that was three parts moss. We picked our way delicately along the rutted track, and the girls called out happily when the two women emerged from the front door to greet us.

As far as a person's physical appearance is concerned, I am a firm believer in the old maxim 'handsome is as handsome does', and hope I am not trivial enough to judge people upon their looks.

But it was the first thing I noticed about the famous Helen Orme – the fact that she was as exquisitely pretty as a china shepherdess, with shining dark hair, porcelain complexion and eyes of that rare, deep blue. She was two-and-thirty, yet her small figure was all grace and youthfulness. Her grey dress was as simple and modest as a servant's – but from her manner, her speech and her bearing, I knew instinctively that she was a lady.

Was this truly the daughter of a poor curate? I watched her as closely as I dared while Blanche and Elizabeth smothered her in their embraces. Dear me, I thought, no wonder

Mr Charles fell in love with her; how could he help himself? She shook my hand with a shy cordiality that was very winning, though I had a strong instinct that she was firmly on her guard.

There was no such mystery about her sister-in-law. Miss Winifred Orme was a toothy, long-faced spinster, of the type you often find among the unmarried sisters and daughters of the clergy. I had an impression that she was a kind, cheerful soul who repaid even a small amount of love with absolute devotion.

We were shown into a little sitting room, square and clean, with plain furniture, a tiny wink of a fire in the neat fireplace and one or two relics of better days – an engraved silver jug, an old sewing box inlaid with ivory and a little wooden stand of books. Above the mantelshelf hung a painting of a horse-faced young clergyman I took to be the late Mr Orme, with a lock of faded brown hair set into the frame. Everything here told a sadly familiar story of making-do, of mending, stitching and scraping, and clinging to the very hem of gentility.

There was one servant, a stooping, grey-headed old woman named Patty, who carried in the tea-board and passed round slices of seed cake. It was all perfectly pleasant, but wretchedly meagre compared to the luxury of Wishtide. Miss Blanche and Miss Elizabeth, however, didn't seem to notice or care; they laughed and chattered like magpies, vying to give Mrs Orme their news.

I did my best to contribute to the conversation, so that no one would notice how intensely I was watching and listening – but Mrs Orme gave me one or two sharp glances, making me wonder what she had to hide.

Mostly, her attention was fixed upon the two girls, and I decided I liked the way she paid attention to them, talked with them, smiled at their drolleries. She had made real friendships with these strangely neglected little potentates, taking the time to listen to them properly when no one else did. If only Mr Charles had not gone and fallen in love with her, she would have been a far better companion for the girls than that sour French servant. I allowed my professional scrutiny to slip for a moment, touched to observe how Blanche and Elizabeth blossomed before me. What a pity it all was.

But back to the task in hand – my chance came when Miss Winifred took the girls out of the room to show them a box of kittens in the scullery. Mrs Orme and I both smiled to hear their cries of adoration.

'They're dear girls,' she offered shyly.

'Yes,' I said. 'They have made me most welcome, and I'm sure I shall enjoy teaching them.'

'Oh, certainly – they are quick to learn – though Blanche is too easily distracted, and not overfond of making an effort.'

'She sang me one of the Italian songs you taught her,' I said. 'It was quite charming, and made me wish I'd had a chance to learn the language myself. But my father was a country clergyman, and could never have afforded such a luxury.'

I kept my tone as neutral as possible; was it my imagination, or had Mrs Orme become a shade more wary of me?

'Mine too.' She met my gaze levelly.

'Our parish was at Greater Moseley in Gloucestershire,' I said, 'in the countryside to the south of Stroud – perhaps you know the area?'

'No, I'm afraid not.' She was (as I was) doing her best to sound light and gossipy, but I thought I heard a hint of unease. 'I grew up on the Suffolk coast – my father's parish was in a

little place called Gallowcross, miles from anywhere of conse-
quence. I learned my Italian when I was a governess, and the
family moved to Italy.'

'What a splendid opportunity,' I said. 'You were fortunate.'

Mrs Orme stared at me in silence for a moment, her lovely
face unreadable.

'In some ways,' she said, 'the move was extremely unfortunate for me – but I met my husband and Winifred, and that was
the best stroke of fortune I'd ever had in my life.'

Winifred, bustling cheerfully into the room with a plate of
muffins, caught the end of this. 'My dear Helen, it was the
workings of Providence and luck had nothing to do with it.
Her employer died, Mrs Rodd; all the money had gone and
poor Helen was left alone and destitute, hundreds of miles
from home.' Her voice was warm with affectionate indignation. 'What is a young woman to do in such a situation?
Helen appeared on our doorstep one night, nearly dead
from fever. We took her in and my brother married her.'
(This story had some gaps, I thought; Miss Winifred rapped
out the facts as if to get them over with.) 'Will you have a
muffin?'

I glanced at the portrait above the fireplace. 'And that, I
take it –'

'Yes, that's Edmund, and not a bad likeness,' Miss Winifred
said. 'Though it doesn't show enough of his sense of fun –'

'Or his gentleness,' Mrs Orme said softly; she looked at her
sister-in-law and the watchfulness melted from her face. 'And
the greatest artist in the world couldn't have painted the sheer
goodness that shone out of him; it was nothing less than the
light of the Holy Spirit.'

This was a large statement to make over a tea-table; I was reminded of Mr Charles's grumbles about 'dead saints'.

But I was sure, in my bones, that Helen Orme had sincerely loved her husband, and was deeply, genuinely attached to his sister. I have a very fine nose for humbug, and would have bet a quarter's rent on it; this little cottage was filled with the kind of happy, wholesome atmosphere that cannot be counterfeited. I did not believe for a moment that Mrs Orme was a ruthless fortune-hunter. I liked the woman. I had not expected to like her.

Neither had I expected to assess the situation as quickly as I did. Likeable she may have been – but I could not tell Sir James that Helen Orme was nothing more fearsome than a poor, blameless little governess. I knew when I was being lied to.

In the absence of both Sir James and his son, the bustle of the great house was muted, as if someone had put it to sleep like the castle in the story of the Sleeping Beauty. Miss Blanche and Miss Elizabeth were called to a private dinner with their mother in her sitting room, and I was free to do a little investigating.

Once I had finished my admirable supper (pigeon pie, roasted potatoes, plum tart and cream – oh, how I wished I could spirit a plateful over to Mrs B), I carried my own tray back to the kitchen. Thorpe, the butler, had gone to town with Sir James. I had calculated that with no formal dinner to cook, it would be relatively quiet belowstairs, and I hadn't yet taken a look at the servants' quarters. Experience had taught me that the domestics are the engine of any house, and I was impressed by the quiet order that reigned here.

The back staircase was bare, clean and adequately lit. The vast kitchen, with its shadowy vaulted ceiling and brick walls hung with copper pans, was empty save for a solitary maidservant scrubbing an enormous wooden table. Somewhere, in another room behind a closed door, there was a comfortable murmur of talk, and occasional bursts of laughter.

'Mrs Rodd – may I help you, ma'am?' Mrs Craik had appeared at my elbow, instantly alert to my invasion of her domain. 'Was your dinner to your satisfaction?'

I knew that I must play this with the utmost care, and gave the housekeeper what I hoped was my friendliest smile. 'I beg your pardon, Mrs Craik; my dinner was excellent; I just thought I'd save someone a journey.'

'Thank you, ma'am. You are most considerate.' By the flickering light of the small oil-lamp she held, I saw Mrs Craik relax a little, now she saw that I had not come to criticize or complain, and knew my place to a nicety (a governess must inhabit that murky hinterland between upstairs and downstairs, belonging to neither; if she is too familiar with the servants they resent waiting on her; if too grand, ditto). 'I was just about to have a cup of tea in my parlour – perhaps you would care to join me?'

It was kind of her, but also an important test of my character – was I about to play the archdeacon's lady and think myself too fine to sit in a housekeeper's parlour? 'Why yes, Mrs Craik,' I said promptly. 'That would be delightful.'

Mrs Craik smiled, and led me through the dark corridors into the sudden light and warmth of a beautifully snug little parlour, the very essence of a good housekeeper's private domain. Rose-patterned chintz hung at the windows and covered the two small armchairs beside the lively fire. The reflection of the dancing flames flickered in the gilded picture frames, the plump yellow Staffordshire lions on the chimney-piece and the gleaming brass fender.

'What a charming sitting room you have here, Mrs Craik,' I said, sinking into one of the armchairs. 'You have made yourself an ideal retreat from the world.'

'Indeed it is, ma'am.' With careful precision, she poured hot water from a copper kettle into a flowered china teapot. 'Wishtide is wonderfully well-appointed; it's not Sir James's way to do anything by halves. In the old house my parlour was dark and all over earwigs – though between ourselves I miss it sometimes.'

'The old house?'

'I mean the place that stood here before, Mrs Rodd – the one that Sir James's father pulled down to build this castle. It wasn't nearly so grand, but a lot more homely in my book. I was born on the estate, and I've lived with the family since I was a girl of fourteen. Do you take sugar?'

'No thank you.'

'Will you have a piece of shortbread? I make it with my own hands – I don't trust anyone else.'

'Thank you, Mrs Craik; that is the best possible advertisement.'

She was pleased, and getting easier with me by the minute; I saw that she was lonely in her solitary housekeeper's splendour, and welcomed the chance to talk to someone (I sympathized; I had known terrible loneliness after Matt died, and would still be a solitary old crow if I hadn't found dear Mary to chat with of an evening). We settled luxuriously beside the fire with our cups of tea. The shortbread was so good that I could ask for the recipe with absolute sincerity, and this broke any remaining ice between us.

Mrs Craik had grown up in the service of the Calderstone family, and spoke of them as her own – in other words, with a mixture of fondness and exasperation. She was devoted to Sir James, whom she had known since infancy, and to his three children. When she talked about Her Ladyship, however, her tone became anxious; she looked at me in a sizing-up way, as if wondering whether or not to tell me something.

Pretending not to have noticed, I changed the subject to the girls, who were her pets; for the next few minutes, I allowed her to tell me how clever they were, how pretty Miss Blanche was, how naughty she had been as a little girl, what a sweet nature Miss Bessie had.

'I must confess,' I said, 'since we are so confidential – please do not repeat this – I have been sorely puzzled by the way these nice, good-hearted girls behave towards their mother.'

'Oh dear,' Mrs Craik sighed, wincing as I hit the nerve. 'Oh dear.'

'We paid a call this afternoon without asking Her Ladyship's leave. Dear Miss Elizabeth told me – cool as a cucumber – that they never listen to her requests. Miss Blanche implied that her mother was an invalid, yet she seemed perfectly healthy when I waited upon her last night.'

'She's no invalid,' Mrs Craik said. 'Between ourselves, it's all the fault of Sir James, for the children take their tone from him.'

'Do they not stand up for their mother?'

'Mr Charlie did once – since when, his father has been a lot more careful to treat her properly in front of him. But he's away a great deal, and the girls have fallen into Sir James's manner of speaking with her. I have taken him to task about it myself, on more than one occasion – I've known him since the day he was born and I feel free to speak my mind. Not that he takes any notice.'

'Good gracious,' I said. 'What does he do to her?'

'It's mostly in the way he speaks to her – contemptuous-like. If I didn't run such a tight establishment, Mrs Rodd, some of the servants would do it too. But I will not have it; I make sure they treat her with true Christian civility, and pity her suffering.' She glanced at me sharply. 'I hope you don't think I'm going too far out of my situation; it's a relief to talk about it.'

'You may rely on my discretion, Mrs Craik,' I assured her. 'I'm not a gossip. But this is all very strange. Did Sir James turn against his wife suddenly? Surely he loved her once?'

'Oh yes, it was very much a love-match; I'll never forget the day he brought her home. She was just eighteen and the two of them were head-over-ears. And then the children came along, bless them – and I would've sworn at the assizes they were happy.'

She pursed her thin lips, obviously longing to say more.

'Miss Blanche said her mother had a serious illness a few years ago,' I prompted. 'She went to the Alps to recuperate.'

'Well,' Mrs Craik said, 'I don't know about any illness, but she certainly went away, and didn't come home until Sir James fetched her back six months later. And that's when it started – his being so cold and hard towards her. It nearly broke my heart sometimes, to hear her sobbing and crying. I wanted to help more, but only the Frenchwoman was allowed to wait on her.'

'Oh, yes,' I said, 'I've met Mlle Thérèse.' (How convenient, and how interesting, that she'd brought the subject up without

47

my asking.) 'And between ourselves, Mrs Craik, she made me a little uneasy.'

'Hmmm,' the housekeeper sniffed. 'You're not the only one. Sir James brought her back with them as a lady's maid. She keeps to herself, does that one.'

'It must be difficult, when she speaks no English.'

'Of course I made allowances. But she has a nasty temper on her, ma'am; she pinches and cuffs my kitchen-girls until they're all terrified of her.'

'I wonder that Sir James continues to employ such a person.'

'I asked him, but he brushed me off like a fly; said nobody else understood Her Ladyship's illness.'

Hmm, I thought, illness fiddlesticks – I smell a classic cover-up.

Sure enough, Mrs Craik whispered, 'It's my opinion – my very private opinion – that there might have been some sort of scandal behind it all.'

'What kind of scandal?'

'I couldn't tell you that; I only know what I've seen with my own eyes. But this was once a happy family, Mrs Rodd – and now it is a sad one.'

Five

M Y QUIET LIFE AS a country governess did not last long. A scant week after my arrival in Lincolnshire, before I had another chance to study Mrs Orme, I received a note from my brother, sent by special messenger at vast expense – 'Come home at once.'

My first reaction was that I could not leave my situation – and then I remembered that I was not a genuine governess, and this *was* my situation. I had to stop thinking about French verbs and Diabelli's exercises for the pianoforte, and apply my mind to the real work in hand.

I went at once to wait upon Lady Calderstone, in that glittering *Arabian Nights* upstairs drawing room where she seemed to spend most of her time; I had barely seen her after our first meeting, but had worn a groove in my brain with wondering about what Mrs Craik had told me.

When I explained to her that my brother had called me back to town, she said only, 'Oh, Mrs Rodd, you're not to worry, Sir James has arranged everything.' Her Ladyship's taut, skinny frame was swamped in a flowing dressing gown of some shimmering pink material, and she was all smiles. 'He has given me leave to take the girls away on a visit to my cousins in

Yorkshire – my dearest cousins, in their dear old house – and we shall be there until at least the end of November.'

This sounded odd to me; why did she need 'leave' to visit her own family, like a servant?

I smiled and thanked her, rather touched by the happiness that shone in her face, sponging away the lines and making her, for a moment, look no older than Miss Blanche.

I found the two girls dancing a polka in their sitting room, whooping with excitement.

'It's not that we won't miss you, Mrs Rodd.' Miss Bessie always took pains not to hurt people's feelings. 'But we haven't seen the Grahames for such ages.'

'Our Cousin Esther was supposed to come to us last summer,' Miss Blanche said breathlessly. 'And then Papa suddenly put her off – you see, she's the girl he wanted Charlie to marry, before he went and fell in love with *La Belle Hélène*.'

I didn't like the pert tone of this, and would have said so if I had really been their governess. But I wanted to hear something about these Grahames, Cousin Esther in particular, and kept up my look of polite interest. 'Did Mr Charles have feelings for Miss Grahame?'

Both girls giggled; Miss Blanche said, 'He loves her in the same way that we all do – but not in an in-love way.'

'Papa was dreadfully disappointed,' Miss Bessie said. 'He'd quite set his heart on it.'

'She must be a very eligible match,' I suggested.

'Not really,' said Blanche. 'They're poor as mice.'

This sharpened my curiosity; why was a worldly, ambitious man like Sir James eager to marry his son to a poor country cousin? It didn't have a bearing on the case as far as I could judge, and I didn't ask any further questions, but only listened with half an ear to the excited chatter of the girls, while I wondered why I had been summoned with such urgency.

'The last letter was bad enough,' Sir James said. 'This one is nothing short of outrageous. All my plans – everything I have worked for – will be ruined if one word gets out. Do you understand, Mrs Rodd? It was one thing to have the business of the Orme woman tattled about – but when the name of my wife – my wife –!' He stopped, trembling with the intense fury that is laced with fear.

'Do I take it there has been a demand for money?' I asked.

'One hundred pounds in gold,' Mr Filey put in grimly. 'And that will merely be a beginning – unless we can find the man who wrote this.'

His veined hand rested on a sheet of paper that lay on the table between us; I saw the words: '*Yr wife is a WHORE. How many WHORES do you want in yr family?*'

'Don't tell me to ignore it,' Sir James said. 'I can't afford to.' His handsome, high-coloured face was haggard and pale in the pool of light thrown out by the oil-lamp.

I took a few deep breaths to clear my head. It was late in the evening and I had spent a long day travelling from Lincolnshire to Fred's house in Highgate. Once there I'd barely had time to wash the smuts of railway soot from my face and swallow a cup of tea before a hansom cab had taken us to a great white square in the West End, choked with magnificent carriages and gold-braided footmen.

'But this isn't Sir James's gaff,' Fred had cheerfully told me. 'It's the London residence of a Mrs Hardy – she's throwing a dinner party for some very important gentlemen.'

'Gentlemen? There will be no ladies present?'

'Without wishing to speak ill of Mrs Hardy, she's not in any position to receive ladies. When Sir James is officially at his London residence, he mostly lives here with her.'

'Oh. I see.'

'It's one of those things the whole town knows, but never mentions.'

He hadn't needed to say more. I ought to have been shocked (I was sorry for Lady Calderstone) but was mostly intensely curious; archdeacons' widows do not often find themselves in the sinful salons of the demi-monde.

Not that I had seen more than a tantalizing glimpse of this wicked world; my brother and I had been hustled down the area steps and into the basement of the house, where we found Sir James and the faithful Mr Filey waiting for us in a chilly butler's pantry. There was another man present, standing awkwardly with his hat in his hands; the slope of his chin and the violent colour of his sparse hair revealed him as Mr Joe Bentley, to whom I had given the task of finding out about the first letter. We exchanged smiles; he bobbed his head in a half-bow. He was ill-at-ease in his thick coat and leather gaiters.

'I apologize for the cloak-and-dagger manner of our meeting,' Mr Filey said. 'When the second letter came, I thought it important to act at once. And there has been a development – Bentley here has a very interesting story to tell.'

We all looked at Mr Joe, who fiddled with his hat, stared down at his boots and mumbled, 'Mrs Rodd wanted me to find out if anyone had borrowed a greatcoat in the livery of the Cross Keys. So I asked around, bought a few drinks, and sure enough someone did.'

'You found him?' Sir James snapped. 'Give me his name!'

Mr Joe clammed up, startled by his sudden violence.

'Please.' Mr Filey laid a gentle hand upon Sir James's sleeve. 'Let him speak.'

'Who was it, Mr Joe?' I asked.

He looked at me and visibly relaxed a little; I wasn't nearly such a forbidding figure as the three gentlemen in their starched white evening shirts. 'It was one of the fellows who hangs around the yards a-looking for a bit of casual work, ma'am. You let 'em muck out the stalls and suchlike, and then they take their wages straight to the nearest tavern. This fellow was rough-spoke and rough-looking, with a beard up to his eyes and his clothes all shiny with dirt. One of the men I spoke to at the Cross Keys said this particular party had given him five shillings to borrow his greatcoat – half a crown down, half a crown on return.'

'And?' Sir James was in an anguish of impatience.

Once again, Mr Filey touched his arm to restrain him. 'And you spoke with this man who borrowed the coat?'

'Yes, sir,' Mr Joe said. 'He wasn't averse to talking in exchange for rum. Said his name was Arrowsmith.'

'Arrowsmith?' Sir James was bewildered. 'That means nothing to me.'

Mr Joe's lips twitched. 'It weren't his real name, sir. He swore all manner of oaths that he'd never sent anyone any letters or borrowed any coats. But he did let slip that he had been in prison. And in them days his name was Savile.'

'By God – I knew it!' Sir James shouted, bringing his fist down on the table with a force that nearly knocked over the lamp. 'All roads lead back to that damned woman!'

The door opened; a soft female voice murmured, 'James?'

He attempted to pull himself together. 'Go back upstairs, my love; I'll join you in a minute.'

In the patchy light I had a brief vision of dark hair and eyes, of glittering diamonds and lustrous lengths of creamy silk, before the door was swiftly closed. Fred and I glanced at each other; no explanation was necessary here. The 'my love' that had slipped out of Sir James said it all.

There was a silence, during which Sir James breathed heavily and Mr Joe's boots creaked.

'Well done, Bentley,' Fred said. 'Did you manage to find out anything else about this man?'

'Was he ever married?' Sir James asked eagerly. 'Did he mention a wife?'

'Well, yes sir,' Mr Joe said. 'He mentioned two or three, but I don't think he was properly married to any of them.'

'Did he mention a lady by the name of Helen Orme?'

'No, sir.'

'Are you quite certain?'

'Yes, sir,' Mr Joe said. 'It's a name I would've remembered, and I don't remember it.' All the Bentleys had a stubborn way of sticking to a story that made them ideal witnesses.

'Why was he in prison?' my brother asked.

'Thieving,' Mr Joe said. 'He worked as a manservant, in the service of several young gentlemen. He was locked up for whacking one of 'em on the head and making off with his watch-and-chain.'

'Thank you, Bentley,' Mr Filey said. 'You've done excellent work; my clerk is waiting outside the door and will show you out.'

Mr Joe – looking relieved – bowed to us all, and left this shadowy room as fast as possible.

'Now, gentlemen,' Fred said, 'you may show us this letter.'

Without a word, Mr Filey pushed the grubby sheet of paper across the table.

Yr wife is a WHORE. How many WHORES do you want in yr family?

I was in Vevey and saw everything. Now I collect or I talk. Bring one hundred pounds IN GOLD to the Goat in Boots in Salt Lane by Wapping Old Stairs. The Prince is at home between the hours of eight and eleven in the evening, until the end of this week. Ask for him at the bar.

Come ALONE.

Fred, reading over my shoulder, chuckled. 'Quite an artist, this Mr Savile. The Prince, indeed! I'm acquainted with the Goat in Boots – it's where the fences hang out, and it's positively swarming with thieves and cut-throats.' His tone was cheerful, almost affectionate. 'The landlady's an old gorgon, but she's very fond of me – I got her off a charge of receiving stolen goods.'

'What are you going to do?' I asked (I had no idea myself what should be done; blackmail leaves its victims with no choices; you're damned either way).

'It's quite obvious what should be done,' Fred said. 'Take the money but fill the area with spies and then catch him red-handed; I have some very good connections around there.'

'No!' Mr Filey snapped. 'Out of the question!'

'Or call the police –'

Both Sir James and his lawyer paled at this suggestion.

'Heaven forbid!' Sir James said. 'My name must not be seen anywhere near this business.'

'Oh, you've decided to pay him, have you?' Fred smiled and shrugged. 'Personally I wouldn't advise it.'

'Sir James,' I said, 'if we are to help you in this matter, I think you should explain to us what happened at Vevey.'

The word made his face twitch painfully. 'I – I hoped I wouldn't need to tell you.' He shot a desperate, drowning-man look at me and Fred. 'This must never get out – but the place has very unhappy links with – with my family. With my wife.' He uttered the last word as if it choked him. 'She became involved with a certain man. He took her away from me.'

So that was it; the trip to Switzerland had been to fetch his straying wife home and cover up a potentially ruinous scandal.

'His name was Villiers – that's what he called himself, anyway. He was rich, with the manner and bearing of a gentleman – his true name quite respectable for all one knew – one of those fellows who goes slumming it on the Continent under a false identity – then disappears before anyone can make him face the consequences.' Sir James's voice was soaked with bitterness and anger. 'Naturally, he deserted her as such men do. There was a child born dead. My wife's servant saved her life and contacted me.'

'Mademoiselle Thérèse,' I said; now it was only too obvious why he had to employ the woman.

He nodded miserably. 'I told the children she'd gone away for her health. They must never know that their mother is a –' The colour deepened in his handsome face. 'Nobody else knew the truth, and so I was able to protect my family name. Or so I thought until that damned letter.'

His mouth puckered with distaste; the word he had not said was 'whore' but we all heard it in our minds. I found that I pitied Lady Calderstone. Poor creature, she had given her heart to a blackguard and lost her baby. And by the look of her husband, she would be paying for her 'crime' for the rest of her life. He had officially 'forgiven' her, but this was not forgiveness as it is known in Heaven.

'Mrs Rodd,' Mr Filey said, 'this blackmailer is connected to Helen Orme. Get down to Suffolk as soon as you can.'

'At once,' Sir James said. 'Do it immediately. I want to know everything about Helen Orme, and exactly who she was before she persuaded some fool of a consumptive clergyman to marry her. In the meantime this vile scoundrel – her true husband, for all we know – must be silenced.'

Mr Filey drew from his pocket a small leather purse, tight and heavy like a clenched fist. 'One hundred pounds in gold.' He placed it on the table. 'We need someone to deliver it; someone we can trust absolutely.'

Six

'DO STOP MAKING DIFFICULTIES,' I told my brother later, as the carriage pulled us eastwards along the river. 'You know I'm the ideal person to do this – all anyone ever notices about me is that I'm a respectable old widow, like thousands of others. We don't tend to have distinguishing features.'

'All right,' Fred said. 'But I keep thinking of Mamma and what she'd say if she could see us now.'

'She'd have fifty fits and accuse me of leading you into mischief,' I said, smiling to remember how often this had happened (and how often naughty Fred had been the leader).

This day had been endless, but I was no longer tired. Beyond the noise of the horses' hooves, we were surrounded by the clamour of the streets by night – shouts, snatches of abuse, bursts of laughter, of rough music. These were sounds that made my blood sing and fizz after the thick silence of the country.

The carriage blinds were tightly drawn. We sat in the dark, each knowing the other's blood was up; the two of us always did love an adventure.

'We must be getting closer,' Fred said. 'This isn't the most salubrious of places. I wish you'd stay inside the carriage.'

'You're too well-known in criminal circles,' I said. 'You'd be spotted at once – you said so yourself. Stop fretting; if anyone challenges me, I shall say I'm collecting on behalf of the Sisters of the Paraclete.'

Fred chuckled. 'Good notion, Letty – you could easily pass for one of those blessed old trouts.'

(These sisters were an order of Anglo-Catholic nuns, mostly genteel and in their middle years, who lived and worked in the most desperate city slums and were locally known as 'Black Bonnets' after their sober headgear; they were excellent ladies and in other circumstances I might have ticked Fred off for making fun of them.)

'I shall take that as a compliment,' I said.

The carriage slowed down and Fred's coachman called from the box, 'This is it, sir.'

Fred pulled the blind half-open to look outside. The carriage had stopped in a narrow court just off Salt Lane – you won't find this now; it was demolished to make way for the new docks. The Goat in Boots stood on the opposite corner of the crowded alley; a crazy, sagging collection of half-timbered gables and broken diamond-paned windows, which had somehow survived the Great Fire and was now on the point of disintegration. All the dirty windows were lit and the smoky bar was packed with sailors and rivermen. More men were gathered on the muddy pavement outside, all smoking clay pipes and drinking heaven knows what out of any vessel that would hold it.

'I can't let you do this,' Fred muttered. 'This is a den of thieves, and it's guarded by the worst-looking ruffians –'

I didn't like the look of them either; I was afraid and I knew it. But my blood was up. I wanted a look at this blackmailer.

'Please don't worry about me,' I said, in a voice that came out sounding surprisingly brave. 'This is a public place; there's safety in numbers – as our blackmailer knows very well.'

'But if you get into trouble –'

'I'll scream.' I was already opening the carriage door. I stepped out carefully, took a couple of deep breaths and walked across the street to the smoky press of men outside the Goat in Boots. A couple of heads turned towards me.

'Good evening, my brothers,' I said. 'I'm collecting on behalf of the Sisters of the Paraclete.'

I'm sorry to say that collecting for charity has always been the most reliable method I know of clearing a room; the crowd melted around me as if I had cast a spell. I was able to see the low door of the tavern, lit by one feeble lantern, and to make my way through into the taproom. A battered brute of a man stood behind the bar.

The moment he saw me, he yelled out: 'MISSIS!'

An odd little wooden door sprang open beside me, revealing a tiny room, a triangular snug with just enough space to accommodate a very small fireplace and one woman in an armchair – a small, sharp, toothless woman, with black eyes that took me in suspiciously. A great bunch of keys hung at her waist.

'I've told you lot before,' she said. 'I won't have you a-begging in my tavern.'

'I'm not one of the Sisters,' I said quietly. 'Kindly tell the Prince that I am here.'

'The Prince?' She stood up, on her guard yet unmistakably interested and bristling with greed; had the blackmailer been bragging about the gold that was coming to him?

'He's expecting me.'

'Wait there.' The landlady lifted up the bar and let herself out of her sentry-box.

I waited for about ten minutes, feeling very awkward in that smoky riverside taproom, and very conscious of being a solitary woman in a crowd of decidedly rough-looking men (good gracious, if Matt could see me now – his ultra-respectable wife surrounded by foreign sailors, thieves, fences and the very scum of the city).

The landlady elbowed her way back to me. 'He says he'll meet you outside.'

'Very well,' I said, leaning disagreeably close to her sullen, toothless face, so that we would not be overheard. 'I'll be waiting at the entrance to the alley across the way.'

'You alone, then?'

'Certainly not,' I snapped back at her. 'Do you think I'm a fool?'

'Oh.' (Frightful woman, I could almost see her regretfully shelving her plan to murder me.) 'He said alone.'

'I daresay that would suit him. But this is the only way he'll get his money.'

That last word sharpened the woman's eyes to flints. 'I'll tell him.'

The men outside the tavern let me pass through them and disappear into the darkness of the fetid court in which Fred had stopped the carriage.

His voice hissed behind me. 'Letty? Thank God – are you all right?'

'He's coming,' I whispered. 'Douse the lamps and stay well back.'

I heard him stumbling and swearing his way back over the broken, slimy stones; a moment later, the two lamps on the carriage were extinguished, and I stood in the shadows where the deepest darkness began. The racket of the tavern was building now; an Irish fiddler started up and there was clapping and stamping.

One figure detached itself from a small group of drinkers and made purposefully towards me – a tall, vigorous man, wrapped in a dirty coachman's cape, his face hidden under the brim of his hat.

He stood in the mouth of the alley, and I whispered, 'Stop there.'

'Where are you?' He stopped. 'No tricks – come out and give it to me. Like I said, I collect or I talk.'

His voice had an exaggerated roughness, as if he were trying to disguise it; I strained for a proper look at his face, and glimpsed in the light of a passing lantern a beard, a mouth, a flash of teeth. Nothing more.

I took a step towards him, holding out the little leather purse in the palm of my gloved hand (the one hundred gold sovereigns had a satisfying weight to them). He snatched the purse so quickly that I didn't even feel it – like a frog shooting out its tongue to catch a fly – and then he turned away and disappeared into the crowd, leaving me gaping foolishly at my empty palm.

'But of course they haven't heard the last of it,' Mrs Bentley said. 'He'll spend the money and come back for more.'

'Undoubtedly,' I said. 'Which leaves Sir James with the ticklish problem of shutting him up. The trouble in that family goes far beyond Mrs Orme; that family was broken when Lady Calderstone lost her heart to a man unworthy of such a sacrifice.'

It was the following morning, and we were busy in the kitchen at Well Walk. The day was cold and blustery, and I hadn't wanted to light more than one fire. I had spent the night at Fred's house, and walked over to Hampstead directly after breakfast. I had now just finished writing a letter to my connection down in Suffolk, and I was trying to keep it out of Mrs Bentley's flour – she was making pastry on the other side of the table.

'So this fellow you saw was Savile,' Mrs Bentley said slowly. 'He wrote those wicked letters – and he reckons he's the lawful husband of Helen Orme.'

'Sir James is convinced of it,' I said. 'He thinks the two of them are working together – though I can't see why Mrs Orme would accuse herself of being a "whore". I think Mr Savile is the kind of person who collects old scandals; he found out something about Mrs Orme, heard that Mr Charles was set on marrying her, and tried a spot of blackmail. He did not risk asking for money that first time – and between the first letter and the second, he somehow found out about the business in Switzerland.'

'The nasty Frenchwoman told him,' Mrs Bentley said. 'I'd put money on it.'

'Yes, Mlle Thérèse is the only person who knew; that's why Sir James is forced to employ the woman. Where would you look next?'

'Hmm.' Mary (still briskly rolling out her biscuit dough) frowned thoughtfully. 'Mrs Orme, of course – no smoke without fire in my experience. Then I'd investigate the Frenchwoman, see if she's working along of Savile. And then I'd want to know about the fellow who ran off with Her Ladyship.'

'Bravo, Mary – setting me right, as usual.' We had all forgotten about this man, whom Sir James had named as Villiers – another person who knew about Vevey. 'I'll get my brother to find out about him; unlike the wretched Savile, a "gentleman" leaves a trail through all the gentlemanly places – schools, clubs, tailors – and someone will know of him.'

'If you ask me,' Mrs Bentley said, 'the lady's been punished enough for what she did. Her husband's got a nerve, treating her like he does when he's living in open shame with his mistress. But that's how the world works, ma'am; gentlemen may do as they please.'

'That's not how it's written in Tidd's *Practice*,' I said. 'But it's about the size of it, and I don't like to think I might be aiding and abetting something that is basically unjust. As far as I can see, I have been hired to spoil the life of a poor young widow, just because she's pretty enough to make a rich man fall in love with her.'

'You liked her,' Mrs Bentley said.

'Yes, though we have only met once. I'm quite sure Mrs Orme has withheld certain facts about her past – but she didn't trust me any further. And how right she was.' I was feeling gloomy about the sordid shape my case was taking. 'Sir James wants me to save his public face, and I don't see what good can come from raking up the past.'

'Well, the truth's the truth,' Mrs Bentley said. 'It may not be pretty, but no one with a clean conscience needs to fear it.'

'I suppose you're right.'

'I'm simply taking the practical view and remembering the money.'

'Ah, that reminds me –' The homely warmth of the fire had induced a splendid calm, and my proper concerns were coming back to me. 'I looked in the Windsor Castle box, and you've spent hardly any of the money I left. Didn't you get my letter?'

'Oh yes, ma'am.' Mary froze into obstinacy. 'I got your letter and did everything you wanted; I gave my grandson Neddy a shilling to bring the apples and put them in the loft.'

'My dear Mary, I meant you to buy yourself decent food and warmth – or how can you expect me not to worry about you while I'm away? Your son Joe told me he called last Wednesday to find you sitting in the dark.'

'Oh,' Mrs Bentley huffed crossly, 'you don't want to listen to him; he's full of fancies.'

'Mr Joe doesn't strike me as a fanciful sort of man; he's a good son and he's anxious about you.'

'I ain't going to live with him, and that's that.'

'He's not trying to kidnap you,' I said. 'He and I had a useful conversation after our meeting last night. While I'm away in Suffolk, Mr Joe's little daughter Anny will come here to help you –' Seeing her mouth open to protest, I added firmly, 'I've paid her in advance, so there's nothing you can do about it.'

'Very good, ma'am; I won't argue, though it's a waste of money.'

I knew she was secretly relieved; the warmth of the extravagant blaze I'd built up in the kitchen grate was already easing the pain in her swollen knuckles. I turned up my petticoats to warm my legs and allowed myself a moment of perfect contentment; it was good to know that I had a home, be it ever so humble, and I wouldn't have swapped my beetle-infested Hampstead kitchen for all the Wishtides in the world.

Seven

THERE WAS, AS MARY observed later, 'no rest for the wicked'.

A scant two hours after congratulating myself for my contentment at home, I was in an upstairs room in another city tavern; a busy and prosperous establishment in Leadenhall Street by the old church of St Katharine Cree. It was the room they used for harmonic meetings, reeking of stale smoke and beer and dominated by a long table. Upon this table was laid the body of the murdered man.

The awful stillness of the corpse contrasted with the bustle around it. A young policeman stood guard at the door, keeping at bay the gawpers and idlers who wanted to stare. Fred had summoned me, Mr Joe Bentley, and a wrinkled, toothless woman who looked at first sight like a bundle of old clothes; daylight did not improve the appearance of the landlady of the Goat in Boots.

'He was found in the early hours of this morning,' Fred told us, 'in the alleyway that runs behind the back yards here. I found out because I pay certain people to tell me when a good corpse comes in. And this one's a beauty.'

My brother had a strong professional interest in corpses, and I'd long ago given up telling him to speak of the dead with more respect. I said a silent prayer for the man's soul, and then went to look at the body. I am not afraid of the dead; only living bodies are dangerous.

'Hmm,' I said. 'A beauty, indeed.'

The man's throat had been slashed and his face beaten to a bloody, shapeless pulp.

'Is it him, do you think, Bentley?' Fred asked, eyes gleaming. 'Is this the man you knew as Savile?'

Mr Joe (just like his mother) was not to be hurried. He came up to the corpse and looked at it with calm concentration. 'Yes sir, I'd say that's the man – the face might be gone but the hair's right, and the scar on his hand.' He pointed to a mark like a thick red worm on the back of the corpse's left hand. 'That's him, all right.'

'Would you swear to it before the coroner?'

'Yes, sir.'

'Splendid! Thank you, Bentley.' My brother turned to the landlady, who was still hanging back by the door. 'Well, Mrs Dooley?'

'I don't know nothing,' the woman said sullenly.

Fred chuckled. 'Peg, my darling, don't you love me any more? I'm the man who saved you from the gallows!'

'I dunno what you want with me.'

'I want you to look at this man,' Fred said. 'Is this your Prince?'

'I dunno what you're talking about.'

'Now come along, Peg – if you help me here, I'll see that you don't get into any trouble.' He added, in a polite and apologetic tone, 'Whereas if you don't help me, I won't be able to stop the peelers turning your gaff inside-out.'

Her face pleated into a furious scowl, but she shuffled across the room to look at the corpse; if she felt any emotion, she did not show it.

'That's him.'

'Excellent – I knew you'd see sense,' Fred said. 'Did you know his name?'

'No; the Prince was all he give me.'

'How long had he been lodging with you?'

'Since late September – just after Michaelmas.'

'Did he tell you anything about himself?'

'No, and I didn't ask,' Mrs Dooley snapped. 'All I know is that he paid cash in advance.'

'I saw you last night,' I said. 'I had a delivery to make to the Prince, and you acted as go-between. Was that the last time you saw him?'

'Yes.'

'I had the impression that you were expecting payment for something; did you get it?'

The woman's poisonous expression of fury told us everything we needed to know.

'We'll leave it at that for the time being,' Fred said briskly. 'You may slink back to your tavern, Peg. And Bentley, thank you.'

Mr Joe bowed himself out of the room. Mrs Dooley followed him a moment later.

'Go with them, Constable,' Fred said to the young policeman. 'Make sure someone takes their names for the coroner.'

'Well, Letty?' Fred asked, when the two of us were alone with the corpse. 'What about you?'

'I can't swear that it's definitely the man I saw last night,' I said. 'But the clothes could very well be the same – and the hair, and the unshaven chin. What's left of it, anyway.' I had glimpsed only the mouth of the blackmailer last night, and only the lower lip was still intact, encasing a row of crooked, discoloured teeth.

'The money was gone, of course,' Fred said. 'I haven't told the police he'd just taken delivery of one hundred pounds – they found nothing on him except three and three farthings and half a meat pie.'

'Does Sir James know yet?'

'Yes, I sent round a note directly I heard – to Mrs Hardy's house, where I was sure to find him. He came to my chambers at once.'

'Was he shocked? Surprised?'

'I'd say more relieved and delighted,' Fred said wryly. 'It's very good news for him, isn't it? He thinks the danger of exposure has gone, and he hasn't yet worked out that if the police knew about the money, he'd be Suspect Number One.'

'In that case, shouldn't we tell the police?'

'No; I want more facts first. Take a good look at him, Letty; you're always noticing little things I've managed to miss.'

'The man who spoke to Joe Bentley was a vagabond and a drunkard,' I said. 'But look at his hands.'

'What about them?'

I touched with my gloved finger one of the dead hands. 'They are dirty, the nails are blackened and cracked – yet the blemishes look fairly recent. And what's left of his linen was once of good quality. All this would fit a former manservant; he had a little education and wasn't accustomed to the roughest labour.'

'Anything else?'

My brother knew me very well, and had picked up my uneasiness; something wasn't quite right. He let the silence stretch on while I tried to get my thoughts in order.

At last I said, 'I'm sure that's Savile if Mr Joe says so – but I really cannot be sure he was the same man that took the money from me last night.'

'Well, it was pitch dark.'

I shut my eyes for a moment, to make a picture of the encounter, and suddenly recalled the glimpse I had caught of the man's mouth.

'Teeth!' I cried out. 'Of course!'

'Eh?'

'The man who took the money had strong, white teeth; nothing like the remaining teeth on this poor creature. This isn't our Prince.'

'I knew it,' Fred said, chuckling. 'I made a bet with myself that dear old Peg was lying; I wonder how long it'll take His Highness to come back for more supplies.'

'Do you think he's still at the Goat in Boots?'

'No, he'll have made off by now.'

'I could try to find out where he went; someone must know.'

'Go to Suffolk,' Fred said. 'I want to know where Helen Orme comes in.'

My 'connection' in Suffolk was none other than my dearest old friend Minnie Gilmore – the lovely, naughty creature who had (so much to Miss Blanche's disappointment) ended her rebellion in Boulogne by marrying the curate. For the past thirty years she had been Mrs Minnie Beswick, wife of the Reverend Jack Beswick, mother of seven children, and a dedicated busybody – clergy wives in general are goldmines of local history.

The Beswicks' parish of Holy Trinity, Pavenham was situated in pleasant countryside between Lowestoft and Yarmouth, a good distance back from the flat, bleak coast. I had braved the magnificent library at Wishtide to search maps and guidebooks for Gallowcross, where Mrs Orme claimed to have grown up, and found no sign of it, probably because the village was so small. I had consulted *Crockford's*, and again found nothing. But that could simply have meant that a tiny parish had been absorbed into the fringes of a larger. Never mind, I thought – Minnie will know.

And my heart lifted with the prospect of seeing her; dear old thing, it had been five years since we met last, though we still exchanged letters every few months. On the final stage of the endless journey, jolting in a farmer's cart, I stopped fretting about the case and tried to make out familiar landmarks through the thick rural darkness. I had always relished my visits to Minnie and her husband, though it made me a little melancholy now to remember that my last stay had been with Matt.

Pavenham was a large and thriving Suffolk village, where very old half-timbered houses and shops clustered around a market square with a quaint stone buttercross in the middle. The rectory lay on the outskirts of the village; it was a handsome, sturdy, grey stone box of a house, covered with wisteria in the summer. The cart turned into the gate; I saw a row of lighted windows. The front door burst open, revealing a stout silhouette, and a moment later Minnie's arms were around me.

When we were girls, Minnie had been an enviably pretty little thing, all pink cheeks, blue eyes and golden curls. Nowadays she wore her curls tucked away under a white cap, and her sprite-like figure had ballooned. But she was still pretty – 'bonny', as Matt would have said – and though she did everything as noisily as possible, she presided over her large household with admirable efficiency. I was too late for the family dinner, but with her own hands Minnie had made me a delicious Welsh rarebit, and while I ate it beside the fire in my room, she rattled out a storm of news. It was odd to me, to hear of her grown-up sons, her married daughter, her two little grandchildren. My world was very small compared with hers, and had stopped turning altogether when Matt died. The contrast between our two lives hurt me a little, but I was too fond of my old friend to hold it against her.

'The two young men you saw on the landing are Jack's pupils,' Minnie went on. 'He has a talent for getting blockheads into the universities and the extra money has been an absolute blessing – mind you, they eat like horses, and Cook's always threatening to leave – and I'm at my wits' end keeping them in mended socks and clean linen.'

We did not get round to the real purpose of my visit until very late, when the household had retired and the perpetual background hubbub had subsided. Mr Beswick came in with the sherry decanter, and laughingly asked where the murder was (Minnie and her husband knew about my work; Jack Beswick had once given me some information regarding the history of a certain rural dean, which had helped solve a particularly sordid case of blackmail).

'Come on, Letty – you didn't come all this way just for the pleasure of our company.'

Jack had been tall, dark and intense as a young man; he had filled out now and the Byronic dark hair had turned grey.

'It's not a murder this time,' I told him (he did not need to know about Savile). 'I'm looking into the history of a local family – the Lyndhursts.'

To my disappointment they both looked blank.

'He was a curate, at a place called Gallowcross.'

'Oh, to be sure – George Lyndhurst!' Minnie remembered first. 'Gracious, I haven't thought of the poor man for years – of course you recall him, dear. You buried him.'

'So I did; I couldn't tell you how many years ago. Poor old Lyndhurst. Why on earth would anyone want to know about him?'

'Did you know him well?' I asked.

'We were acquaintances at Cambridge,' Beswick said. 'He was a sizar; a scholarship man who helped in the kitchens and so forth in exchange for his tuition. A clever fellow, but with no connections whatsoever – only just barely a gentleman. He married a woman of similar obscurity, and managed to obtain the miserable curacy at Gallowcross, a few miles down the coast from here. They don't keep a man there these days. Half the village was gradually swallowed by the sea; the people left and the parish was merged with another.'

'It was a wretched little living,' Minnie said, 'worth barely a hundred pounds a year.'

'Did they have children?'

She sighed and stared into the fire. 'Mrs Lyndhurst had baby after baby, but they kept dying until her heart was quite broken; it was a dreadful shame. There was only one surviving daughter; a sweet, delicate girl.'

'Do you remember her name?' I was not going to prompt.

'Ellen,' Minnie said. 'No – it was Helen.'

(Bingo, as Fred would've said; it seemed that Helen Orme had been telling the truth about her background after all.)

The following morning, armed only with Mr Beswick's rather vague directions, I put on my stoutest boots and toughest bonnet and walked out to Gallowcross. I wanted a look at the place, and I needed to find out where Miss Helen Lyndhurst had gone after the deaths of her parents; there were still some very large gaps in her history.

The day was cold, with a brisk east wind, and the sun trapped behind a veil of thin cloud. The tide was out and the sea far away across miles of sand – this is a very flat piece of coast, where you can barely see the lines between grey sand, grey sea and grey sky. The villages here fight a constant battle with the sea, which the sea appears to be winning; it encroaches a little more each year, giving the little huddles of fishing boats and wooden shacks at the water's edge a fragile, temporary look.

I nearly missed Gallowcross altogether; the solitary finger-post was half grown over with ivy. What was left of the village was nothing more than a couple of dilapidated cottages, one without its roof, and a poor little church with boarded windows. Beside it was a red-brick ruin I guessed to have once been the rectory.

My intention had been to question the villagers, but the place was deserted. I followed the sound of hens to the single inhabited homestead, where I found an old woman with her head tied up in a shawl, digging in her embattled, sand-scoured vegetable garden.

I gave her a friendly good day, and said I was looking up an old family connection in the area.

The old woman, unlike Minnie and her husband, recalled the Lyndhursts at once. 'They were such kind, good people, ma'am – they'd take any amount of trouble to help those poorer than themselves.'

'I was told that the sea had swallowed half this village,' I said.

'That it has, ma'am; we were a bigger place in those days.'

'I believe the Lyndhursts had a daughter.'

'Yes – that was Miss Helen – a little, sickly slip of a thing – used to help her mother with the Sunday School teaching, and making up parcels for the poor, and led all the singing at the services.'

This could easily be a description of the woman I had met; everything I had seen so far chimed with what Mrs Orme had told me. And yet –

Something was not right.

'When did Mr and Mrs Lyndhurst pass away?' I asked.

'I couldn't say exactly, ma'am; he went first, and she followed a few months later. They're in the churchyard along of all their poor babies, waiting for the Last Day.'

'I should like to see their graves,' I said. 'Could you show me?'

'The churchyard's on the other side of the church, ma'am, but I can't show you any graves; they only had a little wooden cross, and a couple of hard winters blew it to bits.'

'Do you know what became of Miss Helen after they died?'

The old woman frowned, thinking hard. 'She was away from home by then. I think she was working as companion to a rich old lady – over in Ipswich.'

'Do you recall the lady's name?'

'No, ma'am.'

'Did Miss Helen never come back here?'

'No,' the old woman said. 'We never saw her again; perhaps it made her too sad.'

It made me sad, too – the whole place was drenched with sadness. Only Heaven remembers it all now. I bestowed a sixpence upon the old woman and turned my steps back to Pavenham. I had learned nothing about Helen Orme, save that her family were so poor as to leave barely a smudge upon the world to show they had ever been in it.

What little information I had I acted upon at once; the Dean of Ipswich was an old friend, and I wrote to him, asking if he or any of his clergy had heard of a lady's companion named Helen Lyndhurst.

Eight

The Deanery

Ipswich

17th November

Dear Letty,

How delightful to hear from you; we were wondering only yesterday when we had last seen you. My scatterbrained Louie says three years but I say more like five – when your great-souled Matt came to preach the Easter sermon. I'm somewhat stouter since then and we are both somewhat greyer. Harriet, our oldest girl, is to be married next spring, and I am to perform the ceremony – and it seems but five minutes since her christening, when I nearly dropped her in the font. As Louie is constantly saying, where DOES the time go?

You wish me to 'ask around' my clergy, for anyone who might remember a young woman named Helen Lyndhurst, but that won't be necessary; both Louie and myself remember her only too well because it was such a sad affair. Miss Lyndhurst lived with a Mrs Gault as her paid companion. The old lady died and poor Miss Lyndhurst, quite alone in the world, was too ill to find any other employment. The vicar of the parish appealed on her behalf to a charitable board of which I am the chairman, but it was too late; this friendless young woman died a month later.

The local people, I'm glad to say, showed her great Christian kindness; but the whole sad business only demonstrates how hard the world can be for such young women. I only wish I could have written you a happier answer to your question.

You are always in our prayers, my dear Letty, and we hope Providence allows us to meet again soon; Louie sends her best love.

Yours in Christ,

Thomas Grant

This mild missive landed on my breakfast tray like a bomb.

Well, well.

So Helen Lyndhurst and Helen Orme were not the same woman.

And that was practically the only part of Mrs Orme's story that I had at least half-believed; at last I had something to work with. I resolved to speak to the lady at once.

If she wasn't Helen Lyndhurst, who *was* she?

After my delightful week in Suffolk with the Beswicks, I had returned to Wishtide on Sir James's orders – and a strange half-life I'd been leading in the great deserted house. Sir James and his son were both in London, Lady Calderstone and her daughters were in Yorkshire (I had been touched to receive a sweet letter from Miss Bessie, full of the fun they were having with their cousin – and without Mlle Thérèse, whom they had left behind), and I had nothing to do except await further instructions.

Until the dean's letter, my only work on the case since my return had been one interview with Mlle Thérèse, most unsatisfactory. It was not the quality of my French that had been the problem, but the obstinacy of the woman's character. Was it my imagination, or had she gloried in giving me so little? I wasted hours poring over her threadbare replies to my questions.

Her name was Thérèse Gabin; born in Paris, nearer to forty than thirty, squat and solid of build, olive complexion. Lady Calderstone had hired her in Vevey, Switzerland, where she had been working for some years. She swore that the name Savile meant nothing to her. She knew nothing either about any anonymous letters. Interviewing her had been (as Mrs B would say) like getting blood out of a turnip.

With the dean's letter in my pocket, I set off for the Ormes' cottage on foot. There had been a hard frost the night before; the ruts in the muddy roads had frozen into ridges and I had to hop between them like a bird. The cold was invigorating and I rejoiced in the sight of hedgerows whitened with hoar, of a plump robin who kept me company for nearly a mile, and the magnificent stillness and silence of the frozen countryside.

The narrow lane in front of the cottage was blocked by a horse; a magnificent beast with a glossy black coat, his breath coming out in great plumes of steam – a gentleman's horse. And a gentleman's voice could be heard inside the cottage.

'I tried, but it's a torment to me; I can't bear it patiently. I won't bear it! You keep harping on about my future, when there is no future for me without you! My father and his expectations can go hang – if you'll only say yes, I don't care where I live or what I do!'

Mr Charles.

This was the first anyone had heard of his being back in Lincolnshire.

The horse and I looked at each other. I went up the front path and knocked briskly on the door. It was opened – after a flurry of whispering – by Mrs Orme; ladylike and composed as ever, though her pale cheeks were spiked with colour.

'Good morning, Mrs Orme,' I said. 'I beg your pardon for calling at such an hour; I wanted to be sure of finding you here.'

'Mrs Rodd.' She couldn't say it was a pleasure.

There's no hiding anything in a house the size of a bandbox, and Mr Charles would have been difficult to overlook anywhere; he towered in one corner of the little sitting room, red as a brick but holding his head up in angry pride.

'Mr Charles,' I said. 'I was most surprised to see that fine horse of yours tied up outside; I had thought you were still in town.'

'I came on an impulse,' the young man said, his eyes upon Mrs Orme. 'I rode through the night to be here. I can't act out this charade any longer.'

'Winifred has gone to market with the maid,' Mrs Orme said quickly. 'Won't you sit down?'

None of us sat down.

'I broke one promise in coming here, Mrs Rodd,' Mr Charles said, 'and I've just broken another; I told Mrs Orme what you're really doing here. I told her to be on her guard against you and your questions.'

I behaved as if I had not heard him, and addressed Mrs Orme. 'I have been away on a visit to some old friends – the Reverend and Mrs Beswick – in just your part of Suffolk.'

Though I kept my 'poker face', I watched her intently; she seemed to freeze where she stood.

'Mr Calderstone,' she did not take her eyes from me, 'I'd be obliged if you'd leave us.'

'Well, I'll do nothing of the kind!' Mr Charles was indignant, ready to fire up on her behalf. 'Why should I leave you at the mercy of some busybody in the pay of my father?'

She quelled the young hothead with one calm, steady look. 'Please.'

He submitted without another word, making a visible effort to control himself for her sake (in a happier situation, I couldn't help thinking, what an ideal wife she would have been for him; how cleverly she would have managed his career). Before he left us, Mr Charles seized Mrs Orme's hand and pressed it to his lips.

And on her face I saw the most extraordinary compound of longing and regret, as if she knew this was the moment she had lost him; I saw then how deeply she loved him, and how strenuously she sought to control her feelings.

After Mr Charles had departed on his horse, Mrs Orme and I continued to stand in the middle of the cramped sitting room, staring into each other's faces.

'I remember the Beswicks,' she said softly. 'They are very good people.'

I said nothing.

'They were kind to my family,' Mrs Orme added.

'But the Lyndhursts of Gallowcross were not your family,' I said. 'Their daughter Helen lies in a churchyard somewhere near Ipswich.'

'Ah,' murmured Mrs Orme, 'then that's all over. What do you want from me?'

'The truth – which I promise to keep to myself as much as it's possible,' I said. 'I'm sure you had good reasons for lying to me, but I must have the true story now. A man has been murdered, Mrs Orme; a man who gave his name as Savile.'

The name hit her like a slap; colour surged into her face; I pitied her mortification but would not look away.

After a long spell of silence, she said, 'I was speaking the truth about Mr and Mrs Beswick; they were kind to my family – my real family. Ask them to tell you about the other Helen.'

'The other Helen – what do you mean?'

'That's all, Mrs Rodd.' She dropped a half-curtsy. 'Good morning, ma'am.'

A week later I received two letters from Suffolk. The first one I opened contained a few lines from Mr Beswick, saying he did not feel it right, in his position as vicar, to delve into an old town scandal. Fortunately, the second was from Minnie, who had no such scruples.

My dearest Letty,

Your inquiry about the 'other Helen' caused quite an uproar in our house. Jack said, 'What on earth is she on about now?' – but I knew at once, for it is still one of the legendary scandals of the neighbourhood. Then he remembered, and we had an argument about 'raking up dead embers' and whatnot; but I really don't see the harm in telling you – especially when you could get the story from pretty well anyone along this part of the coast.

Helen Cooper – the other Helen – was the daughter of a poor fisherman. As you know, the fisher-folk here rather keep themselves to themselves, and I have never been able to help them as much as I would like; the fishing families have always been civil to me and they are often intensely religious, but they tend towards Non-Conformism or the more extreme Evangelical sects, and their contact with the Established Church is confined to what Jack calls the Essential Sacraments, i.e. marryings and buryings.

Their work depends heavily upon the seasons and the weather, and is so dangerous that every year has its sorrowful roll of men who have drowned, too often leaving destitute wives and children. There is much hardship, very bravely and proudly borne, and we do what we can for them (you know too well of course – it's similar to the work you did amongst the charcoal-burners when dear Matt had the living in Herefordshire – there is an insularity, and one is always an intruder). The children came to our school; my ladies and I braved the eye-watering stench of shellfish to visit their homes –

But back to Helen Cooper. Thirty years ago, when Jack and I arrived here as newlyweds, she was a very little child and an orphan; her father drowned shortly after she was born, and her poor young mother died a few months later. There was to be no orphanage nor (heaven forbid) workhouse for this child, however; little Helen was brought up by her uncle, Samuel Cooper – a fine, upright man, who was also raising an orphaned nephew. He was much admired round about for his generosity and rectitude.

This gnarled old fisherman loved his niece with all his heart; Helen was a pretty child with very taking ways and she twisted both her uncle and her cousin around her little finger. She got prettier each year, until people began to whisper that she was 'spoiled' and thought herself too fine for her heaven-sent station in life. She left school and was apprenticed as a milliner and seamstress, and she became engaged to her cousin (very common amongst these people). But this Helen was never cut out to be a fisherman's wife.

Now I have to remember dates and you know how muddled I get. I'm pretty sure it was the year my mother was thrown by a donkey and broke her ankle, and I couldn't go to her in Torquay because the children had mumps. This would be twelve or thirteen years ago. A fine young gentleman came to town wanting to play at being a fisherman – and when he left town, he took Helen Cooper with him.

That, my dear, is the long and short of it. You may imagine the fuss; the young gentleman had made himself popular, and people were mortified that they had been taken in by such a villain. There was a good deal of honest sympathy for the girl's uncle and betrothed, and every bad word you can think of was hurled at the reckless, wicked Helen. There was never the smallest possibility that the gentleman would marry her. She was utterly lost to everyone who loved her, and forever cast out of all decent society.

Jack has just looked over my shoulder; he told me to stop writing a 'penny ballad' and stick to facts.

Very well – though the rest of the story could have come from just such a ballad. Sam Cooper set out in search of his fallen niece (it was thought rather saintly of him to want her back at all) and his travels took him to all kinds of far-flung places. Eventually the stubborn old fisherman tracked Helen down, and the family emigrated to Australia to escape the shame she had brought upon them.

I must stop – I'm writing this in my bedchamber just before dinner and Jack is asking if I intend to go downstairs in my petticoat – but I have given you all I know. It was a delight to have you here, and you must come again as soon as possible, for I have a thousand questions to ask.

Yours hastily and affectionately, Minnie

Nine

S HE KNEW WHY I had come, and showed me into the little square sitting room without a word. It was very cold; the meagre, struggling fire was raw and blue.

All I had to do was hold up Minnie's letter.

'So now you know,' she said.

'I should very much like to hear your side of the story,' I replied. 'I am not your enemy, Mrs Orme, no matter what Mr Charles has told you.'

'It's soon enough told,' she said. 'Please sit down, Mrs Rodd; Winifred has gone to the farm for milk, but you mustn't mind if she comes back – she and I have no secrets.'

We sat in the two armchairs on either side of the chimney-piece, our knees nearly touching.

'I'm not accusing you of anything,' I said, as kindly as I could. 'I'm not sitting in judgement; I'm only interested in the facts.'

Her lovely face had a hardness, a bitterness, that I had not observed before. 'How much did they tell you? Do you know what I am?'

'You did not go to Australia,' I said.

She had not expected me to jump in with this, and a smile twitched at her lips. 'Australia? Is that what they all think?'

'Did your family not emigrate after all?'

She sighed and shook her head; there were a couple of minutes' silence between us, while she chivvied the fire.

'I am not Helen Lyndhurst.' Her manner was very calm. 'I stole her name because my own was ruined. And because the world looks more kindly on a curate's daughter than it does on a fisherman's; but I don't want you to think I'm ashamed.' She raised her head and looked me square in the eye. 'I'm proud to be a fisherman's daughter. My family were kind, honest people.'

'You were brought up by your uncle,' I said. 'Mrs Beswick was full of praise for him.'

'My Uncle Samuel was a very good man,' Mrs Orme said. 'I know that he loved me very much – my mother was his favourite little sister, and he often said I was just like her. I don't want you to blame him for my bad morals. He was forever thundering out verses from the Bible. I grew up with a perfectly accurate understanding of what a bad girl can expect in the way of hellfire and damnation.'

(The hardness of her tone made me wince inwardly, but I kept my face blank; I wanted her to see that she could not shock me.)

'I didn't set out to be a sinner, Mrs Rodd.'

'You met a gentleman.'

'Yes,' Mrs Orme said. 'I met a gentleman – isn't that the usual beginning? A young gentleman with a taste for seafaring paid my uncle for the privilege of going out in his boat. The fishermen thought he was quite daft at first; he won them round with his fearlessness and gallantry. He charmed them, Mrs Rodd, like a snake-charmer; when he was in the grip of one of his manias, he flung himself into it with his whole being.

86

Seafaring was one mania; I was another. One look passed between us, and I was lost.'

'The gentleman's name?' I asked softly.

'Mr Henry Rutherford. But when we travelled together, he gave our name as "Fisher". It was his idea of a joke.'

'I'm assuming,' I said, 'that he was very handsome.'

She coloured, and smiled painfully. 'I'm afraid so. I met him on the very day I allowed my cousin to announce our engagement. I still can't decide if it was the moment of my ruination – or the making of me.' She looked down at her hands. 'You're shocked to hear that, I expect.'

(I was intrigued more than shocked, but held my silence.)

'Think of it this way,' Mrs Orme said. 'I was very young, and only just waking up to the fact that there was a world beyond our little town – a world of light and beauty, in which poverty was unknown, and no man had to risk his life in order to feed his family. Mr Rutherford belonged to that world. When I first saw him in our little house, he seemed so pure, so clean – like a fairytale prince in his blue swallowtail coat, with a cravat as white and soft as a swan's back. His hands were white too, like ivory. And – I know this will sound very foolish –' She glanced up at me, her loveliness suddenly irradiated by a smile. 'But the smell of him! You must understand, Mrs Rodd, that I'd spent my whole life surrounded by the stink of fish – and Mr Ruther-ford carried about him a delicious scent of almonds, that made me almost giddy with delight.'

She was quiet for a moment; I felt her sifting the facts, decid-ing how much to tell.

'It's very important for you to understand,' she said, 'that this wasn't the usual story of the village maiden being seduced and abandoned by a villain. I fell in love with Mr Rutherford the moment I laid eyes on him – and he fell in love with me.'

'I don't doubt it,' I said. 'But could he not have married you?'

'No; he would have been ruined. After he and I had declared our wicked feelings for one another, Mr Rutherford hurried back to London to see his mother. The old lady was not over-joyed to hear that he had fallen in love with a common fisherman's daughter, and threatened to cut off his money if he married me.'

(I could not help sympathizing with Mr Rutherford's mother here; a young man may pick a shell off a beach, but not a wife.)

'But he swore he would take care of me,' Mrs Orme said. 'And for the first few years, he did. I was very happy, and I truly believe he was too. It wasn't just a matter of fine clothes and dainty food. He maintained that I was born to be a lady, and he delighted in improving me. I had masters for French and Italian, masters for music and dancing; I had every book I could possibly want.'

(I had admired her various accomplishments; it was a little startling to hear that they were quite literally the wages of sin.)

She guessed what I was thinking, and smiled. 'Yes, it truly was a primrose path – I mean, at first. Of course I was sorry to leave Uncle Samuel, but it was difficult to be downhearted when I was so very much in love.'

Now that she had told me this, and seen that I had not come to condemn her, Mrs Orme spoke more easily. 'I knew that the day I ran off with him, I would drop out of the world of decent people. The night I left I was dreadfully frightened, and nearly changed my mind a thousand times. But I couldn't live without him.' Seeing the twitch of my eyebrows, she added, 'Oh, I don't mean I'd have died without him, or gone into a decline. It was simply that I couldn't face going back to my old life.'

'I can fully see the temptation,' I said. 'Frankly, I can't think of many girls who wouldn't have done exactly the same, given the same choice – linsey-woolsey versus silk.'

Reluctantly, she smiled at this. 'I can't imagine you doing such a thing, Mrs Rodd.'

I couldn't help smiling back. 'Neither can I – I was a plain-looking girl, and there was never the slightest danger that any passing gentleman would beg me to elope with him. But of course I understand what you're trying to tell me; that Mr Rutherford appeared to you as a saviour.'

'He said I could send money to Uncle Samuel,' Mrs Orme said quietly. 'I thought I'd saved him from the sea. In my dreams, he ended his days in a nice cottage with a garden. Before we left for the Continent, my new protector sent a bank-note down to my old home, more money than anyone had seen in their lives.'

Once again she bent forward to fiddle with the struggling fire, proudly turning her face away to hide the tears that had brimmed up in her eyes; I sensed a dreadful sadness washing through her until the whole room tasted of it.

'That must have been a comfort to you,' I offered.

'Oh, yes!' She looked at me again, and saw that I was not sitting in judgement. 'It made me so happy! But I was too young and silly to see how the money would appear to my poor uncle – the price of my virtue, no less. Long afterwards, I heard that he gave the banknote to the Seamen's Mission. And then he took his own hard-earned savings and set out after us.'

There was a scuffle of footsteps outside, the latch of the front door lifted, and Miss Winifred burst into the cottage bearing a small covered pail of milk.

'Mrs Rodd!'

I stood up. 'Miss Winifred.'

The sitting room was suddenly crammed with our skirts.

Mrs Orme softly said, 'I've always feared the past would come to get me, and now it has; we were talking about the fisherman's daughter.'

'Oh, my dear!' Miss Winifred flinched; the milk slopped in the pail. 'What reason can you possibly –'

'Please don't be afraid that I've come to cause trouble,' I said. 'We are speaking in the strictest confidence.'

Miss Winifred's heavy lower lip trembled. 'Forgive me – but why should we trust you? You came to our house under false pretences; you're in the pay of Sir James.'

This was one of the moments (there are not many) when I was ashamed of my work, and most ashamed of deceiving an honest creature like Miss Winifred.

'You are right,' I said. 'And I am very sorry – but I was employing deceit in order to detect it. The small lie was bait to catch a bigger one. Now that we are all in the open, we can be more comfortable with one another.'

'Winnie, dear,' Mrs Orme caught her hand. 'This is quite all right; I know what I'm doing.'

'Well –' Miss Winifred looked doubtfully at her sister-in-law and then at me. 'Now that we have fresh milk, I can at least make us all a cup of tea. It'll be kitchen tea rather than drawing room, Mrs Rodd; we were not expecting company.'

'You are most kind.' I wanted Miss Winifred out of the room, and so did Helen Orme; I sensed there were certain parts of the story she simply could not reveal to such an innocent.

Miss Winifred retreated into the kitchen.

'I believe,' Mrs Orme said, 'we had reached the part where Uncle Samuel began his long quest to find me and claim me back.'

'A noble quest,' I suggested.

'I didn't ask him to follow me,' was her crisp reply. 'And in the early days, I didn't want to be found and reclaimed. My new life had begun, for better or worse. Mr Rutherford met me in a post-chaise, just outside the turnpike on the London road. I climbed into that chaise as a maiden, and I climbed out of it with a ring upon my finger, and the new name of Mrs Fisher.'

(In the chaise! Good gracious – and how uncomfortable!)

'Everyone at the London inn we stopped at seemed to guess at our situation; greatly to the annoyance of my "husband", some of the servants there treated me with contempt. "Damn them all," he said to me. "When I bring you back, you'll be the finest of fine ladies, and they'll change their tune." Strange as it sounds now, he was protective of my honour; it hadn't yet occurred to him that I had already lost it. We were so very much in love.'

'Tell me,' I said, 'about Savile.'

The name lashed at her. 'Savile was Rutherford's manservant. He was very polite to me, but the way he looked at me sometimes made me dislike and fear him.'

'Could you not dismiss him?'

91

'We needed him; he spoke serviceable French and had a talent for finding us the best lodgings. He knew the landlords who would let rooms to us without asking too many awkward questions.' She sighed, and was quiet for a moment. 'I thought our apartments were the last word in luxury, but Mr Rutherford saw that they were always tawdry and unkempt. He knew that no truly respectable landlord would take us, and the possibility of being judged by such persons made him angry. And if the two of us happened to run into one of Mr Rutherford's old friends, from his former life in England, it infuriated him when they stared straight through him and refused to return a greeting. He wasn't used to being cut, especially by men he considered his social inferiors. The only society we could move in freely was not of the choicest. Mr Rutherford often complained that we met nobody who had not left England under some kind of cloud.'

'He can't have liked being bracketed with such people,' I said. 'Did he blame you for it?'

'Eventually,' Mrs Orme said. 'Once our honeymoon had waned, we moved restlessly between one spa town and another. It was at one such town that I first came across Edmund Orme. Mr Rutherford and I were out for a stroll one afternoon when Henry spotted Edmund, whom he had known slightly at Oxford. As we walked past the young clergyman, he recognised Henry and reddened – of course he had heard of the scandal and knew who I was. Mr Rutherford – meaning to tease him – raised his hat. But Edmund was the greater gentleman; he tipped his hat and returned the bow. And the next afternoon, he came to call on us. I'm ashamed to tell you that I made fun of his meek manners later, but at the time I was moved by his careful respect for me, as if I were truly the wife I pretended to be. Mr Rutherford was impressed – he hadn't thought Edmund brave enough to ignore the conventions.'

'Was this when you met Miss Winifred?'

'Oh, no – he couldn't allow the likes of me to meet his sister. She only saw us once, as she told me much later, when she peeked at us through a carriage window.'

'It's an unfortunate thing in a Christian society,' I said, 'but some conventions cannot be overlooked; Mr Orme had to think of Miss Winifred's reputation.'

'Quite,' Mrs Orme said, rather tartly. 'The only females I mixed with were those whose reputations were as tattered as mine. Some had left well-known names behind them in their old respectable lives. For instance –' She rattled out a list of names, all connected to notorious scandals: Mrs X who had run off with her husband's married brother, Mrs Y who lived openly with one of her former stable lads, Mrs Z who was 'kept' by an Indian prince.

'In any case,' she went on, 'we left that town soon afterwards. My understanding was that Mr Rutherford had won a great deal of money at the casino. For some reason that meant we had to depart in a hurry. We went to Italy, where Savile found us a beautiful villa on the coast near Livorno. Mr Rutherford was restless and things were not easy between us, but I was happier than I had been for a long time. I found a fishing village, and improved my Italian by making friends with the fishermen and their families. Mr Rutherford was angry when he heard that I'd taught the children to address me as "Fisherman's Daughter". He was ashamed of my origins. But I found true friends in that fishing village.'

The door handle turned; Miss Winifred came into the sitting room with the tea-board. I was very glad to have the tea, which was excellently hot and strong and all the better for being served in robust kitchen crockery.

'Gracious, how cold it is in here – Helen, dear, when will you ever learn to keep a fire going?' Miss Winifred made a dive at the tiny grate and briskly dug into the coals with the poker. The fire knew when it was beaten and started to give forth actual warmth. Miss Winifred rearranged the chairs so that she sat on the small sofa beside Mrs Orme, facing me.

'I'm telling everything,' Mrs Orme said quietly. 'Charles must know, and he must have the whole truth. I never intended to marry the poor boy.' The colour rose in her pale cheeks. 'My history makes it quite impossible. But I never set out to deceive anyone. I was simply trying to put the past behind me. I'm sure you are discreet, Mrs Rodd – but please beg Sir James to keep my miserable history to himself, or Winifred and I will be driven from our home.'

'I'll do what I can,' I assured her. 'If you do not intend to marry his son, he won't need to know about your history.'

She was quite right about the danger of being hounded out of her home; country people can be very hard with a 'fallen' woman; when we were in Herefordshire, Matt had to drive away a crowd of locals with blackened faces, who had gathered round a cottage door bearing pitchforks and banging sauce-pans, all because a poor dairymaid had got herself into trouble.

'I'll finish it quickly,' Mrs Orme said. 'It was during this time in Italy that I found I was expecting a child.'

Miss Winifred winced and flushed, though Mrs Orme was perfectly matter-of-fact.

'Mr Rutherford was very angry – he accused me of not taking enough care – of trying to entrap him. And then one day I woke up, and he was gone. After all our time together, all our love for each other, he simply left me – without a word, without any money. I found that he had paid Savile on the understanding that the man would marry me. I daresay Mr Rutherford imagined he was somehow doing the right thing by bestowing me upon his valet, like one of last year's coats. Oh, Winnie, dear – how you hate hearing this!'

'It's a dreadful story,' Miss Winifred said. 'I hate to hear that there is such wickedness in the world.'

'Savile was certainly a wicked man,' Mrs Orme continued. 'He wanted every single thing I had that he could turn into cash – he took my fine clothes, books, ornaments. Mr Rutherford had taken my jewel-box with him, but Savile was convinced I had more. And in fact I did – all the women in our wretched little circle had hidden what they could in case of a rainy day. Savile beat me until I was black and blue and locked me up in my room, but I never told him about the little hoard of money and trinkets that I had squirrelled away behind a loose panel on the wall.'

I was shocked now; she had experienced absolute brutality.

'Fortunately for me,' she went on, 'Savile was a confirmed drunkard and insensible within the hour. I tied my treasures in a handkerchief, tucked it securely into my bosom, and climbed out of the window.'

'Great heavens,' I said faintly.

She smiled a little. 'Actually, it wasn't so very dramatic; I wasn't high up and there was a stout vine to use as a ladder. I took refuge with the only people I could trust – my friends the fishing-folk. I knew they would protect me if Savile came after me. But he never did; I daresay he was glad enough to be rid of me.'

How brave she had been, I thought; she had been abandoned by her seducer, yet she managed to escape falling into a life that was far worse.

'The fishing-people were very kind to me,' Mrs Orme said. 'I lived with a young couple, the only ones who didn't have a swarm of children. The wife was widely known to be barren, and was almost sick with longing to have a baby in her arms. Whereas here was I, great with child, and not wanting a baby in the least.'

She was quiet for a spell, allowing this to sink in.

'I was only thinking of what would be best for my baby; she was a girl, and I gave her to the Gattis to keep as their own. I wanted to give them all my money, all my tainted jewels, but they would take only a few coins – and a gold locket set with pearls, to give to the baby when she grew up. It had two miniatures inside, of Mr Rutherford and myself. Her true parents before God.'

She stopped; her eyes brimmed with tears. Miss Winifred gently took her hand. Though I have not been blessed with children, I can fully understand how agonizing it must be to hand your newborn babe to a stranger, and I allowed the silence to stretch on.

Mrs Orme raised her head. 'As soon as I was strong enough, I kissed my little daughter farewell and made my way home.'

'To England? Not alone, surely?' I was startled. 'How on earth did you manage such a thing?'

'I knew,' Mrs Orme said, 'that I could not possibly travel alone in the guise of a lady. Without Mr Rutherford's protection, I was common again. In the next town I bought myself a set of the coarse clothes worn by the local peasantry. It was harvest time and the dusty roads were busy with men and women in search of casual labour. I spent several weeks working in the vineyards; I pretended to be French, to explain my oddly accented Italian. I kept myself to myself and no one troubled me; a couple of the older women looked out for those of us who were young and alone. I worked my way north, earning just enough to keep me in food, and to pay for my passage across the Channel.'

'Were you planning to return to your family?' I asked.

'No; I don't know that I had any plans, except to make an honest living. But that's a tall order for a woman such as I was. I daresay you can imagine the kind of work that was open to me, once I reached London.'

(Of course I could; I knew of the depravity that awaited friendless women in those wicked city streets, and it made me shudder.)

'In the nick of time,' she said, 'I was recognized by someone from our town who sent word to my uncle. He appeared like an avenging angel, and he saved me.'

'You must have been very happy to see him,' I suggested.

'Oh, I was – at first,' said Mrs Orme. 'Uncle Samuel took me off to a nice clean lodging-house, where I ate the first decent meal I'd seen since Mr Rutherford left me.' She smiled slightly. 'Winifred doesn't like this bit of my tale, Mrs Rodd – she's inclined to take the part of my poor old uncle.'

'But he walked across half the Continent to find you,' Winifred protested.

'He did, and I was very grateful; I'll try to give him the credit he deserves.' Mrs Orme's smile was sour. 'The trouble was, though my uncle went on and on about "forgiving" me, he hadn't really forgiven me at all, and did not intend to. My sin was dragged before me at every possible opportunity. He expected me to spend my entire life in a state of meek repentance. He wouldn't allow me to wear a red shawl and insisted I change it for a black one. "Why?" I asked. "Nobody's died!" He thought I ought to be in mourning for my lost virtue. You should've heard the fuss when he caught me singing a little song in Italian – "'Tis an incantation of the devil! 'Tis the work of Satan!"' She slipped into her uncle's broad country accent for a moment. 'I said, "Nonsense, it's the work of Mozart, who was an angel – and are fallen women forbidden to sing while they're scrubbing floors?"'

(I was rather shocked that I found this amusing; she had such a lively, entertaining manner of telling a story; even Miss Winifred could not help smiling.)

'This was when my uncle took it into his head to emigrate to Australia, where I believe he lives still – though he has never replied to my letters.'

'Why did you not go with him?'

'Oh, I set out with him – but just a few days into the voyage, we had our great quarrel.'

'What was the quarrel about?'

'We had put in at a port on the coast of France, and someone produced an outdated English newspaper. It contained an account of a storm on the Suffolk coast. A schooner from Portugal had gone down with all hands, and one of the dead bodies that washed up on the sands near our old home was that of Mr Henry Rutherford.'

We were all silent for a long moment.

'I was heartbroken,' Mrs Orme said. 'I still loved him; I had not given up hoping to see him again. I wept for him as if he had never left me – and my tears infuriated Uncle Samuel. He thought it was justice meted out by Heaven – "Vengeance is mine," saith the Lord, "and I will repay."'

'So you left him,' I said.

'Yes, Mrs Rodd. I left my uncle and the ship, and set out for Italy. I wanted to see my baby; I had never stopped thinking of her, yearning for her. I just wanted to see my baby.' Her mouth quivered and she hid her face in her shawl.

Miss Winifred put a protective arm around her. 'When Helen returned to Italy, all she found were gravestones,' she said softly. 'The good young couple and the child they had adopted had all died from the fever.'

'And the rest you know.' Mrs Orme uncovered her face. 'I caught the fever myself, and in my delirium I thought Henry was waiting for me in our old villa. Very fortunately for me, the villa had been taken over by Edmund Orme, who recognized me and took pity on me – and who married me in full know-ledge of my history.'

'That's all,' Miss Winifred said. 'I hope you are satisfied now, Mrs Rodd.'

'I'm satisfied that your brother was a true Christian gentle-man,' I replied. 'I should have liked to know him.'

Her long, horsey face softened, making her for a moment almost beautiful. 'Edmund knew that he was near dying; he was so dreadfully worried about what would happen to me after he was dead. My own income was but seventy-five pounds a year, and without him I would be utterly alone. After my brother's death, most of his money would go back to the family and he couldn't leave anything more to me – but in the event of his marriage, seventy-five pounds a year would go to his widow. When Edmund married Helen, it made him so happy to know that he had provided us both with a home, and each other; I know it helped him to a peaceful death.'

I saw it now; Edmund Orme had married Helen as a gesture of brotherly love, to save his beloved Winifred from the life of a poor, dependent spinster. I was moved by his selflessness, and impressed by his practicality – what a sensible man. At one stroke he had given Helen a respectable name, he had given Winifred a sister, and doubled her income.

'I'm sure,' I said warmly, 'that the trumpets sounded for him on the other side.'

Both women wiped their eyes.

'His face looked so beautiful,' Miss Winifred said, 'all bathed in the light of the next world.'

My work is difficult at times like this; moved as I was by Mrs Orme's history, there were still questions to be asked. I left a respectful pause before inquiring, 'Did you ever see Savile again?'

'No, I did not,' Helen Orme said sharply. 'I did not marry the man – and I did not murder him. I haven't set foot out of Lincolnshire since I came here.'

'Murder? What are you talking about?' Miss Winifred's eyes were round with alarm. 'Who has been murdered?'

'You've heard it all now,' Mrs Orme said. 'I have placed the whole truth before you, and I leave you to decide what to do with it.'

I had been wondering myself what I should do with the information I had; it would be a simple matter to find out about

Mrs Orme's movements, but I was certain she had had nothing to do with the death of her old tormentor. Did Sir James really need to know her whole history?

'When I make my report to Sir James,' I said, 'I shall simply tell him you have sworn you do not intend to marry Mr Charles – that is all he needs to know and I'll be as sparing as possible with the details.'

The two women exchanged glances of pure relief.

'Thank you,' Miss Winifred said.

I looked at Mrs Orme. 'It's up to you how much you intend to tell Mr Charles.'

'Everything,' she said, her voice shaking. 'I shall tell him everything. He won't be able to understand why we cannot be married unless he knows it all, poor boy – I wish I didn't have to break his heart.'

My head was whirling as I left the cottage. I hardly knew where to begin.

First, how would the fiery Mr Charles react to having his heart broken? Second, how much of the story should I give to Sir James?

Mostly, however, I found myself thinking of the two Helens – the fisherman's daughter and the poor curate's girl – and how hard life had been for both of them.

Ten

My dear Mary,

I rather think I have reached the wrapping-up stage of my business here. I wish I could tell you exactly when to expect me home, but I am still waiting to make my final report to Sir James; I will give you all the notice I can.

In the meantime, please do not forget to have the chimney swept, and please use Jakes; he may charge a little more than Fulton, but he doesn't leave such a mess. We'll keep a pail of soot for the garden; it's the only thing that kills the black spot and I'm determined to have a better show of roses next year.

If there is sufficient money in Windsor Castle, please place an order (with Nupton, and definitely not with Brown, who sent such bad candied peel last year) for the components of my mincemeat. I fully intend to be at home in time to make it. Please put the currants to steep in brandy as soon as you get them. It will soon be Christmas; of course you and I will be keeping the day itself with our respective families, but Christmas has twelve days and we'll choose one of them for our own private celebration.

It is bitterly cold here; the servants say the wind comes in straight from Russia. I hope Hampstead is warmer – and that little Anny has obeyed my instructions and built you generous fires for your rheumatism. When I am home, I will make you my embrocation of goose-fat and sage leaves.

Talking of 'sage' – I have missed your sound opinions and have a great deal to tell you.

Yours faithfully,

Laetitia Rodd

I opened my eyes in the grubby light of early dawn, and became aware that someone was knocking urgently at the door of my chamber.

It was Mrs Craik, breathless and dishevelled as I had never seen her, in a flannel wrapper with a shawl thrown carelessly over her head.

'I beg your pardon for disturbing you, Mrs Rodd – but I don't rightly know what to do – it's the Frenchwoman, ma'am – the Frenchwoman's been murdered!'

It took me a couple of minutes to get at the plain facts; first I had to hear what a pity it was that the family were from home, what an appalling outrage – et cetera. But the sum of it was that Mlle Thérèse had been found in the stableyard by the head groom, the back of her head beaten to a bloody mess.

Poor Mrs Craik had no idea what to do, and was happy to let me take charge. I hurried into my dress and cloak and went downstairs to the servants' hall, where people stood about in various stages of undress, whispering fearfully to each other.

I sent the oldest footman for the local constable, over in Horncastle, and Mrs Craik recovered her wits enough to notice that the kitchen range had not been lit.

It was a cold, dark morning and I asked for lanterns; I knew it would be important to see all the details of the scene. The stables at Wishtide were a good distance from the house; I had walked that way once and seen a large quadrangle of imposing grey stone buildings around an enormous cobbled yard. I followed the bobbing lights held by the two pale stable lads who were guiding me through the sluggish dawn (the entire household wanted to join us, but a crowd of people would have disturbed the scene of the crime, and I refused to let them treat this tragedy as a spectacle to gawp at).

Brody, the head groom, stood with his own lantern in one corner of the yard, guarding the black, still body at his feet. He was a short, spry little Irishman, a former jockey, with a wizened goblin's face and the bandiest legs I had ever seen.

I told him we had sent for the constable.

'I found her,' he said. 'I nearly fell over her.'

'What time was this, Mr Brody?'

'An hour or so ago – just before first light,' Brody said. 'I was up before the cock had even cleared his throat, ma'am, owing to one of the hunters being poorly with the colic.'

'Have you moved her at all? Is this precisely how you found her?'

'I turned her over, ma'am; when I found her she was the other side up, and the back of her head all beaten in.'

I lowered my lantern to throw a light upon the face of the murdered woman.

As I have said before, dead bodies hold no fears for me; I know they are but discarded husks. As the wife of a clergyman, working amongst the poorest of the parish, I have laid out corpses of every age, often horribly ravaged by illness. As a private investigator I have seen the sad remains of several victims of murder. But the sight of this dead body made me gasp.

The Frenchwoman's face was frozen into a ghastly expression – fury, shock, the shadow of an unspeakable horror lingering in those empty eyes.

And her head lay on the stones like a mask, the back of it quite flattened in a mess of bonnet, hair and a pool of black, congealing blood.

She saw her killer, I thought; she turned her back on him and tried to run away.

The shock of such a sight, combined with the early hour, gave me a moment of giddy sickness; I swallowed hard, and said a silent prayer for the repose of the dead woman's soul.

Aloud, I said, 'I think you may cover her with a blanket, Mr Brody, until the constable arrives.'

Wishtide

4th December

CONFIDENTIAL

Dear Fred,

As I promised in the hasty note I sent yesterday by special messenger, I shall set down the facts I have. The official investigation of this savage murder is in the hands of the local constable – who strikes me as a rather knuckle-headed fellow. So far, all he has done is frighten the younger servants. He brought with him a Dr Walters, from Horncastle, who placed the time of death five or six hours before the body was discovered (in other words, around midnight). There is still no sign of a weapon, though Brody had the stableyard swept to within an inch of its life. He insists that he has no idea what Mlle Thérèse might have been doing in the yard at such an hour, and I see no reason not to believe him; he barely knew the woman and thinks only of horses.

The body of Mlle Thérèse is now lying in the Horncastle lock-up, awaiting the inquest, and order has been restored in the house – though the very walls are whispering with rumours. The fact is that none of the servants here liked the Frenchwoman – 'a spitting old cat' was how one of the young men described her – and there is a regrettable tendency to treat the murder as an entertaining novelty.

They are careful, however, to maintain a proper manner in front of Mrs Craik, who was so dreadfully upset that she was pale and trembling. Once I had observed the body being taken off in a covered wagon, I returned to the blessed warmth of the kitchen and made poor Mrs Craik sit down with me in her private parlour. A girl by the name of Martha (the same obliging little farmer's girl who brings my suppers) was waiting upon us; I sent her off to fetch tea and bread-and-butter.

Mrs Craik is mainly worried about what this scandal will do to the family name. She feels badly for not being as sorry as she might. And she couldn't tell me anything useful about the dead woman – nobody belowstairs speaks a word of French, and Mlle Thérèse made little or no effort to learn English.

Question: what was the dead woman doing in the stableyard in the middle of the night?

Nobody could give me a satisfactory answer to this.

'I'd say she had to be meeting someone there,' Mrs Craik said. 'Though I couldn't say who; she didn't know anybody round about. She spent all her time hovering around Her Ladyship and the girls – I was surprised when they didn't take her with them to Yorkshire.'

'Was Mlle Thérèse angry to be left behind?' I asked.

'Well, you'd have thought so,' Mrs Craik said. 'But she was in a better temper than usual once they'd gone – kept chortling to herself, like she had some private joke at the expense of the rest of us.'

'And she talked a bit,' Martha said (she had just come back into the room with a tray of tea-things). 'She started having a few little drinks of an evening, which I never saw her do before, and it made her want someone to talk to.'

'Did you understand any of it?'

'Not really, ma'am.' The girl's friendly, snub-featured face flushed a little. 'I think she was trying to talk about lovers and sweethearts. She showed me and Ruthie Watson a gold locket with a picture of a man inside it. She went "AMOOR!" and kissed it a dozen times. She was all excited and fluttering her hands about, and she goes, "'Ee comes!"'

These are Mlle Thérèse's only two recorded words of English; I think we ought to assume she was expecting to see the 'amoor' in the gold locket (I will find this when I get a chance to examine the dead woman's effects). Martha added that a month or so ago, she saw the French-woman in Horncastle, which surprised her because the woman normally never left the estate. It was market day and very crowded, but she thinks she saw Mlle Thérèse going into the town's one decent inn, the Calder-stone Arms.

Naturally when I heard this I commandeered a carriage and went to Horncastle to make inquiries at the inn; the enclosed page is a list of men who have stayed there over the past three months; I don't recognize any of the names. The landlord, a Mr Hinton, recalls seeing Mlle Thérèse

107

entering the coffee room of his inn upon the market day in question, but did not see her speaking with anyone. My impression of the Calderstone Arms is that it is well-appointed and so perfectly respectable that I myself could stay there without risk to my reputation.

This, my dear Fred, is all I know. When I return to town we must talk about the Calderstones. I assume Sir James has been informed. I have written to Lady Calderstone; there are questions I wish to ask her about Mlle Thérèse.

You might like to point out to Sir James that both he and his wife have the strongest motives for wanting the woman out of the way. There is a connection to the Savile murder that must be looked into. The business of his son's marriage is pretty much settled; now I must ask him questions that will make him angry and uncomfortable. I don't know on whose behalf I'll be making these inquiries – but I'm in too deep now, and cannot let go of this matter until I know that right has been done.

Your affectionate sister,

L

The girl Martha took me up to the dead woman's room; the attics in which the servants slept were light, bare and spotlessly clean. Mlle Thérèse had been given a room to herself, slightly larger than the others, and set apart on a landing. I unlocked the door with the key given to me by Mrs Craik; though I naturally intended to hand it over to the constable, this chance to get a first look was too good to miss.

Martha was trembling, and I sympathized; there is something deeply disturbing about the room of someone recently dead (entering the study of my beloved Matt on the day after I had lost him was one of the hardest things I have ever done; everything spoke of him so strongly that his absence was an outrage I simply could not understand; how could dumb objects outlive him?).

The Frenchwoman's attic room still had her scent – but it was empty. There were no clothes in the little bureau and no brushes or pins on top of it. Underneath the bed was a small band-box of inlaid wood, open and empty.

'She packed up and left!' exclaimed Martha.

'So it appears,' I said. 'She must've had at least one bundle with her when she met her murderer – yet nothing was found near the body.'

'He robbed her into the bargain, the villain,' Martha said.

I sat up until the fire's last gasp that night, listening to the sounds of the sleeping house and the owls hooting in the great stillness outside, and fretting over a story that refused to make sense.

Mlle Thérèse had known about what happened to Lady Calderstone in Switzerland. Savile had boasted in his cups of being in the same place. They had both been brutally murdered.

I knew what Fred would have said; he believed that the great majority of Murders Aforethought boiled down to matters of money and property, and liked to quote St Paul's maxim that the love of money is at the root of every evil. But I think – especially in cases involving women – that fear can also be the driving force in a killing.

Helen Orme feared exposure of her past, and had the best motives for wanting Savile dead if he knew anything about it.

But why would she need to kill Mlle Thérèse?

Sir James had excellent reasons for wishing the pair of them out of the way – but a man with his means and connections would surely have been able to 'bump them off' (one of Fred's favourite expressions) far more discreetly.

No, I simply could not make it all fit together.

Eleven

THE FOLLOWING MORNING, MARTHA brought in my breakfast tray with the news that the murdered woman's belongings had been found, hastily crammed into a deep hedgerow on the main road to Horncastle.

'The constable sent word that he wants you to have a look at the things, ma'am – on account of all the writing being in French.'

By ten o'clock I was in the carriage, shivering in the frost despite the blanket over my knees, wondering what the French writing would reveal, and hoping for some clue that would identify the person who had arranged to meet Mlle Thérèse in the stableyard at midnight.

It was market day; the little town was thronged with stalls, carts, horses and crowds of people; the carriage slowed to a crawl and I heard the driver up on his box, yelling at a knot of gossiping women with baskets to get out of the way. We drove through an archway into the large cobbled yard of the Calderstone Arms. The landlord had complained to me that things were woefully quiet now that the railway had spoiled his business with the stagecoaches, but today the place was still frantically busy. I found myself relishing the confusion of carts and carriages, and the noise of the metal horseshoes clanging against the stones; how glad I would be, I thought, to see London again, where there was life everywhere you looked.

Early as it was, the public bar was thick with smoke and packed with the more prosperous local farmers, all roaring at the tops of their voices. An overworked waiter showed me into a small private dining room towards the back of the building, of the sort reserved for gentlefolk. To my surprise, two men were waiting beside the fire. Brewer, the constable, a tough-looking man in thick gaiters, with close-shorn grey hair, was in the middle of saying something to a tall, slight young clergy-man with dark hair – something not very temperate, to judge by his mottled red face and growling voice.

'Mrs Rodd, please allow me to introduce myself.' The young man bowed to me. 'I am George Fitzwarren, the vicar of Soking St Mary, and I was trying to explain to Mr Brewer that the town prison is not the place for this poor woman's body.'

I quickly shuffled through my mental notebook for every-thing I knew about Mr Fitzwarren. The Calderstone household worshipped at the old village church opposite the park gates, presided over by Mr Larkin, described by Miss Blanche as a 'Jack-o'-lantern'. He was only the curate, however; his little parish lay within the prosperous living of Soking St Mary, to which Mr Fitzwarren had recently been appointed. Sir James was known to be annoyed that his estate did not hold this par-ticular living; he would never have given it to such a radical.

I took a closer look at the earnest young firecracker of a clergyman. He was decidedly handsome, with fine, burning black eyes; I had a bet with myself that those eyes were wreaking absolute havoc in the pews; until he got himself married,

George Fitzwarren's services would be thronged with eager maidens in loud bonnets.

'And I was trying to explain to Mr Fitzwarren,' Brewer said, 'that the body can't be moved until the inquest.'

'Then allow me to pray beside her.'

'No, Vicar, with all due respect I will not; now, if you will excuse me, I have business with Mrs Rodd.'

'Very well, but you have not heard the last of this.' Mr Fitzwarren bowed gracefully and left the room.

'Meddling young – I beg pardon, Mrs Rodd – but he wants me to lock him up in the town jail so he can kneel beside a corpse –' Brewer was trying to swallow his irritation. 'My darters is mad about that man but I say he's the interferingest –' He cleared his throat a couple of times. 'I'm much obliged to you for coming, ma'am; the French writing means nowt to me, and even the doctor can't make head nor tail of it.'

(If he meant Walters, the man who had given the time of death, I was not surprised; he had a poor enough grasp of his own tongue, let alone anyone else's.)

'Does Mr Fitzwarren not know French?' I asked.

'With respect, ma'am, I didn't ask because I'm not giving him any more chances to poke his nose in. A man can't speak his own mind in his own house these days.'

(From this, I guessed that Brewer's daughters had caught a severe case of religious zeal from their personable unmarried vicar, and were now complaining about their father's irreligious habits.)

I turned my attention to the table, where Brewer had placed the heap of Mlle Thérèse's possessions. How pitiful it was, I thought; this little cairn of tangled dresses and underclothing that amounted to the remains of an entire life. There was also a black silk bonnet bent out of shape, a French Missal with some letters folded inside it and a string of ebony rosary-beads. There was no sign of a gold locket.

'It weren't robbery,' Brewer said. 'She had a little bag full of money – fifteen shillings and ninepence-ha'penny. What sort of robber would throw that away?'

'Someone more interested in murder than money,' I said, carefully pulling the letters from the velvet-bound Missal.

There were five of them; semi-literate scrawls in bad colloquial French. I produced pencil and paper, and after a studious quarter-hour (Brewer watched me with fearful awe, as if I were casting spells), I had come up with a rough but workmanlike translation.

The first two letters, dated the previous year and sent from London, were short requests for money, to be sent to 'the usual place', both signed 'your loving J'.

The third letter was dated the previous September, not three months ago. '*My dearest Thérèse, I have some big news which should bring in some big money. I will tell all when I see you. Please send two pounds for the railway fares and expenses – care of Mr Gammon at the Goat in Boots.*' My heart leapt when I saw the address.

The fourth letter was dated a month later. '*My beloved angel, I beg you to be patient for a little longer. This job is a dead cert. I'll come and fetch you when I've got the goods, your devoted J.*'

The last was the letter that really caught my eye; it was dated only a matter of two weeks ago. '*My dearest Thérèse, the bird is limed and it's all settled. Meet me under the stable clock at midnight on the 1st – the chaise will be waiting and then your generous patience will be rewarded. Your loving husband, J.*'

'Her husband?' Brewer was bewildered; I suspected he spent most of his professional life locking up vagrants. 'I wasn't told about any husband!'

'Nobody had the slightest idea that she was a married woman. She must have had her reasons for keeping it secret.' I smoothed the pages out across the green baize table-cover. The quality of the French puzzled me; it was fluent, and peppered with colloquialisms, but filled with the most elementary mistakes; it was, in fact, the kind of French that might be written by a fairly literate foreigner who was more used to speaking the language than setting it down.

The man Savile had spoken serviceable French.

He had talked, in his cups, of Vevey, where Mlle Thérèse had nursed Lady Calderstone. This was the first connection between the two of them; the second was that they had both been murdered.

'So she was done in by her own husband,' Brewer said.

But Savile could not have written the last of the letters; he was already dead by then. This was the work of another hand.

I was debating with myself how much (if any) of this I would pass on to Brewer when there was a brisk knock at the door and the busy waiter erupted into the room with an armful of smooth white linen. 'Beg pardon, Mr Brewer – the room's booked for luncheon, and I have to set the table.'

I had seen all I needed; I left Brewer grumbling at the waiter about the inconvenience and made my way through the crowded, smoke-filled corridor. As I was leaving, I chanced to look through the glass door of the coffee room, reserved for the gentry.

It was a large, low-ceilinged room, with blackened panelling and a handsome blaze in the old inglenook fireplace; warm and shabby, decorated with engravings of George III and famous local horses, and given an air of musty bookishness with a row of ancient bound volumes of *The Gentleman's Magazine*.

There were three bonneted female groups in the coffee room this morning. The best place, nearest to the fire, was occupied by a grand, white-haired old lady in lavender silk, a fidgety little girl of about nine years old, and a rather elegant lady of about my own age. In the window sat what looked to be the wife of one of the better farmers, plump and prosperous, smiling at her two grown girls, who were giggling and whispering over their new ribbons.

And in the draughtiest spot, just inside the glass door, I saw Helen Orme and Miss Winifred. This being a public place, I was prepared merely to bow – until I saw that Mrs Orme was deathly pale, barely able to hold herself upright. Anxious to be of help if I could, I went into the room.

Miss Winifred was garrulous with relief at seeing a friendly face. 'We only came to the market because the brooms-and-brushes man is here, and Helen needed new knitting needles – and we only came in here because poor Helen suddenly turned deadly faint and it was the only place we could sit down.'

'Please don't make a fuss,' Mrs Orme said softly. 'I shall be well directly.'

Her face was bloodless, her lips the colour of lead; I thought she looked dreadfully ill, and saw that she could not possibly walk home.

'What a lucky thing I was passing,' I said cheerfully. 'Now you can keep me company in Sir James's third-best carriage, which is waiting outside. But my dear Mrs Orme, you ought to have some tea, or at least a glass of water.'

'We – we – the truth is, I'm not sure we have enough money left for tea.' Miss Winifred's long-cheeked face was beaming at me now; my offer had alleviated some of her anxiety. 'As for water, no waiter or servant has come near us, though we've been here for a while.'

Two shabby women in plain grey bonnets were so insignificant in this bustling place that they might as well have been invisible. I marched out to the corridor, collared a reluctant waiter as he pelted past me, and ordered him to fetch tea for three – at once, or I would complain to the landlord – and a glass of brandy for a lady who had been taken ill.

Mrs Orme managed a dim smile as I returned in triumph to the table. 'Thank you, Mrs Rodd; I'm sure a cup of tea is all I need to set me right.'

A few minutes later the door of the coffee room opened and a tall, solidly built woman came in bearing a glass of brandy.

'Are you Mrs Rodd, the lady from Wishtide? I'm Mrs Hinton, ma'am, and I'm very sorry nobody attended to the lady who's poorly; we're run off our feet, not that I'm making excuses.'

Mrs Hinton was middle-aged, neatly turned out in a black dress and starched white cap, and the very embodiment of the traditional innkeeper's wife – welcoming yet formidably capable.

'It won't happen again, ma'am; I shall give those young chaps a dressing-down they won't forget in a hurry.' I didn't doubt it; there was a steely glint in those watchful eyes.

'Thank you, Mrs Hinton.'

'And please give my respects to Sir James.' She bobbed her head, in a mixture of nod and curtsy, and went to the group beside the fire, to tell them that the table was laid for their luncheon – the child made the old lady smile by crying out, 'Hooray!'

As the little group passed us, the brandy glass shook in Mrs Orme's hand. She took a couple of sips, which appeared to revive her slightly.

'I'm so sorry; I'm much better now. I can't think why I turned so faint.'

'I blame that freezing wind from Russia,' Miss Winifred said. 'I should never have let you come out this morning.'

'Oh, Winnie, don't be silly – you'd never have carried all those brushes by yourself.'

'Brushes!' Miss Winifred squeaked suddenly. 'I left them with the cheese-woman when you were taken ill – please excuse me, Mrs Rodd –'

She jumped to her feet and hurried out of the coffee room, nearly upsetting the waiter with our tea-things. Her sister-in-law smiled after her with unmistakable affection.

'Dear old Winnie – and now she'll burst back in here festooned with brushes and brooms, bragging to all and sundry about beating the man down by sixpence.'

'She could give my own dear sister-in-law a lesson or two in thrift,' I said (rather unkindly contrasting Miss Winifred's careful management with Fanny's extravagance).

Mrs Orme smiled properly now, the colour stealing back into her lips. 'She likes to say she can make a shilling stretch from here to Lincoln and back again. But if she sees anyone who needs money more than she does, she turns into a reckless spendthrift and would give the very clothes off her back. And her brother was exactly the same. Whenever I doubt the workings of Providence, I think of the blessed, loving atmosphere of their home.'

The waiter spread a white cloth on our table, and hurriedly put down the tea-things. I set about making the tea (which took a long time; though the leaves were of perfectly good quality, I thought the quantity somewhat mean).

The tea, on top of the brandy, appeared to restore Mrs Orme. She leaned towards me and murmured, 'I have written to – to a certain person.' Her voice was almost inaudible against the noise of the inn. 'I have begged him, if he loves me at all, to let me alone.'

'Will he listen to you?'

'I doubt it. But I had to try one more time. I dread telling poor Charles what I really am. I wish I could make him see that I never set out to lie to him – what choice did I have?'

Once again I sensed how deeply she loved the young man, and how hard she had fought with herself not to love him.

'It's the right thing to do,' I murmured back to her. 'Take courage, Mrs Orme; I will help you in any way I can.'

Sir James sent word that he was coming home for a few days – not because of the murder of his wife's servant, but because the local Member of Parliament had died, and there were preparations to be made for the by-election.

Like a great ship setting sail, the sleeping house cranked and juddered back to life. The empty corridors and echoing staircases were teeming with servants, moving like a noiseless wind through each room, tearing off covers and throwing open shutters.

'It's unexpected, but I'm always prepared,' Mrs Craik told me. 'Her Ladyship and the girls are coming back tomorrow, and the master requests your company at dinner tonight, Mrs Rodd, with himself and Mr Filey.'

She had come to my room to ask if I needed any help with my evening clothes; doing my utmost to keep a straight face, I explained that I possessed no evening clothes and would be wearing my one good black silk. Mrs Craik firmly took it away to be pressed, along with my white cap with the ribbon of black watered silk. I can't imagine what she did to them, but my dress and cap came back beautifully glossy and stiff, and I was rather surprised by the splendour of my reflection in the glass; this exemplary housekeeper had buffed and polished every blessed thing in the place, including the governess.

Dinner was set out in Sir James's library, upon an elegant little table in front of the fire. The two gentlemen stood up when I entered the room and I thought Mr Filey looked very tired after the long journey from London.

Sir James, however, was alight with energy and purpose. 'Well, Mrs Rodd, it never rains but it pours, eh? I beg your pardon if I have seemed neglectful lately – but the business of the letters appears to be settled, and my son's tiresome romance had to take second place. There's the question of who is to be the new member, and the greater question of how to secure enough votes for him – my tenants can be relied on, but a couple of boroughs are full of ten-pound freeholders who may vote as they please, and it's never too early to start buttering them up.' He gulped a mouthful of the excellent steak-and-oyster pie. 'And as if all that wasn't enough, there's this wretched murder of Mlle Thérèse.'

'The voters will like to see you about the town and countryside,' said Mr Filey.

'Yes, and they'll also think it proper that my wife and daughters are coming home, since the murdered woman was their servant.' Sir James comfortably drained and refilled his glass of claret. 'And we owe the countryside some society; if I don't invite the better classes to dine once in a while, their wives won't let them vote for my man.' He dabbed at his mouth with his napkin, as if he had just swallowed his local obligations and dismissed them. 'Now to the matter of the work that you were doing for me, Mrs Rodd. Your brother seems to think it's done and dusted – but as far as I can see, not a thing has changed. My son still insists that no power on earth will prevent him from marrying that woman.'

'Only because he doesn't yet know the truth about her,' I said. 'When he does, he will understand at once that it cannot be. She would have been able to keep her secrets, if your son had not taken it into his head to fall in love with her. She has never encouraged his advances, nor permitted him to hope they might be married – though it is quite plain to me that she loves him with all her heart.'

Sir James listened to this with half an ear, busy with his food and wine. 'So what did you discover, ma'am?'

'You asked me to look into the background of Helen Orme,' I said. 'I did so, and now have her solemn promise that she will never marry your son. She asks only that you will allow her time enough to speak to Mr Charles herself; once he knows everything, there will be no question of a marriage. Even he will understand that it is quite impossible – and then it will be up to you how you comfort him for his first real disappointment in life.'

There was a spell of silence, and then Sir James chuckled. 'By heaven, you're a cool customer, Mrs Rodd; aren't you going to tell us what you found out?'

'No,' I said shortly. 'It is not necessary for you to know the details. Mrs Orme has given her word.'

'Why should I trust the word of such a creature?'

'Because she knows the alternative – her secret revealed to the world. I didn't enjoy blackmailing her, though that's what it amounted to. She's a clever woman, and she knows that discretion is of equal importance to both of you; bear in mind that she has a great deal more to lose than you do.'

'More than I do?' Sir James was astounded. 'What on earth do you mean?'

'Sir James, you are wealthy and powerful; the last shreds of her good name are all this poor woman has in the world. I daresay Mr Charles will tell you all the details – the bare facts are somewhat indelicate.'

'Oh, I see what you're driving at,' said Sir James. 'I beg your pardon – of course as a lady you can't really speak of such matters.'

(In fact I can speak of practically anything without a blush, but it is sometimes useful to hide behind my petticoat.)

'I think we must agree,' Mr Filey said, 'that your task is complete. Thank you, Mrs Rodd; we'll settle what is owed to you in the morning. At least that's one thing less to worry us.'

My heart leapt – I was dismissed, and tomorrow I would be dashing home to the delightful noise and soot of London. But I had not quite finished.

'There is still the matter of the murder on your doorstep,' I said. 'The woman was employed by you.'

Sir James shrugged, helping himself to more butter-glazed carrots from the dish on the table. 'I can't be held responsible for what my servants get up to in my absence.'

'But she was blackmailing you.'

This made him frown. 'You're fond of that word, ma'am.'

'What else should I call it? You told me yourself that you were obliged to take Mlle Thérèse into your household, because of what she knew about your wife. The evidence so far suggests that the woman was working with Savile –'

'But you said you didn't believe the man Savile could have sent those foul letters!' Mr Filey had snapped awake. 'You said we should look somewhere else!'

Though I am extremely good at keeping my patience, I did marvel at the stubborn complacency of these men and their like; they really did not see how the affairs of servants could have anything to do with them. They did not understand that murder, like the cholera, can infect all classes.

'But of course we must look somewhere else!' I said. 'It's as plain as the nose on my face that Savile and the Frenchwoman were working with a third person – the person who cut Savile's throat and bludgeoned Mlle Thérèse to death. Who had the best reasons for wishing them dead? Even if I thought Mrs Orme capable of killing Savile – which I do not – she had no reason to kill his consort. Whereas you did, Sir James; now that she is dead, you are rid of someone who could have ruined you.'

There was a silence; the coals shifted in the grate.

'This must not be traced back to us,' said Mr Filey. 'How much do people know?'

'I left my translation of the letters with the constable,' I said, 'and a brief statement for the coroner, should he care to read it, giving the simplest possible account of the discovery of the murder, nothing more. But I beg you to take care, until this third person has been found – this person who kills coldly and without mercy.'

'Thank you, Mrs Rodd.' Sir James had been a little rattled by my plain speaking. 'You have done excellent work, most excellent; I shall tell my womenfolk you had to go back to town in a hurry.'

'Due to a family emergency,' Mr Filey said.

'Oh – yes, a perfect cover,' Sir James said. 'Women are always having those. As to women,' his attention had turned back to Mr Filey, 'they are never radicals, so they're the key to this election – we may have to resign ourselves to giving a ball.' He shrugged. 'It's a confounded nuisance, but it can't be helped; thank the lord they don't have votes of their own!'

Twelve

THE SECRET OF MY mincemeat was handed down to me by my dear mother. In a word, suet. This must be chopped into the smallest possible pieces, thoroughly mixed with your dried fruits, sugar and spices, and the bowl set beside a hot fire until the fat has melted and the fruit gleams. Then leave it in the pantry or scullery overnight.

Matt was very fond of my mincemeat; under his greedy influence I added more brandy and sugar to my mother's recipe. Every Stir-up Sunday, he would sing 'Dame Get Up and Bake your Pies' – though it was the week before the beginning of Advent, and he was supposed to be thinking of the Four Last Things: Death, Judgement, Heaven and Hell. Pies didn't come into it.

Dearest Matt, he rejoiced in the feasting and fun of Christmas. 'Our Saviour came into this world as a little child,' he would say. 'It never does us any harm to remember the child in ourselves.' I can see him now, tobogganing down Parliament Hill with our nephews – red-faced and wild-haired, a boy amongst boys.

Christmas is a time of looking back and remembering, and it's now a sad time for me; the old joy will never come again in this world.

But gleams and fragments of the joy still return to me. I carry on making my mincemeat, and good old Fred will not allow me to turn into the spectre at the feast; on my first Christmas as a widow, when I was in deepest mourning, he insisted that I spend the day in his turbulent household, as usual.

'You know it's exactly what Matt would wish you to do,' he told me. 'Some things cannot be allowed to change – and if you don't come, who will beat me at Snapdragon?'

(It is understandable that the game of Snapdragon has fallen from favour. I have lost count of the number of cuffs I have burnt over the years, picking currants out of the flaming brandy.)

I set about making my mincemeat the day after I returned from Lincolnshire. Mrs Bentley had taken careful note of my instructions and the ingredients she had assembled were of the highest quality.

'I had to throw out the first lot of currants, ma'am – like a silly old fool I soaked them in brandy but forgot to cover them, and I found two drunken mice on the shelf the next morning.'

'Never mind,' I said airily. 'There's plenty of money this year; we can afford to treat a couple of mice to a night of debauchery.'

Mrs Bentley chuckled. 'I gave them to that one-eyed cat from the tavern – and then, when he ate them, HE got drunk!'

She was spry and bright-eyed; living in a warm house and eating proper meals had done wonders for her health; little Anny had returned to the bosom of her family, but I made a mental note to engage her again next time I was called away.

'Oh, it feels good to be at home,' I said.

I was cutting candied peel (a fiddly job) on one side of the kitchen table, while Mrs Bentley chopped suet on the other. The fire I had made was hot enough to melt the grate, and I had brought the oil-lamp down from the drawing room. The little square basement kitchen was now radiant with light and blissfully warm, and we felt we were working in the very lap of luxury.

'Don't you miss living in that great house?' Mrs Bentley asked.

'Not in the least; I was glad to get away from it. I couldn't breathe freely.'

She nodded. 'You don't like leaving unfinished business, that's the trouble.'

Here was the heart of it – I could not hide anything from her.

'No, I do not.' I laid down my knife. 'There is something in the general atmosphere of Wishtide that makes me very uneasy. I did the job I'd been paid to do and Sir James declared himself satisfied – but a woman has been murdered, and her murderer is still at large. I don't for a moment believe it was the work of some passing vagrant.'

'There's no sense in that,' Mrs Bentley agreed. 'Vagrants don't hang around the stables of great houses. And that French-woman was expecting to meet her husband. She had her belongings with her. I wonder that Sir James didn't keep you on to investigate, ma'am.'

'So do I – but it didn't occur to him to attach such impor-tance to the death of a servant. Mr Filey said they'd look into the Frenchwoman's connection with Savile, and I had to leave it at that.'

Mrs Bentley swept her heap of chopped suet into the big, fragrant bowl of fruits and spices. 'I'd be worried if I were him – who's to say where the killer will strike next?'

This was my fear too, though I couldn't have said who might be in danger. All my instincts told me that the Angel of Death had not finished with Wishtide – or with me.

Early on Christmas morning, Mrs Bentley's oldest son took her off in one of his milk-carts, to spend the day at his dairy farm to the north of Temple Fortune. A little later, when the bells were pealing for morning service, Fred's carriage arrived, to carry me to the elegant new church of St Michael's in Highgate, where his excited offspring filled an entire pew to overflowing.

My brother has always loved Christmas Day; it did my heart good to see his face beaming at me over the children's curly heads and to hear his loud, tuneless voice singing 'Christians, Awake'. Despite the excitement and the fact that the governess had gone home for the holiday, Fanny was unusually serene, and I soon found out why; during the sermon Fred whispered to me that she was expecting another baby, and she was always calm and sweet-natured at such times (I occasionally wondered if Fred kept her in the family way on purpose). I whispered back, 'You'd better rent another pew,' which made him snort with laughter (you can see why our mother did not allow us to sit next to each other in church).

The service over and greetings exchanged with the neighbours, we made a merry party walking back across the green – Fred carried the two littlest children, one on each arm, while Fanny and I each held the paws of the next two up. So the Lord sets the solitary in families. It was a day of noise and jollity; though I ached for Matt, I was never allowed to feel alone.

In the early evening, when the smallest of the small fry were in their beds and the racket had lessened a little, Fred challenged me to one of our games of Snapdragon. This was not a dignified affair; the dish was placed on the hearthrug before the fire and Fred and I knelt on the floor beside it, while the children shouted out our scores and ate the burnt currants.

Fred was three currants ahead of me when the maid came in to announce a visitor – it took her a few moments to make herself heard above the shrieks of laughter.

'It's Mr Filey, sir – he's sorry to trouble you today, but he needs to speak to you and Mrs Rodd and says it won't wait.'

We were sober at once, knowing this must be something serious. Fred settled his singed cuffs, I put my burnt cap-ribbons to rights, and we hurried to the chilly library, where the maid had hastily lighted the lamp and put a match to the fire.

Mr Filey – still in his greatcoat and clutching his hat in one hand – waited beside the desk. 'Mrs Rodd – Mr Tyson – I must apologise for the intrusion.' In the lamplight his furrowed face was agitated. 'The worst of calamities has brought me here.'

'For heaven's sake, sit down,' Fred said. 'Won't you take a glass of something?'

'No – I thank you –' Filey did not sit. 'Helen Orme is dead – and Charles Calderstone has been charged with her murder.'

Thirteen

AND SO POOR HELEN Orme was no more. In my shock and sorrow, I thought of the milkmaid in the old song – '"My face is my fortune, sir," she said.' Helen's lovely face had been her fortune, and probably her misfortune too.

'I can't get away from the feeling that I might have prevented this,' I told Mrs Bentley later. 'I don't know how – but if I had only dug about a little more, and in different places!'

'Now, you stop that – it doesn't help nobody if you go blaming yourself, so drink up.'

Mrs Bentley had returned from her son's house to find me weeping beside the embers of the kitchen fire. Flapping away my protests, she had rebuilt the fire and made a jug of her cure-all hot brandy and water.

'She was a good woman, Mary; as the Lord said, her only crime was that she "loved much". And poor Miss Winifred is as kind a soul as I've ever met in my life.'

'Do you think the young fellow did it?'

'No. The facts may be against him, but my every instinct tells me Charles Calderstone is innocent. I said as much to my brother, and he immediately agreed to defend him – much to the relief of Mr Filey. My brother knows I've never been wrong in cases like this.'

'No more you have – I daresay Sir James wants your services again.'

'He does indeed; he's offered to pay me any sum I care to mention.'

'So when did it happen?'

'Three days ago; the old charwoman let herself into the cottage and found Mrs Orme's dead body stretched across the sofa. She had been killed with a blow – or several blows – to the head, like Mlle Thérèse.'

Mrs Bentley's pale eyes were piercing bright above the rim of her glass. 'Where was the sister-in-law?'

'The old woman heard moaning from the back of the cottage,' I said, 'and found Miss Winifred lying outside the scullery door, horribly injured and unable to speak.' The tears rushed into my eyes. 'She's not expected to live; Sir James would have taken her into his house, but she was not fit to be moved so far; they carried her to the vicarage, a mile or so down the road, to be cared for by Mr Fitzwarren and his mother.'

'They'd better watch out,' Mrs Bentley said. 'That murderer thought he'd killed her; if it wasn't Mr Charles, he might come back for another go.'

'I quite agree – but everyone seems utterly convinced of Mr Charles's guilt. Unfortunately, there's a reliable witness who saw him at the cottage on the morning of the murder.'

'Oh dear.' Mrs Bentley shook her head. 'That looks bad.'

'A farm labourer named Turner was hedging and ditching in the field across the lane. He claims he heard angry voices – or one angry voice – though he was too far off to make out exactly what was being said. As you say, it looks as bad as possible. The inquest was held the following day, the verdict was "wilful murder", and Mr Charles was duly taken up. But I'm convinced this is the work of the same person who killed Mlle Thérèse – and I can't imagine why Mr Charles would want to do that. You've brought up five boys, Mary, and you'd know it as well as I do if you met him; he's hot-headed and impulsive, but he's not a killer.'

'So you think Mrs Orme was attacked after Mr Charles had left her?'

'Yes,' I said. 'There was plenty of time. Unfortunately, the whole countryside knew about the young man's infatuation with Mrs Orme – and there's apparently a lot of local feeling against him, due to the manner in which she was discovered.' I did not need to mince my words with Mrs Bentley. 'Her skirts were pulled up, exposing her in the most merciless manner, and there was every sign that she had been violated – either shortly before or shortly after death.'

We were silent for a moment, letting the horror sink in.

'Dear me!' Mrs Bentley sighed and shook her head again. 'You've got your work cut out this time, ma'am.'

The walls of Newgate Prison, which squatted just south of the Old Bailey, were blank and blackened with soot. Inside this sorrowful place, the condemned waited to be hanged and the suspected waited to be tried. The cells were built to overlook a central yard – the poor locked up on one side, and those who could afford better accommodation on the other. So justice is tempered with money, if not with mercy.

It was early in the afternoon on the day after Christmas but the light was already fading; a dirty yellow fog had descended upon the city, blotting out the struggling winter sun. A heavy door swallowed us into brick-lined darkness, and as I listened to the grind of keys turning and bolts sliding, I felt the dreadful sadness that had soaked into these walls over so many years. The Prayer Book exhorts us to pray for 'prisoners and captives'. The Lord said, 'I was in prison and you visited me.' Matt had great compassion for prisoners, and spent more than one night sitting up with a condemned man; he prayed with them up to the very gallows if he could. 'It's the duty of any half-decent clergyman to walk into Hell itself,' he used to say. 'We're needed most where God is least.'

My brother was extremely familiar with Newgate Prison; he often said he spent more time in here than in his chambers, consulting with his clients or (less often) taking leave of them before they were hanged. The sour-looking gaoler who admitted us broke into smiles as soon as he saw him.

'Mr Tyson – compliments of the season to you, sir!'

'And to you, Mason. How's my godson?'

'Flourishing, sir, thank you – coming up to six now, if you can believe it.'

'Good grief, where does the time go?' Fred dug into his pocket, found a florin and pressed it into the man's hand. 'Buy him something for Christmas.'

'Thank you, sir.'

'This is my sister, Mrs Rodd. We're here to see young Calderstone.'

'Ah,' Mason said, 'I had a bet with myself that it'd be you.' He added, apologetically, 'I'm afraid he's a special-permission case.'

'I have a letter from the governor.' Fred handed over the unsealed sheet of paper.

The gaoler held it up to the light of the lantern he was carrying, and there was a long silence while he worked his way through the few lines. He then returned the letter to Fred. 'I'd better take a look in that basket now, sir – not that I'm suspecting you of smuggling in a file, but rules is rules.'

We had brought a large basket of food and wine, writing paper, ink, candles and other comforts for the prisoner; Mason took a quick glance inside and handed it back to Fred. Then he lifted the lantern to lead us along the maze of whitewashed passages, to Charles Calderstone's prison cell.

It was a bare, cold, pitiless space, furnished with a hard bed, a small table and one chair. The only light came from the lamp that bled in from the corridor, and one fat, slow-burning candle. We found Mr Charles sitting at the table with his head buried in his arms; when he raised his head, I was shocked to see his swollen eyes and unshaven cheeks.

'Chin up, you lucky lad,' the gaoler said. 'Look who your pa's got to defend you!'

The poor young man blinked at us and tried to stand up.

I laid a hand on his shoulder and gently pushed him back into the chair. 'We've come to help you, Mr Charles; this is my brother, Frederick Tyson.'

'It doesn't matter,' he said in a dull voice. 'I'm as good as dead and buried already.'

'Now then,' Mason admonished sharply. 'Mr Tyson's defended worse sinners than you. Show some manners.'

Fred sat down on the bed. 'Ouch – I never can remember to bring in a cushion! You may leave the door open, Mason, and wait outside.'

'Yes, sir.'

The man stepped out of the cell, which gave me room to sit down beside my brother; the space was so confined that our knees touched and I could take hold of Mr Charles's cold hand. My every instinct told me that he was not in a state of guilt, but of grief; he was breaking his heart for the woman he had loved.

'Let's have something to drink.' Fred reached to open the basket, which he had placed on the table. 'We need to keep out the cold, and you look half-dead, Mr Charles; I never forget to bring glasses.'

'He won't be allowed to keep those glasses.' Mason's voice floated in from the passage.

Fred shot a grin at me. 'I hope you'll join us, Mason.'

'That's very civil of you, sir.' The gaoler briefly loomed in the doorway, blotting out half the light and making our shadows leap like demons, to accept a generous glass of brandy. 'I'll drink to your health, sir.'

Fred poured large measures for himself and Mr Charles (I declined) and got down to business. 'You know why I'm here, Mr Charles; to make the case that you did not kill Helen Orme.'

'Of course I didn't kill her.' Mr Charles's bloodshot eyes filled. 'I loved her more than anything. I wouldn't hurt her for the world!'

'But you were seen entering her house on the morning of the murder, and heard shouting at her angrily. There's a witness who'll swear to it. Were you aware of that?'

'Yes.'

'Is it true?'

'Y-yes.'

'Why were you angry?'

Mr Charles tugged his hand from mine, and made an attempt to muster his pride. 'I can't tell you.'

'Let me be frank with you.' My brother had a way of suddenly hardening to steel, though his demeanour remained outwardly genial. 'The only reason I've agreed to take this case is that my sister believes you are innocent. Otherwise I wouldn't have touched it with a bargepole. I can tell you about this witness, though I've never laid eyes on him. He's a reliable yokel, of the type that juries invariably trust, because they assume he lacks the wits to make anything up. He saw you storming into the cottage and heard your voice raised in anger. It couldn't look much worse, could it? I can sometimes heal the sick, Mr Charles, but I can't raise the dead – and I can't do a thing for you unless you tell me the whole truth.'

Fred doesn't like me to interfere with his lines of questioning, but I couldn't help interrupting here. 'Mr Charles, you cannot protect her reputation now.' (I was certain this was what he was doing – but what foolish chivalry, when she was dead and beyond all harm and he was facing the gallows.)

Pain raked across the young man's face, and blood rushed into his pale cheeks. I felt very sorry for him; his idol had confessed to the sin that so many men find impossible to forgive.

He murmured, very low, 'I called her things I would take back a thousand times.'

'So she told you her history, and you were angry with her,' Fred said.

'Yes.'

'Every man on the jury will understand that – and there's our problem. They're also highly likely to regard it as a fine motive for murdering the woman. Can you recall what you said?'

'No.'

'That's not good enough; our reliable yokel will swear he heard the word "whore". Did you use that word?'

'Yes.' This was almost inaudible.

'So she confessed her history, and you reacted by calling her a whore.'

'Don't remind me,' Mr Charles said shakily. 'I can't bear to think about it now.'

'I'm afraid you're going to have to bear it, and a lot more,' Fred said. 'I have a case to build. Was the shouting the end of it, or did you do anything else? Did you strike her, or push her?'

'No!'

'Did you touch Mrs Orme in any way?'

'No –'

'By which I mean, did you force your attentions upon her, disarrange her clothing –?'

'No!' Mr Charles snapped this furiously, his face turning brick-red. 'How dare you?'

I took his hand again, fearful that he would make my brother change his mind about defending him. 'You must try to answer the questions calmly; you will have to face far worse in court. Do you know how she was found?'

He nodded.

Fred sighed and helped himself to a small mutton pie from the basket, giving me a reproachful look – I knew he was thinking of his warm fireside and hot dinner. 'She was violated. Was that your doing?'

'No – I swear! You must believe me!' The young man took a gulp of brandy and made a visible effort to pull himself together. 'I was there because Helen wrote to me that she wanted to talk to me. I still have the letter. She wrote that she wanted to tell me, once and for all, why – why I should forget her. Nothing more than that.'

'Where were you when you received the letter?' I asked.

'At Wishtide – my quarrel with my father can't keep me away from Mamma and the girls. And in any case, my father wasn't there. He was back in town, with that woman of his.'

'Hmmm, no wonder you're angry with him,' Fred said, with his mouth full. 'He wouldn't have turned a hair, I daresay, if you had simply copied him and set Mrs Orme up as your mistress.'

'Fred!' I murmured.

'You're quite right.' Mr Charles frowned, and suddenly looked older. 'He's a hypocrite; he only cares about appearances.'

'So what did you do when you got Mrs Orme's letter?' Fred asked.

'I ordered my horse and rode over at once – I still didn't believe there was anything she could tell me that could stand in the way of our marriage.'

'What time was this?'

'Between eight and nine in the morning.'

Fred said 'Hmm' again; he seldom wrote anything down, but I knew he was listening intently. 'Did you find her alone?'

'No, Miss Winifred was there – but she knew why I had come and she withdrew to the kitchen to leave us alone together.'

'And then Mrs Orme told you her true history.'

'Yes,' said Mr Charles, 'and I have to say I was angry – of course I was angry.' He drained the rest of the brandy; it had put heart into him, and his expression was no longer lost and pitiful. In the shifting candlelight the determined glint in his eyes reminded me strongly of his father. At last he was making a real effort to remember. 'I don't know what I thought she was about to tell me. I was so certain of her purity. It was the light I lived by. I know everyone will laugh at me now – but I was preparing myself for a high-minded argument – I'd got it into my head that she was making one of her noble sacrifices. I most certainly did not expect her to tell me she was another man's discarded harlot.'

'Please –' I could not help interrupting; the poor woman was dead.

But Fred said, 'Sorry, Letty – that's what the jury will be thinking, and we mustn't be shy about it. I'll find some way of using it to get them on our side. Your idol revealed her feet of clay but you were more sorrowful than angry – the duped innocent – yes, that's probably how I'll play it. She made a damned fool of you and you scuttled off with your tail between your legs –'

'Fred!' I was shocked.

For the first time a shadow of a smile crossed the young man's face. 'That's pretty much how it was.' (He liked my brother, I was glad to see.) 'She smashed me to smithereens with a couple of short sentences. At first I begged her to say it wasn't true – and then I was in agonies – I would happily have killed that blackguard if he hadn't been dead already – but I couldn't have hurt Helen. I shouted at her and stormed away. That's all.'

'What time was this?' asked Fred.

'Between nine and ten; I couldn't face going home and made straight for town – I left my horse at the inn, as Hinton will tell you. And the following night I was arrested at my rooms in Half Moon Street.'

'They told you of the murder,' Fred said, 'at which you fainted – oh, don't be ashamed, my boy – fainting was the best possible thing you could have done. The jurors might think you're rather a daisy, but they'll be less likely to believe you had the spunk to kill her.'

From the other side of the door, the gaoler said, 'Time's up, Mr Tyson!'

'Hmm.' Fred brushed away pie-crumbs with a satisfied air. 'We'll have to leave it at that – but it's a pretty good start.'

Mr Charles touched his arm. 'Do you believe I killed her?'

'No,' Fred said. 'I don't.'

'Do I – do I have a chance?'

'More than a chance,' my brother said cheerfully. 'It's my belief you couldn't kill a fly – and by the time I've finished with them, the jury will agree with me. So take heart, Mr Charles; eat and drink, and feel free to ignore the Bible my sister insisted upon bringing you.'

'Fred – really!' I couldn't let this pass; he was wicked to speak in that way about the only source of true light in this dark place.

The young man, however, actually smiled for the first time. 'I'm very grateful, Mrs Rodd; the time hangs so heavy here.'

'Do read it and be comforted.' I took his cold hand. 'Remember that your friends will move heaven and earth to help you. And I also brought you *Robinson Crusoe* and *The Vicar of Wakefield*.'

Fred groaned rudely. 'You poor boy, I'd better get you out of here before you die of boredom.'

Mr Charles smiled outright at this and when we left his cell, I was very glad to see that his brow had cleared, and his red eyes had a spark of hope in them.

Outside the prison I gulped at the dirty air, as if it were as pure as air on top of a mountain, as if a weight had been lifted from my chest.

'Hmm, a good beginning.' Fred checked his gold watch by the carriage-lamp. 'And we'll be back in time for dinner if the roads aren't too bad. When do you go down to Lincolnshire?'

'Very soon, I should think.' (I was not looking forward to the long, cold, sooty journey.)

'They're sending a man down from Great Scotland Yard; you'd better not tread on his toes.'

'Oh, that'll be a simple enough matter,' I said. 'The police never seem to ask the right questions.'

'Question every single person you can think of,' Fred replied. 'Someone has seen Mrs Orme's killer. Someone has fed him, sheltered him, hired him a horse, sold him a pint of ale. It's not the kind of place where strangers go unnoticed.'

Fourteen

'YOU MUST PARDON THE state of the house, Mrs Rodd; we came down in a great hurry to be near our boy and the place has been shut up for several years. My health hasn't been equal to a London season; my husband stays at his club when he's here.'

Lady Calderstone had summoned me and Fred to the official Calderstone London residence; a grand house overlooking Hyde Park, richly furnished but with an air of having been woken up too soon. She knew that we knew about Mrs Hardy; that did not matter now.

I bowed, to show that I accepted the fiction about the 'club'. Frankly, I was startled by the change in her; Lady Calderstone looked older, but also more collected and energetic. She had left off the décolletage and the ringlets in favour of plain black silk, and her anxiety for her son had made a lioness of her (I have often observed that the state of motherhood can turn quite ordinary females into heroines; even fretful Fanny has her moments of magnificence).

'We've left the girls in the country, until the trial, at least.' She spoke of this calmly, absolutely alight with the certainty that her son would be found innocent. 'My cousin Esther Grahame is staying; she'll protect them from the worst of it.'

'Yes, it's a bad business,' Fred said. 'The fact is that if they were in town, those poor girls would not be able to put their noses out of doors. This murder has absolutely gripped the popular imagination.'

He was not exaggerating; it was only the twenty-seventh of December, but the ballad-sellers were already singing the murder around the freezing London streets, and the windows of the stationers' shops were filled with lurid drawings of Mr Charles brandishing a dagger at the throat of a meek clerical widow with her hands clasped in prayer.

'The Metropolitan Police are sending a man from Great Scotland Yard,' Fred went on. 'And he will want to talk to your daughters about the day of the crime.'

Lady Calderstone flinched, and for a moment the light went out of her. 'Can't they be left out of this?'

'They were at Wishtide on that day, weren't they?'

'Yes, but they don't know anything; we had only just come home from Yorkshire!'

'The police will need to ask about Mr Charles's movements,' I told her. 'And the servants will probably have better information; don't worry more than you can help.'

Fred, out of sight of Her Ladyship, shot me one of his wicked smiles. 'The Metropolitan Police are sending a very good man – quite an old friend of ours.'

If we had been alone I would have groaned aloud, for I guessed what he was going to say next.

'Inspector Thomas Blackbeard.'

(Of all the people I could have done without; I had twice crossed swords with the piratically named Inspector Blackbeard.)

For Her Ladyship's sake, I did my best to be reassuring. 'I wouldn't exactly call him a friend, but he's a clever man, and too independent-minded to be influenced by silly local gossip.' (This was putting it mildly.)

Lady Calderstone raised her head proudly. 'Charles is very well loved in the neighbourhood – nobody who knows him could possibly think him guilty.'

The gilded clock on the mantelpiece gave a dusty-sounding whirr, like a genteel cough, and chimed eleven.

'Please excuse me, Your Ladyship,' Fred said, 'I have business with Sir James.'

He bowed himself out of the room with one meaningful look at me; he had brought me here to ask Lady Calderstone about her history, with a view to finding this man Villiers – who just might be a link in what was becoming a chain of murders. If we found the killer of Mlle Thérèse and Savile, it could only benefit Mr Charles.

Lady Calderstone pulled the bell. 'I hope you will take a cup of coffee with me, Mrs Rodd.'

The summons was answered by Thorpe, the butler (I had only seen this deity of the servants' hall from a distance; he spent more time with Sir James than either his wife or Mrs Hardy, and was thoroughly His Lordship's man).

Even at this hour of the morning it was dark; the fog seemed to have gathered in the corners of the great room. Lady Calderstone ordered our coffee and asked Thorpe to build up the fire.

I had already decided how I would approach my dreadful subject. 'My brother feels that Mr Charles's best hope lies in discovering the murderer of Savile and Mlle Thérèse,' I said,

144

once we were alone, 'so that he can establish a connection with the murder of Mrs Orme.'

She bowed her head to hide her stricken face. 'My husband told you about Switzerland.'

'He did.'

'My children don't know – will they need to know?'

'Not necessarily.'

'I – I won't hold anything back if it helps Charles. I can endure any amount of shame for his sake. I have said as much to my husband.'

This rather startled me; was Sir James equally prepared to endure shame? 'I hope it doesn't come to that,' I said. 'Could you tell me something about when you first met Thérèse Gabin?'

'It was in Switzerland. Vevey.'

'Yes.'

Lady Calderstone's voice was level, yet her face betrayed the memory of that anguish. 'You know what I have been. What I am. The gentleman I was with hired Thérèse as my lady's maid.'

'Were you aware that she was married?'

'No.'

'Did you ever meet Savile?'

'No.'

'Didn't your – didn't the gentleman keep a manservant?'

'Mrs Rodd, please let me assure you,' Lady Calderstone burst out, 'none of this has anything to do with Charlie – why would God punish him for my sins?'

I was very sorry for her, all worn down as she was with misery and remorse. 'You must not forget that He is the God of mercy,'

I said gently. 'You have repented, you have been forgiven; your only error now is surely your refusal to forgive yourself.'

'But I was so very stupid,' Her Ladyship said, working her hands together distractedly (she had left off all her rings except the plain gold wedding band). 'Selfish and stupid – I never gave a thought for those who loved me, until it was too late. My children! I deserve this lake of fire.' Her dramatic, impulsive manner of speaking reminded me of Miss Blanche. 'I gave into temptation; I didn't even try to resist.'

She reminded me even more forcibly of Helen Orme; how quick the world was to cast a woman into outer darkness because she dared to fall in love.

Thorpe the butler brought in the tray of coffee at this point; not as good as Mlle Thérèse's coffee, but very welcome in the wretched cold.

'There's one thing I'd like you to know,' Lady Calderstone said, when we were once more alone. 'I'm not telling you to excuse myself, but to show you how things were. At the time of my fall, I no longer had a husband in the accepted sense of the word. Sir James had already met Mrs Hardy. She came first. When I sinned, I had already lost my husband's love.'

(This was surprising, and also sad; it was such a little morsel of an excuse, yet it made all the difference to Her Ladyship; she had not been the first to sin.)

'But men never "fall" as women fall,' I said. 'Love doesn't hurt them as it can hurt us. Their reputations are not as fragile. Was this man Villiers aware of the sacrifice you were making?'

A little colour stole into her cheeks. 'We were rather hurried into the sacrifice; I was with child.'

'Lady Calderstone – I must ask – could Villiers have had anything to do with the murders of Savile and Mlle Thérèse? Was she blackmailing him too?'

'I doubt it,' she said. 'What did he have to lose?'

'Your husband told me Villiers was not the man's true name.'

She shrugged impatiently. 'I never knew him by any other.'

'When your husband came to Vevey to reclaim you, was Mlle Thérèse the only other person who knew the truth?'

'Yes, I'm sure of it.'

Impulsively, I asked, 'Did you like her?'

The question did not surprise Lady Calderstone. 'Thérèse saved my life and stood by me when I was alone and helpless. She had her faults, but I was fond of her.'

'Was it her idea to accompany you back to England?'

'Yes,' Lady Calderstone said. 'She had nothing to keep her in Vevey. And Sir James was only too well aware of the power she had over us, because of what she knew.'

'And you never suspected that she was married?'

'Never.'

I remembered what the girl Martha had told me about the gold locket, and Mlle Thérèse kissing the picture inside it. 'But she had a follower – a lover. Did she tell you nothing about him?'

'No,' Lady Calderstone said slowly, 'not precisely – but she dropped a hint about something when she asked me not to take her up to Yorkshire.'

'She asked you – so it was her own wish to stay behind?'

'Very much so.'

'As I'm sure you know,' I said, 'there's a strong likelihood that she was working with Savile to blackmail your husband.'

'They are both dead now. And they have nothing to do with Charlie.'

I would have liked to probe a little more, but my brother came back into the room with Sir James.

Poor man; the shock that had strengthened his wife had shattered him; his head had frosted over with grey and fresh lines were scored on his cheeks. He leaned towards me, and said, in a shaking voice, 'This is a nightmare, Mrs Rodd. I'd take his place a hundred times over. If they hang my innocent boy, there is no justice and no God.'

Fifteen

IT WAS LATE, AND viciously cold; despite swaddling myself in everything I owned, my knees were stiff and I could scarcely feel my feet when I climbed off the train at Horncastle. I was the only person on the dimly lit platform who had been travelling in the padded comfort of a First Class carriage; the two or three others had ridden in on the pitiless wooden benches in Third.

A straight-backed man of soldierly bearing strode past me, carrying a wooden box on one shoulder; his face flashed out at me as he hurried through a puddle of lamplight, and I knew him at once.

'Mr Blackbeard.'

He halted and turned to me. 'Mrs Rodd!'

Inspector Blackbeard had close-shorn, iron-grey hair, and eyes like two cold grey pebbles. At some point in his past he had been a sergeant in the army; I always thought he looked like a cross between a wicked Renaissance nobleman and a senior clerk. He had some education and a very jaundiced view of his fellow-man, and he scorned anything in the airy-fairy shape of instinct or intuition – even when it was shown to be the truth. 'Crime-solving is not for dabblers,' he once told me. 'Facts, Mrs Rodd; that's all I care about.' (As if I did not!)

'Good evening, Inspector,' I said. 'My brother told me you were coming; I didn't know we were on the same train.'

'Ah, yes.' Blackbeard put down the wooden box he carried. 'I ran into Mr Tyson's clerk yesterday; he told me Mr Tyson will be defending. I suppose that's why you're here. The boy's father has hired both of you.' (He had a way of making everything seem rather sordid.) 'But I'm afraid this won't be the sort of case that calls for your sort of fancy thinking, ma'am. From where I'm standing, it all looks pretty straightforward.'

'All the more reason,' I said, 'to approach the case without prejudice.'

'Prejudice? Take care, Mrs Rodd! I was merely remarking on appearances.'

'I beg your pardon, Inspector.' I had let my tongue run away with me. 'Naturally, I would never dream of making such an accusation.'

'I should hope not, ma'am.' Though his face was in shadow, his voice was curt; I remembered now the great pride he took in the impartiality and professionalism of the police. 'I should hope I know my duty better than that!'

'Of course you do – please accept my apologies.' As Fred would have put it, 'grovelling' was called for. 'My frozen feet have soured my temper.'

'Hmm – yes – well – it was a cold journey, certainly. I was about to remark that the plain facts so far are against Calderstone, that's all.' His voice sounded a shade less cross now. 'Maybe he's guilty, maybe not. We'll have to wait and see.'

'I know Charles Calderstone to be innocent,' I said. 'I'm here to prove it to you.'

'Well,' he said, 'I'll look forward to that.'

'Mrs Rodd?' Someone was advancing out of the darkness behind a lantern.

'Good evening, Brody.' I was startled that the head groom himself had been dispatched to meet me.

Brody took charge of my box and my valise, and asked me to wait at the end of the platform while he turned the horses.

'Don't let me keep you, Inspector,' I said.

'You're not keeping me, Mrs Rodd; I'm awaiting a Mr Brewer, who will drive me to the inn.'

'Brewer is a very good sort of man,' I said. 'You'll find him perfectly helpful.'

'Of course, you're familiar with this place.' Blackbeard's dry-biscuit voice had a hint of cheerfulness. 'I may as well pick your brains while I'm here.'

'I'm sure you know as much as I do,' I said. 'Have you any news of Miss Winifred Orme?'

'The lady is still alive as far as I know,' Blackbeard said. 'But still unconscious.'

'Has she said anything about her attacker?'

'No, ma'am.'

My fine carriage awaited. I wished Blackbeard goodnight, adding that I would be happy to share with him everything I knew – for whatever our personal opinions, we were both on the side of justice.

Wishtide

29th December

CONFIDENTIAL

My dear Fred,

The first person I encountered upon stepping off the train was none other than our Nemesis, Mr Blackbeard; he was annoyingly superior, as usual, but I don't think he knows any more than we do, though I cannot shake off a horrid suspicion that he has made up his mind about the case in advance.

Early this morning, before I had spoken to anyone in the house except the little serving-girl Martha, I took another frosty walk to the Ormes' cottage. And (naturally) Blackbeard had beaten me to it.

'You're in for a disappointment,' was his dour greeting. 'They've gone and cleaned it all up!'

I'm afraid he spoke no more than the truth; the murder scene has been scrubbed and scoured. The sofa cushions and curtains have been burned. The bloodstains on the walls are now nothing more than faint, brownish smears. I could not conceal my dismay.

'It's the landlord's doing,' Blackbeard said. 'He wants another tenant for the place – as if anyone would live here now!'

He had been talking to Patty, the old charwoman who discovered the outrage. She sat stiffly on a kitchen chair in the middle of the newly cleaned sitting room, staring at the inspector in utter bewilderment.

'As a witness, she ain't up to much,' Blackbeard said. 'Deaf as a post, and keeps getting her times muddled. She made a formal identification for the coroner, and that was about it.'

The poor old thing is frightened out of her senses, and doesn't yet realise that she will be relating her garbled tale at the Old Bailey; I doubt she has ventured five miles from Hobley Cross in all her life; London is as remote to her as the moon.

'Patty –' *I took her hand and bent down to her so that she could see my face; I had an instinct that she would be less deaf if spoken to kindly.* 'I'm so sorry – what a dreadful sight for you to see!'

The main problem with Patty's testimony is that she tells the time partly by the church clock over at Soking, and partly by the activities of local live- stock. All I can tell you is that SOME time between noon and dusk on the twenty-second of December, she went to the Ormes' cottage with some pieces of laundry she had taken home with her. The front door stood open; she found the body of Helen Orme on the sitting-room sofa, her head savagely beaten and her clothing disarranged in the shameful manner we have discussed. Patty emphasized, several times, that she had pulled down Mrs Orme's skirt before running across the fields to the farm for help.

It was then that she heard the piteous cry she at first mistook for one of the cats in the kitchen. She is very much distressed (as I am) to think of Miss Winifred, left lying outside on the path for what must have been several hours. She was barely alive, unable to move or speak, and she lies now at the rectory in Soking St Mary, which is the nearest significant house if you take the road; she wasn't strong enough to be carried across the fields.

That is all I can discover from Patty; I don't think her testimony will make any difference to our case. I walked back to Wishtide to take up my post as unofficial guardian of the two young ladies.

You never saw a house as changed as this; it all looks the same as ever, but everything is warped by an atmosphere of fear and sorrow. The servants whisper in corners and I must admit that the family breaks my heart; it touched me very deeply, to see the swollen eyes of Mr Charles's sisters when I found them in their sitting room this morning. Poor Miss Blanche said, 'We know you're not really a governess – Papa says you've come to help Charlie –' and she flung her arms around me.

'He didn't do it – you will make them understand, won't you?' entreated Miss Elizabeth. 'They can't hang Charlie!' And she burst into tears.

The young woman they had introduced as Cousin Esther put down her mending and comforted Miss Elizabeth as if she were a little child. 'Come now – you promised you'd be brave, for your parents' sake.'

This is Esther Grahame, with whom they have lately been staying in Yorkshire, and I must say I took to her greatly. She's a large-boned, rosy-faced girl of two- or three-and-twenty, plain of feature, yet with that radiance of character that is better than beauty (you'll know what I mean when I say she reminded me of Sophia M. at home – who looked like a kind of angelic toad and was such a darling that half the countryside was in love with her). Miss Grahame's boots are thick, her hands are red and serviceable, yet she is a gentlewoman in the finest sense of that word, and I can see how her calm and cheerful manner puts heart into the two girls.

I am curious about Miss Grahame. From what I gather, she is a down-right country lass who can milk cows and make butter. Kirkside Manor, the house in Yorkshire where she lives with her father, is old and quaint but by no means grand. The Grahames are not rich, let alone fashionable. So I would like to know why a man as worldly as Sir James wants to marry Miss Esther off to his son? Please find out what you can about the family.

As you know, I'm convinced that the killer of Helen Orme and the killer of Mlle Thérèse are one and the same. And as you also know, I'm having the greatest difficulty in getting anyone to take me seriously. The verdict at the Frenchwoman's inquest was identical to that of Savile – 'Murder by person or persons unknown'– at which point the poor creature was hurriedly laid to rest in the small Roman Catholic churchyard and forgotten. But she was not killed by Charles Calderstone, who was nowhere near Wishtide at the relevant time. I think the obvious connections between these two murders will be one of the chief pillars of your case for the defence (but I know you hate me telling you how to do your job).

Charles's sisters want very much to see him, and cannot understand why Newgate is no place for them. 'They will only see Charlie in prison if – if the worst happens,' Miss Grahame told me privately, her eyes brimming. 'They will only be allowed inside to say goodbye to him.'

Blackbeard has not called here as yet, though I know he means to; rest assured that nothing the young ladies tell him will spoil your case. On the morning of the murder, at the time their brother claims to have received the letter from Helen Orme, they were at breakfast with Lady C and they

154

all marked Mr Charles galloping off down the avenue just as the clock struck a quarter past eight.

I am very much hoping to visit Miss Winifred, who is still hovering between this world and the next at the house of the Fitzwarrens (the vicar and his mother) in Soking. I know I shan't get anything out of her; I'm mainly calling because she knows me and a familiar face might cheer her up. I'll tell you anything at all that might be of use.

Your affect. sister,

Letty

At the very moment I was sealing this letter ready for the afternoon postbag, one of the footmen came to tell me I had a visitor. The formal rooms of the house were shut up again; I had taken to sitting upstairs with the girls and Miss Esther, and sharing the delicious meals sent up by Mrs Craik (the staunch old housekeeper longed to comfort her pets, and kept up a continual supply of treats), so did not know where I ought to be receiving visitors.

'It's Mr Fitzwarren, ma'am,' the footman said. 'Shall I show him up here?'

The young ladies' sitting room was warm and inviting, and I didn't see any harm in bringing Mr Fitzwarren upstairs; I thought a visitor might improve the tempers of the two girls (the little dears had been bickering all day, until even patient Miss Esther had begun to sigh with exasperation).

'Please do,' I told the footman, 'and tell Mrs Craik there will be one more for tea.'

Miss Blanche groaned. 'And now we must have tea with some horrid old vicar!'

'He's not horrid in the slightest,' I said, thinking that the young lady was in for a surprise. 'And please don't forget that he and his mother are taking care of Miss Winifred.'

'I'm glad he has come,' Miss Esther said. 'I haven't liked to call there without being invited.'

'Perhaps he'll let us visit her,' Miss Bessie said wistfully. 'I should so like to see her.'

'Well, we can't,' Miss Blanche said, 'because everyone thinks our brother tried to kill her. Do get it into your head – we can't visit anyone. And only dull old clergymen can visit us.'

'Blanche, really!' Miss Esther threw up her hands, with a laugh that was half-groan. 'We're all aware of the situation, thank you.'

Poor Miss Blanche, what a torment she was; she had been snapping and scratching all day, scorning any attempt at hopefulness and never missing a chance to snub Miss Bessie; I had to keep reminding myself that she was only behaving like this because she was worried half out of her wits about her brother, and her pretty life had turned overnight to ruin.

She did not care about her appearance nowadays; her curls were bundled back anyhow, and she wore a plain grey school-room gown, which made her look very young. With a scowl that could not conceal her unhappiness, she got off the hearth rug, her cheeks pink from the fire, and flopped crossly on to the sofa – right on top of Miss Bessie's knitting, which would have started another quarrel if the footman had not shown in Mr Fitzwarren.

I was glad to see the young clergyman; he brought energy and hope with him, and a certain lightness and ease. It was another iron-grey frosty day and the cold still hung about him, cutting into the stuffy room in a way that woke us all up.

'Ah, what a pleasure to see a handsome fire,' he said, leaning towards the extravagant blaze. 'I see you share my view that there's no point in building a fire unless it's hot; it's the main cause of dispute between myself and my mother.' He added, turning to me: 'My mother sends her respects, Mrs Rodd; she wanted to come with me today, but I judged it too cold for her.'

'That's a nice way to get round it,' Miss Blanche said. 'We know she couldn't possibly be seen to visit the sisters of someone on trial for murder.'

Such downright rudeness made us all wince. Mr Fitzwarren, however, only smiled, and looked at Miss Blanche so kindly that the colour deepened in her cheeks, and it was pitifully obvious how miserable she was. As he gazed at her, his face became tender.

'Little things like that don't bother my mother, Miss Calderstone – as I hope you'll find out when you come to visit us. She claims to be a direct descendent of Queen Boadicea, and she rides her chariot wherever she pleases.'

The awkwardness passed; Miss Blanche smiled properly. 'May we really visit? We've been so anxious about Winifred, and nobody tells us anything.'

'Of course, that's the first thing you all want to know,' Mr Fitzwarren said. 'I can't say she's well; my mother says she's holding her own. She cannot speak or move, but she does respond to certain signs and plainly has moments of consciousness.'

'Did the Ormes worship at your church?' I asked.

'No, they went to St Peter's at Hobley Cross. The curate there is a Mr Searle, who admits that he did not know the ladies well.'

'I would be most willing to help in any way I can,' Miss Esther said. 'Please tell Mrs Fitzwarren that she must call upon me to share the burden of nursing; I nursed my mother for many years.'

'Thank you,' Mr Fitzwarren said, 'Miss Winifred needs constant care and my mother doesn't trust hired nurses.'

'Has Miss Winifred given any clue about what happened?' I asked.

'No – as I said, she cannot speak. She communicates by squeezing her one good hand. When they carried her to my house, it was assumed that she was only hours from death; I administered the last rites. The person who attacked her thought he had killed her. But she surprised us all by improving a little.'

'Will she ever get better?' Miss Bessie asked, in a quavering voice.

'It's too soon to tell,' Mr Fitzwarren said gently. 'I think she's gaining every day. We must be patient.'

'If only she'd wake up in time for the trial!' Miss Blanche burst out. 'She's the one person who could save Charlie – oh, stop pinching me, Bess! Why won't anyone let me mention it? I'm only saying what we're all thinking.'

'Well, if we're all thinking it, you don't need to mention it, do you?' Miss Esther said.

'You're quite right, Miss Blanche,' Mr Fitzwarren said. 'I'm a great believer in plain speaking; of course you want to talk about your brother.'

'He didn't do it,' Blanche said, clenching her fists fiercely. 'I hope you know that.'

'I don't know anything.' Mr Fitzwarren was calm and cheerful, as if discussing the weather. 'But I believe Mr Charles Calderstone is innocent. I'd stake my life on it.'

This declaration lifted the last shadow of reserve; both girls brightened and the tea arrived (borne by Mrs Craik, the girl Martha and the young footman, Thomas; these were the only servants we saw now, though the rest of them were still downstairs eating and drinking at Sir James's expense; poor Mrs Craik was having a hard time asserting her authority, though she strove to hide it from the girls). I took charge of the tea-urn, while Miss Esther passed round plates of tiny triangular sandwiches and Mrs Craik's own shortbread.

'Mr Fitzwarren,' I said, once the servants had left, 'do you believe in Mr Charles's innocence out of instinct – or do you know anything else?'

'It's mainly instinct,' Mr Fitzwarren said. 'Having met him on several occasions and seen him going about the place. But it's also because I visited the scene of the outrage and felt its atmosphere – I never had such a sense of pure wickedness.'

'Do you think such a thing exists?' Miss Esther asked.

'Most certainly – don't you?' He looked around at all of us, his dark eyes intense. 'It's a sense you get in a place where someone has tried to drive out all goodness, all holiness – where, for a moment, a shadow has crossed the sun. I felt it most powerfully when I went to the cottage on the day following the attack.'

'Was this before the house had been cleaned?' I inquired.

'I believe so,' Mr Fitzwarren said. 'Some items of furniture had been pushed aside by the constable and his men, and there were muddy footmarks everywhere. But certain things had not been touched –' He stopped, unable to say more in front of the young ladies.

I passed him the plate of shortbread and changed the subject. 'Miss Elizabeth has been very worried about the kittens.'

'Er – kittens?' Bless the man, he understood at once, and his face softened to a smile as he turned to Miss Bessie.

'One of the cats from the farm came into their kitchen and had kittens in the cupboard,' she explained to him earnestly. 'You didn't see them, did you? Winifred was feeding the mother-cat and giving her water –'

'I can tell you all about the kittens,' Mr Fitzwarren said. 'Please don't be worried. They come from a famous tribe of very good mousers and they quickly found respectable homes; there were only two left by the time I got there, and I knew my mother wanted a couple of really bloodthirsty cats for the kitchen, so I put them in my hat and took them home.'

Miss Bessie's doughy little face lit up until it was almost beautiful. 'Oh, I'm so glad – I cried so much to think of them being hungry! Are they boys or girls?'

'One of each; my mother named them Solomon and Sheba.'

'Oh, how sweet!'

'Solomon is rather virtuous, but his sister's a little rascal.'

'What does she do?'

'She jumps on my desk and tries to knock over the inkstand.'

It was very pleasant to hear the two girls laughing at this, and to see the care melting from their faces. Miss Blanche in particular was transformed – no longer a sulking child, but an unaffected and charming young woman. The rest of the hour passed very happily.

I made sure, however, that I saw Mr Fitzwarren out, so that I could speak with him privately.

'You could not describe everything you saw in front of the young ladies,' I said. 'But I wish you'd tell me.'

We were walking down the great staircase; there was no fire or light in the hall and I carried a lamp, which cast a net of gigantic and bewildering shadows.

'I beg your pardon, Mrs Rodd; why do you want to know?'

'My brother is conducting Charles's defence, and needs to know everything that might help his case; I'm making inquiries on his behalf.'

He halted abruptly and turned to look at me. 'What I saw was very ugly.'

'Bloodstains?'

'Yes.'

'Where, exactly, Mr Fitzwarren? I'm familiar with the house.'

If he was at all startled by my bluntness, he did not show it. 'There was blood on the path at the back, about six feet from the kitchen door. There was more blood on the sofa in the parlour. There was blood spattered over the walls. It was a charnel house – as if the two ladies had been savaged by a wild beast. It made me feel sick to the very heart, but I prayed there for the best part of an hour.'

'Did you happen to get a look at the body of the Frenchwoman? I'm sure that was the work of the same wild beast.'

'I was at the inquest,' he said. 'And a very confused affair I found it; once it had been established that her so-called "husband" could not have done it, nobody could decide upon a motive for killing the woman. Hence the verdict which only states the obvious – murder by person or persons unknown.' He resumed walking downstairs. 'Where do your inquiries take you next?'

'On the day that I met you at the inn,' I said, 'I met Helen Orme for the last time. I know that she saw something there – something that made her very afraid. I want to know about any strangers who were in town on that day.'

'It's a busy town, Mrs Rodd, and often crowded with strangers; the great horse fair makes it quite a centre for the horse trade right through the year.'

'Yes – but someone outside the horse trade would stand out, wouldn't they?'

'I suppose so. I saw you and the two ladies driving away in a carriage.'

'Did you notice anything unusual?'

'I'm afraid not; I'll tell you if I remember anything.'

'The police inspector may want to talk to you,' I said. 'Of course you must tell him everything you know – but I would be very much obliged if you tell me too.'

'Do you not trust him?'

'He's an excellent man.' I framed my words carefully. 'I only worry that he will make up his mind about Mr Charles too quickly.'

'You have been employed to establish his innocence,' Mr Fitzwarren said. 'You are hardly impartial.'

'I wouldn't have accepted the employment,' I said, 'if I weren't utterly convinced that I'm on the right side.'

The young clergyman regarded me gravely for a moment. 'As a matter of fact, I'm convinced too. The Charles Calderstone I met could not have committed this outrage.'

I must admit, after Mr Fitzwarren had departed, I couldn't help wondering what sort of woman he would marry; with the right wife at his side, there would be no stopping him (Matt would have groaned at this; he didn't approve of my fascination with making matches, though I cannot think of a more interesting subject; so much of people's fortune, good or bad, depends upon how they choose to fall in love).

Later that night, when I was about to prepare for bed, I heard a distant strain of music, somewhere in this great sleeping house. I lit a candle and left my room to follow the sound; someone was playing the Broadwood piano in the shrouded drawing room, and it was beautiful – I recognized one of Beethoven's Sonatas, played imperfectly, but with an expressiveness that stirred me to my soul.

Miss Esther sat in a circle of golden lamplight. She was crying; tears had made snail's tracks down her cheeks. She stopped playing the moment I came to the door.

'I didn't mean to interrupt you,' I said, moving towards her. 'Your playing is beautiful.'

Her round cheeks were pink with embarrassment. 'I didn't think anyone would be able to hear; I'm sorry if I disturbed you.'

'You didn't, truly.'

She shivered, pulling the folds of her blue shawl about her shoulders. 'I had a sudden longing to hear music and it was too late to play the piano upstairs.'

'I'm afraid you have been sad, Miss Grahame,' I said. (I felt kindly towards this young woman, but was also aware that this was a very rare chance to talk to her alone, without having to worry about the sensitivities of the girls.)

'Yes.' She was not the sort to make a pretence of denial, but gave me a look of crystalline candour and trustfulness. 'Sometimes, when I think about Charlie, the horror of it overwhelms me. When that happens I can't be brave. I try to pray – and it's like praying to a brick wall. If I believe in a just God, I must believe that Charlie will be declared innocent. But I'm so afraid.'

'Of course you are,' I said. 'I know you are very fond of Mr Charles.'

'Oh – yes.'

'You spent a good deal of time together as children, I believe.'

'They spent part of every summer at Kirkside at one time,' Miss Esther said. 'Lady Calderstone grew up there.'

'I can't quite follow the family ramifications,' I said. 'Are you and Mr Charles first cousins?'

'My father and Lady Calderstone are first cousins. I don't know what that makes us. Charlie's like a brother to me.'

When a young woman says this about a young man it is almost never true, though it is a forgivable untruth; Miss Esther tried to keep her composure, but a great blush swept up her neck into her hairline. She loved him, of course she did; she was of too honest a nature to hide it.

'Did you ever meet Mrs Orme?' I asked.

'No, never.' If the name of the woman was painful to her, she did not show it.

'But you know Miss Winifred?'

'Yes, though I haven't seen her since I was a child. She and Edmund come from a nearby branch of the family tree; I know my mother was very fond of them. But they went abroad for Edmund's health, and my mother died, and we rather fell out of touch.'

'Quite understandable.' I decided I had made her blush enough for now. 'I'll wish you goodnight, Miss Grahame.'

Sixteen

NOTE ARRIVED ON MY breakfast tray the next morning.

The Rectory

Soking St Mary

Dear Mrs Rodd,

You and Miss Grahame were kind enough to offer help with the nursing of Miss Winifred Orme – and I must now take you up on it. We had an upset in the house last night and my poor mother is dropping with fatigue; an hour or two of respite would be most gratefully received.

Yours faithfully,

George Fitzwarren

'They nearly killed him!' Martha blurted out, before I'd had time to digest this. 'They broke in but he fought them off – dripping with blood, he was –'

It always amazes me how fast news travels in the country, like spores carried in the wind – and how fast the plain facts get mangled in the telling. Martha was babbling out all sorts of nonsense about robbers and murderers; I struggled upright against the bank of pillows and extracted the meat of the story.

The plain facts were dramatic enough. In the early hours of the morning, two men had broken into the vicarage at Soking; the vicar and his mother had fought them off, and managed to capture one of the intruders; the other had absconded.

Martha was assuming that the two men were common burglars, but I was certain the real target had been Miss Winifred, and the thought sent a chill across my blood. Surely even the stubborn Blackbeard would have to listen now. I asked Martha to wait a moment while I scribbled out a reply.

My dear Mr Fitzwarren,

We are delighted to help in any way, and will be with you later this morning.

Laetitia Rodd

As soon as I had dressed and swallowed breakfast, I went to look for Miss Esther, who immediately said, 'I must be the nurse, Mrs Rodd, and not you, though you are very kind to offer. This is a family matter; my mother loved Winifred, and she would expect no less of me.' With her usual lack of fuss, she set about packing a basket of things she would need for long hours in a sickroom: soap, towels, clean dressings, scissors, a couple of books, et cetera.

Mrs Craik helped me to assemble a basket of food and drink for the invalid. The atmosphere in the servants' quarters was strange and troubling. In stark contrast to the frozen silence upstairs, these rooms were noisy with chatter. There was smoking, there was loafing. I glimpsed little groups of them through half-open doors, lying about on chairs, as if the end of the world had been declared and all work abolished.

'They're afraid that Mr Charles will be hanged and they won't get their next quarter's wages,' said Mrs Craik. 'I can't put a stop to it because I don't know any more than they do. Mr Thorpe wouldn't stand for it, but they took him to London.'

'This is very hard for you,' I replied. 'I don't like to think how much you've taken on yourself.'

Mrs Craik bristled proudly. 'Thank you, ma'am; it's nothing I can't manage.'

I was glad to see that the girl Martha and Thomas the youngest footman were still in attendance, as were the cook and her two kitchenmaids. A splendid basket was prepared for Miss Winifred, of beef tea, fresh butter, and a cobwebbed bottle of port from the cellar.

'It's such a relief to have something useful to do,' Miss Esther said. 'I hope you don't mind, Mrs Rodd, but I told the girls they could come too – they swear they'll be as good as gold.'

'I don't mind in the slightest,' I said. 'I dread to think what they'd do to each other if they had to spend another day shut up indoors.'

This fresh crisis, and the prospect of going out to visit someone, had put Miss Blanche and Miss Elizabeth on their best behaviour. The four of us, plus our two baskets, squeezed into the third-best carriage.

Mr Brody himself sat on the box; by the scowling faces of certain servants we encountered, I inferred that some people belowstairs disapproved of Charles's sisters visiting Miss Winifred, and it was possible that Brody did not trust them to drive us. The carriage was a plain one, but of course everyone knew where it came from. I took the precaution of pulling down the blinds. Miss Blanche and Miss Elizabeth were great objects of curiosity in the countryside and I would not have them stared at like a fairground attraction; fortunately the hard frost had kept the roads and fields empty.

The large, straggling village of Soking St Mary lay about four miles to the south-east of Horncastle. When our carriage reached the crossroads, half a mile outside the place, we were stopped by a sturdy labouring man, who put his head in at the window to look at us.

'I don't mean to bother you ladies, but the inspector gentleman put me on guard, on account of the ruffians loose in the neighbourhood.'

(So Blackbeard WAS aware of the danger to Miss Winifred – or why post guards?)

Soking was a single street of dwellings and minor shops. We did not see much of it; the nice little flint-covered church of St Mary was situated a little way outside the village. Another guard had been posted at the lychgate. The vicarage, next to it, was a large and pleasant old house of soft grey stone, which gave me a pang for the beloved home of my childhood. A neat young maidservant opened the front door to us, and showed us into a capacious, stone-flagged hall (you may be sure that I carried out my accustomed lightning assessment of the household; there were touches of elegance here and there that suggested private family money beyond the income from the living).

'Mrs Rodd, Miss Grahame – how do you do?' As soon as Mrs Fitzwarren stepped out to meet us, I saw that she was a feminine version of her son – small and slight of build, straight and slender as a hazel-rod, with the same intense dark eyes and air of energy. Also like her son, she carried herself gracefully, and she was smartly dressed in black silk and fresh white muslin, with a little gold watch at her waist.

'It's good of you to come,' she said, once we had made our hasty introductions. 'I'm afraid you find us in a perfect uproar.'

'We've heard all manner of rumours,' I said. 'We'd be so grateful to know the facts – how is Mr Fitzwarren?'

'My son was injured but no lasting harm was done, thank heaven. He'll tell you all about it; he's shut up in his study with the policeman from London.'

I tried not to be annoyed that Blackbeard had got there first. 'And how is Miss Winifred?'

'She is just the same – there's no way of knowing how much of the upset she took in.'

'I've come prepared for nursing,' Miss Esther said. 'If you tell me what to do, I can take over at once and give you a rest. I have only too much experience of sickrooms. And if Winifred sees me, I think she'll know me well enough not to be distressed.'

Mrs Fitzwarren gave Miss Esther one sharp, searching look; in the way that women often know exactly what another woman is thinking, as if she had uttered it aloud, I knew that this lady was sizing up Miss Esther as a potential bride for her son.

(I must admit, matchmaking once again, that the same thought had occurred to me; if anyone could cure Miss Esther of her love for Charles Calderstone it was surely the handsome young clergyman – and what an excellent vicar's wife she would make.)

'Thank you, Miss Grahame,' Mrs Fitzwarren said. 'I don't like leaving her with strangers, but you are her cousin. And the fact is that I am quite exhausted – if you would be kind enough to come upstairs with me now –'

'Yes, of course; I'd love to see her.' Miss Grahame smiled, and picked up her basket; I could see how she relished having something useful to do, after days of being penned up in the house.

Mrs Fitzwarren turned her attention to Miss Blanche and Miss Bessie; I was glad to see how she softened at the sight of their fearful faces. 'I'm sorry, she's not fit to be seen by anyone else.'

'Mother!' the voice of the vicar called impatiently. 'What are you doing out there? Show them in, or I'll come out!'

His mother, unperturbed, said, 'Be quiet, George. The work is mostly watching, Miss Grahame – I really cannot say how important it is that she is watched at all times.'

A door opened and Mr Fitzwarren came out into the hall; there was a thick white bandage around his head, and I was a little shocked to see how pale he was, but he shook off all expressions of concern or sympathy.

'I'm sure you've heard some incredible stories about last night. The drab reality is that I suffered nothing worse than a crack on the head.' He bowed to Esther. 'Miss Grahame, I can't thank you enough.' (She smiled, he smiled; as far as I was concerned they belonged together like a pair of bookends.)

Mrs Fitzwarren took Miss Esther upstairs to the sickroom; her son showed me and the Calderstone girls into his study (a pleasant, orderly, book-lined room, with a sofa and armchairs beside a cheerful fire; it gave me a pang of longing for Matt's study in our last house in Bloomsbury, and the sight of his head bent over the desk).

The cushions of the sofa were disordered, suggesting that Mr Fitzwarren had been lying down – at least until the arrival of Inspector Blackbeard.

'Mrs Rodd. Miss Calderstone, Miss Elizabeth.' Blackbeard rose from his chair when I made the introductions, giving us each a stiff little bow.

The girls – like every other being for miles around – had heard about the policeman from London, and gazed at him in a state of wonder.

'Well, young ladies,' said Blackbeard. 'I shall have the honour of interviewing you about the movements of your brother – but this matter does not involve him.'

There was a silence; even bold Miss Blanche did not dare to assert Charles's innocence.

'I was telling the inspector about the business here last night,' Mr Fitzwarren said. 'What I remember about it, anyway.'

'Does your head hurt very much?' Miss Blanche asked.

'Hardly at all.' He gave her a friendly smile. 'My mother wants to make an invalid of me; don't take any notice.'

'So your head's feeling better, is it? That's good news,' Blackbeard said. 'Perhaps your memory's coming back too.'

I did not like the suspicious tone of the man's voice – but our attention was diverted when a drab brown hat on the table suddenly began to move. Blackbeard snatched it up, to reveal a little blue-eyed tabby kitten hiding underneath.

We all (including dour old Blackbeard) burst out laughing. Mr Fitzwarren picked up the naughty creature and handed it to Miss Bessie. He was cheerful, but it was an effort. I understood that he was playing down the drama for the sake of Charles's blameless sisters, and I liked him more for it. Both girls (and, really, the poor things were only girls) went happily off to the kitchen to see the other kitten, in the company of a motherly old cook.

The moment the door had shut behind them, Mr Fitzwarren dropped on to the sofa, and I stopped pretending not to be triumphant.

'I see you've changed your mind about the murder, Inspector,' I said. 'We met your guards in the lane.'

Blackbeard was not to be shaken. 'I haven't changed anything – but I must consider every possibility, and it's possible that Miss Orme is in danger.'

'So this break-in was an attempt to kill Miss Winifred?'

'It could have been.'

'Nonsense – of course it was, if you can believe such outright wickedness.' Mr Fitzwarren was very serious now. 'My mother was sitting up with her. I hope you don't mind hearing all this again, Inspector.'

'Oh, don't mind me,' Blackbeard said. 'I can't hear it too often.'

Mr Fitzwarren addressed himself to me. 'One of the maids usually does the night watch, but she was ill – and I very much doubt if she could have acted as my mother did.'

'What time was the attack?' I asked.

'Between two and three o'clock this morning. My mother was dozing in her chair, beside Miss Winifred's bed. She's a light sleeper; she woke to find two men in the room – one of them in the very act of placing a pillow over Miss Winifred's face – and quick as a flash she picked up the silver tea tray and dealt the fellow such a blow on his head that he is still unconscious.'

'Great heavens – how splendid of her!'

'Yes,' conceded Blackbeard. 'She has quite a wallop on her.'

Mr Fitzwarren smiled; I could see how proud he was of his warrior-parent. 'I woke up to my mother's shrieks of "Murder!", I grabbed the poker and dashed across the landing to the sick-room. But it was dark. The other chap whacked me over the head – and the next thing I knew, I was downstairs, being stitched by the local apothecary.'

'Did you recognize either of the men?'

'The one Mrs Fitzwarren knocked out is known to the local authorities,' Blackbeard said. 'Joshua Boggs, a petty thief and drunkard, last locked up in November on a charge of drunk and disorderly.'

'Boggs is well known to me too,' the vicar said. 'And we have no reason to love each other; I threatened to horsewhip the brute if he didn't stop beating his poor little wife. I can easily believe he accepted money to kill Miss Winifred.'

'Yes,' Blackbeard said, 'but I can just as easily believe it was all his own idea, with a view to simple robbery; Brewer tells me Boggs was strongly suspected of a house-breaking job last year, very similar to this one.'

'What – another attempted smothering?'

'With due respect, sir, we only have your mother's word for that.'

'Are you doubting her word?' Mr Fitzwarren was indignant. 'She knows what she saw!'

'But it was very dark, sir, as you said yourself; the man might simply have been beside the lady's bed looking for valuables. We won't know until he wakes up.'

'This other man,' I said, 'the man who struck you – did you see him?'

'I saw nothing but a black shape,' Mr Fitzwarren said. 'A gleam of teeth, a flash of eyes, like an animal on the point of pouncing – and then utter darkness, followed by utter confusion.' He leant back against the sofa cushions; he had stopped putting on a show and I was struck by how ill he looked. 'And a very sore head.'

'We should not be interrogating you,' I said. 'You need rest.'

'How can I rest?' he snapped back. 'There was an attempted murder at my house – there's a wild beast loose in the neighbourhood – I don't think I'll ever rest again!' He took a couple of deep breaths. 'I beg your pardon.'

'You'll be well guarded,' Blackbeard said, 'though I don't think you'll have any more trouble tonight.'

I remembered now why he annoyed me; it was his way of making my forebodings seem silly and hysterical, and nothing more than the overheated imaginings of an old female fusspot. I knew it was pointless to argue with him any further, but for heaven's sake – the murderer of Helen Orme had returned last night to finish off the only witness! What more proof did he want that Charles Calderstone was innocent?

'I'll wish you good day, sir.' Blackbeard stood and picked up his hat – after a comical glance inside it. 'Can't be too careful – my wife had a cat, lord bless her, and I was forever sitting on it.'

I remembered then that the inspector had lost his beloved wife at around the same time that I lost my beloved Matt; suddenly he looked almost human and I found myself – grudgingly – liking the man.

But he really needn't think he could put me off my investigation.

Seventeen

THE CHEESE-WOMAN SAT ON the lower step of the market cross, with her wares neatly laid out around her; it being winter, they were all hard 'keeping' cheeses, of the kind that is so expensive in London at this time of year. Mrs Bentley and I were both very fond of toasted cheese; since I was due to go home in a few days, I bought a pound, which the woman cut and wrapped with wonderful dexterity, though her fingers were red and swollen in the cold.

The market-day crowds were thinning, and the woman had sold most of her produce. She was short and broad (as many of the Lincolnshire women were), with a face as seamed and weather-worn as an old gatepost. Her name was Mrs Todd, and she was happy to answer my questions – indeed, the whole town was seething with gossip about the murder, and the forthcoming trial of Mr Charles, and I doubt she was able to talk about anything else.

'Yes, ma'am, I certainly do remember that day – I can see those poor ladies in my mind as clear as I see you. The older lady was carrying a new broom and two hearth-brushes. The younger lady suddenly stopped in her tracks – right where you're standing – and turned deathly pale. Awful, she looked.'

Mrs Todd's account had a well-worn air; she had been retelling it all morning. 'It's my opinion that she saw someone she knew.'

'Did you see who it was?'

'Well, there was a mass of people, and I couldn't be sure.'

'Could you tell me the types of people you saw nearby? Did anyone look suspicious to you?'

Mrs Todd narrowed her eyes thoughtfully. 'I wouldn't say suspicious. A lot of folks come to town on market day – ruffians and thieves, farmers and suchlike. But I knew most that I saw. Mrs Tapp was there with her daughters –' she reeled off a list of names, finishing with, 'and Mr Drummond, the attorney – riding in a little open carriage with another gent.'

'Was this other gent known to you?'

'No, ma'am. But he was probably something in the horse trade. Mr Drummond's a great one for racing.'

The icy east wind was turning me to stone. I thanked Mrs Todd and hurried across the square towards the inn, picking my way over cabbage leaves, horse-dung, wet sawdust and all the other litter left in the wake of a country market (I wished I had a pair of wooden pattens to protect my shoes; all the women were wearing them and they made a great din on the cobblestones).

Blackbeard had set up his headquarters in the dining room at the inn, and I had undertaken to call on him there. I was very glad to get into that smoky, noisy warmth.

'Mrs Rodd.' The landlady, Mrs Hinton, came out into the passage to meet me. 'The inspector is tied up, ma'am, and asks if you'd be good enough to wait for a few minutes.'

'Of course.'

'The coffee room is busy this morning; please feel free to wait in my private parlour.'

'Thank you, Mrs Hinton.' I was glad I did not have to sit alone in a public place, and was looking for a chance to talk to this woman, without Blackbeard breathing down my neck.

The private parlour was a small room tucked away behind the bar; more of an office than a sitting room, with a good fire. There was a large and businesslike desk, piled with papers and bills, and a broad shelf holding a row of leather-bound ledgers. Mrs Hinton showed me to the chair beside the desk and there was just enough space for her to sit down beside me.

'I beg your pardon for the mess, ma'am.'

'This is a working room, Mrs Hinton,' I said cheerfully. 'It's kind of you to let me sit here when you're so busy – I'll try not to get in your way.'

She relaxed a little, seeing that I was not going to look down my long nose at her. 'You won't do that, ma'am. But you're quite right that this is a working room; many a night I sit here, doing the accounts and suchlike.'

'Does your husband not help?'

'He has more than enough of his own work to do, managing the stables and the livery; everything inside the inn is down to me.' She was matter-of-fact, but I sensed her pride.

'It does you credit.'

She was pleased. 'Well, it wasn't so easy when the children were little, but there's a satisfaction to managing a concern like this. I look at the young wives you get nowadays, and wonder what they do with themselves all day.'

'I've often wondered the same thing,' I said. 'In our day, ma'am, it was understood that if you hired a married man, you got two workers for the price of one.'

Mrs Hinton smiled. 'That's true enough.'

'Talking of married men, I should like a word with your husband, about Charles Calderstone's movements on the day of the murder.'

Her face closed. 'He's told all that to Mr Blackbeard – and given him the ledger from the stables, where it's all written down.'

'I should like to see it for myself,' I said. 'Mr Blackbeard has his job to do, but I have mine: to prove that Mr Charles is innocent. Anything you can tell me will be used to help him.'

Mrs Hinton's eyes narrowed, sizing me up. 'Well – if I can help him –'

'Do you think he did it?'

'No, I do not,' she said promptly. 'When you run a public house, you need to be a good judge of character, and I've known Mr Charles since he was a boy. He's no more a murderer than I am.'

'Did you happen to see him on the day of the murder?'

'As I told Mr Blackbeard, I saw him riding into the yard, just after the stable clock had struck eleven. He was as white as a sheet, all shaken up and trembling – he came into the bar for a glass of brandy before he caught his train – he said it was to keep the cold out. I did notice that he was upset, but that was all. If Mr Charles had done it, wouldn't he have been covered with blood? And there wasn't a drop on him.' She added, with extra firmness, 'I'd have noticed.'

Yes, you would, I thought; nothing gets past you.

'It's possible,' I said carefully, 'that he washed and changed his clothes before riding into town.'

'Hmm, I suppose it's possible,' Mrs Hinton said. 'It's what that Mr Blackbeard reckons he did.'

'But you don't?'

Her mouth pursed up crossly. 'No. If Mr Blackbeard lived around here, he'd know it's well nigh impossible to keep a secret. And nobody – not even those who are against him – saw Mr Charles washing, or trying to hide his bloodstained clothes.'

This was splendid and a lift to my spirits. The wild beast who had killed Helen Orme and tried to kill Miss Winifred would have been plastered with blood from head to foot. With this piece of evidence from Mrs Hinton, we could force the prosecution to produce either Mr Charles's bloody clothes, or a witness who could swear that they had seen him imitating Lady Macbeth and scrubbing out the 'damned spot'.

'Thank you, Mrs Hinton,' I said. 'The other thing I need to ask you about is the day that I met Mrs Orme and Miss Winifred in your coffee room – which I'm sure you remember.'

'That I do, ma'am; when poor Mrs Orme was taken poorly.'

'It's my opinion that she turned so faint because she had seen someone she knew.'

Mrs Hinton nodded. 'That's the story going round – and the inspector's already asked me if I happened to see any wicked murderers hanging about.' She sniffed. 'Well, you were here, ma'am, and you saw how busy we were. I can't be expected to pass judgement on every single person I serve when I'm run off my feet, and I wish you'd tell Mr Blackbeard. He won't take my word for it.'

'Do you have a record of who was here that day?'

She sighed, exasperated. 'I'll tell you what I told him – my records only show who was staying here, or stopping off and leaving their horses with my husband. I can't write down everyone who takes a drink at my bar on a market day.'

'I quite understand, but I should like to see any records you do have.'

'Certainly – excuse me.' Mrs Hinton stood up, to take a large, leather-bound book from the shelf above our heads. She moved a couple of heaps of papers and set the book on the desk. I saw, as she quickly turned the pages, how neatly everything was written down; line after line of black ink, listing every person who had been staying at the inn upon the day in question (I had seen it before, during my inquiries about Mlle Thérèse), and how much they had paid.

'I know Mr Fitzwarren was here,' I said. 'And Mr Brewer.'

'Yes, ma'am, I remember; though they weren't paying customers, so they won't be in the book.'

'Mrs Tapp – would that be the lady I saw in the coffee room with her daughters?'

'Yes.'

'Why is there a star beside her name?'

'To show she paid in cash; Tapp's one of the richer farmers round about, but he has an aversion to credit.'

'A very healthy aversion,' I said. 'Lady Laycock – luncheon three persons – there were some ladies and a child beside the fire.'

'That's right; the Laycocks have a big house up towards Stamford. His Lordship runs a bill with us for keeping his horses when he goes to London.'

I made myself concentrate on my mental picture of that day. 'Was that the elderly lady?'

'No,' Mrs Hinton said, 'Her Ladyship was the younger one.'

'And the child's mother, I suppose?'

'No – the child was with the older lady.'

'Oh.' I was filing away these details rather dutifully; one had to be thorough, but it was hard to see how farmers' wives and local grandees could help Charles Calderstone. 'Thank you,' I said. 'You've been most helpful.'

'It's my pleasure, ma'am.' Mrs Hinton was very serious. 'It's not that I don't trust Mr Blackbeard, but he doesn't know Mr Charles like we do. I've known him since he was a boy, catching the stagecoach here to go off to his school.' Her face softened. 'And you should've seen him bouncing off that coach when he came home for the holidays – he'd give me a big saucy kiss, and tell me he'd been dreaming about my ginger cake. If he hangs, it'll break my heart.'

My own heart contracted a little; perhaps I was as prejudiced as Blackbeard, but I have never had a stronger sense of being on the right side against the forces of darkness.

Eighteen

My dear Fred,

First things first. As you know, the coroner released Helen Orme's body for burial. You wanted a report of her funeral. It was a miserable enough affair; a crowd of country people came to gawp, but Mr Fitzwarren and I were the only mourners (as a female I hung back at the lychgate with Patty, the old charwoman). The Calderstones were represented by an empty carriage, and I'm glad I did not travel in it, as it was pelted with mud on the way.

The service took place at the church of St Peter, Hobley Cross, where the Ormes worshipped. Mr Searle, the curate, officiated. The church is small and squat, and the churchyard cruelly exposed to the east wind. Patty sobbed, the rooks cawed and wheeled above us, and I wept to hear the sad old saw of the funeral service that I had heard too many times before.

In another, better world, Helen Orme would have been able to forget her sad past and marry the young man she loved. I prayed for her, and for Mr Charles. Afterwards, I spoke to Mr Fitzwarren, who says poor Miss

Winifred is 'slowly ebbing away'. Once and for all, we should accept that she will never be well enough to testify in any earthly court.

So the date of the trial is set. I wish I had managed to find anything – or anyone – that could help your case. As Papa would say, this one is a 'puzzler'. Our best hope so far is the absence of blood; many people saw Mr Charles on the day of the murder, but not one saw him bloody, and nobody can say what he did with his bloodied clothes.

As to the other business, you will know the outcome by now. Joshua Boggs is locked up in Lincoln Castle, awaiting the next assizes, when he will be tried for Breaking and Entering – not Attempted Murder. I am still sore about this. The magistrate seems to have followed Blackbeard's instructions as readily as a pet dog – utterly discounting the word of Mrs Fitzwarren.

'Not enough evidence, ma'am,' was Blackbeard's cool reply when I challenged him (I marched straight into his 'headquarters' at the Calderstone Arms while he was in the middle of a plate of roast pork and cabbage, and he didn't turn a hair).

'But you heard her story, Mr Blackbeard! How can you doubt her?'

'It was pitch-dark and the lady had been asleep. All I can see is a scuffle during a botched robbery. Not enough to send a man to the gallows. That is always my first consideration.'

He has such a way of taking the wind out of my sails. I was frankly rather ashamed of myself – of course that ought to have been my first consideration too. The principal question here was not the veracity of Mrs Fitzwarren, but the life or death of a man who might not be guilty.

When Blackbeard saw that he had flummoxed me he turned genial and invited me to stay for a cup of tea. You'd have laughed to see how meekly I sat down with him, in that rather dingy dining room, with a great speckled mirror hung over the chimney-piece.

As a mighty favour, Blackbeard did allow me to interview Boggs before he was taken off to Lincoln. I went this morning, accompanied by Mr Fitzwarren. We were shown to his cell in the town lock-up, where we found a great, sullen, ham-fisted, small-brained fellow, with a lump on his already lumpy forehead where Mrs F applied the tea tray.

When he saw Mr Fitzwarren, Boggs scowled and uttered curses I cannot write (I'm sure you can guess), to the effect that the vicar was a meddling so-and-so who was trying to get him hanged.

'You watch your mouth in front of the lady,' Blackbeard growled, with sudden and startling menace.

'Thank you, Inspector,' I said. 'I'm not easily shocked.'

'To the pure all things are pure, ma'am,' said Blackbeard, and he bowed to me with an old-fashioned gallantry that I found rather touching.

'You owe me an explanation, Boggs,' Mr Fitzwarren said, 'since it was your associate that cracked me on the head. Who was he?'

Boggs shrugged. 'I dunno.'

'Don't be ridiculous, man – you knew him well enough to be his partner-in-crime! What was his name?'

'I dunno.'

'All right – where did you meet him?'

'The George, up at Bagley.'

'It's a village pot-house,' Blackbeard said, 'with no very good reputation – full of thieves and tinkers and passing rascals.'

'He was a flash fellow,' Boggs said. 'I never saw him before. He give me ten shilling and said there'd be more if I helped him break into the vicarage.'

'How much more?' I asked.

'Dunno, do I?' Boggs growled. ''Cos I got caught and he made off, and I never saw a penny.'

'Did this man tell you to attack Miss Winifred Orme?'

'No he did not – that's the vicar's story because he wants to see me hanged.'

Boggs won't be any use to us, as far as I can see; he'll admit to Breaking and Entering but NOTHING MORE. Afterwards Mr Fitzwarren was philosophical and said at least it would be a rest for his wife.

But IF ONLY I could find ONE person who saw the murderer near the Ormes' cottage! Turner, the farm labourer, only saw Charles arriving; I'm still searching for someone who saw him leaving.

The day after tomorrow I shall be escorting the Calderstone girls and Miss Grahame to London. Following your advice to keep them out of the public gaze as much as possible, we are making the journey in a good old-fashioned private coach.

A very Happy New Year to you and yours,

Letty

Before we left for London, the girls and I made one more visit to the vicarage at Soking. So far, we had only been permitted the briefest glimpses of Miss Winifred from the doorway of her chamber: a still, silent figure stretched out on the spotless white bed with her head swathed in a great bundle of dressings. This time, however, Miss Esther gestured to us to come right up close to the poor invalid, and softly told the girls that they could kiss her.

Nobody – not even Miss Blanche – said it in so many words, but we all knew this could very likely be our farewell.

For a long moment, the four of us stood around the bed and, in the silence that fell upon us, listened to the frost-bound hush outside, broken only by the cheep-cheep of a lone blackbird at the window.

This is a death-chamber, I thought, knowing the atmosphere only too well – that numb stillness, and the fearful wonder of

186

the whole world holding its breath; Winifred Orme would soon be taking her place amongst the angels.

'She's very quiet and calm,' Miss Esther said softly. 'I don't know how much she can hear, or if she has any awareness of anything. But I think she's comfortable now, and no longer in pain.'

Miss Winifred's face – what we could see of it amidst the bandages – had the strange radiance I remembered from the face of my beloved mother in her last hours (bless her, she died on a fair Easter Monday morning, with the casement standing open, and a great peace around her).

'Poor thing.' Miss Blanche's pretty features showed how fond she had been of her cousin; she bent to drop a kiss, light as a butterfly's wing, upon Miss Winifred's cheek.

Miss Bessie timidly followed her example.

'I wish I didn't have to leave her now,' Miss Esther said. 'If only I could be in two places at once!'

She had been spending most of her time with the invalid, and was thoroughly at home in the vicarage; it did not escape my notice that both the Fitzwarrens now called her 'Esther', as if they had known her for years.

And she was about to walk into the Valley of the Shadow of Death; the trial and its possible outcome loomed ahead of them all, a great black cliff of impending sorrow. I said a silent prayer – not for Winifred's soul, which didn't need any advocacy from me, but for justice.

Let me find the man who did this.

My visit to Horncastle the following morning had nothing to do with justice. The black petersham ribbon around my travelling bonnet had turned rusty, and I always feel there is something slightly seedy about a rusty widow. My one remaining vanity was a determination to be as trim and smart as possible, and there was a nice little milliner's shop overlooking the market place, its small window crammed with bonnets, rolls of ribbon and lengths of lace, in a gaudy jumble of colours that made my eyes ache. The brass plate beside the door said: 'Madame Cobbold'.

The shop was just large enough to accommodate a mahogany counter and two glass display cases. It was early and I was the only customer. The woman behind the counter – Mrs Cobbold, I presumed – wore false curls under her elaborate lace cap, and I was a little alarmed by the obvious circles of rouge upon her cheeks. She was courteous and helpful, however, and in a twinkling had whisked out three rolls of black petersham ribbon for my inspection.

'This one's a shilling per yard dearer, ma'am, but you'll see it's heavier and better made.'

Matt would have chuckled to see me deliberating over three black ribbons that looked nearly identical, as if I were deciding the fate of the nations (and how he would have hated my black widow's garb – he liked me to wear what he termed 'good, bright colours'). In the end I chose the most expensive ribbon, and also a reel of twilled black silk thread, and I paid in cash – which made the painted shopkeeper positively friendly.

'Amelia – chair for the lady!' she called out. A door opened at the back of the shop and a young apprentice, her bosom stuck all over with pins and needles, appeared with a chair.

I sat down to watch Mrs Cobbold wrapping my purchases.

'I hope you won't take this as impertinence,' she said, 'but might I ask after Miss Calderstone and Miss Elizabeth? And perhaps send my respects and good wishes?'

'Certainly,' I said. 'They'll be very pleased to have your good wishes.'

'I don't hold with all the spiteful gossip that's going round, ma'am; they haven't done anything wrong.'

I looked at her more closely then, stripping away my own prejudices to notice a genuine concern beneath the paint. 'Are they customers of yours?'

'Yes, ma'am,' she said promptly, 'and very good too – I send in my bill every quarter and it's settled immediately.'

'I thought they bought all their finery in London.'

'Finery, maybe – but as you know, ma'am, there are always the little everyday things that ladies need – pins and thread, lace edgings, embroidery silks –' Mrs Cobbold lowered her voice delicately. 'Stay-laces. Even Lady Calderstone sends to me for that sort of article. And I always keep in a bit of good, plain silk ribbon for them. These bright-coloured ones –' she nodded towards the rainbow riot of ribbons in the glass case '– are more for my local customers.'

Something nudged at my memory: the farmer's daughters in the coffee room, whispering over their new ribbons.

'Was Mrs Orme a customer of yours?' I asked.

The question did not surprise her; nobody in this town was talking about anything else. 'Not regular – she came in for a paper of pins once. I thought she was very nice-looking and very ladylike.'

'Did you happen to see her on that last market day before the attack?'

'No, I was too busy here to look outside.'

'Mrs Tapp came in with her daughters.'

'Yes, I believe she did.' Mrs Cobbold was thoughtful. 'She bought the dark-red silk bonnet I had in the window, and she treated her girls to my best new ribbons. Ready money too.'

'Do you remember any other customers that morning? Anyone out of the ordinary, I mean.'

'Well, now,' Mrs Cobbold said, 'there was Lady Laycock, with an elderly lady and a little girl. Her Ladyship brought in last season's bonnet to be made over, and the old lady bought a bag for the child; blue velvet with a gilt clasp, six-and-sixpence.'

'Did you happen to catch her name?'

'Yes, it was Mrs Rutherford.'

It came out so simply, so flatly that it took me a moment to recall where I had heard it before. And then it hit me like a steam-hammer. Rutherford was the name of the man who had first seduced Helen Orme.

Rutherford.

Could this old lady be the mother of the dead man – or aunt, or cousin?

Of course it might be nothing more than a coincidence. But I've never really believed in coincidences.

Nineteen

'I DON'T CARE ABOUT ANY Rutherfords – old ladies or drowned seducers or any Rutherford whatsoever! This is a disaster! Oh, this is a gift to the other side!'

It was two days after my return to London, and there had been a development. My brother had immediately called me to his chambers in Furnival's Inn. When I got to his private office, I found him pacing furiously up and down a shabby, dirty scrap of rug, in front of a sooty, ashy, unswept fireplace. He had just come out of court; his black gown had been flung across a chair and his white barrister's wig lay in a careless heap on the desk.

'You've let your sentimentality cloud your judgement,' Fred said. 'And I've let you make a precious fool of me – Hockley will be dancing a jig!'

'That's Mr Julius Hockley,' Fred's clerk murmured to me. 'We've just heard that he'll be acting for the Crown in the Calderstone matter, and we never like having him over the way.' With sublime, almost ethereal calm, he dodged the heaps of papers and my rampaging brother, to pick up the gown and put the wig on its wooden stand; Mr Beamish had been Fred's clerk for more than twenty years, and knew him at least as well as I did (he was thin and dry, withered yet oddly ageless like a piece of parchment, and though he had a wife and family, it was impossible to picture him out of the office; he looked as if he slept in a drawer).

'All right,' I said, 'I'll admit it's a setback.'

'A SETBACK!' Fred roared. 'Bloodstained clothes and a new witness, and you call it a SETBACK! Beamish, where do you think you're going?'

'Down to the tavern on the corner to get the brandy,' Beamish said, picking up his dusty hat (to save me writing the word too often, you may take it that everything in Fred's office was dusty). 'Because we'll be calling for it any minute now. Excuse me, Mrs Rodd.' He bowed to me with a distant smile, as if we had met outside church, and softly left the room.

Fred caught my eye and gave a sudden snort of laughter; his rages never lasted long. 'Damn the man, I was just about to send him out for brandy – he knows me far too well.' He dropped heavily into the chair at his desk. 'But oh God, Letty – what's to be done? This is a catastrophe!'

I chose my words carefully, not wanting to set him off again. 'At least we have advance warning, and can plan accordingly. It won't be sprung on us in court.'

'And that's supposed to cheer me up, is it – advance warning that I'm going to look like an absolute idiot, before the entire legal profession?'

'Fred, please stop thinking about your professional reputation,' I said. 'A young man's life is at stake here. And I believe he's innocent.'

'Your belief isn't going to be enough to save him.'

'Tell me again about the clothes.' Now that I was over my initial dismay, I wanted every detail. 'Where were they found, and who found them?'

'I'll tell you if I can smoke.'

'You can set fire to yourself, for all I care.' I hated the smell of the little black cigarillos my brother liked to smoke (so did Fanny; on this matter at least we were in perfect accord), but this was not important now. 'Stop being in a temper and concentrate. It strikes me as a somewhat last-minute discovery.'

'It happened the day before yesterday.' Fred rummaged about his desk, found his silver cigar-case, and once he had lit one of the nasty things he calmed down a little. 'A labourer from a farm on the Horncastle Road climbed into the hayloft to get feed for the animals; shoved away in a dark corner was a bundle of clothes, stiff with blood. He took them to his employer, a Mr Raven, who carried them straight to Blackbeard.'

'Do we know for sure that they're Mr Charles's clothes? And is it even human blood? The real murderer could easily have soaked some clothes in pig's blood, and planted them near the scene.'

Fred made a rude noise, indicative of brotherly scorn. 'If you think I'm going to spin such a ridiculous tale to a jury –'

'But it's possible – it might have happened.'

'Tall stories don't work in court; you of all people should know that murder is never that complicated, and this one is beginning to look beautifully simple. Here we have a young man with a clear motive – a young man who was seen to enter the Ormes' cottage, and heard to shout at the murdered woman – listen to me, I'm practically making the case for the prosecution.'

'Have you spoken to Mr Charles?'

'I went straight to Newgate this morning, the moment I got Blackbeard's message,' Fred said. 'Naturally Charles denies all

193

knowledge of the clothes. They are the clothes of a gentleman, however, and apparently made by a West End tailor; I won't be surprised if they turn out to fit him perfectly. Who else could they belong to? Is the countryside swarming with murderous young gents in fine London-made garments?'

Of course I could see how it looked; I tried to ignore my growing sense of dread. 'And who is the witness?'

'A man by the name of Drummond.' Fred blew out an immense plume of smoke that did not dissipate in the small room, but hovered about us in noxious streaks. 'Not a reliable yokel this time, but a respected local attorney who is prepared to swear he saw Charles Calderstone on the day of the murder, just outside the farm where the clothes were found – washing himself hurriedly under a pump in the yard.'

'Drummond – yes, the cheese-woman saw him, on the day I met the Ormes at the inn.' My heart sank. 'Why did Mr Drummond take such a long time to come forward?'

'He's been away in the wilds of Scotland,' Fred said. 'He didn't know about the murder until he was on his way home and read about it in a newspaper in Glasgow.'

'And what did Mr Charles say? Does he recall seeing Drummond?'

'No,' Fred said. 'And he denies washing himself under any pump. So it's his word against the attorney's.'

'Do we know anything about Drummond – apart from what the cheese-woman said about his fondness for horse-racing? Should I go back to Lincolnshire?'

'Absolutely not,' Fred said. 'They're on to you now, old girl; the whole countryside will know you're trying to discredit the witness.'

I couldn't argue; that was precisely what I wanted to do. We sat in silence for a moment, listening to the racket of the street outside. Now that I had digested the first shock, I took a moment to examine my feelings (which are of importance, no matter what Blackbeard might think).

'My instinct hasn't changed,' I told Fred. 'I'm still sure I'm on the right side. I don't care what Blackbeard comes up with – Charles Calderstone did not kill Helen Orme.'

'You're just stubborn.'

'Yes, and I'm proud to be stubborn, if it means keeping true to what I know in my bones. You said it yourself – I've never been wrong before.'

'Hmm,' Fred said, veiling himself in smoke; I knew he was considering this seriously; a relief when it was practically my only argument. 'But you are a terrible old romantic, Letty; are you sure you haven't been persuaded by his good looks?'

'Oh, Fred – don't be silly!' Worried out of my wits as I was, I couldn't help smiling at this reminder of my foolish girlhood. 'I am "persuaded" by the fact that Charles cannot be placed anywhere near the other two murders.'

There was another spell of silence while Fred frowned and gazed into space (deep thought; the expression hadn't really changed since he was a baby). And then his brow suddenly cleared, and he was back to his usual brisk and genial self. 'As it happens, my instincts are the same as yours. Charles is not a killer; I can far more easily believe someone planted the bloody clothes to discredit him.'

It was a vast relief that Fred still believed in Charles's innocence. 'I'll write to Mr Fitzwarren; he can be trusted to ask a few discreet questions about our Mr Drummond. How did Charles take all this?'

'Pretty well; he's a spirited young fellow. When I asked him, had he put his head under a pump at any time on the day of the murder, he laughed outright – said he wasn't such a fool in the depths of winter. As for Drummond, he swears he knows nothing of the man. Tell Fitzwarren to get what he can. Tell him to work upon the assumption that Drummond is a scoundrel.'

'Very well,' I said. 'And please, Fred – try to find out about the Rutherfords.'

'The who?'

'The Rutherfords, Fred; someone must talk to this Lady Laycock.'

'Oh – the drowned seducer.' My brother rolled his eyes. 'Yes, yes; no stone unturned, and all that; I'll put Beamish on to it.'

The short winter afternoon had darkened by the time the cab set me down in Well Walk. The narrow street was half-blocked by a carriage, directly outside Mrs Bentley's house – a sleek, gleaming, expensive carriage, with no coat of arms or monogram on the doors, and the blinds drawn over the windows. A coachman sat motionless on the box behind the fine pair of grey horses.

Mrs Bentley was in a high state of curiosity. 'It's someone for you, ma'am – I don't know who – I told 'em you weren't at home, but the driver said they'd wait till you came back. They've been outside for a good half-hour. I got a nice fire going in the drawing room – which I hope was right.'

'Exactly right,' I said. 'Give me ten minutes to run upstairs and take off my bonnet, and then you may tell that magnificent coachman we're at home.'

'Yes, ma'am – and the kettle's on.'

'Mary, you're a trump.' I was every bit as curious as she, and the mystery was a very welcome distraction; I had spent the cold and tiresome cab journey from the city fretting about Drummond and the bloodstained clothes. It was pleasant to be in my little drawing room, warmed by a generous fire, in the mellow golden light of the big china lamp from my lamented drawing room in Bloomsbury.

I heard Mary going outside, saying something to the coachman; I heard footsteps coming into the house.

And then she was in the room with me; all gleam and shimmer of silks and pearls, filling the whole house with a scent of summer flowers.

'Mrs Rodd.' She bowed to me. 'My name is Christina Hardy.'

I'm not often lost for words, but this was the last thing I had expected, and for a few moments I could do nothing but gape at her foolishly.

She was not in her first youth – I judged her to be in the region of five-and-thirty – with dark hair and large, expressive eyes, and a tall, elegant figure. Her dress, her fur mantle, her feathered bonnet and the diamond rings upon her slender fingers would provide me and Mrs B with many hours of conversation later.

'Mrs Hardy.' I found my voice and returned the bow. 'Please sit down – Mary, we'll have some tea.'

It was rather like entertaining a bird of paradise; the exotic creature settled in my fireside chair in a waft of scent and rustling silk.

'This is very good of you,' Mrs Hardy said. 'I'm sure you know who I am.'

'I have heard of you, yes.'

'I'm not in the least a good woman.'

'That's not for me to judge,' I said.

'But I am truthful – and I wanted to tell you something about Sir James.'

'Does it relate to the murder?'

'Absolutely not! But I'm so afraid people will think – I mean, if it gets out at the wrong time –' She drew herself up proudly. 'Whatever you've heard about Sir James and myself is – is – no longer the case.'

'Oh?'

'He has left my house, and he doesn't want to see me any more; he says his wife needs him.' Her eyes filled with tears. 'Naturally, I didn't argue with him; I knew from the beginning that there could be but one ending.'

My first reaction, I'm sorry to say, was unkind; her protector had thrown her over, and now this fallen woman would need to cast about for another.

But what did I know of her heart? What did I know about the forces and misfortunes that brought about her so-called ruin in the first place? I despised myself for making assumptions based purely upon prejudice.

'I overheard your brother asking Sir James about Miss Grahame,' Mrs Hardy said.

'Esther Grahame?' It was surprising, and (I must confess) not entirely wholesome to hear the name of that blameless creature on such a tongue.

'Sir James put him off with only half an answer. He doesn't like admitting how angry he was when his son wouldn't marry her.'

'Why was he so set on it?'

The tears on Mrs Hardy's lashes hardened to diamonds. 'Money, of course – isn't it always money?'

'But – I understood Miss Esther was penniless!'

'She might think she is; I believe she and her father are very unworldly people. Mrs Rodd, I want you to tell them something that Sir James has found out about their estate –'

'A new coal seam?' I cried out excitedly. 'Oh – I beg your pardon –'

Mrs Hardy gave me a faint, sour smile. 'Actually, you're not far off. But it wasn't coal he found – it was copper.'

'Copper?' I could hardly take this in, or see where it fitted.

'Sir James owns an estate next to Kirkside; he was testing his own land when he made the discovery; though they don't know it, the Grahames are sitting on a fortune.'

'And he didn't tell them?' This was disgraceful; I could hardly believe it of the man.

'He told himself it didn't matter because Charles would bring the fortune into the family by marrying Miss Esther.'

'Thank you, Mrs Hardy,' I said, as warmly as I could. 'All sorts of things are becoming clear now. It will be my pleasure to tell Miss Esther as soon as possible – though it probably won't mean much to her at the moment.'

A little colour crept into her face. 'You mustn't think I'm doing this from a desire for revenge; I simply felt uneasy about the situation and wished to set it right. James won't listen to me – he refuses to see what fearful trouble he'd be in if anyone found out. And please don't think too badly of him – at the time everyone assumed Charles would marry Miss Esther. It was a dreadful shock when he declared his love for someone else.'

I heard Mrs Bentley outside the door, and went to take the tea tray; far too much for her to manage, as I was constantly telling her. While I made the tea, I turned the new information over and over, trying to see how – or if – the picture had changed.

'Why was Sir James so upset?' I asked. 'Surely he has money enough of his own?' I think I knew the answer before the question was half out of my mouth. 'He doesn't, does he?'

Of course, of course – so much was explained! Miss Blanche had not come out this year because her parents couldn't afford a London season. I now understood why Lady Calderstone had said that if Charles married Helen Orme they would all be 'ruined'.

'They told me you were sharp,' said Mrs Hardy.

'Is he in financial difficulties?'

'Yes, very grave difficulties.' She accepted a cup of tea. 'Thank you.'

'Can you tell me anything more?'

'I shouldn't even have told you this much. There was some kind of overseas venture, to do with railways or mines; it all went wrong and Sir James was very badly stung. He lost a vast amount of money. A great sword of debt hangs over his head by a single hair.' Mrs Hardy was mournful; she loved this man. 'The blade would have dropped months ago if I hadn't been paying his expenses.'

'I beg your pardon?' I had run up against another of my prejudices, assuming it was Sir James who had paid for her diamonds and carriages.

'I'm a fallen woman,' Mrs Hardy said, 'not a kept one.'

'I'm sorry – I didn't mean –'

'You needn't apologize; I'm aware that it's a singular situation. When I met Sir James, we were both wealthy enough to think money was of little importance.'

'When was this?'

'Seven years ago, in Baden-Baden.' She smiled slightly, and seemed to look at me more closely. 'Mrs Rodd, I wish I knew what you're thinking about me. Do you despise me – or perhaps you pity me? It's usually one or the other.'

'Neither,' I said, as earnestly as I could. 'I'm most grateful to you for coming here; I can see that you're only trying to untangle some of the mess Sir James has got himself into.'

'Everything has gone to smash for him,' she said. 'And so quickly! You must understand, he is a man who has never known adversity. His rank and wealth have protected him up to now. He's accustomed to a world that bends to his will, and he knows nothing else. Poor man, he's in a state of absolute bewilderment.'

'He looked very worn and anxious when I saw him,' I said.

Mrs Hardy eyed me thoughtfully over the rim of her teacup (I was glad to note that Mrs B had put out my mother's beautiful blue-and-white Minton tea set, and not the workaday Lambethware we used in the kitchen).

'I think you have known adversity, Mrs Rodd,' she said.

'I know how it feels to have a comfortable world suddenly turn against you,' I replied. 'My husband died, and poverty made my sorrow ten times more painful.'

I tried to see the world through Sir James's eyes; how far would such a man go to save himself? Come to that, how far would Mrs Hardy go to save the man she loved? I longed to know what was in her mind.

'I have money,' Mrs Hardy said, 'but – up to now – I thought I'd had more than my share of unhappiness in this life.' Her eyes glazed over with tears; she pursed her lips to stop them trembling. 'I had a wretched childhood; my father was a cruel man, who married my poor mother for her fortune. When I turned eighteen, he married me off to the Mr Hardy whose name I still bear. I thought I was escaping from my unhappy home – but it was a case of "out of the frying-pan and into the fire". How would you advise a young woman, Mrs Rodd, if she confided to you that her husband beat her, bruised her, shamed her?'

She hit a raw nerve here; many years ago, just such a young woman had come to me for advice. And I had not been able to do a thing to help her. Under the law she was the property of her husband; he could beat her as much and as often as he pleased. And hadn't I secretly wished I could urge the poor wife to run away?

'I ran away from him,' Mrs Hardy said. 'And I'm still glad I did it. I met a certain man who was decent and gentle-hearted, and I placed myself under his protection. I didn't care that I was ruined; I'm afraid you won't find me a repentant sinner. This gentleman and I went to Baden-Baden, where we lived together very happily, and perfectly honourably, for a good number of years. His death left me in dreadful solitude, but it was a gilded solitude – my father and my husband had both died in the meantime, and there were no more men standing between me and my poor mother's fortune.' As if she had heard the cogs of my brain turning, she added, 'And before you ask, my dear protector couldn't marry me when my lawful husband died; he was married himself; his wife is alive and kicking to this very day.'

She was daring me to be shocked, and her history was certainly shocking in the conventional sense. But what I found most shocking of all was the fact that the laws of this country were squarely on the side of the various men who had hurt her. Society at large had refused to protect her from a brutal father and later a brutal husband; I could not condemn her for choosing to be happy outside it.

'I wore black for him when he died,' Mrs Hardy said. 'He was a true husband to me. It was at this point in my life that I met James – I'm sure you won't wish me to go into detail.'

'I like details,' I said. 'Details are meat and drink to me.'

'If you insist.' She gave me a reluctant half-smile. 'We met at one of the at-homes I used to hold, for all the interesting people who were passing through Baden. It was a larger gathering than usual; Franz Liszt was playing.'

'You know Liszt!' I gasped this out like a schoolgirl; I had never forgotten (and never will forget) seeing and hearing this stormy genius in 1843, at a concert given by the Archbishop of Canterbury.

'Yes; my late protector was a patron of his. When I moved my household to London, my at-homes had a more political flavour – and were very useful to James.'

She was telling me this so that I would know why he had fallen in love with her; Lady Calderstone could never have competed with this intelligent, worldly, independent woman.

'I'm sure Sir James told you,' I said, 'of the murdered woman's past history. When she was alive, I did my best to conceal it. But of course the murder will bring it all out into the open.'

Mrs Hardy raised her eyebrows a little satirically. 'Yes, he told me. And before you point it out, I'm well aware of the similarities to my own history. Mrs Orme lived with a man out-side the blessing of marriage, and so did I. We both chose to make ourselves outcasts. For all the differences between us, Sir James has but one word for the pair of us.'

The unspoken word resounded between us; I guessed that Sir James had flung it at Mrs Hardy, and that she was in equal measure broken-hearted and furious.

'I liked and respected Mrs Orme,' I said. 'She told me a little about her life on the Continent – about the shifting population of "outcasts", moving from town to town.'

'There are some who live in that way,' Mrs Hardy said. 'Certain ladies used to turn up again and again – sometimes with a new protector in tow. I did my best to avoid such society; it wasn't always possible.'

It was an effort to keep my composure when my mind was a ferment of questions. 'Did you ever meet Helen Orme?'

'Not to my knowledge. Really, Mrs Rodd – if I had, don't you think I'd have mentioned it before now?'

'Perhaps you did not hear enough of her history,' I said. 'Before her marriage, she went under the name of Mrs Fisher.'

'Fisher.' She repeated the name blankly. 'When was she in Baden?'

'I'm afraid I don't know – but I think you would recall her if you had met her. She was small and dark-haired, and very pretty.'

'Fisher.' Mrs Hardy said it again, with a quickening of the voice. 'Good heavens, I do believe – how extraordinary, when I haven't given her a thought for ten years, at least – you mean the Fisherman's Daughter!'

My heart leapt. 'Yes, she was the daughter of a fisherman – but wasn't it a deadly secret?'

Mrs Hardy was amused. 'Deadly secrets were ten-a-penny in that little world; everybody had one. It was good manners to pretend you didn't know. And in any case, Mr Fisher was dreadfully fierce about it; he wanted us all to think her a most perfect lady.'

'What was Mr Fisher like? Did you know him?' (I apologize to my female readers for taking so long to ask this burning question.)

'Not well.' She set down her cup, eyeing me warily. 'My – the gentleman who rescued me from my husband – didn't care for him. He said Fisher was a spoilt young wretch, who would discard his little fisher-girl as soon as he tired of annoying his family.'

'Sadly, he was perfectly right,' I said. 'He treated her brutally.'

'I heard something of that later,' Mrs Hardy replied. 'Someone came from Italy with the story that Fisher had left her high and dry. And then someone else heard that she had died. Well, well – so Mrs Orme was the Fisherman's Daughter all along! It's a great pity that I didn't get a look at her when Charles fell in love with her; I would have recognized her at once, and James would not have needed your services. But he always kept his two lives as far apart as possible.'

'Did you ever see Fisher's manservant Savile? Or Savile's wife?'

She shook her head. 'Not to remember.'

'Mrs Orme told me a little about Mr Fisher,' I said. 'According to her, he was as handsome as a prince in a fairytale.'

'I wouldn't go so far – poor creature, it was obvious that she worshipped him. But yes, he was a very good-looking young man; tall and graceful, with his hair in long brown curls, and eyes of a famous blue.'

'How long did they stay in Baden-Baden?'

'Six months or so, and then they were simply gone. We didn't go in for formal leave-takings. What happened to him, in the end?'

'He drowned,' I said. 'His body was washed up on the east coast, and sent home to his unfortunate mother.'

'Oh.' Mrs Hardy sighed and shrugged. 'Such romances are always doomed, one way or another. This is why one never asked too many questions.'

'If you had seen Mrs Orme, would you really have recognized her?' I asked.

'Of course – the Curate's Widow act wouldn't have fooled me for a moment.'

The hard matter-of-factness of her tone made me wince a little. 'She didn't set out to deceive anyone, Mrs Hardy. I don't think she was putting on an act.'

'But of course she was,' Mrs Hardy said. 'It was a question of survival; women like us must disguise what we are at every turn.'

'Let me refill your cup; the second is always the best.'

'Thank you, I can't think why I'm so thirsty.' Smiling, she held out her cup. 'Today has been rather a strain; somewhere along the way I forgot to have luncheon.'

Mrs Bentley had sent up some slices of currant cake, buttered and cut into triangles; blessing her foresight, I held the plate out to Mrs Hardy. She took two slices and attacked them eagerly.

'What will you do now?' I asked.

'I have a house in Ireland; that's where James expects me to go. But I won't leave at once. He might change his mind and decide he needs me after all.'

'You don't seem to realize, Mrs Hardy.' There was no delicate way of putting this. 'You've just given him a good motive for murder. He wanted Helen Orme out of the way, so that Charles would marry Miss Grahame and keep the copper in the family.'

'I can vouch for him,' Mrs Hardy said. 'So can all the dozens of people who saw him at my house in London at the time of the murder; he didn't go down to Lincolnshire until the following day. He's not the man you're looking for – as you'd see if you knew him as I do. Please try to sort out the business with the copper, Mrs Rodd.'

I assured her that I would do my best, which was all I could do.

'For the past few months I've been keeping the worst of the wolves from his door. But I'm not wealthy enough to prevent what's coming.'

'What do you mean?' I asked.

'I'm afraid you'll know about it soon enough,' Mrs Hardy said. 'Thank you for hearing me out, Mrs Rodd. If there is anything – anything – I can do to help him, you will find me at my house here in London.'

Once she had gone, I carried the tea tray down to the kitchen, to wash and dry my mother's china and compare notes with Mrs Bentley.

'Well, Mary? Did you catch all that?'

'She don't half talk quiet – but I think I got the gist of it. Sir James Bigwig is heading for a smash, and it's a good thing we got paid up front.'

'Yes, in a nutshell. And I haven't had time to tell you the latest news. We'd better have one of our conferences to clear my addled brain.'

There was a routine we had at such times. I made things neat in the kitchen, while Mrs Bentley built up the fire and made the inevitable jug of brandy and water. On this particular evening, I toasted slices of bread and we were extravagant with the butter.

Mrs B's response to the news about Drummond and the bloodstained clothes was simply: 'Oh, lor'!'

'Quite,' I said. 'My brother was in a terrible taking.'

'He doesn't think the young man's guilty, does he?'

'No, thank heaven – but of course he's worried about how it will appear to the jury.'

'You'll need to dig up some dirt on this Drummond fellow,' Mrs Bentley said thoughtfully. 'He couldn't be the murderer, could he?'

'I'd have said not, but I know next to nothing about the man.' I let out a long sigh; what a day of frustration and puzzlement this had been. 'I've met the murderer, don't forget. The man who took the money from me in Salt Lane was little more than a voice and a shadow – but there was nothing of the country attorney about him, that I do know.'

'And in the meantime,' Mrs Bentley said, 'I suppose you'll have to do something about that business with the copper.' She refilled our glasses. 'Makes you think, doesn't it? If young Mr Charles had just done what everybody wanted and married his cousin – but he had to go and fall in love with someone else. Love! The trouble it causes! There was none of this nonsense about falling in love when I was a girl.'

I couldn't help laughing at her indignation. 'For shame, Mary – you, the mother of five and landlady of John Keats! Didn't you fall in love with Mr Bentley?'

'I didn't lose my head over him, if that's what you mean.' She was not to be shaken from her point. 'I've never known such a case as this for folks falling in love in the wrong places.'

This last phrase came back to me much later, when I lay awake listening to the ghostly, hooting noise our chimney made in windy weather. Mrs B was quite right, I thought; this case truly did boil down to people falling in love. There were broken hearts wherever I looked – I was knee-deep in broken hearts.

But Helen Orme was not killed for love.

What I needed to know was who had hated her.

Twenty

'SHE GIVES HER NAME as Mrs Jane Arrowsmith,' my brother said. 'Her age as three-and-thirty, her address as Bates Buildings off Cursitor Street.'

It was the morning after Mrs Hardy's visit, and Fred (before I'd had a chance to tell him anything about it) had summoned me to a police station in the depths of the city near the Monument, where he exhibited Mrs Arrowsmith with the glee of a fairground showman.

'She was locked up last night on a charge of Drunk and Bloodthirsty, having allegedly caused an affray at the Goat in Boots, during which she assaulted the landlady.'

'I weren't drunk, sir,' said Mrs Arrowsmith, in a low voice.

She sat in the middle of the bare, cold, brick-lined room, looking anything but bloodthirsty; poor creature, it was impossible not to feel sorry for her. She was faded and shabby, lined and grey before her time, and carried with her that poignant air of having once known something better. Hope had died in her. She had a fine bruise over one cheekbone (her hand fluttered painfully over it) and her sparse hair was all torn down at one side. Once, I thought, she would have been astonished to see herself in this fallen state.

'You were certainly bloodthirsty,' Fred said, smiling. 'They told me it took two policemen to drag you off her.'

'All I want is my husband, sir – she knows where he is, and she won't tell me!' An exhausted tear slid down her cheek.

'Arrowsmith' was one of the names used by Savile; now I understood Fred's totally unsuitable air of jollity. He could be dreadfully thoughtless sometimes. I raised my eyebrows at him meaningfully, and he had the grace to look a little ashamed.

'I'm afraid you'd better believe me, Jane,' he said, in a softer voice. 'The man you described to me sounds awfully like the dead man who called himself Savile.'

'My husband's name is John Arrowsmith.' She was breathing hard, as if trying to fight off the truth. 'We've been married seven years. Anyone can tell you.'

'Where would I find a record of your marriage?'

'It weren't in a church,' Mrs Arrowsmith said. 'But we lived together and everybody in our buildings knows us as man and wife.'

'She last saw him the day after the last of Savile's letters to the Frenchwoman,' Fred said, over her tattered head. 'Unsurprisingly, she hasn't heard anything since.'

'Why did you think he was at the Goat in Boots?' I asked.

'Because that's where he went to meet this man that he called the Prince.'

No wonder Fred was smiling. Here, at last, was proof of the link between Savile and his killer.

'Did you ever see the Prince?' I tried not to sound too eager.

'No. But my husband said he knew him. I didn't ask where from.' She hung her head, tired out with repeating her story. 'When he said it like that, he usually meant it was someone he met in prison. He was locked up for robbery with violence – but it was only the drink made him like that.'

'He once lived on the Continent,' I said. 'Could the Prince have been someone he knew from that time?'

Mrs Arrowsmith was confused. 'I dunno – he only talked about it when he was in his cups. And he talked French sometimes, on account of he used to be quite a gentleman.' (It was touching to hear the remnants of pride in her voice as she told us this.) 'The Prince gave him a job to do – he didn't say what job, but Arrowsmith swore blind there was money in it.'

'Did you see any of it?' Fred asked.

'No, sir; Arrowsmith said it was coming, that's all.' A single sob shook her. 'I can't believe he was murdered and I didn't even know it!' At last, the news was sinking in. 'Oh, what shall I do?'

'Did you ever hear the Prince's true name?'

'No, sir.'

'Did your husband ever let slip any little thing about the Prince's background?'

'No, sir. The only thing he said was one night when he was brought home drunk, and he kept going on about how he was going to give the Prince a taste of his own medicine.'

'Had they argued?'

'I dunno, sir,' Mrs Arrowsmith said. 'He shouts his head off sometimes, and all I care about is keeping him quiet because of the neighbours.'

'Do you remember anything he said?' I asked.

'Something from the Bible – the dead will rise again. But it was only the drink talking, sir – he was such a good man at heart!'

It was plain to me, if not to my brother, that this woman had deeply loved the man she called her 'husband', and I did my utmost to sound kindly – which was difficult when I had been given a high chair behind the duty sergeant's desk, and felt I was looming over her like an ogress. 'Can you remember the last time you saw your husband?'

'It was just like any ordinary morning,' Mrs Arrowsmith said. 'That is, except for him getting out of bed before noon. I know I'd only just sat down to my work when he left – I take in bits of sewing when I can.' She wiped her face with her shawl. 'He gave me a kiss and took what money I had – well, just like any other day.'

'When were you expecting him to come home?'

She raised her head, to fix me with her stubborn, hopeless eyes. 'He took off sometimes, for days on end. But he was always back home inside a week – even if it was only to get money. This time, when he'd been gone for more than a fortnight, I went out a-searching for him.'

(I am often astounded by what a woman will endure from a man; for two pins I would have told Mrs Arrowsmith she was a great deal better off without her 'husband', but didn't have the heart when she was only just getting acquainted with the fact of his death; the tears rained down her frozen face, and I couldn't help recalling my own state when I lost my beloved Matt.)

'Where did you look for him?' I asked.

'The places he went when he wasn't with me.'

'What places?'

'The inns where he worked sometimes, in the stables and suchlike. When I didn't find him, I knew he must've gone to the

Goat in Boots and the Prince. Mrs Dooley said the Prince had gone and she'd never seen my husband. She kept on turning me away – I went back again and again. I was sure she was lying to me.'

'Why would she do that?'

'I thought she was covering up for him because he had another woman.' Mrs Arrowsmith touched her swollen, wounded cheek delicately, wincing with the pain. 'It wouldn't have been the first time. But he always came home to me, or he sent word – for clothes and money, and suchlike. I was his wife, you see.'

'I'm afraid you're not the only woman to claim that honour,' Fred said briskly.

'Yes, sir – but I'm the wife he lived with.'

There was a certain dignity in the way she insisted upon this ('I am Duchess of Malfi still!') that could not fail to move me.

'Constable,' I said to the policeman inside the door, 'Mrs Arrowsmith is shivering; would it be possible to move her chair closer to the fire?'

There was a very small fire in the grate, nothing on such a bitter day. Mrs Arrowsmith and her chair were placed in front of it; she held out her hands to it like a sleepwalker.

'Did you suspect any woman in particular of harbouring your "husband"?' Fred asked.

'Sarah Gammon. He let her cook for him sometimes.'

'Gammon! Another of Savile's names,' Fred said. 'This job your "husband" was doing for the Prince – let's assume it was blackmail. Did the Prince know something juicy about somebody important?'

'No, sir – not exactly,' Mrs Arrowsmith said. 'At least, he thought he did, but Arrowsmith said the joke would be on him – he reckoned he knew something about the Prince that was going to set him up for life.'

That last word hung on the air with awful irony; the poor woman remembered that he was dead, and dissolved into a flood of tears.

Fred paid Mrs Arrowsmith's fine of fifteen shillings, and we both watched her bent, ragged figure vanishing into the crowds that jostled on the narrow city pavements.

'Don't feel too bad, Letty.' He gave me a friendly clap on the back. 'I talked them out of locking her up any longer. And she can keep her own money for herself now.'

My brother was in a very good mood today – despite the biting winter weather, and the lamentable lack of progress in our case.

(The fact is that Fred was born in a good mood; I well recall the enchanted morning when I had just turned three and Papa woke me up with the astounding news that a baby brother had appeared overnight; I still swear that this small, lusty, scarlet personage grinned at me when we met, and I adored him at once; according to Mamma, I grabbed his little hand and shouted, 'Mine!')

Today, when I needed to tell him about Mrs Hardy, he kept brushing me off. 'Yes, yes – I can't listen properly until my feet are warm. At the moment, I wish to get as far as possible from any sort of penal institution. We're off to Newgate this afternoon, and I always like to fortify myself beforehand. I can go no further without beefsteak.'

'Fred, what has got into you?'

'I'm not telling you until lunch has got into me.'

Matt always said the only people who knew more about bodily comfort than clergymen were lawyers. Fred whisked me off to a delightful old private dining room, on the first floor of a bustling chop-house in Fleet Street, a traditional haunt of the legal profession. There was a blazing fire, and a round table spread with a crisp white cloth. Fred ordered glasses of hot negus, and the establishment's celebrated beef-steak pie.

The negus was strong and spicy, and spread delicious warmth to the ends of my toes. I held my frozen hands over the fire, and thought sadly of Mrs Arrowsmith, shivering in her thin shawl. At times like this, I am ashamed that I ever considered myself poor; how rich was my life compared with hers. I wondered where she was at this moment.

'Knock it off,' Fred said, lounging royally in his chair. 'There was nothing more you could've done for the woman. Don't you ever take a holiday from the sorrows of the world?'

'I can't help it; I see sorrow wherever I look.'

'My dearest sister, the first thing I learnt as a lawyer was that no murder is big enough to stand in the way of a good luncheon.'

'Fred – really!' (I was laughing in spite of myself; this was exactly the sort of thing he did with juries.) 'I don't know how you can shake it off so easily. What's put you in such a jolly mood?'

'It's the result of a conversation I had yesterday with Filey,' Fred said, ladling more hot negus into his glass. 'I confronted him with a snippet of rumour that I picked up in the city. He knew the jig was up, and spilled a bean or two about the Cal-derstone estate. Would that be along the lines of what was imparted to you by Mrs Hardy?'

'Yes.' I was a little crestfallen that he knew. 'I thought you'd be anxious about your fees.'

'Anxious?' He let out a rich, satisfied chuckle. 'Quite the reverse. I took the information I had from Filey, and dropped it into the ear of a friend of mine who works at the Stock Exchange. And a nice bundle of cash he made of it.'

'But surely Mr Filey told you in confidence! Doesn't this count as an abuse of privilege?'

'No,' Fred said shortly. 'You said yourself, when Sir James folds I'll have to whistle for my fees. I simply decided to help myself – perfectly legally, I hasten to add. A case of "fore-warned is forearmed".'

'Even if it wasn't against the law, it was very unprincipled of you; think what Papa would've said.'

'Papa would have given me his sermon about keeping the letter of the law while breaking the spirit. God bless him and rest his soul – but I have ten children and another on the way, and my unprincipled behaviour has paid a lot of bills.'

'But Fred – don't you dare make your wise-monkey face at me! Oh, what's the point? I know you won't listen.'

'I'll be able to move the mob down to the seaside for a couple of months this summer,' Fred said happily. 'Which will be pleasant for Fanny and the new nipper. You should come down for a few days, old girl – put the roses back in your cheeks.'

'Stop it – you know my cheeks have never had any roses. You're a disgrace.'

But I knew he would refuse to listen until his ample stomach was full. Two immaculate waiters arrived with our luncheon, and the rich scent of the beefsteak pie made it impossible to think about anything else. I am but flesh, after all; the sorrows of the world were left to take care of themselves for a few minutes, while I lost myself in the base pleasure of eating.

Afterwards, when the cloth had been drawn and my brother reclined luxuriously beside the fire with a glass of port, I began again.

'What did you make of Mrs Arrowsmith?'

'Not much,' Fred said. 'As far as the case goes, she's another dead end; I was hoping she could tell us a little something more about the famous "Prince"; I'm sick of hearing about this mysterious character when I can't get my hands on him! But His Highness plainly doesn't want to be found.'

'I'd like to talk to Mrs Dooley,' I said. 'We only have her word that he left the Goat in Boots. He's the murderer, Fred – we must find him before Charles Calderstone goes to trial!'

'Yes, he's our man,' Fred replied. 'And yes, we must catch him as soon as maybe.' He leaned towards me across the fire, suddenly very serious. 'But it's no job for you, my dear old thing; I want you to give me your solemn promise that you'll stay as far away from him as possible.'

Twenty-one

'NEVER IN MY LIFE have I had so much time to think,' Charles Calderstone said. 'I've managed to avoid dangerous amounts of thinking up to now – I could always call for my horse and go out for a gallop. But that's hardly possible here.'

I was impressed by how greatly Mr Charles had improved since the last time I had seen him; all traces of the grieving boy had gone. Here was a straight-backed, keen-eyed man, fully in command of himself – and uncannily like his father. We were not in his cell; Fred had pulled strings, and we met Mr Charles in a large, bare room of whitewashed brick, furnished with plain deal tables and chairs.

He showed me to a chair as if we were in a drawing room. 'Please sit down beside the fire, Mrs Rodd; it's streets ahead of your usual Newgate fire – I sent Mason out to get proper coals.'

'Give it a minute.' Mason – the warder I had met on my last visit to the prison – was blowing on a small, smoky fire in the rusted grate. (He had become very friendly with Mr Charles, and though money undoubtedly played a part in the relationship, I sensed a genuine kindness between them.)

Once we were alone, my brother whisked a flask of rum from his pocket and took a mighty nip. 'Well, my boy –

what has all this thinking of yours turned up? Why did you wish to see us?'

Mr Charles had been pacing to and fro across the brick floor, like an impatient young horse ramping in the stall. He now sat down at the table.

'It's not about the case, exactly.' He was very serious. 'I know – and heaven knows – I did not commit this crime. But innocent men have been hanged before, and I cannot help being aware of the public feeling against me – I hear them out in the street, calling me a vile monster and baying for my blood. No disrespect to your genius, Tyson – but I have to consider the possibility that I'll be found guilty. And I want to know what will happen to my estate if I die.'

He was admirably calm and businesslike, without a trace of fear or self-pity.

'That's more Filey's department, surely,' said Fred.

'If I'm found guilty, will my property be forfeit to the Crown?'

'Hmmm.' My brother's eyes narrowed thoughtfully. 'I see no reason why it should be.'

'In that case,' Mr Charles said, 'who will inherit?'

'Your father – unless you make a will leaving it to someone else.'

'But if my estate goes to my father,' Mr Charles said, 'won't it all be swallowed by his debts?'

This was a very good question; I had been so certain Charles would be found innocent that I had forgotten the fortune he had inherited from his maternal grandmother.

'You're thinking of your mother and sisters,' I said.

'I can't stop thinking about them,' Mr Charles replied. 'My father has made ducks and drakes of his own money; I want mine to go to Mamma and the girls. I've spoilt their lives quite enough as it is, without leaving them in poverty.'

'What does your father say?' I asked. 'Did he tell you about his losses?'

'Yes.' Mr Charles reddened a little. 'He came yesterday and made a clean breast of it – even to the point of asking my forgiveness – which made me feel an absolute hound. Of course I did it readily, and asked the same of him.'

'I'm glad you and your father are reconciled,' I said. 'You were very angry with him.'

'We've been at odds for a long time – since he lost his head over that woman, and made my poor mother so unhappy. But the fact is that I've no right to condemn him. I made a far greater fool of myself with Helen Orme.' He looked down at his hands. 'Please don't think I'm blaming her – Helen tried again and again to make me see that marrying her would never have made me happy. Now that I think of it, I realize that she was quite right.'

(I was surprised to feel a pang of regret on Mrs Orme's behalf; he had fallen out of love with her and consigned her to history with surprising ease; if she had not been murdered, a trip to the Pyramids would have been enough to cure him; a young man's heart bounces before it breaks.)

'A man should never marry his first love,' Fred said, smiling. 'I'm sure my sister remembers mine.'

(I did indeed – Belinda Duffield, fading belle of our local Assembly Rooms, abundant flesh bursting out of unsuitably youthful dresses, who enslaved twenty-year-old Fred during a dull long vacation; she would have been insupportable as a sister-in-law: Fanny was an angel beside her.)

'But Helen didn't die because I loved her,' Mr Charles said, with a sudden flash of energy. 'Have you discovered anything about this Drummond fellow?'

'We are looking into him as a matter of urgency,' I assured him. 'Are you certain there's nothing more you can tell us?'

'Mr Drummond and I don't exactly move in the same circles,' Mr Charles said. 'I know him to nod to, and I'm sorry to say we've both been present at certain – er – rather illicit local gatherings.'

Fred let out a rich, rumbling, rum-scented laugh. 'Cockfights, eh? Lor', that takes me back! I got my first and only thrashing from my father for being caught at a cockfight.'

'Fred, how can you make light of it?' I remembered this shameful incident only too well; I had never seen Papa so angry (he had been preaching against the barbarism of cockfighting for years).

'It wasn't illegal in those days,' Fred said. 'But naturally it still goes on – legal or not.'

Mr Charles, I'm glad to say, looked a little ashamed. 'Yes, I'm afraid you're quite right; I beg your pardon, Mrs Rodd – but I last saw Drummond at a cockfight in Hobley Cross.'

There was a brief rap at the door, and before we could say anything else, Inspector Blackbeard was among us.

'Mrs Rodd.' He bowed to me. 'Gentlemen.'

He looked tired, I thought; there was a frost of grey stubble on his chin. He stared at us in silence for a moment.

'I've just come down from Lincolnshire,' he said. 'I've been travelling all night; I wanted to bring you the news myself. Miss Winifred Orme died yesterday.'

We had all been expecting this, but that did not lessen the shock, or the sadness. The kindest of women had found her peace at last.

'May God rest her soul,' I said.

'Amen,' said Blackbeard. In a softer voice, he added, 'She slipped away very peacefully, I'm told.'

Mr Charles, pale and shaken, murmured, 'And now I suppose you'll charge me with her murder.'

'Yes,' Blackbeard said, cold grey eyes fixed to the young man.

'How can anyone believe I could've done such a thing?'

'I only believe in solid evidence,' said the inspector. 'And the evidence is all against you.'

'You've met me, you've spoken to me – do you honestly think I'm capable of killing two defenceless women?'

'That's not for me to decide,' Blackbeard replied.

'But look at me! Can you really see me committing such an outrage?'

We all looked at Mr Charles; he was very handsome, his face flushed with what seemed to be entirely honest indignation.

'Keep your mouth shut, my boy,' Fred said, 'until you're before a jury.'

Our business was ended, for this day at least. My brother and I took our leave, and Blackbeard stuck to us on the way out like a burr. Though I suspected him of feeling triumphant, his cold eyes expressed only fatigue, and a certain thoughtfulness.

When we were all outside in the noisy street, he said, 'Well – this changes things, don't it?'

'Not really,' Fred said, heaving his stout self into the carriage. 'Unless you have something new to add.'

The inspector was looking at me. 'There's nothing new; just a few loose ends. Where do you go next, ma'am?'

Where indeed? At this moment I had no idea. While Fred was talking to his coachman, however, I quickly told Black-beard of the Rutherford coincidence. It sounded, even in my own ears, quite extraordinarily feeble – but I thought I saw a latent glimmer of interest, though all he said was, 'If you find anything else, Mrs Rodd, I wish you'd keep me in the picture.'

I would like to say that I found my next clue with my intellectual brilliance. In fact, it was entirely the work of Smudge – a lively brown-and-white cocker spaniel who belonged to Fred's tribe of children. As a puppy, Smudge had increased the general chaos in that household by chewing everything he came across, from Fanny's shoes to Fred's blue legal bags. He might have grown up into a better-behaved animal if my older nephews hadn't tumbled him about so much, and tried to hunt with him on the Heath (entirely without success, unless you count the old umbrella he once dragged out of the pond).

On this particular afternoon, Tishy and I had taken the irrepressible Smudge for a long walk, in the hope of wearing him out.

Tishy – short for Laetitia – was my oldest niece. She had been named for me, and I was her godmother. It would, of course, have been very wrong of me to have a favourite among Fred's children, but I must admit that Tishy had a special place in my heart. As a little girl of seven, she nearly died of scarlet fever, and was afterwards so pale and feeble that she came to spend a summer with me – Matt and I were still in

Herefordshire in those days, and our dear old house was very pleasantly situated.

(Such a happy summer; we both loved having the little elf running about; though we never spoke of it, our childless state was the only sadness in our marriage.)

At the time of the Calderstone trial, Tishy was fifteen years old; tall and coltish, with shining dark brown hair, and solemn, sherry-coloured eyes (Fred kindly maintained that she looked like me; I'm glad to say she was a great deal prettier). She was a pattern oldest daughter – her mother's right hand, her father's repose and comfort, and one of the very few who could keep the little ones in some semblance of order.

It was one of those bright, hard winter days; so rare in smoky London. Tishy and I had chased Smudge across the Heath, and I was clutching his lead as we trudged up Swain's Lane towards Highgate village. Here were the gates of the large new cemetery that had opened a dozen or so years before. It was a pleasant, wooded, ivied place – or would have been, if not disfigured by enormous memorials made of granite and streaky marble.

(I don't care for such large and strident expressions of grief, shouting their sorrow to the empty air; my dearest Matt was laid to rest in the clerical dust of St Paul's; my parents sleep in a quiet country churchyard where the sheep graze amongst the graves – but I know that I must not seek my darlings anywhere in this world.)

Tishy and I were cold and tired, and (in my case at least) longing for a cup of tea. Smudge, however, had other ideas; the lead jerked from my hand and the naughty creature bounded gleefully through the iron gates of the cemetery.

Tishy galloped after him like a young deer. 'Smudge! Here, Smudge!' Her clear voice rang in the freezing air; the day was waning, and the frost clenching around us like a fist.

I followed them as best I could, hobbling on my frozen feet past a row of marble mausoleums, each the size of a small house, family names blazoned in gold over the doors. Turning a corner in the gravelled path, I found Tishy, breathless but victorious, clutching Smudge's collar in the shadow of a huge stone angel weeping over an urn.

'Bravo, my dear,' I said. 'I'll let you have the lead again, if you don't mind – he nearly took my arm from its socket!'

'He was only chasing another phantom rabbit.' Tishy rubbed the dog's ears affectionately. 'He thinks he's a mighty hunter.'

She dragged Smudge away from the towering angel – and that was when I saw, carved upon the plinth, the inscription:

IN LOVING MEMORY OF

HENRY EDWARD MUIRFIELD RUTHERFORD

BORN 1810 – DIED 1841

'I AM THE RESURRECTION AND THE LIFE'

'MANY WATERS CANNOT QUENCH LOVE, NEITHER CAN THE

FLOODS DROWN IT'

Twenty-two

I T WAS HARD NOT to see the hand of Providence at work; I had wanted to find Mrs Rutherford, and here was the grave of the 'drowned seducer', positively on the doorstep; it had to be him.

'I'm still shaken by the coincidence,' I told my brother later, when Tishy had taken the dog to the nursery, and I sat thawing beside the fire in the study. 'I'd never have seen it if Smudge hadn't led me right to him.'

'The cemetery company will have a list of the owners of the plots,' Fred said. 'But I'm bound to say that I don't understand why you're so keen to find the sorrowing mother.'

'Mrs Rutherford was in the coffee room at the inn; I'm more and more convinced that Helen Orme saw her killer that day.'

'Letty – I'm warning you, my darling – no jury in the world is going to believe that those two ladies were bludgeoned to death by a sweet old grandmother.'

'Of course not – but my every instinct pulls me back to her.'

'You and your instincts!'

'They've never let me down before.'

'Evidence!' Fred groaned. 'Get me some good, hard evidence! Get me a respectable witness that saw any other living being near the murder scene!'

He was frustrated and anxious, and I couldn't blame him, when all of London was looking forward to Charles's downfall. The popular press was also predicting the downfall of my brother ('Take note, Mr Tyson; this is one "miracle" you won't be able to pull off!'). I was gloomily aware that I was clutching at straws because there was nothing else.

Providence, however, decided to give me another helping hand.

All the time we were talking, Mrs Gibson had been busy putting fresh coals on the fire. She was a sturdy, grey-headed, bustling woman, a mixture of housekeeper, butler, chief nurse and sergeant-major in that establishment, and essential to the running of it.

She put the fireguard back in its place, stood up straight, and said, 'Excuse me, sir; if Rutherford's the name, there's a Mrs Rutherford lives up by the Spaniards Inn.'

Fred burst out laughing. 'Thank you, Gibby! My sister was prepared to go to the ends of the earth – and here she was all along, not a mile down the road!'

'I knew she wouldn't be far away – I'm not at all surprised to find her on the doorstep, near to her son's grave. Do you know her, Mrs Gibson?'

'No, ma'am, I've never seen the lady. A cousin of mine was in service there, until she got married a couple of years back. It's a house called Fortune Hill, behind a wall with a big gate.'

The pleasure-gardens around the Spaniards Inn, on the road that runs between Hampstead and Highgate, were surrounded by open fields; on a summer Sunday, the place was always crowded with what would now be called day-trippers – that is, city-dwellers in search of green meadows and fresh air (and very unpopular they were among the better class of inhabitants, who resented the traffic, the noise and the litter of the visitors). On a frosty winter's weekday, however, fields and heathland were as empty and remote as the Sahara.

Fortune Hill was a little difficult to find; once we had passed the old tollgate, Fred's coachman nearly missed the small, obscure turning off the principal thoroughfare. At the end of this narrow lane we saw the wall as described by Mrs Gibson. Behind the gates stood a long, low red-brick house; not grand, but comfortable and well-kept – an old farmhouse, hiding itself away from the tide of new buildings that was poised to engulf it.

I was visiting in state, attired in my best black silk, and I had commandeered Fred's carriage (Fanny had wanted it for one of her expensive jaunts to the West End, and was very put out when Fred gave me priority). The house and gardens were trim and clean, but without a single sign of life. I pulled the bell on the gatepost.

After a long moment when the silence and stillness seemed to deepen, the front door opened. A young maidservant tripped down the path to open the gates.

'Yes, ma'am?'

'I'm calling upon Mrs Rutherford,' I said. 'Is she at home?'

She was doubtful. 'I don't know, ma'am; is she expecting you?'

'No – my name is Mrs Rodd, and I'm calling on behalf of the Hampstead Ladies Blanket Collection.' (A small enough fib; I really was a member of this charitable committee, and had written so many tedious letters on its behalf that I felt quite justified.)

The maidservant – still doubtful – took in my carriage, my black silk gown, and the pasteboard visiting card I put into her hand. 'Please come inside, ma'am, while I ask.'

I walked down the short path to the front door, and was shown into the hall (quiet, gracious, lavender-scented, Persian rugs scattered across the uneven stone flags, age-blackened portraits of soldierly ancestors – my all-important first impression was of solid, unshowy prosperity).

'Mrs Rodd?' A woman came out into the hall to meet me, holding my card gingerly as if it might explode – a woman instantly recognizable as a lady despite her very modest grey dress and plain cap. She was about forty years old, very dark, with a high, rosy complexion, sour brown eyes, and a scar upon her mouth that sliced through both her lips. 'I'm Miss Muirfield; how may I help you?'

I began my speech again. 'My name is Mrs Rodd; I would very much like to speak to Mrs Rutherford about our blanket collection; this is a harsh winter, and there is a great need for common comforts; not only warm blankets, but clothes and fuel –'

'Oh, yes, to be sure.' Miss Muirfield cut me short rather impatiently. 'We had the vicar's wife round a few months ago – I must give you ladies points for persistence.'

'If it's inconvenient, I could call again another time.'

'Oh, it's not particularly inconvenient – you might as well come in, I suppose.'

It wasn't exactly a hearty welcome, but I pretended not to have noticed her rude, offhand manner, and followed her into a room leading off the hall.

And there she was, in a high-backed chair before the fire – the same old lady I had seen at the inn, white-haired, handsome and imperious, in a gown of grey silk.

It was a gracious room, with rose-patterned wallpaper and large windows looking out over a pretty walled garden. The first thing I noted, however, was a portrait above the fireplace, of a young man with long, brown, curling hair, keen blue eyes and the same imperious gaze as the old lady.

The drowned seducer, I thought, in all his glory.

And all but a couple of the portraits were of the same young man, at various stages of his life – a peach-faced baby, a little boy with a hoop, a schoolboy, a swaggering youth. This room was a shrine to his memory, and to his mother's endless sorrow.

A wax doll lay in a drunken heap on the window-seat, beside a game of cup-and-ball; signs of the little girl I had seen at the inn. I had been told she was Mrs Rutherford's grandchild – though there was no clue to her parentage here.

'Mrs Rodd,' Miss Muirfield said shortly, by way of introduction. 'She's collecting for the poor.'

'Good afternoon, Mrs Rutherford,' I said quickly. 'Please forgive the intrusion. My name is Laetitia Rodd; I'm calling on behalf of the Hampstead Ladies Blanket Collection.'

'Please sit down, Mrs Rodd.' Mrs Rutherford gestured towards the chair facing hers. 'I'm perfectly willing to help, but my health doesn't allow me to go into society as much as I'd like – Emma, dear, go and hurry up the tea.'

Miss Muirfield raised her eyebrows. 'I thought you wanted to wait for Lina.'

'Yes, but now we have a caller – I hope you'll have some tea, Mrs Rodd.'

'You're very kind, ma'am,' I said.

Miss Muirfield sighed and shrugged, and left the room without another word.

'You mustn't mind Emma,' Mrs Rutherford said. 'She's my cousin, on my mother's side of the family, and my trusted companion. But her manners can be a little brusque; her life has not been easy.'

(A poor relation, in other words; I felt a twinge of sympathy.)

'Any fault is mine,' I said smoothly, 'for calling unexpectedly. That is a very striking portrait, ma'am.'

She saw that I was looking at the painting above the fireplace, and her rather majestic face melted into a smile of mingled pain and pride. 'My son, Henry – I had it done to mark his twenty-first birthday.'

(I regretted that I had to trample on her feelings, but this chance was too good to miss.) 'A very handsome young man.'

'Oh, yes – from the day he was born! But no picture fully does him justice. He was brilliant and charming, and might have done anything!' Her voice trembled; the wound was an old one, yet still fresh as the day it was made. 'He died nearly ten years ago. It doesn't seem so long.'

'I'm very sorry to hear it,' I said (as gently as I could, and meaning to be gentle; this woman had loved her son to the point of idolatry, and his death had broken her).

There were still flashes of that old pride in her manner, like fragments of a smashed mirror. 'At one time, I was sure he would go into politics; he could command any room he was in, and he had great compassion for the poor, the unfortunate – the lesser creatures, who did not have his gifts. It was a loss to the country as well as to me.'

(Hmm – was it, indeed? This was one of those times I was thankful for my poker face; Henry Rutherford's mother had clearly decided to forget great swathes of his life story.)

'But you have recently been widowed.' She nodded towards my black dress and bonnet, with queenly kindness. 'I'm sure you don't need me to tell you about the burden of grief.'

'My husband died two years ago,' I said. 'It was very sudden and unexpected.'

'Ah, yes –' Mrs Rutherford's interest in me quickened. 'I know something of that; my son was drowned, when his ship foundered off the east coast. My only blessing was that they recovered his remains, and I could properly lay my child to rest.'

(She spoke calmly, yet her anguish was in the room with us like a howling beast; part of her would be in a fresh state of horror until the day she died.)

'You are right to describe grief as a burden, ma'am,' I said. 'And I know it never grows any lighter. But would one wish it to? My grief keeps my memories green.'

'Yes, yes,' Mrs Rutherford said. 'I dread forgetting my darling. He was all my joy. Do you have children, Mrs Rodd?'

'No, to my sorrow.'

She looked at the fire. 'I was nearly forty years old when he was born, and his father was over fifty; we had long resigned ourselves to our childless state. Henry was our miracle.'

There were voices outside the door; a child's voice snapped, 'Ow! Let go of me! I want to get Hatty!'

Mrs Rutherford smiled. 'My granddaughter – back in time for tea after all.'

'You'll have to wait,' Miss Muirfield's voice said. 'She's with a visitor.'

'I don't care! I want Hatty NOW!'

The grandmotherly smile became radiant – as if I had over-heard the child reciting a psalm instead of shrieking like a little fishwife. 'Let her in, Emma! Forgive me, Mrs Rodd, but we'll have no peace otherwise.'

The child erupted into the room like a tornado – my first impression was of long, skinny limbs, a banner of dark-brown curls, rosy cheeks, fair skin, and arresting eyes like sky-blue stained glass. Taking no notice of either of us, she made a dive for the window-seat and snatched up her doll.

'Oh, Lina!' Mrs Rutherford said indulgently. 'Don't you see that I have company? Come here, my little savage, and make your curtsy to Mrs Rodd!'

Like a kingfisher arrested mid-flight, the child reluctantly stopped running and came to the side of the doting old lady.

'My granddaughter, Adelina.' Mrs Rutherford caressed the child's hair.

Adelina briefly turned those blue eyes towards me as she dropped an indifferent curtsy.

'Now run along with Emma.'

'I don't want to.'

Miss Muirfield stood in the doorway, arms folded. 'You'll get no tea until you wash those hands, miss.'

'No!'

'There might be plum cake,' Mrs Rutherford said, 'but only for good little girls.'

Adelina's scowl melted into a smile – a charming smile, a smile that made whole armies walk up and down my spine.

'I must apologize for her manners,' Mrs Rutherford said, once Miss Muirfield had removed the child. 'She's not always such a harum-scarum; she's sensitive, just as her father was at her age.'

'Her – father?'

Mrs Rutherford stiffened, with an imperious air. 'My son lived abroad during the latter part of his life, and he married an Italian lady, from a very fine old family.'

'Oh.' I hoped this did not come out as a squeak.

'Sadly, she died giving birth to Adelina. After my son's death, I sent to Italy to bring the baby home.'

I found enough of a voice to offer, 'That must have been a great consolation to you.'

'Yes – since the day she came to this house of mourning, she has given me a reason to live. I know that I have a sacred duty to bring her up as my son would have wished – as an English-woman and a lady. Though I don't care to insist upon it, the fact of the matter is that she has some very good blood in her veins. And she's the image of Henry!' She nodded compla-cently at the portrait over the mantelpiece. 'Perhaps you noticed the resemblance.'

'I – yes, she's very like him.' And so she was – but another face had flashed out at me when little Adelina smiled.

Helen Orme.

Was it the sight of this child that had given her such a shock, on that famous day in the coffee room? Could she have known Adelina as her own lost baby, the child she thought was dead?

In which case, did Mrs Rutherford know that half of her granddaughter's 'very good blood' came from a long line of fishermen?

And how did she discover the child's existence in the first place? According to Helen Orme, the only people who had known about the baby were herself, Henry Rutherford – and Savile.

My mind was too numb to process the tempest of questions. I stayed for one cup of tea, making a mighty effort to show nothing but politeness. I was afraid, however, that the sharp eyes of Miss Muirfield had noticed something suspicious in my behaviour; the woman would not stop watching me.

At last, Mrs Rutherford presented me with a half-sovereign for the blanket collection, and Miss Muirfield marched me smartly to the front door.

I began to thank her, but she interrupted, in a tone that dripped with venom.

'Please don't call again; visitors upset my cousin for days afterwards.'

'Really? Mrs Rutherford doesn't appear to be upset today.'

'It's not wholesome for her to talk about the past,' Miss Muirfield said. 'You have your money. I wish you good afternoon, Mrs Rodd.'

Twenty-three

WHERE DID THIS VISIT leave me? I had no time to digest what I had seen, because the storm broke the very next day.

I know very little about money or stock markets, but I have lived through several Great Smashes, and they all had one thing in common – people behaved at the time as if the world had ended, and then a couple of months later they got excited about something else and forgot all about it.

This is my apology for understanding so little about the Smash of Sir James Calderstone; a financial expert could probably explain how it was that a mighty fortune could simply dissolve overnight. I can only report the visible effects.

The newspapers – particularly those opposed to Sir James's politics – gleefully accused him of all kinds of villainy. His debts were exposed, and a legion of creditors clamoured for their money. That hysterical creature the Stock Exchange took fright; many suffered losses or were ruined. Ignorant people decided that his father's Smash made Charles yet more guilty of murder; the gutter-press printed fantasies that were nothing short of ludicrous.

As far as our case was concerned, there was only one minor spark of information. Mr Filey sent me a cutting from an

English newspaper printed in Switzerland, which contained a laconic announcement of the death of one Mr Horace Villiers. He did not need to tell me this was the man who had once been the lover of Lady Calderstone.

'We can rule him out as the blackmailer, then,' Mrs Bentley said. 'Unless he was horribly murdered like all the others.'

'According to the paper, he died of a "long and debilitating affliction",' I replied. 'So we may lay this red herring to rest, at least.'

'I suppose – though it's a bit rum that everyone who knew about Villiers and Lady C is dead now.'

'Maybe, but I don't see how an invalid in Switzerland could get to Lincolnshire from his deathbed, to kill Mrs Orme and Miss Winifred. Or why.'

I liked to have something to do with my hands while thinking hard, and we were in the process of cleaning my few remaining pieces of silver, which had belonged to my mother.

'I know it has nothing to do with Charles Calderstone,' I said, 'but I can't stop thinking about that child.'

Mrs Bentley, gamely buffing the cream-jug, said, 'And you're certain Mrs Orme was her mother?'

'Mary, the resemblance took my breath away – when she smiled, I saw the Fisherman's Daughter. And there was the old lady, bold as brass, telling me that her son had married an Italian lady from a "fine old family"!'

'A fine old fiddlestick,' Mrs Bentley said. 'But you'd want to cover things up, wouldn't you? I mean, you're hardly going to tell the world that your precious young lady is a common little girl, and a bastard into the bargain. If you'll forgive the language.'

'Mrs Rutherford believed every word she was telling me,' I said. 'Or her pride has allowed her to rewrite the past. But I'm utterly convinced that Helen Orme turned faint that day because she recognized her lost baby.'

'Hmmm,' Mrs Bentley said. 'There must've been a bit more to it than that.'

'I'm assuming that she overheard the old lady's name, saw the child and did the arithmetic. Miss Adelina is evidently very much like her father. The shock must've been appalling.'

'Well, I don't know. It don't fit, that's all.' Mrs B was sceptical (Fred said her natural scepticism was very useful to him in the art of managing a jury). 'I thought Mrs Orme went back to Italy and saw the baby's grave.'

'That was her story.' My own brain was numb with wondering about this. 'I really don't think she was lying. She was ill with the fever. The epidemic had laid waste to the fishing village where she left the child. I doubt those people could afford much in the way of gravestones.'

'So Savile told Mrs Rutherford about the baby,' Mrs Bentley said. 'And Mrs R went to fetch her home – or sent someone else to do it.'

'That much is obvious,' I said. 'And if Mrs Rutherford knew that the child's mother was still living, she would have had a very fine motive for killing her. In just a few years she'll want Adelina to enter society, and to make a good marriage. And her position is doubtful enough as it is; that "fine old family" in Italy won't bear much looking into. If her true parentage got out, every door would be closed to her.'

'Yes, but would her granny commit brutal murder to cover it up?'

We both smiled grimly, for the idea was preposterous.

I had not seen Miss Esther and the two girls since our journey from Lincolnshire, and decided to pay them a call that afternoon. I travelled to the West End on foot and by the omnibus, knowing that I could no longer expect my unfortunate employer to 'stump up' for a cab. His Smash was all over the streets, on every tongue, in every newspaper and scandal-sheet.

A young policeman, stamping his feet in the cold, stood guard at the entrance to the Calderstone house. At the foot of the front steps, half a dozen creditors shivered in a stubborn huddle.

I gave the policeman my name. He simply pushed open the heavy front door and nodded me inside, into the grand echoing hall (the marble floors and pillars reminded me uncomfortably of the ostentatious tombs I had seen in Highgate Cemetery). It was emptier than I remembered; some paintings and items of furniture had already disappeared. There was a litter of straw across the floor, and not a servant in sight until the butler emerged from under the stairs.

'Good afternoon, Mrs Rodd.'

'Good afternoon, Thorpe; is Lady Calderstone at home?'

'Her Ladyship is from home at present. The young ladies are in the small sitting room, if you'll be kind enough to follow me.'

He led me up a flight of stairs, through an obscure door, along a narrow passage, and signs of desolation were everywhere I looked – blank squares on the walls, chairs and tables all awry, fireplaces cold and ashy, an air of chaos and neglect. I felt deeply, sincerely sorry for the two innocent girls, who surely faced a most uncertain future, even supposing their brother was not hanged for murder.

The 'small' upstairs sitting room, however, was a little haven of warmth and light amidst the encircling gloom. Here I found the three young ladies, and – to my surprise – Mr Fitzwarren.

'Mrs Rodd – how nice!' Miss Esther jumped up to meet me. 'Come and sit by the fire.'

The young ladies wore the plain black dresses of deepest mourning; the sight disconcerted me like an omen, until I remembered Miss Winifred.

'I'm glad you have come,' Miss Blanche said. 'As you see, we're under siege here. We can't sit in the drawing room because someone threw a brick at the window.'

'I think this is much more comfortable,' Miss Esther said. 'The drawing room is impossible to heat, for one thing.'

'Sweet are the uses of adversity,' Mr Fitzwarren said.

Miss Esther smiled. 'I was going to say, "It's an ill wind," but Shakespeare's better.'

'Please accept my condolences,' I said. 'I was very sorry to hear about poor Miss Winifred.'

I'm always interested in the ways that outward events can reshape a person, for good or ill. My first impression was that Miss Blanche had got older, while Miss Elizabeth had got younger. It wasn't that Blanche had hardened in any way; there was a sense of inner strength that I had never seen in her. The stark simplicity of her black dress made her face absolutely beautiful. Whereas poor Miss Bessie was a frightened child, with a bewildered look in her eyes that went to my heart.

'I was speaking of her last hours,' Mr Fitzwarren said. 'There's not much to tell; it was a slow, calm sinking away. My mother and I were with her at the end. I hoped that she would try to speak, as the dying sometimes do. But there was nothing – and it was profane of me to wish for it, when the room was filled with peace and holiness.'

There was a silence.

'I know Lady Calderstone wishes to thank you and your mother,' Miss Esther said, 'for taking Winifred into your house.'

'It was a privilege.'

'Mamma's not here because she's gone to see Charlie,' Miss Bessie said. 'I wish we could see him too. But he sends us such kind messages; he says I must be a good mouse.'

'And so you are,' Miss Esther said, kissing her cheek. 'The very best of mice!'

As usual, she was the embodiment of quiet comfort, effortlessly warming this house of doom into a home. Had anyone yet told her the extraordinary news about the hidden wealth at Kirkside? I could hardly mention such a subject before the two girls.

I noticed that Mr Fitzwarren watched Miss Esther a great deal, and that the two of them exchanged jokes like old friends; a proposal was surely in the air, once the immediate horror of the trial had passed. I sensed a gentle conspiracy between them to protect Blanche and Elizabeth, and thought that some good might yet come from this catastrophe. Though we were all in mourning, though the Angel of Death hovered above us, these two strove to keep the atmosphere light, if not cheerful.

A tray of tea came in – carried by Thorpe, the only servant I had seen in the house.

'The others all ran off, apparently,' Mr Fitzwarren said to me later, when the two of us were making our way out by the light of a single candlestick. 'Like rats leaving a sinking ship.'

'How long are you in town, Mr Fitzwarren?'

'I'm staying for the trial,' he said. 'Now that I know the family, I can't bear to desert them; too many of their supposed "friends" have forsaken them.'

(Bless the man, I thought; he was here because he couldn't keep away from Miss Esther; he loved her and felt that his place was at her side.)

'Have you found out anything about Drummond, as I requested in my letter?'

He smiled suddenly. 'You'd have been proud of me, Mrs Rodd; I was an absolute model of discretion. I didn't ask questions outright, but merely listened to the local gossip – and that was enough to tell me that Mr Drummond doesn't move in the best society.'

'That I can believe,' I said. 'Mr Charles saw him at a cock-fight.'

'He's a gambler, and there are whispers that he owes money to some gang of villains or other – this is only hearsay, of course, but I can easily believe such a man would stoop to committing perjury – either from necessity or greed, or both. Though I don't have proof of anything at the moment, I'm sure it can be obtained.'

'Thank you, Mr Fitzwarren,' I said. 'You've been most helpful.'

I took my leave and started the long trudge back to Hampstead. It was a cold, disagreeable journey through dark, chaotic city streets, but I hardly felt the discomfort, for my head was racing.

Never mind the proof; I knew in my bones that the killer had purchased Mr Drummond. Fred would be delighted; there was no sport he enjoyed more than discrediting the other side's chief witness.

But there was more. The cheese-woman at the market had seen Drummond in a carriage with another man; at last I had a sighting of my Prince.

Twenty-four

I'M RATHER ASHAMED OF what I did next. My only defence is that I was in pursuit of justice. I am not a spy by nature. I did not set out that day with spying in mind.

Or not precisely.

It was the morning after my meeting with the Calderstones. The weather was fine and clear, and I was out walking. And I just naturally found myself turning my steps towards the toll-booth by the Spaniards, and the old house where I had met Mrs Rutherford.

Hampstead Lane was busy that day, with carts and carriages lining up to squeeze through the narrow tollgate, and many foot-passengers taking advantage of the dry conditions. I stood aside to make way for a laundress hauling an enormous basket – and my eye was suddenly caught by a dark, slight figure, moving determinedly towards Highgate village.

It was Miss Muirfield, wrapped in a close black cloak and bonnet. She did not see me. Where was the harm in following her? Or – to put it another way – how could I miss such an opportunity? I was very curious to know where she was off to in such a hurry, and with such an air of purpose. Luckily for me, she was so intent upon her journey that she did not bother to look behind her.

And it was quite a journey; I followed her down West Hill, along Highgate Road and through Kentish Town, until she climbed into an omnibus just by the Mother Redcap in Camden. I could not climb in with her, or she would have seen me at once. Again the fates were on my side; there was a cab-stand nearby, and I was (for once) well supplied with cash. I had to lean out of the dirty cab window to keep my eyes on the omnibus. Where was she going, for heaven's sake?

At last, when we were in the roaring depths of the city in Ludgate Hill, and I was starting to worry that I had lost her, I saw Miss Muirfield climbing out of the omnibus; I paid the cabby (over-tipping him by at least sixpence in my haste) and hurried after her.

She turned into the great arch that led into the yard of the Bell Savage, a famous old coaching inn that was now crumbling and empty due to the decline of the old stagecoaches and the march of the railways (I am not an enemy of progress and can fully see the benefits – but I hated the great gashes those steel roads had made across countryside unchanged since the days of *Ivanhoe*, and now lost for all eternity).

Miss Muirfield kept her head bowed as she hurried through the public dining room, towards a glass door with 'Coffee Room' painted in letters of flaking gilt. In she went, closing the door smartly behind her.

It was risky, but I had come too far to turn back; I took a quick peek through the glass. And I was rewarded by the sight of Miss Muirfield falling into the arms of a gentleman. He had his back to me, so I could make out nothing except that he was a good head taller than she, and attired in a blue greatcoat of elegant cut.

Her face, however, spoke volumes; she was all afire with passion, and clung to him almost with abandon. The spinsterish poor relation had a lover.

The coffee room was divided into wooden booths, like little sentry-boxes or pews in a very dissolute church. Miss Muirfield's lover pulled her into one of the snugs. My blood was up now; I went inside and whisked into the booth next door to them (my heart was hammering fit to burst out of my ribs with nerves; even if these two didn't see me, I was doing something that was abominable in the sight of Heaven and I mentally apologized to Matt, but at the same time I was consumed with curiosity). As I had hoped, I could hear the voices of the lovers and make out most of what they were saying.

His voice was light and well-spoken, and not loud – I had to put my ear right up against the wooden wall. Concentrating to my utmost, I understood that he was talking (rather disappointingly) about the fireplace in his new lodgings, which was smoking him into 'a Suffolk ham'.

'But it won't be for long,' Miss Muirfield said. 'Do you remember, my darling, years ago, when I swore I'd follow you to the ends of the earth? That hasn't changed.'

'Please, Em!' His voice became coaxing. 'I thought we agreed to stop going on about last time.'

'I just want you to know that I'm ready, and I won't falter at the last moment.'

'I have every faith in you.'

(My curiosity was now at boiling-point; what were these two planning? An elopement seemed unlikely, when Miss M was plain, middle-aged and penniless, but stranger things have happened; they had a 'past', after all.)

'I can't stay long,' she said, more matter-of-fact. 'She won't remember that I told her I was going out; she never really listens to me; I might as well have told her I was off to join the circus. But she's as sharp as a needle when she chooses; I can't keep her in the dark for ever.'

'It'll have to be soon, anyway,' he said. 'My supplies are dwindling.'

'You had the legacy from your godmother; don't tell me you've run through it already!'

'Darling girl, you said yourself I must take my rightful place in the world. I was starting again from scratch – and gentlemanly clutter don't come cheap.'

'As soon as you like, then – I'll wait for a letter in the usual place.'

I was agog to hear more, but the room was filling up and Muirfield and her lover were preparing to leave; I quickly got myself out of the Bell Savage and on to the street, before they could see me.

Fred always said that I ran after a new scent like a bloodhound; I took a cab directly to my brother's chambers in Furnival's Inn. Mr Beamish told me he was with Charles Calderstone at Newgate. I duly ordered the cab on to the prison, my mind in such a ferment that I barely even thought of the expense.

I was cold, exhausted by the long route-march of the morning, and faint with hunger – but what did I care?

I had seen him and heard his voice, I was sure of it; one thin plank of wood had separated me from the killer.

'I've told you absolutely everything,' Mr Charles said. 'You know what I ate for breakfast, what I said to the stable boy, exactly where I was when the clock chimed. You have the clothes I wore that day. We've been over every detail.'

'I know, I know – but one little detail can be all it takes to make a case, or break it.' Fred brushed pie-crumbs off his waist-coat. 'Wouldn't you agree, Inspector?'

'I don't like generalities,' Blackbeard said.

I had found a strangely convivial party in that brick-lined Newgate room – Charles, Fred and the inspector in a huddle around the fire, drinking hot punch. The seething punchbowl on the table overlaid the lysol smell of the prison with giddying scents of cinnamon, lemon peel and port wine.

'Mrs Rodd, you look frozen; you'd better have some punch.' Mr Charles put a glass into my stiff, gloved hands. 'Among his other talents, Mason makes an excellent bowl of Smoking Bishop.'

(People don't seem to make Smoking Bishop nowadays: it's a fragrant concoction of red wine, port wine and spices, and my beloved Matt was very fond of a glass directly after a chilly Matins; you must first stick a lemon with cloves and sugar-lumps, roast it beside a medium fire until caramelized, then place in your pan of wine to simmer gently for twenty minutes.)

Mason, the affable gaoler, handed me a glass. I took it grate-fully, suddenly aware that I was numb with cold and half-dead from exhaustion. I was longing to tell Fred about Miss Muir-field, but that would have to wait until we were alone.

I could, however, pass on the promising snippets about Mr Drummond.

'By God, I knew it!' Fred shouted triumphantly. 'Now, Black-beard – what do you say to that?'

'Well,' the inspector said, slow and thoughtful, 'that's your job, ain't it? The jury will expect you to have a go at him, on account of its being his word against yours. It's not my business unless he's committed a crime.'

'He's lying his damned head off,' Mr Charles said fiercely. 'He did NOT see me reeking with gore and washing myself at that pump.' He glanced at me. 'I beg your pardon, Mrs Rodd; you can't imagine how awful it feels, to know that people will believe such a blackguard before they believe me.'

'My informer says he can easily find out more about Drummond without arousing too much suspicion,' I assured him. 'The jury will only need to know that he's heavily in debt and fond of low company – though it's rather a pity, Mr Charles, that some of the low company included you.'

Fred chuckled. 'Never mind that – I'll bet you fifty guineas Drummond was paid by the killer! Don't let us keep you, Inspector. You'll want to be rushing up to Lincolnshire to arrest the man.'

'Well, I'll have to see about that,' Blackbeard said, blinking like a tortoise in the fumes of the punchbowl. 'It might bear some looking into.'

I wanted to argue with him, but there was a rap on the door. Mason went to open it, and we were all startled to see Miss Esther.

She looked small and slight in her plain black dress, and very young.

'Essie!' Mr Charles jumped up, the colour rushing into his face. 'My dear old thing – but what are you doing here? What's happened?'

'I'm so sorry, I know you didn't want me to come here – but Charlie, I had to tell you before you heard it from somewhere else –'

'What? For God's sake –' He seized both her hands in his. 'Mamma – the girls –'

'Please, you mustn't be alarmed; they're very well. It's your father, Charlie.' It was singular to see the way she gripped the hands of tall Mr Charles, as if transmitting waves of strength to him. 'He had some kind of fit, late last night; he's paralysed down his left side, his speech is dreadfully muddled and impaired –'

'Papa – oh, my God –' Mr Charles was now deathly pale.

'But the doctor says he can recover,' Miss Esther said fervently. 'Do you hear me? That's what you must remember! If he has sufficient rest –'

'Rest? That's a good one – when his son's about to be tried for murder! This is my fault, isn't it? Now I've killed my father.'

'No, indeed, Mr Charles.' I could not allow him to believe this, though it was at least half-true. 'Your father had all kinds of strains and worries in his life that had absolutely nothing to do with you.'

'You'd better hang me at once before I kill again!' He pulled his hands away pettishly. 'Which I can apparently do without even leaving the room!'

Miss Esther's lower lip trembled, and tears spilled down her face. This brave young woman suddenly looked no older than Tishy (oh! seven-year-old Tishy, making such valiant efforts not to cry when she parted with her mother! Matt said it made him want to 'slay beasts'); I knew that Fred was thinking along the same lines, for he murmured, 'My dear little girl!' and gave her the huge white silk handkerchief that he used for flourishes in court.

Blackbeard blew his nose loudly. 'Excuse me, ladies.' He bowed and left the room, discreetly followed by Mason.

'Essie – oh God, I'm a complete monster! I'm so sorry, old thing – don't cry!' Mr Charles was now all tender penitence, and took the weeping girl in his arms. 'Don't, my dearest.'

'I'm sorry.' Miss Esther was making a mighty effort to stop. She pulled away from Mr Charles, her face flaming scarlet.

This was when I knew, with absolute certainty, that George Fitzwarren had no hope. Miss Esther was in an anguish of love for Mr Charles; there it was and there it would be until the last crash of the spheres; women like us lose our hearts but once, and for all time.

Mr Charles, however, did not seem to have noticed this, and still treated her as a beloved old playmate (I had been very cross with him for making Miss Esther cry, but was now touched by the way he joshed her and coaxed her – just like a ten-year-old Fred, wheedling forgiveness for the most outrageous crimes).

'Sit down beside the fire, your hands are like ice! How about a glass of punch?'

'Oh, Charlie – don't be silly!' She couldn't help smiling at this. 'You know I can't drink! And if ever there was a time when I needed a clear head –'

'Miss Esther, you look dreadfully tired.' I gently pushed her into the chair Mr Charles had set for her. 'When did you last sleep – or have anything to eat?'

'I can send Mason out to the pie-shop,' Charles offered.

'No, really; I was overcome for a moment, that's all. I didn't mean to upset you; that's the last thing I – Charlie, you truly must believe that everything is being done to help your father.'

He sat down close beside her and took her hand. 'How did you find a doctor, when the whole world knows he's ruined?'

'Not all his friends have deserted him,' Miss Esther said. 'Sir Marcus Astley came at once, and said right at the outset that he expected no payment.'

'That's decent of him.' Mr Charles was moved. 'He's a good old cove. But there'll be other expenses.'

The door opened; Blackbeard entered, bearing two steaming cups and looking pleased with himself. 'Some tea for the ladies,' he said. 'Compliments of Mason and the gatekeeper.'

'How splendid!' I said. 'Exactly what we needed.' Or, more accurately, what Miss Esther needed; hope and strength flooded back into her face the moment I took the thick, white cup from Blackbeard and put it into her shaking hands.

And very good tea it was – just the right side of scalding; strong, with a good dash of fresh milk. One sip and Miss Esther revived before us, like one of those paper flowers that expand when you drop them in water.

She gave Blackbeard a proper smile. 'Thank you, Inspector.'

'You've had a rough night, Miss Grahame, and I know you ladies like your tea,' Blackbeard said (with the gleam, deep in those stony eyes of his, that I was beginning to recognize as kindness). 'My wife was a great one for a cup of tea.' He jerked a stiff bow at the room in general. 'Now I'll leave you to get on with your family business. Good afternoon.'

For a fraction of a second our eyes met, and I knew that the inspector wanted to speak to me; though I hardly dared to hope for such a thing, I sensed a softening in him – but that's the wrong word. It was more like a slight shifting deep beneath his hard exterior. Blackbeard, I remembered, liked to work with dogged, trudging slowness, ignoring flighty things like instinct and intuition and holding out for 'cold, hard facts' (as if facts became colder and harder the more true they were).

This was promising; in each of our last encounters there had been a turning-point, when Inspector Blackbeard had chewed all those facts to a pulp and finally admitted that he could not make them fit together. I had noticed (watching him while he watched all of us) that he sometimes looked at Mr Charles with what I can only describe as the puzzled fascination of a scientist who has found a new sort of beetle. At last, he had got around to forming an opinion of the young man.

'A rare instance of tact,' Fred said, after Blackbeard had left us again. 'The fact is, though he's as stubborn as a gatepost and makes abominable slurping noises when he drinks, the inspector is a very good sort of a man. You look a little better, Miss Grahame.'

'I'm much better; please forgive me for breaking down like that.'

Mr Charles gave Miss Esther's arm a friendly squeeze. 'I'm the one who should be begging forgiveness – the last time I made you cry, we were fishing for tadpoles at Kirkside – do you remember?'

Well, of course she remembered; the colour surged back to her cheeks. 'You pushed me into the pond.'

'But then you forgave me, and begged Uncle George not to take a slipper to me – which he was obviously longing to do,

254

little beast that I was. You always were ridiculously good to me. Tell me about Papa, so that I can get it straight. When did it happen?'

'Just after midnight,' Miss Esther said. 'The girls and I had gone to bed, and were woken up by your poor mother's cries for help. Thorpe ran across the square to fetch Sir Marcus, who was very fortunately at home giving a dinner party. Sir James was insensible for a long time, and when he regained his senses he could not speak plainly, or move his left side.'

'How's Mamma? Oh God – if I could be there!'

'She was very frightened at first, thinking your father was dead. I was at my wits' end trying to calm her down – but then Blanche took her away, so that Thorpe and I could assist the doctor. You'd have been proud of Blanche.' A ghost of a smile flitted across Miss Esther's face. 'She was as brave as a young lioness and as gentle as a lamb – and an absolute angel to poor little Bessie, who thought she'd woken up to the end of the world.'

'Poor Mouse,' Mr Charles said shakily. 'What a bad sign it is when they're not squabbling! I miss them so much – and I can't drive away the knowledge that I've ruined their lives. Tell me exactly what's needed for Papa and I'll tell Filey to give you the cash. My father can't raise a farthing in his own name, but my name is still good; if I'm hanged –' She flinched as if he had whipped her. 'I had to say it, old thing. If Tyson breaks the habit of a lifetime and loses this case, Grand-mama's estate will go to Blanche and Bessie. It's in pretty good order.'

'So I believe,' Fred said. 'Fortunately, you were only ever an amateur dissolute; according to Filey, your debts were piffling.'

Charles ignored this, still thinking about his father. 'You'll need professional nurses, for a start – and I'm sure Sir Marcus has prescribed food and wine, and that sort of stuff. He must have the very best.'

'You mustn't worry about it,' Miss Esther said. 'He has the very best nurses, and a gigantic basket of the very finest food and wine. They all turned up together on the doorstep this morning.'

'Who sent them?'

She sighed, and that was enough.

'Mrs Hardy.' Charles had forgiven his father for the affair, but could not utter the woman's name without contempt.

'Don't, Charlie – I saw her in her carriage, and I couldn't bear to let her go without a word. When she saw me coming to the window she put a veil over her face as if my eyes burned her, poor soul. She was half-dead with weeping and worry. I told her all the hopeful things Sir Marcus said about your father.'

'Hmm,' Mr Charles said. 'That's just like you, and I can't scold you for it. At least she's standing by him.'

'More than that – she has been settling the most pressing of the bills, to protect your father from being taken up for debt.' Miss Esther had recovered, and her voice was firm. 'You can't imagine what it has been like for us. Of course we tried to keep the worst of it from you. But the moment the news was out, we were beset with wave upon wave of grocers, tailors, saddle-makers – all with bills from a few shillings to hundreds of pounds. Mrs Hardy has been seeing off dozens of them, and with perfect discretion. She has been very kind.'

'I've met the lady,' I said. 'And she left me in no doubt of her good intentions. Rightly or wrongly, Mr Charles, she loves your father.'

'I'm grateful, and I'll try to think better of her.' Mr Charles was very serious. 'Lord knows, I'm hardly in a position to judge the woman. You were a trump to come, Ess; the sight of you is like – I don't know – like sunshine – like champagne –'

'Oh, don't be silly.' Once more, her cheeks blazed scarlet. 'I had to tell you myself.'

'And Mamma – how is she now?'

'Please don't worry about her,' Miss Esther said. 'After the first fright had worn off, she was splendidly calm. She's already talking to Sir James about the new life they will have in the country after – when all this is behind us.'

There was a silence.

'Wishtide will have to go,' said Mr Charles. 'The Smash swallowed it whole.'

'Not Wishtide; she means to bring him to dear old Kirkside. Sir Marcus says that with peace and quiet, and good country air, your father can hope to make a reasonable recovery. What-ever might happen –' her voice shook a little '– I want you to know that I'll take care of them.'

'My dear thing.' His face was tender, smiling down into hers. 'I know you will. And it's a great burden lifted; I shall like to think of them all stowed safely away at Kirkside, beyond the reach of the outside world. Are the lavender-beds still there?'

'They've grown since the last time you came,' Miss Esther said (trying to sound matter-of-fact while blazing love for him from every pore). 'The scent can make me giddy sometimes.'

'You're an angel,' Mr Charles said. 'Heaping coals of fire on my father's head. I suppose you know how he tried to cheat you.'

'No!' Miss Esther spoke with ringing firmness. 'He did nothing of the kind!'

'He kept his discovery from you and Uncle George, which amounts to the same thing.'

'Please, Charlie – I can hardly bear to think of it now. He told me everything, as far as he could form the words, and asked my pardon. I'll say to you what I said to him.' She drew herself up proudly. 'You're my family, you loved and comforted me when I lost my mother, and all that I have belongs to you – no, please don't say anything! What else would I do with it?'

'It comforts me to know you're with them,' said Mr Charles. 'I know I can trust you to take care of them for me.'

He took her hand and kissed it; the two of them looked into each other's eyes.

At last, in the very shadow of the gallows, Mr Charles gazed at his cousin as if seeing her for the first time, and I saw the first spark of love in his gaze – nothing like his boyish passion for Helen Orme, but the deep love of a grown man.

What a fine couple they would make, I thought sadly; if only he could be allowed to live (I sent up a swift and rather strictly worded prayer for the two young people, pointing out how unfair it would be to let them fall in love if Charles was to be hanged; Matt would have roared with laughter and told me to stop giving orders to the Almighty).

Blackbeard was waiting for us when we left Charles.

'I'd like to catch up, Mrs Rodd,' he said. 'Might I call on you tomorrow morning?'

'You may, Inspector.'

Despite the solemnity of the situation, I was joyful; 'then shall the eyes of the blind be opened, and the ears of the deaf unstopped'.

Twenty-five

'I T WAS DOWN TO my son David,' Mrs Bentley said. 'He's in the dairy business; he knows the fellow that does the milk-round along that way – name of Dixon – and he arranged for me to ride on the cart. I met it first thing this morning, at Jack Straw's Castle, and went off along Hampstead Lane towards the Spaniards.'

She was pleased with herself, and had every reason to be; the milk-cart had been entirely her idea. I could not go back to the Rutherford house without a very good excuse, but no one takes any notice of an old woman in a tradesman's cart, and she had returned in triumph, bristling with observations.

'You chose a cold enough day for it,' Inspector Blackbeard said.

We had woken up to an iron frost and though I had wrapped Mrs B in every scarf and shawl I could find, and my own thickest cloak, I had been dreadfully worried that the bitter grey weather would aggravate her rheumatism. Before she made her report to us, I insisted that she thawed herself at the kitchen fire, and drank a mug of hot ale.

'Cold! It was cold, all right,' Mrs Bentley said. 'Whitestone Pond was one solid sheet of ice – the little boys will be all over it later, you wait and see. My lot would've gone wild.'

'That takes me back,' Blackbeard said. 'Best day of the winter, when the pond froze over.'

The inspector, who had appeared on the doorstep a few minutes before the return of Mrs B, was comfortable and unhurried – since the loss of his wife, I suspected, his life had been rather short of domestic comfort (later, when I had time, I wondered about that pond of his, and whether it was in a town or village; it was very difficult to picture Blackbeard as a boy).

'Well, this Dixon was a nice enough fellow,' Mrs Bentley went on. 'He packed my feet in straw to keep them warm, and off we went.'

'Not many houses along that road,' Blackbeard remarked.

'No,' Mrs B said. 'But there was a fair bit of meandering up and down lanes, before we came to the Rutherfords'. I couldn't tell you exactly what time it was, but I'd heard the church clock striking half past nine not long before. Dixon drove his milk-cart round to the back door, and out came a servant – a cook, maybe, or a housekeeper. She wanted a quart more milk than the usual order, on account of Mrs Rutherford had a cousin staying with her. A gentleman, she said.'

'A gentleman!' I seized upon this eagerly. 'I'd be prepared to bet it was the same gentleman I saw with Miss Muirfield!' (I had already gabbled out an account of what I had seen and heard at the Bell Savage.) 'Did you see him, Mary?'

'I dunno if it was him, ma'am – but I certainly did see a gentleman. There's a stables round the back of that house, and the gentleman was out in the yard, giving the little girl a ride on a pony.'

'What did he look like?' I asked.

Mrs B narrowed her eyes thoughtfully. 'Youngish, I'd say – though everybody looks young to me these days. Tall and thin, with brown hair close-cropped. The servant said his arrival had put the ladies of the house into an uproar, and they'd been giving big orders to the butcher and the wine merchant – properly killing the fatted calf, she said.'

And then I had it, and nearly laughed aloud. 'Of course! Oh, I've been so slow – just because I take gravestones in good faith! Don't you see, Inspector?'

'See what?'

'For whom did they kill the fatted calf?'

'The Prodigal Son,' Mrs Bentley said. 'I remember that much from Sunday School.'

'Precisely.' I could not help my voice shaking with excitement. 'That's not Mrs Rutherford's cousin – he's her son!'

Blackbeard's reaction to this thunderclap was disappointingly calm. 'But she buried her son; you've seen his grave.'

'I've seen someone's grave; who's to say Mrs Rutherford buried the right body? You and I have both seen the remains of people who have drowned. They are often disfigured and bloated beyond recognition.'

He nodded. 'True.'

'I can go back to Suffolk, Inspector; I can seek out whoever it was that identified the body; suppose they decided it was Henry Rutherford from the clothes he wore, or the papers he carried?'

'Hmm,' Blackbeard said, turning this over. 'So you're saying Rutherford deliberately dressed a corpse in his clothes, because he wanted the world to believe he was dead?'

It sounded ridiculously far-fetched when spoken in that flat voice of his.

'Perhaps the dead man robbed him,' Mrs Bentley suggested.

'No, that won't do.' Blackbeard shook his head. 'A mistake like that would've come to light much sooner. I'd have to believe it suited Mr Rutherford to drop out of sight for a while. But why would he do such a thing? Didn't you tell me he was tied to his mother's purse-strings?'

'Yes – but there might have been more to it than money.' In my mind's eye, I saw the face of Helen Orme as she related the story of her past. 'Mrs Orme mentioned to me that she and Rutherford had been forced to leave a certain town in a hurry – perhaps he decided to allow the false reports of his death, as a means of saving his life?'

The inspector took a slow sip of his ale. 'You think he was escaping from foreign bandits?'

Now he was making it sound like the plot of a light opera.

'Foreign bandits may look more picturesque than the home-grown variety,' I said, 'but they're every bit as dangerous. I think Henry Rutherford had to die before somebody killed him.'

'What's brought him back, then?'

'Money, of course – but mainly his daughter. Even wild beasts love their young.'

'It's a fine story, Mrs Rodd.' The inspector loudly drained his mug. 'But it's a castle in the air; by which I mean, it don't make any difference to Charles Calderstone; he's still going to be tried for murder. Get me evidence, ma'am – get me witnesses!'

My frustration made me snappish. 'Not that I'm telling you how to do your job, Inspector – but you could always speak to

263

Mrs Rutherford's mysterious cousin and ask him for his where-abouts at the time of the murders!'

'Yes – and I could always look like a fool when he turns out to be exactly who he says he is! You still haven't given me one good, solid reason why young Charlie shouldn't be in that dock.'

'Not yet.' I was not to be snubbed. 'But Henry Rutherford had every reason to want Helen Orme out of the way. Henry Rutherford is the lover of Miss Muirfield, and the man who called himself the Prince. I will bring you proof that Henry Rutherford's neck is the one that belongs in a noose.'

'I'll look forward to it,' Blackbeard said.

'Poor Mrs Arrowsmith named another of Savile's "wives" – Sarah Gammon.' I drew the name out triumphantly. 'By the time I have finished, Inspector, my castle in the air will be fully built and furnished.'

'I'm sure I hope you're right, ma'am,' Blackbeard said. 'I've taken rather a liking to young Calderstone, and it would be nice to hear that he didn't murder those two ladies. I'm sure I hope your Sarah Gammon doesn't turn out to be so much gammon-and-spinach!'

We found her two days later in a narrow city court near to the easternmost gate in the old London Wall.

'Jane Arrowsmith told me the whereabouts of her rival,' Fred said, 'in exchange for half a crown – which buys quite a bit of information round here.'

The woman who called herself Mrs Sarah Gammon worked at a laundry, situated in the basement of one of the soot-encrusted buildings; my brother and I had to fight our way through a dense forest of damp linen, hanging from the washing-lines that criss-crossed the yard. We plunged down some stone steps into a great cloud of steam. Fred parted with another half-crown, and we were directed to a woman feeding wet clothes through a large mangle while another woman turned the handle.

'I'm looking for a Mrs Sarah Gammon,' my brother said.

'That's me; what d'you want?'

She was a good deal younger than Jane Arrowsmith, and even rather handsome in a coarse, red-faced fashion (what on earth had all these women seen in a man like Savile?).

'We'd like to talk about your late husband,' Fred said. 'But not in this Turkish bath; I refuse to be steamed like a suet pudding.'

Several half-crowns later, Mrs Gammon was walking out of the laundry with us, blinking in the daylight and shivering in the sudden assault of the cold after the damp heat. She was, however, delighted by this unexpected adventure in the middle of her working day. Fred marched us into the back room of an obscure tavern, where there was a good fire and plentiful hot gin and water, and she was positively smiling.

'Good health to all!' She raised her pewter mug to us. 'Now, what's this about my husband? It was him, wasn't it – that fellow that got murdered? I knew it when I heard about that scar on his hand – which I give him with a hot iron, one time when we had words.' (It was a relief to me that this woman did not appear to be dying of sorrow; she was evidently made of more robust stuff than the unfortunate Mrs Arrowsmith; I couldn't help rather admiring her casual boast about the hot iron.)

'Did you know his real name was Savile?' Fred asked.

'Not when I first met him, sir.'

'And did you know that you're the third "wife" we've found?'

Mrs Gammon shrugged crossly. 'If you mean that Jane Arrowsmith, she weren't his wife nor anything like it! He told me he only went along with her to get his clothes looked after.'

'Mrs Arrowsmith told us he let you cook for him occasionally,' I said.

'Did she, indeed! That's just her nonsense, ma'am; she's mad with jealousy. She knows perfectly well, me and Gammon were living together as husband and wife. He only went back to Jane when we'd had words and I stopped the money.'

'Where did you meet him?'

'At the –' She suddenly stopped; her eyes narrowed warily. 'At a tavern where I was working behind the bar.'

Fred grinned. 'More gin, Sal?'

'Thank you, sir.' She held out her empty mug.

'What tavern was that, my dear?'

'The Goat in Salt Lane. Mrs Dooley's my aunt.'

'Well, well – all roads lead to Rome!' My brother was enjoying himself. 'So you met this Adonis at the Goat in Boots!'

'Yes, sir.'

'And set yourself up as his wife.'

'Yes, sir. And I was with child by him, though it didn't take. He didn't bring in a wage, which was why I started at the laundry – my aunt wouldn't let me back at the Goat – here, you did square things with Mrs Jones, didn't you? This is a good job and I don't want to lose it.'

'Fear not,' Fred said. 'The entire establishment has been tipped and bribed up to the nines. So rest and take your ease, Sally; and I'll keep the gin coming.'

'I've no objection to that, sir.'

'My sister and I are searching for someone I think you know – the man who calls himself the Prince.'

She certainly knew; the mention of the name made her wary and beady-eyed. But the gin, which she was putting back in amazing quantities, was doing its work.

'Yes, I know him.'

'Do you know where he is?'

'No, sir; I ain't seen him for months.'

'When was the last time you saw him?'

'I dunno.'

I was getting a little impatient with Fred's line of questioning; this woman was not in the dock, and hectoring would get us nowhere.

'Mrs Gammon,' I said, 'I'm afraid your late husband treated you very badly.'

Something in my tone made her look at me sharply. 'It don't matter now he's dead.'

'I can see that you were a good wife to him.'

'I always meant to be.' She had softened; such women can often be disarmed with a little sympathy.

'You must have been very distressed to hear of his death.'

'I didn't know about it until he was cold and in his grave.'

'Surely you were anxious when he was missing?' asked Fred.

'Not at first,' Mrs Gammon said. 'He was given to taking off, and not coming back for days. Oh, we had some fights!' She shook her head sadly, as if recalling a golden romance. 'I didn't get worried until old Jane came round my place, screaming blue murder at me. And then I heard the description of the murdered man – it was the scar on his hand, like I told you

267

– and knew it was him. Can't say I was all that sorry. At least I got to keep my wages.'

'You're a philosopher, my dear,' Fred said. 'And if you tell me a good story, you'll get more gin, a hot mutton pie and another half a crown.'

Mrs Gammon smiled, showing many gaps in her teeth. 'What story would you like to hear, sir?'

'I know you'd tell me anything for that price, my Scheherazade, but I want fact rather than fancy. I want to hear about the Prince.'

The smile vanished; despite the gin she was strictly on her guard. 'Nobody must know it comes from me. And don't expect me to say where he is because before Heaven I don't know – and don't want to, come to that.'

'You can tell us how you met him,' I said.

'It was last September – just after Michaelmas, which I remember because the quarter's rent was due, and Gammon had gone and drunk all the money I'd saved, and I had to borrow off Mrs Jones at the laundry. Anyhow, late one night he comes back and wakes our whole building – he's got two men with another man on a stretcher – Jenkins downstairs says the man on the stretcher is dead – that starts off a whole lot of yelling. But my Gammon was that determined; he shouted them all down and took this fellow into our room. He looked like a corpse, all right – thin as a skeleton, he was, and barely breathing. And there's only the one bed!'

A waiter in a decidedly dirty apron entered at this moment, bearing a tray of disreputable-looking meat pies (I won't call them mutton; in this sort of establishment it could just as well have been donkey-meat). Mrs Gammon's face lit up; she fell on her pie with ferocious hunger that made me wonder how long it was since she had eaten a hot meal.

Two pies vanished and she was ready to take up the story. 'I said to Gammon, what d'you want with this dirty beggar? And he says, I couldn't leave him. He was down by the river, he says, and he stepped on what he thought was just a bundle of old rags in the gutter – but then a voice says, Savile! For the love of God, have pity! And my man nearly started out of his skin – nobody's called him by that name for years. It was his old master, from when he was abroad – name of Mr Henry Rutherford.'

'Bingo!' Fred cried out. 'Letty old thing, you've done it again!'

My pulse raced with excitement – my instinct had been entirely correct.

'That was kind of Mr Gammon,' I said.

His 'widow' snorted scornfully. 'It didn't last long, I can tell you – when he woke up next day he swore the air blue, calling his old master all sorts of names – said he was a scoundrel and deserved to die in the gutter, and he would've thrown the man out if I hadn't begged him not to. Now that he was in our room, I couldn't help taking pity on him as a fellow-creature. For two or three days he was near to dying – rambled about his mamma, and once or twice called me Helen and tried to kiss my hand.' She sighed heavily. 'Gammon took off somewhere – said he wasn't coming back until Rutherford was gone, and so I was left alone with him. I didn't know what to do, except give him water and gruel off a spoon.'

Angels look out of the eyes of the most unlikely people; this draggled woman had taken pity upon a complete stranger, sharing with him what little she had. I saw her dignity, her humanity, and was ashamed of certain assumptions I had made about her.

'You did a very good thing,' I told her. 'Heaven will bless you for it.'

Mrs Gammon's ravaged face coloured; for one moment she looked young and confused. 'I didn't set out to be good. I told you, I didn't know what else to do.'

'You could've left him at the door of the workhouse infirmary or simply turfed him out on to the street,' Fred said. 'The point is that you did not. You have all a woman's heart, my dear.'

'Thank you, sir.'

'Heaven will bless you – though I can't help rather wondering what Heaven had to do with saving the life of that blackguard.'

'I didn't know he was a blackguard,' Mrs Gammon said. 'When he started to come back to himself, I really took to him. He was that polite to me it would've made you laugh – all please and thank you, like I was the Queen. And the stories he told – about when he was a gentleman and my Gammon was his manservant – it was like a play!'

This chimed exactly with Helen Orme's account of her seducer, if there had been any more doubt that he and the Prince were one and the same; Henry Rutherford had the gift, when he chose to use it, of enormous charm. The Fisherman's Daughter had fallen in love with him, along with her entire family and half the town. The man had been a ragged, bearded skeleton when Mrs Gammon saved his life; his charm had evidently been the first thing to recover.

'When did your man deign to come back?' Fred asked.

'It was a week or so later,' Mrs Gammon said. 'The Prince was sitting up by then, and before my husband could have a go at him, he says, Savile, I owe you everything, and if you help me to get my ma's money I'll cut you in and do it handsome.'

'Hmm,' Fred said, 'or words to that effect. What did Gammon say?'

'He got sharp then; he knew the old woman had money – they'd had some sort of dealing, a few years ago.'

'Do you know what it was?' I asked.

'No, ma'am.'

Well, that did not matter; I was sure the 'dealing' concerned the recovery of Rutherford's daughter.

'So the Prince and his Good Samaritan were reconciled,' Fred said. 'Thick as thieves.'

'Yes, sir, as you might say. They got some money and Rutherford took a room at the Goat along of my aunt.'

'How did they get money?'

'It was the Prince's idea – he found a place down by the river where the rent-collector wasn't overlooked and Gammon bashed him over the head.'

'By God, the Limehouse rent-collector!' Fred burst out laughing. 'So that was the work of Rutherford and Savile! One of my customers was very nearly hanged for that outrage! You remember, Letty – my finest ever closing speech to a jury!'

(I was not present at this triumph, but the newspapers were full of it next day; Fred famously pointed out that the accused was 'quite plainly a feeble little pipsqueak', who could not possibly have overcome a burly rent-collector; the jury roared with laughter and the man was found innocent, at the cost of being known as Pipsqueak for the rest of his life.)

Mrs Gammon's hand flew up to her mouth; through the haze of gin, she was alarmed. 'I shouldn't have told you nothing! If he ever finds out –'

'Who?' Fred asked. 'The Prince?'

'Yes, sir – he'll have me killed!'

'And yet you were so fond of him! Unless that changed.'

'I don't feel like saying anything else – please, sir!'

Fred leaned forward to lift the copper pan off the hob. 'We're your friends and admirers, Sal – you have nothing to fear from us. In fact, if you play your cards right, you could be on to a very good thing. So take a little more Dutch courage.'

'No, sir – I shouldn't – and I must get back to work –' Mrs Gammon was afraid, and making a visible effort to resist my brother's blandishments, but she could not help holding out her empty mug like a sleepwalker, staring at the hot, sugared gin and water as Fred dispensed it – with the exact expression he used to have when we were children, and he was trying to get something out of me.

(I am never sure about the morality or effectiveness of bribery, and in this case I strongly disapproved of the veritable gallons of gin my brother was pouring into the woman; on the other hand, I had to admit that it was likely to buy us the most splendid potential witness; while I am not proud of my behaviour, my excuse is that a young man's life was at stake.)

'I'm afraid you're still hungry, Mrs Gammon.' (I brought out my kindest voice, and Fred gleefully flashed me his partners-in-crime face, which made me want simultaneously to laugh and to slap him, and which I loftily ignored.) 'Won't you have another pie? You must not be afraid of telling us the truth. And if you help us, we'll see to it that you are protected.'

She was still very afraid, but want had weakened her and she could be purchased, lock, stock and barrel, with large amounts of food and drink (I don't condemn her for it; she had never known sufficiency, let alone excess).

'He'll find me.'

Fred, suddenly deeply serious, leaned across the fireplace to take Mrs Gammon's red, damp-bloated hand. 'Not if we find him first. And as things stand, my dear, you are our one solid link between the Prince and Henry Rutherford. It may be that we need you to tell your story in court.'

'No!' She pulled her hand away, horrified.

'You're very precious to us, Sally – and we take proper care of our treasures. There'll be no more laundry for you – like Curly Locks, you'll sit on a cushion and sew a fine seam – and you won't be returning to your lodgings. You'll be warm and well-fed, which I daresay will do wonders for your memory.'

Sarah Gammon's bloodshot eyes widened; he might as well have been describing a palace in the *Arabian Nights*. I gave her another of the suspicious pies and she crammed it into her mouth.

'Fred, can you truly promise all this?' I asked.

'Yes; our Mrs Gibson has a sister in Hornsey who has been known to shelter my more delicate female witnesses –'

'Oh, to be sure; where you sent the scullery maid during the Heaton case.'

'The woman is built like a prize-fighter,' Fred said. 'She could give me a couple of stone. Our girl will be safe as houses.'

My brother and I were speaking of Mrs Gammon as if she was not present; I find upon reading back that this makes us sound too unfeeling. The fact is that Mrs Gammon had suddenly deflated into insensibility, with half a pie sticking out of her mouth. We would not get much more out of her now.

'An unexpectedly fruitful day's work – well done, old girl!' Fred tipped back the last of the gin. 'I'll send for Beamish; he knows the drill and he'll take her there.'

'Wait a moment.' I looked at Sarah Gammon – drooling, wretched, tattered. 'She needs more than guarding, Fred; can Mrs Gibson's sister prepare her to face a jury?'

'Hmm.' He looked at her too. 'See what you mean; we don't want the jury to dismiss her as another whore.'

'Fred – that word!'

He ignored this, gazing at her and almost talking to himself. 'How would I present her? Let's see – as an innocent dupe who was led astray – a respectable and industrious woman – an Angel of Mercy who saved the life of a stranger – or is that too much?'

At this very moment, the slumbering 'Angel of Mercy' let out a long, deep belch, and Fred and I fell into a dreadful fit of laughing (I wonder sometimes if we ever grew up completely, and I do try not to succumb to this sort of behaviour in front of the children; when St Paul exhorted us to 'put away childish things', this was just the sort of thing he meant).

Once recovered, I knew what we must do. 'Let me take her home to Well Walk.'

Fred chuckled. 'My dear old thing, please take it from me, Sally is not a fit companion for an archdeacon's lady.'

'I know Mrs B will help; between us, we can give her shelter, and make her appear at least halfway respectable in the witness box.'

'But we don't know if we'll ever get her into a witness box. And as things stand, she can't help Charlie Calderstone.'

'Remember the break-in at Soking,' I reminded him. 'The man Boggs was paid to kill Miss Winifred – don't shake your head at me like that! I'm sure Mrs Gibson's sister is a fine protector of witnesses, but I'd be a great deal easier in my mind if I had Mrs Gammon where I can see her.'

Twenty-six

THE GREAT THING ABOUT Mary Bentley was that nothing shook her; she met every situation with the same equilibrium, and she did not turn a hair when I came home with a bedraggled, ragged, toothless drunkard. It was very odd to see Mrs Gammon's incongruous figure swaying in the middle of my drawing-room carpet.

'Look on the bright side,' Fred said. 'At least she's clean, coming from a laundry; be thankful she didn't work at Billingsgate.'

Mrs Bentley made up a bed in the narrow, empty back room upstairs. She then came down with the candle to light our way – Fred and I were half-dragging Mrs Gammon between us.

We dropped her on the makeshift heap of bolsters, blankets and quilts (I entered widowhood with piles of leftover bed-furnishings; it was oddest of all to see Sally Gammon sprawled across the flowered curtains that had once hung around our old-fashioned, four-poster bed, in Herefordshire and in another life).

She was immediately insensible. The narrow slip of a room reeked of gin – the gin-fumes in the cab on the way here had been almost overpowering. I held the candle over her and saw that though her entire being was soaked with alcohol, Mrs

Gammon was strong and sinewy; try as she might, she had never had the wherewithal to drink herself to death.

When we were downstairs again, warming ourselves at the kitchen fire, Fred briskly said, 'I'll leave some money behind the bar at the tavern, so you may feel free to ply her with strong drink; you've seen how much she talks when she's had a few. I'll add it to the optimistic bill I'm drawing up for young Calderstone, on the assumption that he won't be hanged.'

'No, that won't do.' I had been thinking about this. 'We want her sober.'

He snorted rudely. 'You'll be lucky!'

'Let me see what a few days of rest and good food will do for her. We need her. She's given us enough to take him up, Fred – for arranging the murder of the rent-collector, if nothing else. You must tell Mr Blackbeard.'

My brother sighed at me and shook his head. 'But that won't be any use to young Charlie; what he needs is a solid link between Rutherford and the murders of Mrs Orme and Miss Winifred.'

'You think I'm clutching at straws,' I said.

'My dear quixotic old sister, I think you're taking a very big risk – if you insist upon taking that drab into your house, lock up your valuables and keep a weapon under your pillow.'

I admit that I was a little apprehensive, but something made me want to stick up for the 'drab'. 'Do you know her to be a thief?'

'No – but I doubt she's ever been inside a place like this, and the temptation might well be too much for her.'

'I don't have anything worth stealing.'

'To someone of her class, absolutely everything that isn't nailed down is worth stealing.'

'For shame, Fred; I refuse to condemn her on the grounds of her "class".' I was on my high horse because my brother was laughing at me. 'She's innocent until proven guilty, like everybody else.'

'And even if she doesn't sell your fire-irons for gin, she's hardly fit company for a lady. Oho – you'll hear some interesting language! Don't imagine you can make a silk purse from a sow's ear.'

She was up and downstairs a good half-hour before I was the next morning; a pale, pasty-faced creature with bloodshot eyes and rough dark hair – and a look in her eyes of fearful amazement, as if she had awoken in another dimension. Mrs Bentley had given her a mug of strong tea and a bowl of porridge.

'Good morning, Mrs Gammon,' I said. 'I hope you slept well?'

'Yes'm.'

'I caught her trying to go off to work,' said Mrs B. 'She's worried sick about her job.'

'It's a good job, ma'am; I dunno as I can get another.' Mrs Gammon's sober voice was quiet and hesitant.

'You'll keep your job,' I assured her. 'Or we'll find you a better one.'

'I hope I didn't do nothing bad yesterday, ma'am. I hope I didn't say nothing to cause trouble. Why did you bring me here, anyway?'

'You gave us some very useful information about the so-called Prince.'

'No! I didn't!' Her eyes were wide with horror. 'I was drunk and talking rubbish!'

I sat down with her at the table, making sure I was gentle and friendly; Fred had prepared me for some savage harpy, but the sober Mrs Gammon turned out to be rather meek – and dreadfully frightened of the Prince. I swore to her that she would be safe in this house, and hinted that she could be of great help to us. I don't know how much of it she took in; she was stymied with the astonishment of it all.

Once breakfast was finished, Mrs Bentley carried the dishes to the sink in the scullery, a dank and freezing space with a stone sink and a pump, tacked on to the back of the house. She firmly told Mrs Gammon to wash the dishes, and the woman jumped up at once.

'But I don't like setting her straight to work,' I protested, once Mrs B and I were alone. 'It doesn't seem fair.'

'She's happier when she's working,' Mrs Bentley said. 'She's not a lady like you, ma'am; she don't know how to sit and do nothing.'

'My dear Mary! When have you ever seen me "sit and do nothing"? I ought to be very insulted.'

'You know what I mean, ma'am.' She was not to be teased out of making her point. 'You can read books and write letters. But a woman like this only knows about hard labour. And when she ain't labouring, she's drinking to forget it.'

'You're quite right, of course.' I was starting to understand what I had taken on when I insisted upon bringing the witness into my home. 'What do you think we should do with her?'

'Keep her going with little bits of washing and sweeping and suchlike,' Mrs Bentley said promptly. 'Because when she's idle is when she wants her gin.'

'Should we give it to her? If she's so dependent, it might be cruel to deprive her –'

'She's not far gone enough for that,' Mrs B cut me short. 'My son David's wife had an uncle that drank himself to death. Bright yellow, he was – and shaking. And there's a smell they have. But this one still wakes up pretty sober. Let's see how far we get with beer.'

We spoke in low voices, listening to the crockery-noises from the scullery (nothing had smashed yet).

'Very well,' I said. 'And we should fill her up with decent food. My brother thinks it's only the drink that makes Mrs Gammon talk; I thought the pies worked just as well. I don't want Mr Blackbeard to see her in this state – she's our only witness, and if he doesn't believe her, he won't take up Rutherford.'

'Leave her to me,' Mrs B said. 'I'll clean her up to pass as a respectable widow-type. And I'll keep a good eye on her, in case she decides to make off again.'

The door of the scullery creaked open. Mrs Gammon came diffidently back into the kitchen, wiping her red hands on her ragged apron.

'Well now,' Mrs Bentley said. 'Do you know how to griddle a nice rasher of bacon?'

She shook her head.

'Sit down, and I'll show you.'

To Mrs B and myself, bacon was a treat for a Sunday breakfast. To Sally Gammon, it was the rarest of luxuries; I left her gazing at the pan with what looked like the beginnings of cheerfulness.

We had advanced – but not nearly enough. It was no good to anyone if Rutherford was arrested for the killing of the rent-collector. The rent-collector would still be dead. And Charles Calderstone would still be days away from being tried for murder.

I wrote a short note to Inspector Blackbeard, stating the times I would be at home.

Twenty-seven

'I T'S A MATTER OF the utmost delicacy,' Lady Calderstone said. 'And you are the only person I trust to carry it out discreetly.'

It was the following day. She had summoned me with a note, carried by a messenger from Filey's office and stating only that she wished to see me. We were alone in the small sitting room at the back of the great mansion; she had invited me to sit down in one of the chintz-covered armchairs, but did not sit down herself.

'It's about Christina Hardy,' she said.

'Oh?' I was taken aback; this was the last thing I had expected to hear.

'You know her, I believe.'

'I have met her.'

'Mrs Hardy's carriage comes to the square every day,' Lady Calderstone said. 'Hour after hour, day after day, she sits inside it with the windows covered – waiting, waiting, heaven knows for what.'

'That must be distressing for you,' I suggested.

'Distressing?' She shrugged this off a little impatiently. 'That's not why I sent for you. I need someone to speak to her; I know Esther has done so, but this is no job for Esther – and my daughters have no idea of Mrs Hardy's existence.'

Yet again, I was struck by the change in Lady Calderstone since our first meeting. She was thinner, there were new lines etched around her eyes, but it was more than that; the enamelled shell had fallen away to reveal a woman of quiet, steady courage.

'Do you wish me to ask Mrs Hardy to leave?' I asked.

'No, not at all; I want you to bring her into the house.'

'I – I beg your pardon?'

'My husband wants so much to see her; they parted in anger, and now he can't stop fretting about her. I believe it's holding back his recovery; he won't be easy until he has seen Mrs Hardy and asked her forgiveness. Now, will you do this for me, Mrs Rodd? I can tell that you are surprised.'

This was putting it mildly – I was vastly surprised. But I was also moved. 'You love your husband very much,' I said, 'to make such a concession.'

'I can't make him less anxious about Charlie,' Lady Calderstone said, 'but this is one weight I can take off his mind; God knows, I'd cut off a limb if it would help him.'

'Tell me what I must do.'

'Thank you.' She gave me a faint, brief smile. 'Everything is arranged – Esther has my entire confidence, and she has taken the girls out to Richmond for the day, to visit a great-aunt of mine. You must use the back door; Thorpe will show you out to the carriage.'

'Thorpe is as good a man as he is a butler,' I said. 'What should I say to Mrs Hardy?'

'You must assure her that she will not see me; she will only see James,' Lady Calderstone said. 'And you must warn her about his appearance; his face has dropped on one side, and his speech is very laboured and indistinct. Tell her that he seeks her forgiveness – and that I would take it as a great favour.'

And so I set off on my odd errand – sent by the wife to fetch the mistress.

Discretion was vital; a small, persistent crowd of ten or so debtors, gawpers and loafers had taken up residence outside the Calderstone house. Mrs Hardy's carriage was half-hidden in the entrance to the mews at the back, the blinds closely drawn, the black-clad coachman perched on the box like a waxwork.

I indicated that I wished to speak to Mrs Hardy; a moment later, I was sitting inside the carriage (the seats were wondrously soft and luxurious) and we were face to face. Poor woman, her eyelids were red and sore as if she had cried herself half-blind.

When I explained to her why I had come, she wept again – but immediately wiped her eyes, and begged me, 'Take me to him!'

The excellent Thorpe ushered us through the back door of the house, and up the dusty, narrow servants' staircase. Mrs Hardy was visibly nervous, yet I had the impression that no force on earth could now keep her from the man she loved.

We emerged on to a broad landing.

'You're to have half an hour, ma'am,' Thorpe said. 'And you're to go in alone.'

Mrs Hardy seized my hand. 'Please tell her that I thank her! Say that I thank her with all my heart!'

Thorpe opened the door to Sir James's bedroom, giving me a brief picture of a bright fire, a respectable-looking nurse, and a sagging figure on the bed, awkwardly propped up by a great bank of pillows.

He saw her on the threshold and gave a wordless cry; before the door shut, I watched the flurry of her silk skirts as she hastened to his side.

I have never felt able to condemn a person for loving, even if it is in the wrong place, and I honoured Lady Calderstone for her greatness of heart in engineering this meeting. She had forgotten everything else in her passion of love for her husband, to the point of admitting her rival into her home.

'I know he'll be easier now,' she told me, when I returned to the sitting room. 'He has been in such torments of remorse since Charlie was taken up; he frets over every single person he feels he has wronged in the past.'

'Was he such a great criminal?' I asked.

'Not in the sense of breaking the law,' Lady Calderstone said. 'He worries that he caused pain, and longs to make amends. I believe this is the key to his recovery.' She hung her head and, after a moment of silence, added, 'After Charlie comes home, of course. Everything depends on that.'

'He will come home,' I said. 'Even Inspector Blackbeard is beginning to doubt his guilt. Take courage; Heaven will bless you for what you did today.'

Matt would have said this was another instance of my 'giving orders' to the Almighty, and perhaps it was at the time. Now I see that I spoke only the truth; Heaven did bless Lady Calderstone, for I firmly believe it was her selfless action that led directly to a very important piece of information. But this was still in the future.

At the end of the allotted half-hour, I met Mrs Hardy at the door of Sir James's chamber and accompanied her back to her carriage. Her eyes were reddened with fresh tears, yet there was a sense of calm around her.

'We begged each other's pardon for our last quarrel, and parted again as friends,' she said. 'I think he'll be more peaceful now. Please tell his wife that I will never forget her kindness and please be assured, Mrs Rodd, that you can call upon me for any sort of assistance.'

Neither of us guessed how soon I would need her help.

Twenty-eight

I T HAPPENED A SCANT three days before Charles's trial.

The hammering on the door was loud enough to make us all jump out of our skins.

'Mercy!' Mrs Bentley cried. 'Who's that at this time of night?'

'It's the poliss!' said Sally Gammon.

It was indeed the 'poliss', in the shape of Inspector Black-beard. He stomped down to the kitchen, where the table and chairs were covered with snowdrifts of white linen because the three of us had been turning my worn bedsheets 'sides-to-middle'.

'I beg your pardon for disturbing you so late, Mrs Rodd,' Blackbeard said. (It was only about four in the afternoon, but one of those murky January days when it never gets properly light.) 'There's been a bit of a development.'

I had been tired, winking away yawns; now I was galvanized as if struck by lightning; I leapt to my feet, scattering pins and cotton-reels. 'You're going to take up Rutherford! I knew it! And this is my witness, Mrs Gammon, who can identify him –'

'Now, hold your horses, ma'am; it's a bit of a development, that's all.' He looked at the chair Mrs Bentley had hastily cleared for him. 'Perhaps I'll stay for a sup or two of something hot, if you have such a thing.'

'Yes, of course – Mary, please give the inspector some hot ale.' (Mrs Bentley had prepared a large jug of ale, as a means of keeping our witness off the gin.) I was trembling with impatience; for two pins I would have shaken the information out of the man. I forced myself to stay calm and steady until Blackbeard was comfortably settled beside the fire in the carver's chair. 'Do I take it that you've come round to my way of thinking?'

'Well, I wouldn't know about that.' Blackbeard, with customary and maddening slowness, took a sip of the ale and rolled it thoughtfully around his mouth. 'Let's say certain occurrences have made the case look somewhat different.'

'Occurrences?'

'Well, I like to be thorough, you see. I don't like loose ends. So when you came at me with your story, ma'am, I felt I had a duty to follow things up. Just out of curiosity, I sent down to Suffolk for an account of Henry Rutherford's inquest.'

This sharpened my interest still further; I had written to Minnie Beswick about the same matter, but Blackbeard had the authority to demand any information he wanted, and from any source.

'Did you discover anything interesting?'

'It was rather like you said, ma'am; the corpse was battered out of recognition, so he was identified as Henry Rutherford by his watch and seals, and what was left of the papers in his pockets. Well, that's common enough with drownings. But I thought to myself – what if Mrs Rodd got it right? What if they buried a stranger, and Henry Rutherford is still alive?'

'Oh, he's alive, all right!' Mrs Gammon blurted out. 'And that's my fault because I took him in and nursed him – and then he kills my man by way of a thank you!'

The inspector took a long, searching look at her (I wished we'd had more time to prepare the witness before he saw her, but she was already greatly improved, both in appearance and demeanour; in just a few days, Mrs Bentley had hunted out and made over an old dress of brown wool to replace the woman's steam-bleached rags; I had been very struck by the clever way Mrs B 'managed' our guest, stuffing her into a state of calm with more good food than she had ever seen in her life).

'Do you know for sure that he killed your man?' Blackbeard asked.

'It's quite obvious that he did,' I said. 'At least four people have died because they knew too much about Mr Henry Rutherford.'

'When you put him into the picture,' Mrs Bentley added, 'it all starts to make sense.'

'The inquest report wouldn't have been enough to go on by itself,' Blackbeard said. 'I've taken a personal liking to Mr Charles Calderstone – but that ain't enough either. Unlike you, Mrs Rodd, I can't afford to work with nothing but my feelings to go on.'

(I allowed this little stab to pass without comment; the important thing here was my 'feeling' that Blackbeard had moved an inch or two closer to my way of thinking.)

'But then there came this development, as I said – which I daresay Mr Tyson will tell you about, once he's finished jumping for joy.' This time, the glint of humour was quite unmistakable. 'The chief witness for the prosecution has gone up in smoke.'

'Drummond!' I cried out (resisting the temptation to whoop with triumph and throw in the air the cotton-reel I was holding; this was not a game). 'I knew it!'

'That she did, sir,' Mrs Bentley put in loyally. 'She said all along that Drummond was a rascal. What's he done, then?'

'He was taken up for fiddling about with the wills of his customers,' Blackbeard said. 'And that's not even the half of it; Brewer wrote to me that the man came to him with two black eyes and a broken nose, begging to be locked up for his own safety. He's fallen foul of one of the big gypsy families who trade horses at the fair.'

'Did he say anything about Rutherford?'

'Well, ma'am, Brewer ain't much of a writing man, but he did report that Drummond was now eager to tell the truth, in full co-operation with the law, because he don't want to be hanged. So now we have two witnesses: Drummond can testify that Rutherford bribed him to commit perjury, and Mrs Gammon here can finger him for the business with the rent-collector. I ain't got enough to take him up for murder – but I reckon this will do to be going on with, don't you?'

'It's a ticklish business, arresting a gentleman,' Blackbeard said. 'A ruffian might black your eye, but a gentleman will get up on his high horse and tell you his cousin's a judge – or a colonel or a bishop – as if that made a blind bit of difference to the facts of a case. Which is why I'm glad to have your assistance, Mrs Rodd; I know you won't be bamboozled by that sort of talk.'

We were in a plain black carriage, with two policemen riding on the box (this vehicle had caused a minor sensation in Well Walk; when I emerged from my house and climbed inside, one of the local urchins yelled, 'Wot you done, you wicked old bird?').

'I am only too happy to help, Inspector,' I said. 'I hope that where this case is concerned, I am now beyond bamboozlement.'

There was a rough, scraping sound in the darkness beside me, which I identified as Blackbeard's version of laughter. 'I give credit where credit is due, ma'am; it's down to you and your spying that we know where to find our villain; a lesser lady than yourself would've said "I told you so".'

(Despite the seriousness of the situation, I could not help being amused; for Blackbeard, this counted as the handsomest of apologies.)

'It's his mother who is most to be pitied,' I replied. 'She lost him once, and now faces losing him again, in the most dreadful fashion.'

'Well, that's another reason to have you aboard, ma'am,' Blackbeard said, 'in case of vapours and faintings and so forth, which might distract me from the real task in hand.'

In the light of the carriage-lamp I could see a half-inch or so of linen sticking out of his drab sleeves and, excited as I was, I could not help observing that the cuffs of his shirt were dull and beginning to fray; a doleful reminder to me of his widowhood.

Hampstead Lane was clear, and the going tolerably smooth. We halted outside the Rutherford house; it was nearly swallowed by the darkness, but there were lights visible behind the wooden shutters.

Blackbeard helped me out of the carriage. He gave a few laconic orders to the policemen – one was to wait outside the front gate, the other was sent round to the back door. Nobody was to leave the house. One blast of the whistle would mean one thing; two blasts would mean something else. I wasn't really listening; to be quite candid, I was in what my nephews would have called 'a blue funk' and the blood was roaring in my ears.

I tugged at the bell. The sound died away and there were no signs of movement in the house.

'Pardon me, ma'am.' Blackbeard gently set me aside, to grab the bell for himself and jangle it without mercy, until the front door cautiously opened.

'Who is it?' a woman's voice said. 'What do you want?'

'Police!' Blackbeard snapped at her. 'Open that door in the name of the Queen – and don't try running!'

There was a brief, hard silence, and then someone emerged – not the maid, as I had thought, but Miss Muirfield. She walked down the short path to the gate, into the light shed by the carriage-lamps, and I was shocked to see that she had one eye badly swollen and bruised.

'You're too late,' she said. 'He's not here.'

'Open up, ma'am, if you please.'

She unlocked the gate.

'Miss Muirfield,' I said. 'You are hurt.'

'You! I know you!' She saw my face and was suddenly furious; she hissed at Blackbeard, 'What's she doing here?'

'Mrs Rodd is assisting me,' Blackbeard said.

'Well, she can't come in.'

'She can if I say so.'

'This woman is a busybody and a spy – but what difference does it make, anyway?' Miss Muirfield scowled at me. 'Poke and pry as much as you please – you won't find anything!'

I was not about to be put off by her rudeness; the principal note that I heard in her voice was pain. In the hall of the house there was lamplight enough to see the ravages of her grief; her

292

eyes – as far as I could make them out behind that cruel bruise – were pits of despair.

'Emma!' Mrs Rutherford's voice cried out from the drawing room. 'Is it him?'

'Him?' Miss Muirfield clenched her hands in a sudden spasm of fury. 'No – of course it's not him!'

'Emma! Tell him to come to me!'

'Why won't you listen? I've told you a hundred times – it's not him and it never will be him!' She whipped around to face Blackbeard. 'Did you hear that? He's not here! You can search every inch of this house if you don't believe me!'

'That's exactly what I intend to do,' Blackbeard said. 'I'm here to take up Mr Henry Rutherford, and I will find him, ma'am; it's no use anybody trying to hide him.'

'Emma! I heard the bell! Is it him?'

'No,' Miss Muirfield shrieked, 'for the last time!' She picked up her skirts and positively charged into the drawing room, where the old lady sat, swathed in shawls, in her armchair beside the fire. 'He's GONE! And now the police have come for him, because he's a DAMNED VILLAIN!'

In the shifting light of the flames, Mrs Rutherford's face had an expression that pierced me to the quick; a compound of bewilderment and raw horror.

Miss Muirfield suddenly began to weep, and swooped down to take the old lady tenderly into her embrace, crooning as if to a child. 'Dearest, dearest – Emma's here!'

Mrs Rutherford wept (oh, how many tears had she shed for that son of hers?). 'He took my baby!'

I had assumed the child Adelina to be in the house. But of course he had taken her; that had been Rutherford's intention all along. Now Blackbeard and I could see, only too plainly, the wreckage he had left behind him.

'He has run away with the little girl,' I told the inspector. 'She must be found; you must set up a search for her at once!'

'Do you think he will harm her?'

'I think he is capable of any outrage; though he loves his child, she is not safe with him.' I drew Blackbeard back a few feet, so that the two weeping women would not hear me. 'Muirfield helped him, believing that she was going with him – and he plainly betrayed her at the last minute, leaving her with nothing but a black eye for all her trouble.'

'Hmm, yes, I see,' Blackbeard said thoughtfully. 'Dear, dear.'

'I saw how she looked at him,' I murmured. 'She loved him, and he has broken her heart; I know that doesn't excuse the fact that she was apparently quite prepared to desert Mrs Rutherford, but we'll get nothing out of her unless we treat her gently. And is there any need to turn the house upside-down? I very much doubt you'll find Henry Rutherford anywhere near here.'

'I'm of the same opinion,' Blackbeard said. 'I'd say that bird has flown.'

'Let me talk to these ladies, Inspector; they may have an idea about where Rutherford has taken the child.'

'Well,' he said, 'you do have a way of winkling out a story, Mrs Rodd. And I'm quite happy to leave you to deal with the tinderbox.' (He meant, of course, the volatile Miss Muirfield, still sobbing quietly, but liable to explode at any moment.)

I moved back to the fireplace.

'Miss Muirfield,' I spoke as softly as I knew how. 'Your eye looks very painful; may I ring for a hot compress? And perhaps someone might build up the fire.' (The coalbox was empty, the grate covered with ashes, the fire swiftly shrinking to a single ember.)

'The servants don't know,' Miss Muirfield said. 'I haven't been able to tell them; it all happened too fast.'

'Mr Blackbeard, would you very kindly go to the kitchen, to ask for clean towels and a bowl of hot water? And a good pot of tea, naturally.' I flicked a glance at him; he understood that I would coax out the facts more easily if he left us alone. 'The fire must be mended too, and the lamps trimmed.'

He nodded to me and left the room.

A very short time later, the maidservant appeared with the towels and steaming bowl of water. Miss Muirfield permitted me to help her to an armchair, and to make a hot compress for her eye (a cold compress being unsuitable in cold weather). Another woman brought us tea and revived the fire (by their frightened faces, I saw that the servants did not need to be told about what had happened).

And all the time, the portrait of Henry Rutherford above the fireplace smiled down on us like a young god.

Miss Muirfield, clutching the compress to her face, said, 'I was right to be suspicious about you; you're a spy for the police.'

'Not at all,' I said. 'I'm making inquiries on behalf of a private client.'

'The Calderstone boy.'

'Yes; you know as well as I do that he's innocent.'

'Do I?'

'Miss Muirfield, if you know where Rutherford has gone, it is your duty to tell us – before an innocent man is hanged for murder.'

'What do I care about him?' Another spasm of passion twitched through her exhausted body. 'If I knew where to find Henry Rutherford, I wouldn't tell you – I'd be with him! He promised he had changed – and like a fool I believed him.'

'What was the original plan?' I asked.

'I don't know what you're talking about.'

'How long have you known he was alive? When did he first approach you – and how did he do it?'

'It doesn't matter now,' Miss Muirfield said. 'I ought to have seen through him; I could always see through him when we were young. He used to say he loved me because I knew him right through to his backbone.'

Mrs Rutherford, half-dozing in her armchair, suddenly raised her head and glanced about the room with a kind of polite interest, finally settling upon me.

'Mrs Rodd,' she said. 'Of course, you came collecting for the poor.'

'Oh God,' Miss Muirfield hissed, 'here we go again! I've had to tell her fifty times – she forgets five minutes later.'

'I'm not surprised,' I said. 'The shocks she has suffered would addle anybody's mind.'

'She never listens to me! She lives in the little world she's built around herself!' Miss Muirfield jumped out of her chair to stand over the old lady. 'Henry's gone – Lina's gone! And all my money – and God knows how much of yours! Do you hear? Are you satisfied? This is the man you made! Look at my face – see what he did to me!'

Mrs Rutherford narrowed her eyes, and looked hard at Miss Muirfield, as if trying to make her out through a mist. 'Oh, my dear, your lip will soon heal; it's only a scratch, and poor Henry is so sorry now!'

'Didn't you hear me?' Miss Muirfield shrieked. 'Henry's GONE!'

Just as I was putting out a hand to restrain her, fearing she was about to pounce on the old lady, she collapsed into another fit of weeping, sank to the floor at Mrs Rutherford's feet and buried her face in her cousin's grey silk skirts.

'Oh, my dear child!' Mrs Rutherford tenderly stroked the younger woman's shoulder. 'You have made a sacrifice, and I will never forget it; you confided in me, to save my darling from the first impulse of his undisciplined heart!'

I was stirred by a genuine (as opposed to dutiful) pity for Miss Muirfield as I saw these glimpses of her history. The scar on her lip was thick and white, and had plainly been a great deal more serious than a 'scratch'; had Mrs Rutherford truly excused her son's behaviour in such a way? Was this truly what she had said to a young woman covered with blood he had spilled? And it was only too easy to guess about the 'sacrifice'; better men than Henry Rutherford have enlivened a dull summer with an unsuitable romance; he had broken both her head and her heart.

Mrs Rutherford's old-fashioned white cap began to nod and droop; she had drifted back into sleep, which could only be a mercy.

I helped Miss Muirfield back to her chair and made her a cup of tea. She was quite exhausted by the strong passions that had been raging through her, and her hostility towards me had vanished.

For a few minutes, I allowed the silence between us to settle, and listened to the sounds of voices and footsteps elsewhere in the house.

'He threw a hammer at me,' she said.

'I beg your pardon?'

'The scar upon my mouth.' Miss Muirfield touched the white seam that cut through both her lips. 'Henry made that, when I refused to do something or other for him. He said I was a charity-case and no better than a servant, and he could order me about as much as he pleased. He was fourteen years old.'

'A charming young man, indeed,' I said.

'He was the Prince.' Miss Muirfield's voice was tight and soaked with bitterness. 'And I was the Beggar-maid – the poor, dependent female relation, condemned to a lifetime of apologizing for my existence by making myself useful.'

'Have you always lived with the Rutherfords?'

'Since I was twelve, when my father died. Henry was a few years younger; his had died when he was an infant, and his mother devoted her whole being to the worship of her golden boy. She has been very kind to me, very generous – except where he is concerned. She truly does not see the monster she has made.'

'And yet,' I said softly, 'you fell in love with him.'

'That was a few years later,' Miss Muirfield said, 'just before he went up to Oxford. He wanted me to fall in love with him; he demanded it, and I could not resist him. It was summer, he was bored – and far-fetched as it might sound, I was passably pretty in those days. My cousin said it was inevitable, and blamed herself for putting temptation in his way. She was very kind to me, thinking my broken heart only right and proper.'

I now understood the particular expression she had when she looked at Mrs Rutherford, of mingled love and resentment. We did not have enough time, however, to dig up the distant past.

'When did you find out that Henry was still living?' I asked.

She leaned over the table to refill her cup, and went on as if I had not spoken. 'But then came the next assault upon our hearts – oh, that was a good one! Prince Henry dropped in unexpectedly one afternoon, to announce that he meant to marry some common little trollop he picked up on one of his sailing jaunts.'

'Helen Orme,' I said.

'Yes – but of course the infatuation wore off eventually, as they always did, and he got rid of her – and then he died, and we buried him.' She smiled grimly. 'You should've heard how he laughed when he saw his own grave; he said the angel didn't look half sorry enough.'

'Miss Muirfield, please tell me what happened today.' I was striving to keep my patience. 'Where was Rutherford planning to take the child?'

'He said we were moving abroad, that's all. He allowed me to believe, right up to the last minute, that I would be going with them. I packed a box for myself and a bag of Lina's belongings. As we had arranged, I left them behind the shrubs at the front gate. At the appointed hour of two o'clock this afternoon, I dressed Lina in her warm outdoor clothes and told her we were going for a walk. The carriage was waiting outside. Oh, it all went perfectly!' She fixed her fierce, wounded eyes upon me. 'I'll say it, to save you the trouble; I was fully prepared to run away from my cousin, from my respectable home, to be with him; I couldn't face losing him a second time.'

'When did you realize you had been betrayed?' I asked.

'Only afterwards; it happened so fast. I bundled Lina into the carriage – and while I was climbing in after her, Henry knocked me off the step with a single blow that sent me sprawling in the mud. By the time I had picked myself up and collected my wits, they were long gone. All I could do was come back into the house, to tell my poor cousin her beloved son had risen from the dead to cheat her, and break her heart all over again. It was only the child he wanted!' She picked up something from the small table at her elbow. 'I came to my senses clutching this, though I don't remember grabbing it; he gave it to Lina.'

She dropped something cold into my hand – a gold locket, set with seed-pearls, with a crude little picture inside it of a young man with luxuriant brown hair. A companion picture had been rather roughly removed.

Mlle Thérèse had reportedly kissed a picture in a locket, under the impression that it was of her 'husband' (it could have been almost anyone).

Helen Orme had left a gold locket with the Italian couple who took in her baby – in those days, it had contained the faces of both parents.

I held the trinket in my palm, tracing its journey. In the beginning, Rutherford had given it to Mrs Orme as a love-token. Mrs Orme had left the locket with the Italian couple who took in her baby. Mlle Thérèse could only have been given the locket by Savile, who must have appropriated it when he found the child. And Henry Rutherford could only have found it when he murdered Mlle Thérèse.

A small enough link – but a link, nevertheless. I dropped the locket into my bag, to give to Inspector Blackbeard.

'Does Miss Adelina know that Rutherford is her father?'

'We told her he was a cousin,' Miss Muirfield said. 'I daresay he has revealed himself by now.'

It sickened me to think of the little girl, alone and perhaps frightened, at the mercy of such a man. 'Will he harm her?'

'Ha!' The expression on her face was sour enough to curdle milk. 'He'll treat her like a princess – as if she wasn't spoilt enough already. He'll deck her in silk and satin, not to mention the diamonds and pearls he took from his mother's dressing table on his way out. You're looking down your nose at me, for being jealous of a child – yes, I'm so jealous of her that I hardly care what happens to her!'

'Miss Muirfield,' I made an effort not to look down my nose, if that was really what I had been doing, 'you don't mean that.'

'Yes I do – why should she have him? She's a common little bastard, and her mother was a whore.' She pursed up her mouth suddenly; the ugly words echoed between us.

There was a soft knock at the door and the inspector came back into the drawing room. 'Well, Mrs Rodd? Do you know where he was headed yet?'

'I told her – I don't know,' Miss Muirfield said. 'He kept changing his mind. One day it would be the Low Countries, another day it would be Italy – and then it was France, then Russia, then America. You're right to despise me as a fool; I despise myself for trusting him.'

'Thank you, ma'am,' Blackbeard said. 'I'll send out word around the ports to watch for a lone gent travelling with a little girl. And do you happen to know, Miss Muirfield, if Henry Rutherford has visited Lincolnshire in the past few months?'

'No,' she said flatly. 'After he made himself known to me, he would disappear for days at a time, sometimes weeks. If I asked him where he was going, he would feed me some lie – it pains me very much, to know how easy it was to lie to me. He could have travelled to the moon and back, for all I knew about it.'

'Emma –' Mrs Rutherford's head bobbed up; she gazed around at us all, and her face crumpled. 'Where's baby? Did he bring her back?'

I was afraid this would provoke Miss Muirfield into another fit of fury, but she was all tenderness now, soothing and rocking the old lady, murmuring to her that the police would find Adelina and bring her home (what a bundle of contradictions she was; though she had snapped at me that she didn't care about the child, I could see now that this had only been bad temper; she loved Adelina almost as fiercely as she loved Rutherford, and was half mad with anxiety). When the inspector and I took our leave, I carried away a vivid mental image of the two women, weeping in each other's arms beneath the portrait of the smiling villain.

Twenty-nine

'I wish I'd known about it sooner,' Blackbeard said, in the carriage on the way back to Well Walk. 'He's had a good head start on us; if the tides are on his side, he could be out of the country by now.'

'Do you have enough to free Charles Calderstone?' I asked.

'Now, hold your horses, ma'am.'

'You know he could never in a thousand years have murdered those two ladies. You know he is innocent – you cannot possibly allow the trial to go ahead now!'

'All in good time, ma'am.' He was not going to commit himself. 'I shall have a little talk with Drummond; I daresay he'll be happy enough to tell us about Rutherford's adventures in Lincolnshire.'

I like to think I am a patient, forbearing person, but Blackbeard's obstinacy made me want to shake him. 'You must ask him about Joshua Boggs,' I told him. 'If Drummond talks, Boggs will have to change his story; it's obvious that he was paid by Rutherford to murder a potential witness. Obvious to me, at any rate.'

'Hmm,' said Blackbeard.

'Is that a yes or a no, Inspector?'

'It won't hurt young Calderstone to wait a bit longer, ma'am, until I can put some salt on Rutherford's tail. If I swallow one bit of your story, I have to swallow the lot – by which I mean, this is a man without a conscience, who commits murder without turning a hair.' His voice hardened. 'But I will get him; I will scour every corner of this city until I have him. In the meantime, I'll be leaving a man on guard outside your house tonight.'

'Is that necessary?'

'You're sheltering a fine witness for the Crown in the shape of Mrs Gammon. I don't want to take any chances.'

A chill ran through my blood; I had been assuming that Rutherford was already miles away from London, but I remembered the attack at Soking; if Mrs Fitzwarren had not been a light sleeper and direct descendant of Boadicea, Miss Winifred would have died that night. This was how 'a man without a conscience' dealt with potential witnesses.

I had been feeling rather splendidly triumphant, imagining the joy of the Calderstones when Charles was exonerated; this brought me down to earth. I was very glad to have the policeman standing guard upon our doorstep in Well Walk, though I made light of it to Mrs B and Mrs Gammon.

My journey through the Valley of the Shadow began with hot currant pudding.

Mrs Gammon had made it that afternoon, under the benign supervision of Mrs Bentley. It was very good and I was famished. I ate a very large helping; I can taste those spiced currants now. As Matt would have said (and how that man loved a hot pudding), it 'lay heavy'; the Lord did not send me on my journey with an empty stomach.

The summons came when we were on the point of retiring for the night. The policeman outside knocked at the door, to inform me that someone had sent me an urgent message. I did not know the messenger, and I did not recognize the handwriting on the cover of the packet he handed to me.

'I'm to wait for a reply, ma'am,' he said.

'Yes, of course.' I had broken the seal and seen the signature: Christina Hardy. 'Please come inside.'

Leaving Mrs B to entertain the man down in the kitchen, I put a match to the lamp in the drawing room; I needed to be alone to concentrate.

MOST URGENT

Dear Mrs Rodd,

I have seen Henry Rutherford and know where he may be found. I came upon him this morning, quite by chance, at the shipping office in the city. He is much changed – but I knew him at once as 'Mr Fisher'. Fortunately he did not know me, and did not notice that I was eavesdropping. He took places for himself, one other party and a large carriage, on the next steam packet to Antwerp – the Dreghorn Castle, *which leaves Blackwall Dock at midnight. I have informed the police.*

In case he slips through their fingers, however, I enclose your First Class ticket, and a Letter of Passport signed by a trusted old friend of mine. The banknotes are to meet any further expenses. My carriage is at your disposal,

Yours sincerely

Christina Hardy

She had thought of everything. The banknotes were crisp and white. And as for the Letter of Passport – well, that signature certainly showed off the quality of Mrs Hardy's connections. Her 'trusted old friend' was Sir George Grey, the Home Secretary.

I first encountered the English Channel as a schoolgirl, on my way to be 'finished' in Boulogne. My last encounter had been some ten years before the time of which I am writing, when Matt and I had a delightful holiday in Paris, with an old friend who was a chaplain at the Embassy. I was, therefore, well prepared for the noise and tumult of the docks – the forest of masts, the ant-like swarms of men loading and unloading the ships, the sailors shouting, the great heaps of boxes and bales, the chaos of travellers departing, the flares of gaslight that filled the darkness with demonic shadows.

I found the *Dreghorn Castle*, a large paddle steamer, about an hour before she was due to depart. Before I boarded, I scanned the weaving crowds on the quay for Rutherford and his child – and, more urgently, for Inspector Blackbeard.

Before I left Well Walk, I had written a letter to Blackbeard, which I ordered the young policeman outside our door to deliver to him. I had also written to Fred, and to Mr Filey, in case they knew better where to find him.

There was, however, no sign of the inspector, nor anything to do with the forces of law and order – not so much as a single policeman. Fear fluttered in my stomach. He had not received my message; I would be pursuing the murderer on my own. If Fred had been present, he would have told me to give up and come home – but I had no intention of allowing that steamer to sail without me. I was confident that nobody would take much notice of a lone woman wrapped in a black cloak and close black bonnet (if anyone was too curious, I could always tell them I was a governess travelling to her new situation). I had brought with me one small carpet-bag, containing only the bare essentials for the continental traveller: smelling salts, soap, lavender water, book (Keble's *Sermons*, in a conveniently compact edition), spare handkerchief, flask of medicinal brandy, two russet apples, a moist parcel of bread and cheese (quickly made up by dear Mrs B, while I was scribbling my letters) and a little folding canvas stool. I picked up my luggage and joined the line of people walking up the gangway on to the deck of the *Dreghorn Castle*.

The deck of a steamer before departure is always a maelstrom; I dodged and wove my way through the throng of passengers, the friends who had come aboard to wave them off and the sailors who were loading the last of the boxes, crates and trunks.

I was a First Class passenger, entitled to retreat to the relative seclusion of the Ladies' Saloon – but I was determined to avoid this for as long as I could, and not just because I would not find Henry Rutherford there. The Ladies' Saloon on a channel steamer is a dreadful, dreadful place – strewn with bodies, the air filled with sobs and moans and piteous cries for help, like a picture from Dante's *Inferno*.

I confess here, though some will hate me for it, that I am an excellent sailor. I have never in my life experienced the smallest twinge of sea-sickness. But I have observed its horrors at close hand – for instance, while travelling to Calais on my honeymoon, when dearest Matt was so sick that he begged me to kill him, though the sea was as smooth as a millpond. On this winter night, there was a boisterous wind that promised to turn ferocious once we were out at sea. I decided to set up my canvas chair in some sheltered spot on the deck (easier said than done; the deck was already packed with other good sailors, plus a few bad sailors who imagined fresh air would make them feel better).

One section had been set aside for private carriages (those with money enough were thus able to avoid being rattled about in the 'diligence' or stagecoach when they arrived on the Continent). There were six handsome travelling carriages chained to the deck, all with names chalked on the backs, and one of them was 'Rutherford' – he had not taken the trouble to conceal himself behind a false name, though he must have known by now that he was only one step ahead of the police. He was all set, I thought, to do his usual trick of disappearing as soon as he touched land. I decided to pitch my canvas chair where I could keep an eye on the carriage, and found a space nearby between two big wooden lockers.

We set off at peak tide, in a great cacophony of bells and shouts – as the mighty paddle-wheels began to turn, the whole ship shuddered and heaved.

The pallid lantern that was nailed to the wall above my head did not shed sufficient light to read by. But I was too keyed-up to read. I sat listening to the thrum and churn of the paddles, staring out at the blinking points of light on either side of the river – and saying a prayer for the innocent child.

The weather turned on us while we were battling into the open sea. The wind became violent; the *Dreghorn Castle* pitched and thrashed like a walnut shell in a drain. Only the hardiest passengers were outside now.

I heard them before I saw them – a thin, keening, wailing sound underneath the noise of the wind. A dark shape passed in front of me, of a tall man swathed in a travelling-cloak, with a weeping child in his arms. My senses leapt and I sent up a fervent prayer of thanks, for of course it was him; the Lord had heard me, and delivered him into my hands.

I quickly folded my canvas seat, tied my bonnet down more tightly, and went out into the savage wind to stand just a few feet away from him. I'd only ever seen his back, but now I saw his face – Henry Rutherford, the Prince, the 'man without a conscience'.

As far as I could make out under the brim of his hat, he was just as Mrs Bentley had described him: thin and spare, his brown hair close-shorn and peppered with grey. The child was an invisible hump under the many capes of his cloak. He looked, at that moment, nothing like the devil of my imagination. In the fitful light of the lantern above the First Class door, his face was anxious and exhausted, and he was no more forbidding than any harassed parent.

I went to his side; our eyes met.

'Please excuse me,' I said, 'may I be of any help? I can see that your child is distressed, poor little thing.'

Rutherford's face suddenly melted into a smile – a delightful smile, which gave me a glimpse of the young man he had been. 'How very kind of you; I don't know what to do with her, and she utterly refuses to be left in the Ladies' Saloon without me.'

'Has she no nurse or governess?'

'No, I'm travelling alone – and I'm frankly at my wits' end.' He lifted one of his capes, to reveal the head of Adelina, cowering against his shoulder.

Of all the terrible sights in this world, the face of a frightened child is one of the hardest to bear. Adelina had been weeping for hours; she was white and limp with exhaustion, and with a fearful expression in her swollen eyes that cut me to the quick. As I had hoped, she did not recognize me.

'Her name is Adelina,' said Rutherford.

'How do you do, Adelina,' I replied. 'My name is Mrs Rodd. You are very cold and tired, my dear – would you allow me to take you into the saloon?'

'No!'

'But you'll feel a great deal better out of this wind –'

'No!'

'Lina, for God's sake! I don't think she knows what she's saying, Mrs Rodd, and it would be most awfully decent of you.' With his free arm, Rutherford pushed open the door and we all dived through it, into the relative stillness of the First Class corridor. The *Dreghorn Castle* was a new ship, built on an ambitious scale; I had an impression of brass and mahogany and red plush, rather confused because we were pitching violently; one enormous wave would have sent me flying half across the room, if Rutherford had not grabbed my arm.

'Thank you, sir.' (I remembered not to call him by his name, which he had not yet told me.) It was odd to be touched by him; his fingers gripped like steel.

'It's pretty rough today; you're the first person I've seen who's not dying of seasickness.'

'I never get seasick.'

'Neither do I,' Rutherford said. 'I've been a sailor in my time, and love nothing better than being out at sea. My daughter doesn't appear to have inherited my sea-legs, however, and I'm most grateful to you for your kindness, Mrs Rodd. I shall be on deck if you want me – or if there's any service I can do for you in return.'

He tried to put the child down on the floor; at first she wailed and clung to him like a limpet. But she was quite worn out and had no more resistance; he set her down and she staggered and blinked, and let me take her frozen hand.

The Ladies' Saloon was large and handsomely appointed, furnished with sofas, chaises and soft chairs. As I had predicted to myself, it was a veritable hospital, with groaning bodies stretched out everywhere you looked, and grey-clad steward-esses moving between them. I saw a vacant armchair with a footstool beside it, and gently pushed Adelina into the chair. I sat myself down on the stool and began to rub her freezing hands. She was quiet now; the warmth of the saloon was making her drowsy.

'You are as white as a sheet,' I told her softly. 'How long is it since you have had anything to eat?'

Listlessly and without conviction, as if unsure of being heard, she said, 'I want Grandmama, I want Emma.'

I had to tell her; she was dying for want of comfort. Bending close to her ear, I whispered, 'You must be a very brave little girl; your papa does not know it, and you must keep it as a great secret – but I'm going to take you home to Grandmama and Emma.'

For a moment she stared at me dully, and I wasn't sure she had heard me.

Then she said, in a very small and cautious voice, 'He hit Emma.'

'I know, my dear. But she was not badly hurt. And now she's waiting for you.'

'Good evening, ma'am.' A solid, muscular middle-aged woman in a dress of grey serge stood over us. 'I'm Murphy, your stewardess; is there anything I can do for you?' She had a pleasant Irish voice, and generally a kindly look to her, and in a moment she had covered Adelina with a rug and provided us with cups of tea (words cannot express how welcome this was to me, after hours spent out in the cold and wind). The poor child was quite used up now, and allowed me to feed her little spoonfuls of tea, until her eyes grew heavy and she sank into a deep and merciful sleep.

I sat watching her for a good while, tracing likenesses in her face, and thinking how extraordinary it was that she existed at all – this living, breathing reminder of her parents' shame. What sort of life would she have if her 'natural' father managed to spirit her away into his murky underworld?

In a purely practical sense, it was useful to have Adelina safely out of his reach in the Ladies' Saloon. I could guard her here – but only until we arrived at Antwerp. And I did not entirely trust Rutherford not to change his mind about his daughter. He had cheerfully betrayed everyone who loved him; I doubted such a man was capable of real, disinterested love as it is known in Heaven. Everything he did, every impulse he had, was deeply and unashamedly selfish (he reminded me of Tibs – short for Tiberius – the beautiful but wicked cat from my childhood, who thought his fine tortoiseshell coat put him far above the vulgar work of catching mice). He'll tire of her, I thought, just as he tired of her poor mother; he'll stow her away in some convent school and forget all about her.

The seas rose – and the wind – and the piteous groans of the sick.

Two moaning maidens lay on the broad sofa beside me. One of them kept saying, 'When, Mamma? When will we get there? When?'

And Mamma – cowering in a chair under a heap of shawls – kept sighing, 'Oh, why won't anyone let me sleep?'

Murphy came back, to whisper that the little girl's father had sent something for her – and she handed to me the wax doll with tumbled skirts that I had seen at Adelina's home. Against my will, I was touched that he was thinking of her comfort. He must have taken this favourite toy from the bag packed by Miss Muirfield – he had been cool-headed enough to snatch this along with his daughter.

I placed the doll beside Adelina. She stirred and sighed in her sleep, and put her arms around it; I thought she slept more sweetly after that.

'Dead to the world she is, bless her,' said Murphy. 'I can keep an eye on her, ma'am, if you want to slip out for some fresh air – you look as if you need some.'

Yes, I was certainly ready for a good gulp of fresh air; the saloon was stuffy and too crowded. And if I was watching Rutherford, I could safely leave Adelina with Murphy. There was a large First Class Saloon on the other side of the corridor, but I knew I would not find him there. This was a man who hated confinement and loved nothing better than a stormy sea. He would always want to be outside, in the thick of it.

The wind pounced at me like a wild beast the moment I opened the door, spitting icy spray into my face and nearly knocking me off my feet. The deck was pitching like a seesaw; it took me several minutes to get my legs into the rhythm of the waves.

Rutherford was standing out of the worst of the wind, smoking a cigar, in the tainted yellow light of a dirty lantern above his head.

'Mrs Rodd?' He saw me. 'Is she all right?'

'Miss Adelina is fast asleep,' I told him, summoning my most reassuring voice as best I could. 'The poor little creature was so dreadfully tired, she closed her eyes almost at once.'

'Thank you, ma'am; I'm most sincerely grateful. I hope she wasn't too much of a nuisance.'

'Not at all, she was as good as gold.'

'Did she happen to say anything?'

I lied to him boldly, even with slight enjoyment. 'Not a word.'

'Well, you have been my saviour, Mrs Rodd. It was splendid of you to take pity on us.'

'Perhaps you had a difficult journey?' I suggested.

'We set off in rather a flurry, and she wouldn't stop crying, though I tried everything.'

(How convincing he was, how sympathetic – if you didn't know he had abducted the child.)

The air had revived me a little, but I was very tired. I tried to pull my canvas chair from my carpet-bag; my hands were clumsy in the wind, and Henry Rutherford gently prised it away from me, to set it up himself.

'Thank you, sir.' All of a sudden, it was a great relief to sit down.

'May I help you back inside?'

'No – I'd much rather stay out here.'

'I thought you would,' Rutherford said. 'I had you down as the sort that actively enjoys rough weather. I'm exactly the same. The sea wind cleans my mind – if not my conscience. It helps me to organize my thoughts efficiently, without giving into sentimentality.'

I did not reply; I could see him and hear him, but everything around me was turning faint and dim. It took all my strength to hold up my heavy head.

Rutherford bent down, to speak close to my ear. 'There are times when I must force myself to be ruthless; it doesn't come naturally. I really should have been ruthless with Sally Gammon – but I made the fatal mistake of sparing her because she was kind to me. For once in my life I did something decent. You'd think Heaven would reward me, wouldn't you?'

He knew me; all pretence was at an end.

'I never imagined that the one good deed of my life would be my undoing. If I had hardened my heart – I'm sure you think it's quite hard enough already, but I have to be practical, Mrs Rodd. I'm afraid I shall be forced to keep a hold of you, until I've decided what to do with you.'

I wanted to reply, of course I did – but the words would not come. My head was a lead cannonball; his silken voice came from a great distance, and at a distance I was very afraid, but a dreadful, sick fatigue was washing over me, and I knew no more.

I was in the pond at home and Fred and I were rushing up to the sunlit surface, scattering drops like diamonds.

And then Matt was with me, and it felt quite unremarkable; I was telling him something that made him smile.

Tishy was playing the piano and singing, but I looked into room after room and could not find her.

I was dragged back to consciousness by a raging thirst – dreadful thirst, worse than I had ever known – and a mouth lined with sandpaper. At first I could not move; my limbs were heavy and seemed to belong to someone else. I was lying upon something soft. I opened my eyes and saw a low ceiling, crisscrossed with ancient beams.

My thirst drove me to sit upright. There was a jug of water on the small table beside me; I could not pay attention to anything else until I had gulped down three glassfuls.

I was alone, in a large and comfortably appointed room, furnished with heavy continental beds and armoires, and well heated by a large, tiled stove. Heaven alone knew how I could be here, when I had no memory whatsoever of leaving the boat. Slowly, slowly, my wits began to collect themselves. Here was my carpet-bag; Rutherford (or someone) had thoughtfully placed it within reach.

As my eyes adjusted to the lamplight, I saw that I was not alone after all. Adelina lay in the bed beside mine, so white and still that at first I thought she was dead. She was still breathing, however, and I could just about feel a little fluttering pulse in her neck. Her hands were freezing; I rubbed them between mine, and gently shook her shoulder, hoping to bring her round. When she did not stir, but lay like a limp rag doll, I began to be frightened. She needed a doctor, or we would lose her.

I tried to stand up. I fell down. I tried again, and managed to get to the door. It was locked – and made of such thick, carved wood that I knew screaming for help would probably be a waste of time.

There was a flask of brandy in my carpet-bag; I fished it out, poured a few drops on to a spoon, and put it to the child's colourless lips. Her eyes remained shut, but she coughed and

316

spluttered, which I took as a good sign; she drew some deep breaths and seemed to fall into a more peaceful sleep.

Behind me I heard the lock, and felt Rutherford's presence in the room like a chill wind in the small of my back. I had an instinct that a lot depended upon my ability to hide my fear.

'You must find a doctor,' I said shortly. 'I can't wake her; you gave her too much.'

Rutherford came to the child's bedside and gazed down at her, his expression unreadable. 'She'll come to no harm; I know what I'm doing.'

'It was the tea, of course.'

'Yes,' he said. 'I slipped in the sleeping powder while the woman was looking the other way.'

'Where are we?'

'Oh, somewhere or other.' He flashed me a smile. 'It's probably better for you not to know.'

'How on earth did we come here?'

'I stuffed you inside my carriage,' Rutherford said. 'And then the carriage was unloaded by means of a crane – I was immensely glad you didn't wake up to find yourself dangling in mid-air.'

'Adelina should be at home.'

'But she is at home,' Rutherford said. 'I'm her home now. She is my daughter, she belongs to me.'

'She is not a belonging,' I said sharply, 'she is a human child – and you have frightened her almost to death!'

'She'll get over it. Once she has got used to me, she will be very happy.'

'Don't you think she'd be happier – and altogether better off – with your mother?'

(I remember now that I was not afraid of him, and that this was a surprise to me; here I was, shut up with a man I knew to be highly dangerous, a man who was debating how and when to kill me, yet I felt quite calm; we circled each other with the utmost politeness.)

'I'm grateful to my mother,' Rutherford said, 'and I fully intended to leave Adelina where she was at first – but then I saw her, and knew at once that I would never be able to part with her.'

'She is certainly a handsome child.'

'Yes, she's beautiful – but there's more to it than you think, Mrs Rodd.' He was very much in earnest, his fine-boned face looking almost noble in the mellow lamplight. 'I saw her as my chance to make amends with Helen.'

'You – I beg your pardon?' This nearly took my breath away.

'I tried to fashion Helen into a lady – but I never quite eradicated the stink of fish. This time I mean to do the job properly. Adelina must not grow up in the shadow of her mother's shame. Her background must be without blemish.' He leaned towards me with polite concern. 'Are you unwell? You seem lost for words.'

'Her mother's shame?' I found my voice. 'Good gracious, Mr Rutherford, you astonish me! Isn't her father's shame a thousand times worse?'

'It depends on your point of view.'

There was a sharp rap on the door; my heart gave a lurch of hope, but Rutherford said, 'Please join me for breakfast; I give you my word as a gentleman it won't be drugged. And please don't imagine you can run away.'

'You know perfectly well, I'm not going anywhere without the child.'

'I guessed that would be your view of things; ladies of your type are so delightfully predictable.' He went briskly to unlock the door. 'You will sacrifice yourself with all the fervour of an early Christian martyr – possibly to the point of singing hymns while the lions are tearing your flesh.'

I saw it then – the look, the expression, that I had seen in the eyes of those who were truly wicked.

I was very frightened.

Rutherford, however, was suddenly all smiles; he showered the inn servants with coins and pressed me to sit down with him beside the stove. I obeyed him in silence. The gallant attentions continued, even when we were alone again.

'Some slices of ham, Mrs Rodd?'

'No, thank you.'

'A bowl of coffee?'

The smell was delicious; I was giddy with longing for coffee. Rutherford smiled at my eagerness as he placed the bowl in my hands (our continental neighbours make lamentable tea, but their coffee is ambrosial) and I could have gulped it down like a dog. How long was it since I had eaten? I demolished two soft brioches, suddenly so ravenous that I did not care what he thought of my manners.

We ate and drank in silence that was oddly amicable. Rutherford lit a cigar.

'I think you loved Helen Orme,' I said.

He looked at me sharply, as if stung.

'As much as you're capable of loving anyone,' I added.

'You think me incapable of loving? You couldn't be more wrong about me, Mrs Rodd. My entire life has been driven by love.'

'Self-love.' I was getting bolder with him, reasoning that he was going to kill me anyway, and I may as well be hanged for a sheep as for a lamb. 'You have never loved unselfishly; you don't know what it is to put another person before yourself. That is why you killed Mrs Orme, and Miss Winifred – and Savile, and Mlle Thérèse –'

'And Uncle Tom Cobley and all.' He smiled wryly. 'Yes, it has been a rather eventful career.'

'You don't deny that you have killed so many?'

'Why should I deny anything? You won't be telling anything to anyone. Ask me any question you like, Mrs Rodd; you will leave this world with your curiosity thoroughly satisfied, at least.'

'Very well,' I said. 'Who is lying in your grave?'

He gave a snort of laughter. 'Someone dead.'

'Why did you need to disappear?'

'To save my skin. Certain people were hounding me; they said it wouldn't stop until my death, so I decided to die.'

'How did you do it?'

'Oh, it wasn't planned in advance,' Rutherford said. 'Let's say that I saw my chance and took it.'

'But how did you live without your mother's money?'

He chuckled outright at this. 'I went to South America and married an ugly heiress. But that's not the story you want, is it?'

'No,' I said. 'I'd like to hear about your return to England – when your former manservant found you dying in the gutter.'

'Well, all right – why not? I hope the cigar-smoke doesn't bother you, by the way; I ought to have asked your permission.'

'I don't mind it at all. Had you come from South America?'

'My wife's brothers were after me – another story – and I had to make a somewhat hasty exit. I worked my way back to

England on a sailing ship. And do you know, Mrs Rodd, it was the best time I'd had in years? I sometimes wonder if I would have been a happier man – a better man – if I had stayed a sailor, and left the genteel world behind me.'

'When did you decide to reveal yourself to your mother?'

'I couldn't bear to until I'd got myself some money. I was destitute.'

'But then you saw an opportunity for blackmail,' I said. 'You sent that first letter to Sir James.'

'Yes – when I still assumed Helen had married Savile all those years ago.'

'When did you recognize her?'

I was trying to sound calm, but could not hide my curiosity. He was well aware of this, and smiled at me with a kind of glorious insolence, which reminded me strongly of the cherished portrait above his mother's mantelpiece.

'It was quite by chance, at a country horse fair.' He was laughing. 'Lord, she gave me a turn! I was there to pick up casual work – and there she was, a few feet away from me – my little Helen, heavily disguised as a respectable widow, and hardly a day older! It did not take me long to hear the gossip about "Mrs Orme" and Charles Calderstone. I sent off one letter, but before I could collect, I caught the fever. A beautiful plan was on the brink of extinction; I was on the very point of carrying it off with me to the next world – and then the gods sent me poor old Savile.'

'And he knew so much more about the Calderstones,' I said drily. 'You extracted your first pound of flesh from Sir James with very little trouble.'

'Ah, yes – our first meeting in Salt Lane,' Rutherford said. 'I needed that money to turn myself back into a gentleman. My mother is a proud woman, and I am a proud man; it would never have done to present myself to her as a beggar. Fortunately for me, Emma Muirfield wasn't as finicky.'

'Did you always intend to betray her?'

'I wasn't really thinking about her at all, to be truthful. She was a means to an end.'

'It was cruel of you,' I said, 'to let her believe you loved her.'

'Would you have believed it? No, you're far too sensible. Poor old Emma swallowed it all because she wanted to. And as a matter of fact, I did consider bringing her along, at least for the first part of the journey. Frankly, I had no idea Adelina would make such a fuss.'

'Really, Mr Rutherford – of course she made a "fuss"! She was terrified! Did it never occur to you that she would be?'

He looked at me for a moment, turning this over with mild interest. 'Not really.'

'I assume it was Savile who told you of her existence.'

Rutherford smiled. 'He blurted it out one evening, when we were sharing a bottle of rum down at the Goat – after the Limehouse job.'

'The rent-collector,' I said.

'Yes, the rent-collector; he made rather an untidy job of it, otherwise I couldn't have done it better myself. And during our celebration afterwards, he launched into the rambling story of finding Adelina. The couple who took her in died from the fever before she was a year old. When Savile happened to return to that part of the coast, a few months later, Adelina was living as part of a large local family – he told me she looked like a little pink-and-white changeling in the middle of that dark-haired brood.'

'How very kind of that family,' I said. 'Mrs Orme found her true friends in that poor fishing village.'

'The irony was not lost on me – the fact that our child was growing up as a fisherman's daughter. The local peasants were very good to her; when Savile reached the maudlin stage of intoxication, he told me that the child's adoptive mother had wept to part with her. Poor as they were, they had kept a valuable item of jewellery left by the child's true mother.' He held up one hand like a conjuror, dangling the famous gold locket on the end of its chain.

'That was in my bag,' I said. 'What else have you stolen from me?'

Rutherford laughed loudly, delighted by my indignation. 'Well, the apples were tempting, and so were the sermons – but this was never your property, was it? I had it made for Helen, during our first summer together in Switzerland.'

'You took it from Mlle Thérèse,' I said, 'after you killed her.'

'I wanted to give it to my child.'

'You admit that you killed Thérèse Gabin – just like that? Without one hint of remorse?'

'You can't imagine what a nuisance she was turning out to be.' He said this coaxingly, as if he expected me to agree with him. 'She was threatening to come to London and Savile was too lily-livered to keep the harpy in order; I saw that she would have to go, even before the unfortunate end of Savile.'

'Had you never wondered about the child Helen was carrying?' I asked.

'I never thought about her after I left her – not much, at any rate. I have a habit of shedding my past selves. But I was interested enough to go and take a peek at my mother's house. And then I saw my child – and I felt as if my heart had been washed clean and born again – but you look startled.'

'Born again?' I could almost have laughed at this. 'Mr Rutherford, you immediately embarked on a frenzy of killing!'

'But don't you see? Everything had a purpose, at last; everything was pure, if done for her sake.'

'What – including the murders of Mrs Orme and Miss Winifred? Pure?'

Rutherford sighed and winced, as if I had said something distasteful. 'That was different. I had to act quickly; I may have been too hasty.'

'She saw you, that day at the market,' I said. 'You were riding in a chaise, beside your friend Mr Drummond – apparently risen from the dead! I can understand now why the poor woman was so shocked.'

'You think I have no heart,' Rutherford said, very serious. 'But how little you understand me! If you could see the battles between my good and bad angels! You are right that I loved Helen – when I came to the cottage that day, my first impulse was to take her in my arms! My better angel urged me to spare her, to love her again.'

'Please, Mr Rutherford – I know how she was found, and any mention of love is perfectly grotesque.' The ill effects of the sleeping powder had cleared by now; I was myself again, and angry. 'You killed two innocent women!'

'They didn't fit the new history I was making for myself.'

'Did you know Charles Calderstone was going to be there – or was that another stroke of good fortune?'

He smiled. 'Now you are being sarcastic, Mrs Rodd, and it doesn't suit you. Let's say that I know how to make the most of a golden opportunity.'

'I presume that means you arrived at the cottage in time to see Mr Charles leaving.'

'I heard him first – dear me, the language! The boy was yelling his head off, and I even had a potential witness, in the shape of some local clodhopper who was mending the hedge in the next field. I simply waited until they had both gone and the women were alone. I admit to you, I gave into a moment of weakness, and – the deed was not cleanly done. That I regret.'

'In the past, you have killed in cold blood,' I said. 'But not this time.'

'No – my blood was boiling. The embers of the old passion engulfed me.'

'Have you decided how you are going to kill me? I'd prefer not to have my head broken.'

He was taken aback, and slightly amused. 'A tidy death – is that your last request?'

'If you like.' My heart galloped, but my anger burned through my fear. 'I leave the details up to you. And please tell Adelina I was very sorry that I couldn't keep my promise to take her home.'

'It's kind of you to think of her; my better angel is urging me to thank you for taking such good care of her.'

'If I were you, Mr Rutherford,' I snapped back at him, 'I would dismiss that feeble "better" angel of yours without a reference – it's obviously quite useless.'

He smiled. 'I'm sure you keep your angels in much better order.'

'I don't care where you go or what you do – if you leave Adelina with me, I promise I won't try to follow you –'

'You mean well.' He cut me short; his face suddenly turned to stone. 'And that only makes matters more difficult. You will now put on your outdoor clothes. I will carry my daughter. Don't imagine you can scream for help, or run away from me.'

'I told you, I won't leave Adelina – but where are you taking us?'

'That does not concern you. Don't look about you.'

I put on my cloak and bonnet, and picked up my carpet-bag. I was glacially calm, though I knew that every passing minute was bringing me closer to my death.

Rutherford wrapped his unconscious child in a thick rug and gathered her into his arms. He unlocked the door of our chamber and we walked out on to a broad landing. Without moving my head, I dared to look about me; we were making our way through a prosperous inn, probably in Antwerp, since there were shipping timetables pinned to every wall.

He made me walk in front of him, and kept so horribly close behind me that I could feel his breath on my neck. I sent up a silent prayer for courage.

It was night again; I had no idea of the time. Rutherford propelled me out into the cobbled street where his carriage stood waiting – a large and expensive travelling carriage, with no fewer than four horses stamping and steaming in the traces.

It took me a few moments to make sense of what happened next; there were shouts, and a brief scuffle – and a voice that made my heart leap heavenwards.

'Henry Rutherford, you are under arrest for the murders of Helen and Winifred Orme – hold him tight, lads! He's not giving me the slip again!'

Thirty

'INSPECTOR!' MY PRAYERS HAD been heard; my own good angel had arrived, in the drab and tousled shape of dear old Blackbeard (I won't go as far as saying I could have kissed him), and two young men in plain clothes.

'Damn you!' Rutherford was appalled, astonished, thunderstruck. 'Damn you to hell! This isn't England – you have no power here!'

'That's why I'm taking you home,' Blackbeard said. 'So you can have a proper English trial, and swing from a proper English noose.'

I will never forget the expression on Rutherford's face then – thoughtful, as if working out a puzzle.

'There must be melodrama, I'm afraid,' he said. 'You leave me with no choice.'

He pulled a pistol from the folds of his cloak, and placed it against the forehead of his unconscious child.

'NO!' It came out of me in a banshee's scream, and I would have tried to snatch her, but Blackbeard gripped my arm to stop me; we watched him fearfully, knowing this man was quite capable of carrying out his threat.

'On the other hand,' he said, 'it'll be better for my immortal soul if I take this journey alone.'

He dropped the child in a heap at his feet and turned the pistol on himself – with a look of triumph that haunted my dreams for many months afterwards.

I said a prayer for his soul; I have never stopped saying prayers for Henry Rutherford.

I wish I could find a good piece of Shakespeare to illustrate the scene, or a sonorous verse from the Bible. All I can think of, however, is the Punch and Judy booth at the fair, and Mr Punch's crow of victory when he beats the hangman. Rutherford had beaten the hangman by choosing to bypass all earthly courts and stand before the Judge of Judges.

Blackbeard stared at the body for a long spell, before he covered it with a tarpaulin.

'Well,' he said, 'this time he'll stay buried.'

My first consideration had to be the child. Adelina was still as limp and white-faced as a little ghost; I dreaded to think how much of the drug Rutherford had given her. On the steamer back to England we were allocated a tiny cabin of our own, and Blackbeard sent out an appeal for a doctor. Somehow, in such circumstances, there is always a doctor; on this occasion, it was a Scots army surgeon with bristling white whiskers, who assured me that 'the wee gerr-ull' would suffer no ill effects, and should be left to 'sleep it off'.

Once this weight was off my mind, I could surrender to my own fatigue; I fell into a sound sleep as if falling into a feather-bed, and knew no more until the splendid Murphy woke me with a cup of tea.

'And I do assure you, ma'am, that nobody has slipped in any powders this time – I'm very sorry about that.'

A sigh issued from the narrow bunk; I leaned over to take Adelina's hand, and to my very great relief, she opened two bright blue eyes.

'Good morning, Adelina,' I said. 'I don't know how much you remember, my dear, but it's all over now, and you will soon be at home again.'

She smiled and squeezed my hand, and whispered: 'I'm hungry!'

Murphy fetched a bowl of warm bread and milk; I fed it to Adelina, and saw her gaining strength with every spoonful. By the time we were nearing England, she was chattering as if she'd known me all her life. She remembered her father striking Miss Muirfield, but the sleeping-drug had wiped all the other horrors from her memory.

Before the day was over, I had the happy experience of returning the child to her home, and the two women who loved her with such devotion; she threw herself into Miss Muirfield's arms, and Muirfield hugged her as if she would never let her go.

Blackbeard and I stayed in the carriage.

'There'll be time enough to tell them,' he said. 'Let's leave them alone for the moment.'

It was over.

I will never forget the surge of gladness I felt when we drew up outside my dear old front door in Well Walk.

Mrs Bentley had lit the big lamp in the drawing room, and the window shone out a welcome home.

'Here you are then,' Blackbeard said. He cleared his throat. 'I hope you'll forgive me for staying out of sight like that, Mrs Rodd.'

'All's well that ends well,' I said. 'And you came to our rescue like Sir Galahad.'

'What I mean to say, ma'am, is that it has been a pleasure working with you. I freely admit, I was a bit slow with this one. Next time I'll have to take your word for it.'

'But you won't,' I said, laughing. 'You'll be just as obstinate as ever.'

'I'd call it cautious.'

'No more arguing,' I said. 'Let us agree that we have each learnt from one another's methods, and drink a toast to Justice.'

'Always happy to raise a glass to that, ma'am.'

Blackbeard helped me from the carriage, and we went into the house together.

Extreme old age does strange things to my memory. The past is fresh to me, vivid in every detail, felt in every sense. People who have been dead for years are suddenly filled with life again, and I hear their voices reminding me of things I had long buried. Whereas I couldn't tell you what happened yesterday if you paid me.

I am working out in the garden, in the drowsy shade of the big oak tree, and it is that soporific hour after luncheon on a warm afternoon. Everything sleeps (children, birds, livestock) except the bees – and me. I'm too old to feel the heat, and I have been utterly caught up in remembering.

Tishy, who is a great romantic, wants to know if Charles Calderstone married Esther Grahame. I'm happy to say that he did; they went to Kirkside and lived happily ever after. Mr Fitzwarren was not disappointed, however, because he was not in love with Miss Esther after all. I am mortified to admit that

I was completely wrong about this. Three months after Charles's release, he married – even now I can hardly believe it – Miss Blanche.

And this was the young lady who had sworn never to fall in love with a clergyman!

The birds are stirring; a breeze nudges at my papers on the table. The children have come out to play on the lawn.

Tishy comes to my side. 'Is it finished yet, Aunty?'

She's not my Tishy, but her daughter, and so like her that I sometimes feel, near the end of my life, that no time has passed at all.

'Yes,' I say. 'Quite finished.'

Afterword

MY LOVE AFFAIR WITH Victorian fiction began when I was a teenager. I spent hours lying in front of the gas fire at home, guzzling chocolate and immersing myself in the mighty novels of that golden age. There were certain books I read again and again, until the characters were like people I had met, and the book I returned to most obsessively was Charles Dickens's *David Copperfield*. It is still my favourite novel – but every time I come back to it, I find myself more annoyed by the one line in the story that doesn't give the modern reader full satisfaction. I mean, of course, the bit about Little Em'ly, the fisherman's daughter who elopes with the dazzling James Steerforth.

As my fellow Dickens-nerds will have guessed, the plot of *Wishtide* was directly inspired by my issues with *Copperfield*. In Dickens's version of events, Em'ly spends the rest of her life repenting in the Australian outback. In my version she leaves her uncle in order to search for her baby – and why wouldn't she have had a baby? Dickens, as the father of nine, knew as much as anyone about where babies come from. Helen Orme is my Em'ly, Henry Rutherford is Steerforth, and Emma Muirfield is his mother's companion, Rosa Dartle. It is not necessary to know a thing about *David Copperfield* before you read this – but how I envy anyone reading it for the first time. I have written with the deepest respect – and nothing I do could hurt one of the greatest novels in any language.

Mrs Bentley is based on a real person – wife of the Hampstead postman, mother of a swarm of red-headed boys, and a kind landlady to the poet John Keats. It was a pleasure to imagine her in vigorous old age.

Thanks to the many who have helped me with this book – especially Caradoc King, Alexandra Pringle, Sarah-Jane Forder, Amanda Craig, Marcus Berkmann and (as always) my wonderful family: Bill, Charlotte, Louisa, Etta, Ewan, Ed, Tom, George, Elsa, Claudia and Max.

About the Type

The text of this book is set in Baskerville, a typeface named after John Baskerville of Birmingham (1706–1775). The original punches cut by him still survive. His widow sold them to Beaumarchais, from where they passed through several French foundries to Deberney & Peignot in Paris, before finding their way to Cambridge University Press.

Baskerville was the first of the 'transitional romans' between the softer and rounder calligraphic Old Face and the 'Modern' sharp-tooled Bodoni. It does not look very different to the Old Faces, but the thick and thin strokes are more crisply defined and the serifs on lower-case letters are closer to the horizontal with the stress nearer the vertical. The R in some sizes has the eighteenth-century curled tail, the lower case w has no middle serif and the lower case g has an open tail and a curled ear.